EVIDENCE

EVIDENCE

EMMA TOM

flamingo

An imprint of HarperCollins*Publishers*

Flamingo
An imprint of HarperCollins*Publishers*, Australia

First published in Australia in 2002
by HarperCollins*Publishers* Pty Limited
ABN 36 009 913 517
A member of HarperCollins*Publishers* (Australia) Pty Limited Group
www.harpercollins.com.au

Copyright © Emma Tom 2002

The right of Emma Tom to be identified as the moral rights author
of this work has been asserted by her in accordance with the
Copyright Amendment (Moral Rights) Act 2000 (Cth).

HarperCollins*Publishers*
25 Ryde Road, Pymble, Sydney, NSW 2073, Australia
31 View Road, Glenfield, Auckland 10, New Zealand
77–85 Fulham Palace Road, London W6 8JB, United Kingdom
Hazelton Lanes, 55 Avenue Road, Suite 2900, Toronto, Ontario M5R 3L2
and 1995 Markham Road, Scarborough, Ontario M1B 5M8, Canada
10 East 53rd Street, New York NY 10022, USA

National Library of Australia Cataloguing-in-publication data:

Tom, Emma.
  Evidence.
  ISBN 0 7322 7396 X.
  I. Title.
A823.3

Cover design by Christa Edmonds, HarperCollins Design Studio
Internal design by Darian Causby, HarperCollins Design Studio
Typeset in 11/14 Sabon by HarperCollins Design Studio
Printed and bound in Australia by Griffin Press on 80gsm Econoprint

5 4 3 2 1   02 03 04 05

Author's Note

This book is a work of fiction inspired by a real life death. The character of Samuel Leadhead, his life, his family and the circumstances leading up to his death are complete inventions. No identification with any actual person or persons, living or dead, is intended or should be inferred.

A few of the books and pornographic items mentioned in *Evidence* are real. The Most Life-like Female Doll Ever Invented is real. *Titzapoppin, Dr Pauline Messemer & Dr Johann Hauser's World of Good, Safe and Unusual Sex, Sexual Positions* (Book 1), *Sexual Positions* (Book 2), *40 Plus Pleasure Chests, Intercourse Illustrated, Encyclopedia Sexualis, Sex Stars Fav. Positions, Interracial Sex* and the advertisements for phone sex are real. *The Shorter Oxford English Dictionary* (published by Oxford University Press in 1993) and its definition of 'legs' are both real, as is *Why Haven't Marijuana Smokers Been Told These Facts — 758 Short Digests and Warnings, With Love From Dad* by Malcolm E. Smith.

Evidence was assisted by the Commonwealth Government through the Australia Council, its arts funding and advisory body. Thank you, Australia Council.

There were a bunch of other people who helped out, including Helen Corben, John Merrick from the NSW Institute of Forensic Medicine, Laura Armesto, Sydel de Zoysa, Cindy Pan, David McCormack, Martin Rico, Fiona Inglis, Vanessa Radnidge and Linda Funnell. Thanks also to my former colleagues at *The Northern Star* newspaper in Lismore who assembled the 'Darcyisms' that inspired Max Grippa's malapropisms, as well as to Steve Walsh who knew the difference between brie and camembert.

In other news, the first chapter of *Evidence* appeared in an edited form in *Dumped* published by Bookman Press in the year 2000.

Prologue

The one good thing about Samuel Leadhead's murder was that he had no nerves left by the time he died. That's what the police told Cheryl Kiss and her mother the night they were brought in for questioning. They said it was the one good thing.

'The point is he didn't suffer as much as you would of thought from looking at him,' the constable told Cheryl in the dark police corridor. 'Second degree he would of really known about. Second degree would of really got him hopping. But third degree burns'll strip a man's nerves right back to their stumps.'

The policeman said you had to look on the bright side.

The policeman said you sure you're all right?

The policeman said look sharp Cheryl Kiss, if the wind changes your face'll stay like that forever.

Cheryl thought about the bright side as she sat with her knees to her chest in the dark in her bedroom. Over the racket outside the door, she could hear her mother screaming from the laundry and Zeus yapping his head off, uselessly strapped to the iron spine of the clothes line.

It was only a matter of time until the whole story ran full circle.

Cheryl pulled her Personal Pocket Journal out of her school bag.

'I, Cheryl Kiss,' she wrote. 'I, Cheryl Kiss write this only half a mile from the river where Samuel Leadhead was burned alive. I, Cheryl Kiss, write these words before it is too late and I am also snatched.'

Cheryl stopped.

She peered through the gloom at the page then adjusted the elastic waistband on her trousers.

It was typical really.

Minutes, maybe only seconds left to live, and she had writers' block.

Violet Kiss's daughter had no idea whether the distance between her bedroom and Samuel's pyre at Advantage Creek was really half a mile. She'd been raised on the metric system. And *snatched*? What sort of bullcrap word was *snatched*?

Minutes, maybe only seconds to live, and she was still as pointless as ever.

Whatever happened next she deserved.

Whatever happened next she was asking for.

What was going to happen next?

'Not the Pulitzer Prize,' she said aloud. 'I can tell you that for free.'

'Pull-its-a-what?' Zeus barked back from the clothes line. He still couldn't believe the sheer cheek of the invader. The outrageous inevitability of the enemy that had crunch crunched its way right past him.

The banging on Cheryl's bedroom door grew louder.

Burning skin.

Burning hair.

If Samuel Leadhead had no nerves left to feel the pain why had he screamed the way he had?

Just for the fun of it?

Cheryl didn't have all the answers. Cheryl only knew as much as she knew. Evidence was thin on the ground for the lonely detective, but the things her mother had suggested were unforgivable.

Wood splintered.

'Oh for fuck's sake,' she barked, reckless with fear. 'There's no need to have a coronary. I'm coming out, all right?'

'All right.'

Outside in the dark, Samuel Leadhead's killer stopped pounding his fist against her bedroom door and waited.

1

A Little Gory Don't You Think, Cheryl?

Murray Ramsbottom was the one they sent to tell her. (It struck Cheryl as an odd choice as well.) Murray Ramsbottom brought the message through a late-summer scorch when entire schools scratched with the heat rash and stained babies rolled in the rocky orange sand along the beaches until they were mistaken for the dangerous prawn cutlets Dora Knockers served in fistfuls of greasy newspaper at lunchtimes and up until 8.45 p.m. on Thursday nights.

Murray Ramsbottom brought the message the month Samuel Leadhead swept the hot town of Tantanoula into a deadly tango.

'Hey Cheryl,' Murray called as Cheryl walked across four squares of burning school concrete while watching her reflection shrink to half its size in the dark glass of the headmaster's offices.

'What?' Cheryl replied, looking into Murray's marble eyes for only a moment.

But Murray seemed to have forgotten.

Cheryl waited for Murray to Rock Her World and scratched Lance Seldom's initials into a patch of dried Erraway on her yellow school bag. Erraway was a correction fluid which could be used to create an opaque film over errors of judgment committed in biro. Lance Seldom was the American rock singer of the same name. Rock Your World was from verse two of the Seldom hit single *Lance-A-Lot (I Am Your)*.

Was Murray ever going to say anything else *ever again*?

'Hey Cheryl,' said Murray.

'Yes?' said Cheryl.

'How you going, then?' he said, hopping from one foot to another as the chilli bitumen chewed through his soles.

Cheryl wanted to tell Murray she couldn't think of a single question quite so meaningless. Except perhaps for 'what do you know?' or 'nice day for it' (which wasn't even a question now she thought about it). Cheryl wanted to tell Murray Ramsbottom 'how you going?' was problematic enough. His addition of the word 'then' made it absolutely impossible to answer with accuracy.

'I'm good,' she said. 'How you going, then?'

'All right,' said Murray.

And there was this silence.

To tell you the truth, Cheryl wasn't surprised. To tell you the truth, Cheryl hadn't had a thing to say to Murray Ramsbottom since they'd played Spin The Bottle in Lou's mother's carport in full daylight.

Spin The Bottle, the game was called.

Not: Close In The Bucket Cupboard With Murray Ramsbottom And His Trail Bike Helmet.

Not: Can There Be Any Satisfactory Explanation For The Slipperiness Of The Human Tongue?

Just: Spin The Bottle.

Murray Ramsbottom was no Lance Seldom. His thighs were as thin as fuse wire, he had a dripping nose spread a good half-inch wider on one side than the other and his spit was as thick as glue made from flour. But for a full week after Spin The Bottle, Murray Ramsbottom's sticky lips were all Cheryl could think about.

Later, when Murray and Rachel Roulette were observed dribbling beneath the basketball hoop at the school social, Cheryl wondered whether Rachel also used her pillow for a horse in bed after playing Spin The Bottle with Murray Ramsbottom.

Perhaps the Roulette girl had also noted that spinning the bottle comprised only a fraction of the total game playing time.

'Why are you staring at me like that?' said Murray.

He jabbed a fist against his nostril to see if it was spilling a twig of dried snot. It was. For three whole seconds he wondered how much his green trail bike might weigh in hot dogs.

'Hey, listen.'

His voice was finally urgent.

'Hey listen. Reb and Lou and the rest of them don't want you hanging round them any more. They told me to tell you.'

Cheryl froze, a smile hammered across her face like a piece of wood. She glanced past the headmaster's office to the wide cement staircase where her best friends sat in a crooked circle down the slant. Reb was eating something pink out of a plastic bag while Lou sang from the chorus of *Lance-A-Lot*. Neither of them looked up at Cheryl.

You'll tear me in two
You'll tear me in two
You'll tear me in two if we part
(Cos there's)
Nothing but blood
Nothing but blood
Nothing but blood in my heart

Lou had the song wrong of course. The word was love, not blood. But this new version reminded Cheryl of the nuclear holocaust and the way Louise's skin would peel off her face in long red tongues after the blast.

'I'll be off, then,' said Murray.

'OK,' said Cheryl.

'Hey, Murray,' she called as he turned away.

'What?' he said over one shoulder.

'You didn't have to tell me about Lou and Reb and the rest of them I knew already you know.'

It was a lie and an unpunctuated one at that, but Cheryl was past caring.

'Right, then,' said Murray. He was hopping again, looking down at Cheryl's bag.

'Are you wearing perfume?' he asked.

'No,' said Cheryl.

'I thought I could smell something.'

'It's just this,' she said, opening her school bag and pulling aside the books to expose a broken banana in all its obscene spread.

Cheryl turned from Murray Ramsbottom and walked back the way she'd come. She walked to the art rooms and then to the library where she stole the book called *Why Haven't Marijuana Smokers Been Told These Facts? — 758 Short Digests and Warnings, With Love From*

Dad. Samuel Leadhead and Bradley Spam spied from their losers' hide-out beside the atlases but declined to alert the relevant authorities.

Six-and-three-quarter minutes later, the thief swayed in a conga line outside the canteen window. She bought a meat pie bleeding Kiddy Litter Tomato Sauce then threw it in the bin. After that she walked three steps towards the school gates. Then she stopped. Then she thought about going back to get another pie. Then she stepped on a crack in case she broke her mother's back. Then an electric hoon sounded the end of lunch and Cheryl finally had somewhere to walk.

'Video time,' Mrs Stint told Modern History. 'Pay close attention because at the end of this educational feature presentation there shall be a short test and any student who doesn't know how many times the narrator uses the phrase "Pocket Chancellor" will have to pray to the baby Jesus for forgiveness.'

Mrs Stint was a former primary schoolteacher specialising in religious instruction. The video program she showed her class that afternoon concerned the shooting murder of Engelbert Dollfuss — a genuine personality involved in the historical occasion known as World War II. Mrs Stint had shown the Engelbert Dollfuss film on three previous occasions. Each time she had snored loudly enough to cause the pigeon living outside the window to empty its bowels in fright.

'SnhgrrGGGGH,' said Mrs Stint as the five-foot Christian Democrat trading as Engelbert Dollfuss trading as The Pocket Chancellor raged against the Nazis in Austria.

'SNHGRRGGGGH.'

Half an hour after the video ended, Mrs Stint woke with a snuffle and handed out crossword puzzles on the

Japanese occupation of Manchuria in 1931. After that she handed back the poster assignments on World War II and read out the marks in order. Reb and Lou's median mark was B+. They high-fived at the news and did not look up at Cheryl.

The lowest scoring assignment belonged to Samuel Leadhead. He got an E because he hadn't handed in a World War II poster at all. Murray Ramsbottom's brother, Mort, had rubbed it in human stool and flushed it down the toilet two days before it was even due in.

Cut Your Own Arms Off Save Hitler's Time

That was the slogan on Cheryl's World War II poster. It was also the reason she had only scored a C-.

In the margin next to the mark, Mrs Stint had written: 'A little gory don't you think, Cheryl?'

As usual, Mrs Stint forgot to ask how many times the film actress Lurex Imperial had said 'Pocket Chancellor' during her narration of *The Darkening International Scene*. (For the record, it was 16.) Fortunately there was plenty of time for the history teacher to catch up on more sleep while her overhead projector clicked through a meaningless card deck of maps, dates and critical developments. The lesson was what was known as a double period, which meant two 40-minute lesson slots in a row, which meant a total of two electric hoons before Cheryl could escape.

Aoooba, the electric hoon rang out.

And then again: *AOOOBA*.

Reb and Lou fell over each other in their race for the door.

Once, Reb told Cheryl a secret. She said her father played Spin The Bottle with her each night after her mother left for work. Reb told Cheryl not to tell anyone. She made her cross her heart and hope to die. Then Reb told Lou and Lou told her hairy mum and she told the school counsellor and now Reb's dad was serving time in a low-security prison on the outskirts of the city.

'How's that mother of yours, Cheryl Kiss?' Mrs Stint called with a grotesque wink as Cheryl reached the doorway. (Sometimes Cheryl thought she actually preferred Stint back in primary school before she was medicated.)

'A little fucking personal don't you think, Mrs Stint?'

'I'm sorry, Cheryl?' the teacher asked in a specially high voice. 'What was that?'

Cheryl smiled with only her bottom lip. It was a trick that reduced her mother to tears.

'I said "my mother's fine thank you very much, Mrs Stint".'

'That's good to hear, Cheryl,' said Mrs Stint. 'You tell that mother of yours she's got a lot of fans here in Tantanoula.'

Worst of all, the snory old bitch had a point. Violet Kiss had never received an eviction notice from Murray Ramsbottom in her entire life.

Cheryl waited in the girls' toilets until she knew for sure Reb and Lou and the rest of them had left the building. The trick to passing time was counting. Eight cubicles. Two cigarette butts. Ninety-two square white tiles. One piece of graffiti offering Rachel Roulette's home number for 'a root and a half'.

Cheryl held her hand against the fluorescent light and audited her blood. Once, Lou had suggested she and

11

Cheryl and Reb and the rest of them slice open their thumbs and become blood brothers. By then, the gang was so large that by the time the knife reached Cheryl's flesh, it was as blunt as cardboard.

Cheryl waited in the toilets behind the swinging door with the stick figure wearing a skirt until she was certain her blood brothers had gone, until she was sure that if she waited much more she'd faint from the stench of trough lollies and disinfected tiles. The perseverance paid off. By the time she walked across the sports field towards the bus shelter, Reb and Lou's crimson double-decker was hauling itself into a stream of traffic. Behind the bus a cloud of black ash filled the air like the speech bubble of someone with a vocal impediment.

'Reb's got a fucking impediment,' Cheryl thought to herself. 'Her name is Lou.'

Cheryl checked for Samuel Leadhead and his sisters to make sure she hadn't missed her own bus, then sat on the grass slope with her knees pointing in at least a dozen directions.

The Leadheads lived next door to the Kiss family. Leadhead wasn't their real last name. It was Lead-something else, but everyone called them Leadheads because there were so many of them and because they lived in connected caravans by a dam the colour of shit and because sometimes when the bus pulled up in the morning the oldest Leadhead of the lot — Old Grandma Leadhead — was stretched out beside one or other of the big tin cans with a brown bottle asleep in her fist and red dirt clawing through her beard.

The Leadheads were Leadheads because even after water rained fresh from the sky their dam stayed the colour of shit.

Cheryl checked for Samuel Leadhead and his parliament of sisters and spotted them beneath the dying gum tree — splattered like fallen avocados across the dying grass.

She took out her Personal Pocket Journal and wrote the first line of her memoirs.

It was her name, as usual. And what a ridiculous name it was.

Cheryl signed her name on the page again and wondered if anyone in the history of the world had had such a ridiculous name, EVER. It wasn't the name of a novelist or a dancer from 'Boog Tube' or a confidante of Lance Seldom, that was for sure.

She signed for the third, fourth and fifth times.

Cheryl 'The Fuckface' Jane Kiss
Cheryl Jane Kiss — Fuckface
Fuckface: Cheryl Jane Kiss

After more work of this calibre, Cheryl gave up on her memoirs and looked up her age in the *Spikeman New Budget Edition Dictionary*.

It said: One more than 13.

She could have wept.

Cheryl pushed one of the Leadhead girls aside to take the seat opposite the emergency exit.

'Fuck off,' said the Leadhead girl.

'You fuck off,' said Cheryl.

The exchange could have continued for hours but it was still too, too hot.

Cheryl looked round the bus without moving her head. Murray Ramsbottom wasn't on board. But his older brother, Mort, was there all right. And hundreds of

Leadheads. The red bus paint shrieked in the sun. The vinyl cushions were torn and spewed foam as hot as volcanos.

Clearly it would never be winter again.

Cheryl's legs prickled with sweat. What's more, the splay of fat round the top of her thighs was taking up more than half the double seat. Well, wasn't it? Wasn't it taking up more than half, more than HALF the damn bus seat? Cheryl stared. Her brain was the size of a pea. She was a pea attached to an entire butcher shop of legs and thighs that took up half the bloody block.

Cheryl was using her ruler to measure how much hot vinyl was full of thigh and how much was free of thigh when Mort Ramsbottom yelled from the back of the bus: 'You want a dead leg, Leadhead?'

Mort was the biggest of Murray's big brothers. He had burned potato hair and a yoyo. Once, Mort and Lou had spent a full 45 minutes in the bucket cupboard playing Spin The Bottle. When Lou finally surfaced, she wore a red shawl of hickies. Mort, on the other hand, had lost another tooth.

'Well do ya Leadhead, do ya?'

Samuel didn't say a word even though Mort's gappy grin was so close he could have kissed it. Loser Leadhead was in all Cheryl's classes at Tantanoula High School and spent lunchtimes hiding with loony Bradley Spam in the encyclopaedia fortress in the library. If he had $1 for every time he'd been offered a dead leg by Mort Ramsbottom, he'd have $54.

'Cat got your tongue, cunt?' Mort said to Samuel.

'You're a tongue cunt,' said the smallest in a long line of dirty green-brown Leadhead sisters — the one they said would grow up pretty if she wasn't a Leadhead. 'You've got the biggest tongue cunt of anyone in town.'

(It was true, too. Mort's tongue was bushy and monstrous. It unrolled from his mouth like a wet dog.)

Mort ignored the girl but the yoyo strung from his finger snapped faster and faster. It was the official Lance Seldom fan club yoyo. The slogan was 'Lance Adds Love'.

'Murray saw you,' Mort hissed into Samuel's neck as the bus fell into another corner on the hot, airless road. 'Murray saw you and your stinking friend in the dunnies you pair of fucking poofs.'

Samuel's dark eyes flapped. The elastic sister swivelled round so far she could have been a dishcloth.

'Shut your trap,' she said in her deep Leadhead voice. 'Shut your smelly trap or my big sister Christy'll deck you, she bloody will.'

'We don't put up with filthy poofs like you,' Mort hissed at Samuel again. 'We'll slice you in half, we'll cut you in pieces no questions asked. We get all you faggots in the end just you wait and see if we don't.'

And there was this silence.

Cheryl looked at Samuel Leadhead sunburning himself from the outside in. She looked at Mort Ramsbottom and the Leadhead sisters and the endless faces on the bus and for no reason in the world she laughed. Snorted through her nose the way she and Reb used to laugh in assembly before Mrs Stint sent them both out to the cement gutter to think about what they'd done.

Cheryl thought of Murray Ramsbottom with his Clag glue tongue and Mrs Stint with her elephant armpits and Lou with her heart full of blood and she laughed and laughed and laughed. She remembered the time Reb had drawn eyes and a nose over her appendix scar and the time Reb moved into the Kiss residence for a week while they sorted out the business with her father. Then, for no

15

reason at all, Cheryl thought of Sarah Beth Anderson who would have been Sarah Beth Kiss if she'd lived and eventually she was laughing so hard she wasn't laughing any more she was crying.

'What's so funny Cheryl Kiss My Anus,' asked Mort Ramsbottom.

Cheryl had no idea.

'But the Leadhead's right, you know,' she said, seeing it all wetly through fly eyes. 'You really would do everyone a favour if you shut your face for once.'

Mort's fleshy lips peeled over a tortuous parade of teeth. Anyone who played Spin The Bottle with him was definitely asking for it.

'I'll pretend I didn't hear that, Hunch.'

Hunch was short for *Hunch For Men* — a gentlemen's magazine specialising in exotic jackfruit lubricants, convertible sheep, latex tennis socks, 'Hound's Toot' love rods and photographs of naked women the size of entire lounge suites. Naked women so fat they needed special cranes to move them in and out of *Hunch*'s makeshift photographic studios.

Mort put two fingers on each side of his head.

'Oooowooo,' he mooed at Cheryl. 'Had any calls from the *Hunch* talent scouts lately, heiferlump?'

Cheryl whipped her mother's autographed sewing scissors out of her school bag and cut Mort Ramsbottom's dancing yoyo string in half. There was a brief whiff of banana as the red-and-white plastic world somersaulted down the middle of the bus.

Mort moved fast. He wrestled the sewing scissors out of Cheryl's hands and hurled them out the window. (If he'd known what Mrs Kiss usually did with the clippers, he would have pulled Cheryl's hair instead.)

Did Mort say anything else after that? Did anyone say anything at all? Cheryl couldn't remember. Later, when she thought back, she wondered whether she'd met the eyes of Samuel Leadhead one last time as she'd stepped from the bus that reeking Tantanoula afternoon. But all she could recall with clarity was the image of the scissors' twin swords spinning in slow motion through the air. Catching the hot light like steel water.

Also, Mort may very well have pulled down his pleated grey school shorts and mooned her.

2

The Tantanoula Newsreader

When the Kiss girl regained her sense of things she was standing beside the road watching the bus shake itself into action and imagining future headlines.

MORT RAMSBOTTOM!
(The front page of *The New York Hurrah* would trumpet).

Cheryl Jane Kiss Tells How She Came to Write Her Celebrated Autobiography and How the Ace Raper Tried to Stop Her.

Ace raper or arch? It was hard to know. Lou had sworn blind that Mort tried to stick an Icy Fright up her bottom behind the bus shelter after the sports carnival but Lou had also sworn blind she didn't have nits.

The celebrated autobiographer brought it to her own attention that she had gotten off the bus ten stops too early.

It was 4.30 p.m. and still as hot as a pot's spot as she poked miserably through the sticky roadside paspalum looking for Violet's autographed sewing scissors. The sole role of the yellow secateurs was the trimming of Mrs Kiss's intimate hair growth. Cheryl knew this for a fact because she'd seen the lawn clippings around the toilet bowl.

Also, late the night before, there'd been an accident.

'Sugar,' came the cry from behind the bathroom door. 'Holy sugar and Caesar I've done it now.'

Violet Kiss — who could never bring herself to explete with gusto even after amputating half her right labia — had staggered out of the toilet with her thighs knotted and one hand clutching her crotch.

'Back in a tick, sweetheart,' she'd gasped to Cheryl, hitching herself towards the car. 'Don't answer the phone and if your stepfather rings tell him I've ducked out to borrow butter.'

When Violet returned an hour-and-a-half later, she was wearing what looked like a nappy beneath her pencil skirt and couldn't stop giggling.

'Cakes darling!' she'd cried. 'What are you still doing up? Have you eaten? Did you do your homework? Ha ha ha. Mix mummy a vodka, there's a good girl. I hope you didn't answer the phone. Homework done? HA! Eaten already? For God's sake Zeus, take it *outside*. OUTSIDE. There's a good boy. Vodka darling, not gin, darling. Ha ha ha. Dr Salmon sends his love. He always makes mummy feel so much better. Mr Medicine, darling! But he said it really is time you lost a bit of that puppy fat, it really is. We won't be telling Jackson now, will we sweetheart? This will be our little secret. Homework? HA!'

Cheryl had retrieved the sewing scissors and rinsed their bloody blades while her mother lay on the couch laughing at the ceiling. Violet had never seen such a hilarious ceiling in all her life. She laughed and laughed and laughed. Cheryl put the scissors in her school bag. She personally had nothing worth trimming down in the darkroom department but Lou had plenty. Bush, they'd called her the night she and Reb and Cheryl and the rest of them skinny-dipped in the cold creek out the back of the Kiss residence on Panorama Way. Babushka.

Cheryl had presented the scissors to Bush during assembly that very morning. 'Everyone reckons it's time for you to cut down a little,' she'd said. Then she told the others about her mother's hairdressing habits, wondering aloud whether the hair down in Violet Kiss's famous darkroom looked like one of those boxy hedges snipped into the shape of an animal. A circus elephant. Or a poodle up on its hind legs, perhaps.

Tragically, Cheryl was the only one to snort uncontrollably through her nose at the joke. Lou told her for the 100th time she was fucking disgusting, Reb looked away and then, after a wordless recess, Murray Ramsbottom came calling.

Cheryl's car park of clothing origamied beneath her arms as she stood in the heat beside the road. 'If you didn't insist on wearing a parka in the middle of summer, maybe you wouldn't smell so bad by teatime,' was her mother's usual line.

Then: My God, Cheryl, you're not leaving the house dressed like that, you look like one of the Leadheads.

Cheryl tried, unsuccessfully, to put her mother out of her mind. She seized a piece of road with a heart of sparkling quartz and let fly when it burned her fingers.

Heatwave, she said in her head.

Heatwave.

The words were electrifying.

Cheryl didn't find the scissors. She found three mango seeds with prickly fibres dried into sun flares, a hair clip with a glued glass budgerigar and a broken beer bottle half-full of spit and black dirt. She found an abandoned sandwich with crusts as hard as nails, a skinned tennis ball with lime skin flaps and an injured tin can trapped in a chicken-wire fence.

Cheryl walked for another 15 minutes and found herself passing the Ramsbottom's letterbox. There was no sign of Mort or Murray. Their brick house was resting peacefully on the side of the hill, attached to the main road by an umbilical driveway. Booga, their red setter, streamed up and down the fence with his frayed ears and broken nose. It was Booga's own fault that the Kiss's dog, Zeus, kept shredding him. According to Cheryl's stepfather, Booga had bitten Zeus while Zeus was still a puppy and Zeus wasn't the type to forgive and forget. Also there were his bloodlines to consider.

'*Slim killer with slavering attacker spirit, lockjaw reflexes and ability to hold grudge,*' Zeus's entry would read if he was ever to advertise in *Hunch For Men*'s personal column. '*Must have independent food source, pedigree bloodlines and GSOH. No poodles, neuts or red setters. Don't make me come and find you myself. You know I will.*'

'It's your own fault,' Cheryl barked back at the idiot orange dog as she walked down the road towards her house. 'If you hadn't messed with Zeus while he was little he wouldn't keep tearing your ears off now.' Booga scratched the back of his head against the barbed-wire fence until a swollen black tick fell to the flaming bitumen and fried.

'*Huh?*' his personal advertisement would read.

Panorama Way was the name of the road that was home to the Kisses and 25 other upstanding Tantanoulian nuclear family units. Panorama Way wasn't in the town and it wasn't in the country. It was somewhere in between. Rural suburbia, was how the area was classified by the Tantanoula Local Government Authority. Zone 87B. Milk runs but no garbage collection.

Panorama Way started wide with dark and shiny bitumen. It turned off City Road next to Dora Knockers' takeaway food shop, then snaked along the side of a hill, past the Balstrups and the Spadgeways and the Zaxmaxes and the Keefs and the Weleslys and the Spudics and the Ramsbottoms and the Kruegers and the Hatts and the Okes and the Ketteringhams and the Surfs and the Domotors and the Knotts and the Lavertys and the Goslings and the McMaxwells and the Nids and the Proudfoots and the Scrimshaws and the Towers and the Wetherills and the Chungs and the Kisses and finally, past the Leadheads.

At the top of Panorama Way, the backyards shared fences. But down where the Kisses and Leadheads lived, the tar turned to dirt and the houses got farther and farther apart until eventually you could drive for hours and see nothing but starched grass. Panorama Way was the tail of a dog. It started strong in the spine of things, then frizzled out to nothing but empty hair, Leadheads and useless roosters.

Who was it that first dumped live roosters at the Local Government Authority rubbish tip next door to the Leadheads?

The old depot guard, in fact. Under the cover of a dust storm the old man and his dog left a spray of useless he-hens from the Easter hatchings to fend for themselves among the pelted pyramids of slag and local scrapings. Then Mr Wiblen from Clerical and Ancillary at Tantanoula Primary School downloaded two kicking hessian sacks. Then the husband of the daytime newsreader ditched a fighting cock that had lost its nerve. And after that there was no telling how many of Tantanoula's fine citizens had left leached white leghorns with missing combs or flaming bantams with fireworks for tails or Turkish Silkies with faces like blue trifles at the Panorama Way tip.

Why was the town plagued by such a surplus of unwanted roosters?

Ask Jackson Kiss! Cheryl used to cry. As far as she was concerned the world would be a better place if there was a similar dumping ground for useless balding stepfathers. Not to mention thick-lipped Ramsbottom brothers. Imagine Jackson, Murray and Mort wading in circles through pools of household bilge, discarded undergarments and crisping orange rinds with the rest of the roosters. What a sight for sore eyes that would be.

The Kiss residence sat in a dip two kilometres down the road from Dora Knockers' fish and chip shop at the Panorama Way turn-off. The walls of the fibro house were so thin, Cheryl had left dints on three separate occasions just by hurling tins of mangos.

'Who would have guessed?' Cheryl announced to Sprawlin' Pauline on the cover of the latest edition of *Hunch For Men* (she'd packed the magazine into her school bag for show and tell along with the sewing scissors, but reneged at the last minute). 'They weren't even family-sized tins.'

Sprawlin' Pauline had nothing to add. But the distributors of Phwoar Adult Entertainment video products did note that When It Came To Sports, Nothing Burned Calories Faster Than Wet, Wild Facial Action. Sally McSlab, November *Hunch For Men*'s 'Plumper of the Month' had this to contribute:

> We can't all express ourselves in some lasting way. We can't all write a blockbuster or compose music of lasting interest just as there is no guarantee we can achieve a vital medical breakthrough. However, thanks to my fiancé's skill in the kitchen and interest in fuller-figured American women, my body has become a work of art. What's more, now it can be enjoyed by generations to come thanks to November's sinsational *Hunch* pictorial! In other news, my hobbies include dancing, gardening and good old-fashioned front-end loving, especially out of doors. I am an Aries with a personal weight of 300 pounds and rising!

The Kiss residence would never qualify for Plumper of the Month. Its fibro walls were so thin, Cheryl could hear the crackle of her mother unwrapping pantyhose from 40 paces. Out the front was an anaemic scar of eucalyptus trees and a sign dangling by two dark chains from the letterbox. Kiss residence, it read. The closest neighbours were an old couple across the road with a dog called Chiko Roll. Chiko was a miniature fox terrier with a crocheted collar. He was also the only dog on Panorama Way Zeus hadn't tried to shred. Jackson Kiss said it was because Chiko Roll respected Zeus's superior bloodlines, but Cheryl knew it was because the Chungs fed Zeus steamed dim sims the colour of storm clouds whenever he stopped by to snap at their thistles.

Down the hill from the Kiss residence was a long valley with a distant rectangle of shining water that turned such a bright gold at sunset, it lost its shape completely.

Oh How Beautiful, Violet! What An Absolute Knockout Of A View! the verandah visitors would pirouette to tell the hostess with the mostess.

And Cheryl's mother would laugh with her hands fluttering and her yellow hair swishing, which meant once again it was up to her daughter to explain: It's The Sewage Plant, Don't You Know.

Violet didn't like Cheryl telling the visitors the view was shit but facts were facts.

'What they can see shining,' Cheryl would sometimes tell Zeus after she'd been sent to her room in the cement carport in disgrace, 'is their own shit. They're in love with their own shit.'

'Nothing is as it seems,' Zeus would reply, losing another swivel of hair as he made good with his mouth across open back. 'Everything's hidden. What's there? Did someone say gristle?'

'Nothing wrong with being in love with your own shit but at the very least you could own up to it,' Cheryl would add.

'Please don't say "shit" in future darling, it's grubby.' That wouldn't be Zeus. That would be her mother after the visitors had left and lipstick bubbled in each corner of her mouth and the smell of her made Cheryl want to bury her face into Zeus's ripply neck to escape. 'Very grubby indeed.'

No prizes for guessing what would happen after Violet Kiss wall-to-walled her way back inside the skeletal white house. No prizes at all. But here's a hint: Mmmm. Hmmm. Oh Jackson. OH JACKSON.

Exactly.

Cheryl crunched up the gravel driveway and wondered how long it would be before her mother noticed the sewing scissors were missing. Maybe the accident the night before would put her off pruning for good.

Zeus shouted and bounced from the end of his rope.

'Hey, listen,' said Cheryl, unclipping his leash. 'I'll let you off but Reb and Lou and the rest of us don't want you hanging round us any more.'

'Can't stop now,' said Zeus and ran at a white bird picking dried dog balls out of his bowl.

'Can't stop now,' said Zeus and sniffed in zigzags along the barbed-wire boundary.

'Can't stop now,' said Zeus and made one last pass at that bewitching temptress his lashing tail.

'It's because you're too rude and too rough and too much of a fat pig,' she said.

But Zeus wasn't listening. He said something about having to see a man about a dog and vanished.

Three strands of barbed-wire fence separated the handkerchief of land that came with The Kiss Household from the 100 acres owned by the Wetherills up the road.

'Can I have a horse now we live on a farm?'

'No, Cheryl, there's not enough room.'

'Can I have a bullock?'

'No, Cheryl, there's not enough room.'

'Can I have a goat?'

'No, Cheryl, there's not enough room.'

'What about a dog?'

'For God's sake shut up, Cheryl. Do you want to give me another one of my migraines? Is that what you want? IS IT?'

Subdivision.

That's how Panorama Way had turned from horizon farms to horrible halfway-between land. Farmers drawing lines through their land and selling off squares to people like Cheryl's mother and stepfather. Not that anyone expected the Leadheads to subdivide. Their 20-acre block was a wasteland, a mess of weeds and camphor laurels and cattle missing eyeballs. Grandma Leadhead was always too busy sleeping outdoors to sift the dead magpies out of the water tank and Old Man Leadhead's birthmark just got redder and redder. Their land wasn't going anywhere.

When Violet had driven Cheryl away from their house in the city, she'd promised they would only live in the country until she found her feet or got her head together — whichever came first. That was seven years ago. Cheryl remained hopeful. She knew stranger things happened at sea. And just imagine how good it would be once Violet was vertical and clear-headed and no longer living in la la land (which was the address she once gave a police officer after being caught driving with two cocktail bottles of white rum tucked behind her ears).

Things That Would Change Once Violet Kiss Found Her Feet
(Five examples which came readily to mind)

1. Fame and fortune all round.
2. Never having to attend Tantanoula High School again in your whole life.

3. Trail riding with Miss Carlos beneath the skyscrapers.
4. No more YOU KNOW WHAT.
5. The rooster dumping of Jackson Kiss.

Well there was no harm in thinking positive, was there?

Once, deep within the previous summer, Cheryl became convinced that December 31st would be the occasion of her mother's transformation. This was the date the old depot guard had nominated via cardboard body poster that the world would end without warning, as well as the night 100 local luminaries had been invited to attend the Kiss residence for the purpose of celebrating the end of the old year and the birth of the new. Cheryl's anticipation was misspent. Apart from Kenneth Vulpine's dramatic recycling of Jackson's crème margot and Violet and Dora Knockers' fisticuffs, the night came and went like any other. In fact, on New Year's Day, Violet was even less foot-sure than usual. Cheryl and Zeus had turned their back on the retching figure in the bathtub and made the first of a series of decisions to move into the thick throng of bamboo on the hill on the way down to the river. But the morning wind transformed the gleaming yellow stems into a witch's circle and the dynamic duo lasted only four hours in the still heart of its moaning body before the mosquitoes and the rat got the better of them.

'Maybe next year,' said the woman with fifty pounds of Jiggling Juicy Juggs in Phwoar's Limited Edition Video Catalogue as the girl and the dog schlepped homewards. 'Maybe next New Year's Eve or the Easter holidays or in 1000 sleeps.'

Cheryl told the girl in the magazine to shut up. She

wanted Violet to get her head together as much as anyone, but sometimes she couldn't remember why she'd wanted to move back to the city in the first place. Leeroy and Leon Evensly had once asked for underwear in exchange for freshmint chewing gum and a dog called Princess once had puppies, but that was about it.

'Neither incidents were particularly recommending,' she explained to Zeus. 'The Evenslys didn't speak to me once they were awarded proper bikes and Princess couldn't even hunt cockroaches.'

The truth was Cheryl would have been happy living anywhere with a less hilarious ceiling and less depressing lino. Actual physical pain, was what those peeling lime floor squares at Lot 28 Panorama Way caused Violet Kiss. Actual physical pain.

Off the cement carport of the Kiss residence was a small room with a screen door facing the road. This was Cheryl's bedroom. Up on the wall was a poster of Lance Seldom reclining on a chaise lounge and two photographs of the film actress Lurex Imperial sitting on a motorbike with enough plastic fairing to feed a hungry family of four. The bedspread and curtains were in matching shades of smalt blue and there was a bucket hidden in the wardrobe in case Cheryl couldn't make it back to the main house before she threw up.

On the afternoon of Lou's school d'état, Cheryl balanced on a cardboard carton full of empty scotch bottles to reach the top of the electricity box containing the keys to the house and to her room. The box hummed and the keys were hot from a sparking blue wire. A plane passed overhead and Cheryl pointed her finger and shot finger bullets until it fell in flames.

'Can't stop now,' said Zeus observing the carnage. 'Must bark. Must roll. Must glare down cow. Must chew on poo. Must sleep. Gotta run.'

Cheryl blew the end of her trigger finger. If she didn't shoot planes out of the sky they were only going to fall out themselves. Like the one carrying her real father, Frank Anderson, over the ocean between Mexico and Australia. Suitcase dinghies floating on the ocean. Shoes and pillows and elbows and legs and ribbons of safety belts. That's what plane wreckage looked like in Jackson's collection of *Whoops!* videotapes. A disgorging bag of human groceries.

'Get those disgusting tapes out of my house,' Violet had shrieked the night she'd discovered episodes I–IV of *Whoops!* filed under Comedy in the video cabinet. 'How many times have I told you my nerves simply won't stand this sort of insensitivity?'

Jackson agreed that Violet had indeed presented him with this information on quite a number of occasions and tossed the tapes out with an eiderdown of potato peelings. Cheryl didn't care. She'd watched them all a hundred times. There was no footage of her father's plane crash, but there had been a daredevil speedway stuntman who looked a little like him. Richard Variety-Slim was a retired Formula One test racer who caught fire after leaping a motor bike over six children's swimming pools noodling with toddlers. The firefighters who hosed him down couldn't understand why he'd kept rolling and screaming and churning up the lawn even though he was as damp as a dishcloth. It was only after he passed out in a steaming heap that they realised his hair was on fire beneath his helmet.

'Richard Variety-Slim learned a valuable lesson that day,' the presenter beamed at the conclusion of the segment.

He declined to explain exactly what.

Violet Kiss didn't like answering questions about Cheryl's real father and the day his plane had fallen out of the sky into the ocean.

She said it was morose.

She said it wouldn't do anyone any good anyway.

She said why was Cheryl so obsessed with Frank Anderson when it was Violet Kiss who worked day in and day out to give her the opportunities she'd never had. Well? WELL?

Cheryl opened her school bag and discovered that the broken banana had infiltrated the marijuana book. The smeared biro inscription in its front cover now read:

Son, you're old enough now to read this (smear).
And it is worth reading, because it's the truth, love
always, Mom, x (smear smear)

According to the confidential records of the school librarian, *Why Haven't Marijuana Smokers Been Told These Facts?* had been stolen from the Tantanoula High School library more often than any other title except for *When A Man Loves A Woman*, *101 Infectious Diseases*, *The Anatomy of Deviance* and *Grammar Fundaments* (which contained an artist's impression of the breasts of various senior netballers).

The air inside the Kiss residence was dark and green from the vindictive kitchen linoleum. Cheryl performed a half-hearted Lance Seldom-style fist 'n' spin move in front of the pantry. For breakfast she'd picked at a cup of her stepfather's savoury rice and pineapple goulash. For lunch she'd ignored the banana and also the meat pie. All day she'd hoped dinner would be nothing more than a vicious rumour.

noteating noteating noteating NOTEATING

Cheryl hopped from one end of the house to the other — a procedure which took some time. She picked through the contents of her mother's bedroom bin, tried on the knee-high boots and pulled out strands of her own hairs until there was a small floor pile of mousy brown.

She wondered if Reb would go and stay at Lou's place the next time her father went to jail.

'One last time,' she said to Zeus. 'One last time then never again.'

Tins of spaghetti and tins of sliced mangos and tins of custard and tins of fish, slaty and soft boney, scraping, scraping and salt and vinegar Crispy Cracks and sickly thick Nutmad and eat through your teeth Chocorocko and neverenough Nicerice and Lutbutter straight from the jar and crab meat in pressed plastic blocks and sweaty cheese with green pepper and two plates of ice-cream with chocolate syrup and pink milk direct from the carton and more ice-cream and another plate of whipped Beam Cream and a worn silver spoon tasting of steel and meat.

Cheryl ate until she was invisible. She ate until she was the brain pea on top of the butcher's shop. She swallowed solidly for an hour. It wasn't like it was food. It was just something going in.

She lay in the coarse green carpet in the lounge room, shag elbows rubbed bare by chair legs and repeat feet. She lay back and stared the bookcase into angular nightmares and threatening spines. Up on the television was a circular vase of purple flowers inverting themselves in a spew of purple spray and yellow-tipped stems — petal sharks regurgitating their stomachs in shock.

Cheryl the body wept into the synthetic lime whirls of the floor, the last person left alive in the whole world.

Later, she threw the empty cans and bottles into a white garbage bag. Her fingernails swelled with dirt as she dug a shallow bush grave beside the stand of bamboo on the hill. Back in the kitchen was a trail of red-and-yellow fluid where she'd dragged the evidence.

'Tomorrow it will be different,' she told Zeus, wiping the floor with a sponge alive with secret bacteria. 'This was absolutely and definitely the last time.'

But Zeus had taken issue with a bruised purple tongue fluttering from the vase of flowers on top of the television and was in no mood to engage.

Cheryl felt sick.

She lay on the couch.

Outside, calves shrieked for their mothers and the gold rectangle in the valley reflected the colours of the afternoon sky in all its shitty glory. There was a distant call from the rooster dump down the road as Jackson's car breaststroked through the driveway gravel.

'How was school, CJ,' he asked over a sinkful of potatoes, minced steak and sprinkling pepper.

'OK,' said Cheryl.

An hour later he asked again.

'How was school, CJ?'

'All right,' she said.

Violet's fourth husband decided not to exercise his right to remain silent and told Cheryl it was 7 p.m.

'Well?' he said.

'Well?' she said.

'Aren't you going to turn on the television?'

'OK.'

'You're a bundle of joy tonight, CJ.'

'I'm all right.'

'How was school, then?'

'It was OK.'

'Is that the only thing you can say?'

Cheryl glared through her fringe.

'We all know how important it is for you teeny-boppers to be individuals, Cheryl, but have you looked at yourself in the mirror lately? You're really starting to pork up, young lady.'

'It's 7 p.m.'

'Put the news on, then,' said her stepfather. 'No-one's stopping you.'

Outside, the afternoon changed colour but not temperature. Hot, dark light fell over the dog curled in a dried bean on the green carpet, over the bald man skinning carrots at the sink, over the fat girl in front of the television.

'And turn a light on would you, Cheryl?'

The Tantanoula newsreader related a story about the surf carnival at Zip Point. There had been a record number of hospitalisations in the heatwave. Human vegetables on stretchers. Talking faces, an oceanic engineer, a worried aunty, a keeper of supernatural lighthouse goats who knew about the tides.

'Holding a beach volleyball competition in this weather is just asking for trouble,' said the doctor in the white coat during a live cross from the Tantanoula Base Hospital. 'It's a disgrace and a blot on the landscape and another black mark against the increasingly putrid reputation of the Tantanoula Local Government Authority. Where do they think they get off? Hollywood?'

'That was local general practitioner and mayoral hopeful Dr Razz Salmon,' said the newsreader, half-smirking with eyes a deep, rectangular blue. 'And the weather's not the only thing getting the good folk of Tantanoula hot under the collar. Local small businesswoman Miss Dora Knockers has finally come head to head with the long arm of the law thanks to her flagrant disregard of basic hygiene during her alleged food preparations.'

Another half-smirk followed by an eyebrow raise and forehead head tilt. Headatorialising, *The Chinese Whisper* called it. Who did that newsreader think she was? And who would have guessed she'd increase the nightly news ratings by a whopping 16 points?

The headatorialising made people think the Tantanoula newsreader knew things they didn't. That's why they stopped her in the street to ask her advice about thin-finned versus blue-eyed pilchards or whether Dr Salmon's impotence potion cut the mustard or if Dora Knockers was really selling under-the-counter calamaris disallowed by the Fish Board. To some, the newsreader's headatorialising and half-smirking was arrogant, callous even. To dozens of others it was as good an excuse as any to send ornamental pots of succulents, alive with ribbons and Sealed With A Loving Kiss.

'. . . six-month suspension of her cabaret licence . . .'

'. . . denied the allegations . . .'

'. . . celebrated her 101st birthday . . .'

'. . . disarmed seven fox traps . . .'

'. . . redeveloped the brickworks . . .'

'. . . reignited the yowie debate . . .'

'. . . and for Christ's sake if you're going to dump your dinner in the bin then do it when Jackson's not looking, it's not nice when he's gone to so much trouble . . .'

Cheryl sat so close to the screen the newsreader's smile exploded into hard squares of colour.

'Hello?' she said, her face pressed into the screen. 'Hello?'

Cheryl sat so close to the screen the woman's face gathered around her, the television mouth stretched huge and deep like the jaw of a beast.

'Hello?'

'Hello?'

'Can't you even hear me?'

After the news, Cheryl sat at the table pushing a green bean around the outside of her plate. When she tired of the bean she pushed a pea. When she tired of the pea she pushed both. Construction had begun on a mashed potato replica of Mrs Stint's bosoms when her stepfather finally spoke.

'Are you sure you're all right?' he asked.

'Yes,' said Cheryl.

'"Yes, thank you",' said her stepfather.

'Yes, thank you,' chanted Cheryl.

'Well, you've hardly touched dinner and you haven't said a word to me all night.'

'It's definitely more like 20.'

'I'm sorry?'

'It's definitely more like 20 words.'

'Do you want me to send you to your room, Cheryl? Because if you're going to act like a child, I'm going to treat you like one.'

'Fuck off,' said Cheryl with all the maturity she could muster.

Behind the screen door of the room off the carport she shredded the report card she'd been hiding from her mother and thought again of the dictionary definition of

14. The dictionary definition of 14 was what was wrong with the whole world. The logic was internal. If you weren't already in possession of inside information, you'd never get it.

'One more than 13' explained nothing.

3

Cheryl Has Considerable Physical Ability But Is Inclined Not To Use It In The Correct Way At Times

TANTANOULA HIGH SCHOOL 'Success through Strivation' YEAR 9 OR 10 REPORT NAME: Cheryl Jane Kiss CLASS: 9–1 ASSESSMENT: Final					NOTE: The Letter Grade indicates such things as attitude, industry and co-operation in the subject according to the code: A: Excellent B: Very Good C: Satisfactory D: Needs Improvement E: Poor The average mark is 65.
SUBJECT	CLASS	MARK	POSITION IN GROUP	LETTER GRADE	
English (Adv)	1	97	1/135	C	Despite a good overall result, interest, effort and performance have declined since Terms 1 and 2. (Mrs Waist)
Maths	1	54	59/60	D	Cheryl has become a problem. She does not co-operate and do as she is told, or do the work, and sometimes tries to start arguments. I feel maybe she is finding the work difficult and this has caused it.
Science	1	60	24/30	C	Makes very little effort. Lacks basic knowledge of short-answer section and at times gives the impression that Science is boring.

SUBJECT	CLASS	MARK	POSITION IN GROUP	LETTER GRADE	
Televisual Studies		84	10/21	B−	Cheryl keeps up to date but her concentration is poor. Eliminating these lapses might improve results. PRUE BLOCK
Geography		66	24/37	D	Satisfactory yet disappointing. Cheryl is capable of much better results but has developed a negative attitude to her work. CY
Modern History		71	31/65	C+	Cheryl has a growing sophistication in historical analysis and has worked consistently to produce a pleasing result. Perhaps next year she could follow her mother's example and become more like her wonderful mother! Mrs Stint!
Home Economics			58/59		CHERYL DERIVES LITTLE SATISFACTION FROM HOME SCIENCE AND TEXTILES. Katherine Whitebait
French		75	16/27	B	Disenthusiastic about language study. Rob Bruce
Art		68	29/37	B−	This student has been unsuccessful with ceramics. V
Physical Education			56/56	C	Cheryl has considerable physical ability but is inclined not to use it in the correct way at times. (Pete Scoob.)

Over the past SIX MONTHS Cheryl's marks have fallen CONSIDERABLY — a situation which has caused great concern to *everyone* here at Tantanoula High School. Despite being a potentially very BRIGHT YOUNG STUDENT, this young lady finds it hard to work without disturbing others, is poorly motivated and rarely dresses in a manner suitable for given occasions. *Please encourage Cheryl to wear correct school uniform in future* (this is a high school *not* a CIRCUS). A much more determined effort is needed in Year 10 if this student is to achieve the *above meritorious standard requirements* we all know she is capable of.
P. Roper (YEAR ADVISOR)

4

The Enormity Of The Situation

The morning after Lou's school d'état, Cheryl and her mother took breakfast together over an ashtray of White City cigarettes. Next to them, the tinny little kitchen transistor vibrated madly with the effort of bringing them The Dick Lyndon Sextet's acclaimed instrumental version of the sentimental favourite, *Onion Tears*.

Violet had locked herself into a life or death stare-off with a square of green lino. She sent an arrow of blue smoke shooting down its throat and it curled its thin, lime lips into a cutthroat snarl.

'You disgust me,' she said.

'Pus forever,' the floor replied, strands of yellow lino glue pulling free from the floorboards. '*Gleet mucor rankling copro scato defo uronic PUS.*'

Violet sucked even harder on the cigarette and sent her stomach into a relief map of sand dunes.

Not really a morning person, Violet Kiss. Not really an afternoon or an evening person either, but there was no need to get snippy.

'Skipping breakfast this morning, Cakes?' Violet smiled crookedly as Cheryl toyed with her food. Violet's privates were killing her. The medical dressing beneath her mauve leisure slacks was as discreet as a surfboard on a roof-rack.

'Maybe,' said Cheryl.

'Breakfast is the most important meal of the day,' said Violet.

'I know,' said Cheryl.

'Good on you, Cakes,' croaked Violet. 'I'm proud of you.'

Violet was full of good ideas about how to stay trim, taut and terrific. For one unforgettable weekend while Jackson was out of town, she and Cheryl had used dog bowls instead of plates as a novelty reminder that food was for pigs. The gold lettering on Cheryl's bowl read *Blackie*.

'It's the only way, Cakes,' Violet the Swinelette had spat at Blackie the Pig, local produce smeared over her perfectly painted face.

'My neck's sore,' Cheryl had grumbled back. 'Can't we at least eat from dog bowls up at the table?'

'Grhjhg blugh furlugh,' Violet had reprimanded. 'Ghgflug bluglt!'

The woman was gargling solid lamb.

A pink joke of a skull materialised at the bathroom door.

'Morning ladies,' said Jackson, towelling away at what might have once been his hair. 'How are the famous Kiss sisters this morning, then?'

41

Violet giggled in an excitable fashion and adjusted her private padding. The only person who ever mistook Violet and Cheryl for siblings was Jackson — religiously. But when the Kisses were out in public, Cheryl had been instructed to call Violet Violet rather than mum. It was all part of the Kiss commitment to keeping the romance alive. Jackson even had a book on the subject. It was called *Keeping The Romance Alive*. He had recently reached Chapter Three: Romantic Cookery.

'How's my grapefruit foam and rice medley muesli then?' he asked.

'Delicious as always, my sweet,' cooed Violet.

'Excellent, excellent. Fish meuniere tonight. With quick Betsy noodles, prune souffle and weekend Christmas cake no less.'

'You're spoiling me again as usual, darling.'

'If I don't there's plenty of others who will.'

'Oh, Jackson.'

'Oh, Violet.'

Cheryl was dry-retching.

'I'm an intravenous drug user,' she said.

'You're too good for me, Jackson.'

'No you're too good for me, Violet.'

'I cut off my blood supply with barbed wire and inject heroin through my eyeball with a needle.'

'I wuv you.'

'I wuv you more.'

'In fact I'm about to get a prosthetic vein built into my anus because all the real ones are infested with gangrene, syphilis and household bleach.'

'Did you say something, Cheryl?'

'No, mum.'

'That's just as well, darling, because it's almost time for school.'

Jackson shovelled down two plates of ricey grapefruit muesli and topped it off with the leftovers of his thatched taties. He told Zeus to get on his mat. He said he hadn't imported a genuine ram skin 4 Legs Good 2 Legs Bad water-rug just so Zeus could look at it. Then he coughed into the bathroom sink for 10 minutes and then he washed up.

Cheryl ran odds on how Violet had explained the underwear surfboard to her life partner.

Women's troubles: 18/1
Fishing accident: 29/1
What surfboard?: 2/1

There was a low scream from the front yard.

'Looks like the dog has got himself another koala,' Jackson said, wandering outside into the heat. 'Anyone seen my glasses?'

Violet was also moving in for the kill. She wanted to know why Cheryl had failed to implement a single one of her flesh-abbreviating exercise suggestions.

'Skipping breakfast is all well and good but the trick is to get really puffed at least three times a week. You don't want to have those rolls on your wedding day, do you Cakes?'

'Yep — it's a sticky one,' Jackson called from the masticated koala site. 'Anyone seen my shovel?'

'No pain no gain remember, Cheryl.'

'It's a complete soup. *Zeus — drop it for God's sake . . . At least till I'm finished . . .*'

'Are you listening to me, Cakes?'

'It doesn't make any difference,' Cheryl grouched. 'No matter what I do it makes no difference and I don't care if I'm a fat pig anyway.'

'Do too.'

'Do not.'

'Do too.'

'Do not.'

'Could one of you young ladies remind me where I left the exterior dust buster? No, don't get up. Here it is. Now if someone could just switch off the power point in the laundry before I — *oh bugger* . . .'

The thrashings in the front yard were becoming increasingly distracting. Breakfast was the only time Cheryl saw Violet during the week. Sometimes she heard her skittling bottles or horse-laughing late at night but that didn't really count as quality time.

Didn't anyone have anything better to do than lip push-ups?

'I don't know where you get this bad attitude from, Cakes, I really don't. Do you want to be refloated every time you turn up at the beach? Is that what you want?'

'Wiglet,' said Cheryl.

'Negativity will get you a big EN OH nowhere, my girl.'

'Wiglet, wiglet, wiglet.'

'Get those spoons out of your ears while I'm talking to you.'

'Wiglet, wiglet, wiglet, wiglet, wiglet, wiglet, wiglet, wiglet, wiglet, wiglet, wiglet, wiglet, wiglet.'

'For Christ's sake, Cheryl, it's too early for your rubbish, it really is.'

And she was right. It was only 8 a.m. and already the day was impossibly fiery.

What's more, someone was about to die.

Cheryl and Violet didn't know that, of course. Cheryl and Violet had taken a brief break from shouting to simultaneously consider the size of their stomachs. Violet was wondering whether one could gain any real satisfaction from looking a young 38. Cheryl couldn't believe she'd spent another afternoon in the pantry. Beneath the table, evidence of the afternoon before oinked over her lap. Her belly was the size of the local television station's promotional blimp. It had a life of its own. The only consolation was that she was never going to eat again. The only consolation was that it would only be a matter of time before Mrs Stint rotted off with disfiguring scabs and Lou was hounded by head lice the size of dogs and Murray Ramsbottom finally realised what he'd been missing out on all these years.

'A thousand apologies,' Cheryl would say as Murray begged endearingly from the ruins of his trail bike. 'But it can never be. And now I'm afraid I shall have to whip you into little bits and pieces and wrap you up in shopping bags and dump you in the shit-maker to teach you a valuable lesson.'

'I'm speaking to you, Cheryl,' said Violet.

'Yes mother?' said Cheryl.

'What I said, and believe me this will be the last time, is am I wrong in assuming it is 8.05 in the a.m.? And if I am not wrong, why, pray tell, are you not in your school uniform?'

Cheryl shaped a breakaway muesli pod into an exact replica of Lou's fat arse and cast her memory back to the first page of the chapter entitled '*Warning: Distorts Time, Impairs Memory and Reduces Ability to Reason*' in the stolen library book.

'According to United States Senator James O Eastland, pot smokers will remain partial mental cripples even after they give up cannabis,' she told her mother.

'Don't change the subject,' snapped Violet. 'Where is your uniform?'

'In my bedroom beneath a vital publication on the dangers of marijuana.'

'Then for Christ's sake shut up and get dressed.'

Cheryl considered the best method of telling one's mother one was no longer attending one's educational institution because one had nowhere to walk to at lunchtime.

'I'm not wearing my school uniform because I've grown a third arm,' she said.

'Why are you doing this to me?'

'What difference does it make to you?'

'Because I'm your mother, that's why.' (Look out! Logic!) 'Do you want to end up on night fill at Bi-Mart with the rest of the breeders? Is that what you want?'

Bi-Mart was a supermarket chain that sold ten-packs of unbleached toilet rolls for $3.69 per unit. 'Night fill' was the official description of a position in which paid workers restocked its shelves between the hours of 9 p.m. to 7 a.m. It was a thankless task, but it did pay $5 an hour. That was a lot of toilet rolls.

There was a roar on the road outside, and Cheryl and Violet both turned to watch the school bus steam past.

'I can't go to school because I don't have any friends,' said Cheryl.

Violet twisted a strand of blonde hair around a red fingernail.

'Don't be ridiculous,' she said. 'Everyone has friends. Especially at your age. What about Reb and Lou and the rest of those nice young ladies who gave so much help to Jackson in the kitchen on the day of your party?'

'They sent Murray Ramsbottom around to say they don't want me hanging round them any more.'

'Murray Ramsbottom?' said Jackson walking in from the front yard with a racing stripe of blood and koala fur down one leg. 'That was an odd choice.'

'Shut up,' said Cheryl.

'Shut up,' said Violet.

The enormity of the situation had finally penetrated her blonde tangles.

'But Cakes,' she said as if she was putting her foot down. 'You *need* friends.'

'Exactly,' said Cheryl. 'That's why I can't go to school.'

Violet Kiss lit another cigarette. She sank her head into her hands. It was another stinking hot day and Tantanoula's enigmatic newsreader had no idea what to say to her fat daughter.

5

A Statistical Introduction To Violet Kiss And Her Flight To Amsterdam

Violet Kiss hadn't always been an enigmatic newsreader in a deadbeat coastal backwater.

Once, she almost became an internationally successful catwalk model. Once, she ate pig intestine frankfurters on a dare in Paris. Once, Italian businessmen showered her with wristwatches. Once, she stepped out with a bona-fide inventor of plastic women. (Delilah, The Most Life-like Female Doll Ever Created, had a 7-inch penetrable vagina and was billed as being at least ten years ahead of her time.)

By the time Violet Kiss was 38 years old and sat taking breakfast with her daughter in Tantanoula she had also gone all the way with 172 gentlemen callers. That was some legwork. In fact, that was an average of 3.44 men per annum (or 5.06 if you commenced counting the year Violet commenced courting).

A tally of this calibre meant any educated listing of the good woman's menfriends would require the use of some grouping mechanism or another.

'The Dewey Decimal system should do the trick!' Violet's best friend, Rashani Bail, used to shout after deportment lessons.

There you have it: Even back in the schoolyard it was unhelpful to rely on simplistic models when introducing the subject of Violet's conquests.

EXHIBIT A — A CHRONOLOGICAL PRESENTATION OF VIOLET KISS'S FIRST NINE BEAUS

1. *Dylan Anchovy*
2. *Alan Dubious*
3. *Frank Stomp*
4. *Glynn French*
5. *Ian Beanland*
6. *Davo 'Horse' Kellogg*
7. *Shift Randhorn*
8. *Trevor Putz*
9. *Baron Romeo*

EXHIBIT B — ALPHABETICAL PRESENTATION OF SAME

1. *Dylan Anchovy*
2. *Ian Beanland*
3. *Alan Dubious*
4. *Glynn French*
5. *Davo 'Horse' Kellogg*
6. *Trevor Putz*
7. *Shift Randhorn*
8. *Baron Romeo*
9. *Frank Stomp*

As you can see, both techniques are convenient enough as memory joggers. Yet each displays the candidates in an unfortunately unrepresentative fashion. Under both systems, Dylan Anchovy pulls rank whereas in reality nothing could be further from the truth. His brief stab at the undergarments of his designated 'beaker buddy' in the demountable science storage unit during Inter School Meet and Greet was so monumentally unmemorable, even Violet herself would have forgotten the incident if she hadn't made a note in her logbook. (The sciences were never her forte, after all.)

And what of Shift Randhorn, inserted so inconspicuously in the grey, no-chap's-land of 'neither first nor last in the list'? How was anyone supposed to ascertain the importance of this unpleasant photographer in the chain of events that eventually led Violet to the hellfires of Tantanoula?

The point is that if listings were problematic back in the days when Violet was sentenced to 14 years of school trombone lessons, the difficulties faced by the time she reached 38 were tenfold.

Or 10.29 fold to be completely accurate.

Violet's mother was the first of many people to have absolutely no idea her daughter was developing a sexual filing problem. Edna Opus-Worthington was too busy wearing embolism undergarments and making sure Violet was free from Satanic influences to notice what she might or might not have been getting up to during youth orchestra practice. Edna's commitment to developing new clichés was also taking up a criminal amount of spare time.

'It's for today!' the antsy old Catholic would shout at Violet after commandeering her for tea or another Minimiser brand brassiere fitting. 'And I *am* planning to close for business before the year 2020, in *case* you were wondering.'

Violet's mother's favourite cliché was 'before the year 2020' followed closely by 'it's for today' followed closely by 'what do you take me for — a pint of lint?' All three were Edna Opus-Worthington originals, therefore requiring constant conversational application in order to justify their status as platitudes.

Many of Edna's DIY clichés missed the proverbial mark or required 'lint' to be pronounced 'line-t' in order to scan. But back in Edna's day, the year 2020 did seem an incomprehensibly long time off and if one was planning to close for business, one would hope it was well and truly before that date.

Youth is wasted on the young, life is wasted on the living and hindsight is wasted on historians. Three pieces of information that would have been of vital interest to Mrs Opus-Worthington when she was still summonsing her teenage daughter to dinner via Swiss Army whistle:

a) The fact that at the time of Edna's official closure of business, her head would be completely separated from her body due to the devilish combination of immutable force (in the form of her husband's car) and immovable object (in this case, the razor-sharp cuff of a sign offering the information: 'Pounce Street Nos 14–102').

b) The fact that at the time her death, Mrs Opus-Worthington had been wearing a heavily elasticised Minimiser brand brassiere 24 hours a day for 37 years.

c) The fact that at least one of Edna's clichés would eventually pass into general usage. Surely Cheryl Jane Kiss was not the only film buff to document the fact that millionaire vegetarian and film starlet Lurex Imperial began bellowing 'it's for today' at hapless extras as early as the filming of *10 9 8 7 6 5 4 3 2 Terror!* and *Sugar Daddy Deadly*)?

Anyway.

'It's for today,' Edna cried up the stairs at her daughter, blowing the whistle for all she was worth. 'Do you think I fry liver for the fun of it, Violet?'

'Coming,' Violet replied, shuffling louvre flaps like great glass cards as she ushered another suitor (possibly Alan Dubious or Frank Stomp) out her bedroom window.

Violet Kiss's most hated nickname at primary school was 'Squid'. Blame it on the trombone. The moment she brought the thing to her mouth, her beautifully ribboned lips were transformed into the beak of an octopus. Mrs Opus-Worthington had forced her daughter to take up the trombone because she believed it was the least sensuous instrument on the market. She was right. The most sensual act Violet ever performed after being viewed playing the trombone was offering Tony and Bernard Patio 'one dollar for one look' the afternoon they wheeled their school bags home in a shopping trolley.

What Tony and Bernard said that afternoon was: Sure thing, Squid.

It was the 200th time Violet had been called Squid that year.

Violet's phenomenal scores in the mating game were no secret. Once or twice she had even presented the figures to her daughter in an attempt to hurry the dear girl along in what she referred to as 'the boyfriend department'. But not even Cheryl was aware that 28 of the 172 aforementioned parties had marriages unconnected to Violet's own and only three were capable of arousing in Violet physical sensations any more exciting than, say, a mouthwash. Only one punter took advantage while the little trooper was down and out for the count, but before anyone calls the vice squad over that one, it should be remembered that

Violet had authorised proceedings a good five minutes before losing consciousness into the incoming tide of the Formula One test racer Richard Variety-Slim.

'Sugar,' she was heard to cry late the next morning when she finally woke. 'That was the worst night's sleep I've had in years.'

Then: 'Who on earth are you?'

By the time she was 38, Violet Kiss had also had three general anaesthetics, four husbands and at least 17 experiences she mistakenly assumed to be near death. The woman four tabloid publications had referred to as a 'leggy blonde' had paid approximately 401 visits to hair salons for bleaching purposes. She had been involved in 14 traffic incidents, three times considered faking her own kidnapping, eight times used the pseudonym Flora Torres and once watched a midwife die of a brain haemorrhage in the front seat of a Glans Four Wheel Drive. The five resolutions she wrote en flight to the European city of Amsterdam at the age of 18 were:

1. *Stop thinking bad thoughts.*
2. *Be own person.*
3. *Change hair?*
4. *Do something about money.*
5. *Don't ever use lipstick for rouge ever again.*
   (You can tell.)

But at the end of the day, most of these figures were neither here nor there.

Jackson Kiss would have disagreed, of course. He found Violet's personal statistics most influencing indeed ('172 gentlemen callers' being of particular note). But what caught or failed to catch the eye of Violet's fourth and final husband was hardly of lasting concern. Violet's mathematical details were only of note because eventually they resulted in the birth of two girls: One buried in an unmarked grave on the outskirts of the Mexican resort town of Cabo Roto and the other pummelling the rolls of flesh on her stomach beneath the Kiss family kitchen table like no-one's business.

Violet's flight away from suburbia and towards her tragic fate in Mexico began on a wintry Thursday morning in May when she boarded Flight RA 865 to Amsterdam for the purposes of expanding her horizons, establishing herself as an international modelling star, obtaining some sort of foreign husband and never seeing her mother again.

At least 50 per cent of this quest would prove to be a dismal failure.

Not that Violet was taking odds.

She was only 18.

'Am I jet set or am I jet set?' she asked her cat, rotating stiffly through the dining room in the very first pencil skirt she had ever owned.

The crusting tabby waited until his mistress had packed her shoes, then settled into the suitcase with a cheated drool. If the human with the high voice thought she was going to expand her horizons by restricting her ability to walk then let her. Moses was going to stick close to the food in the bowl in the white room if it was all the same with her. In the meantime, he scratched a nest in Violet's suitcase and gazed into the middle distance with jelly eyes as dull as toilet water.

On the morning of the great escape, Edna Opus-Worthington found herself deeply distracted by a discounted slab of rump steak in the meat section of the new Bi-Mart. She had no idea her daughter had discovered the nest egg she kept hidden inside an oven bag inside a sock inside a hollowed *Abraham's Old-Testament Encyclopaedia* inside the mattress on her version of the marital bed.

Edna Opus-Worthington was living in a state of ignorance. It wasn't blissful owing to the insomnia and back pain (the corners of that nest egg were nothing short of villainous). But it was ignorance nonetheless.

The Monday Violet spent Edna's savings on a one-way ticket to Amsterdam, Edna thought her daughter was at school.

The Saturday Violet spent queuing in the Dutch embassy for a visa, Edna thought her daughter was busy learning to keep her eyes diverted at Ludmilla Merriweather's Applied Deportment For Debutantes.

The afternoon Violet returned home with her arm right-angled from a stampede of vaccinations, Edna assumed she had received yet another caning at Wart's Catholic Ladies' College as punishment for frivolity or consorting.

And as for *that* personal advertisement Shift Randhorn had placed in *Gush* magazine guaranteeing modelling work on the international catwalks to All Genuine Applicants . . . Edna Opus-Worthington had discovered the heavily-fingered clipping in Violet's dirty clothes basket during a surprise linen raid. She'd taken one look at the international post office box at the bottom of the notice, frowned at the unbridled licentiousness in evidence in a neighbouring advertisement for nail polish remover, then thrown the lot into the garbage and thought no more about it.

'Since when do you ignore the dinner whistle?' the highly strung old Catholic shouted at her daughter's closed bedroom door after returning from the Bi-Mart with not one, but four polystyrene display plates of cut-price rump. 'I *am* planning to close for business before The Year 2096, in *case* you were wondering.'

But the only reply came from a thrillseeking black cockroach that leapt at the neckline of Edna's housedress in a half-hearted shot at what Mr Opus-Worthington might have jokingly referred to as 'the title'.

By then, Violet was halfway to Bangkok.

Rashani Bail and Amanda Joint had taken the future Mrs Kiss to the airport in a car borrowed from one of Rashani's dreaded uncles. Rashani didn't like asking Uncle Hector for favours but it wasn't every day your best friend ran away to Europe to become a superstar.

'My God, it's a symphony in hideousness,' Violet exclaimed, when she first laid eyes on the transport. 'Isn't there a towel or something we can put on the back seat before we sit down?'

'Symphony in hideousness' was a direct quote from *Janet and The Gaberdine Trousers* — the short story in the latest edition of *Gush* magazine. It was an inspirational tale about a young American woman who travelled to Europe to seek fame and fortune as a nanny and was soon married to the richest army general in Austria.

'Symphony in hideousness' was also a more than apt description of the strange, pouncing machine with the bonnet shaped like a half-opened umbrella and headlights slanted like the eyes of death-row cats. The yellow upholstery in Rashani's uncle's car was irretrievably perished. There was something perverse about the way its cracks and crevices spat folded tongues of vanishing seatbelt. The mere act of placing one's bottom on its tight, mustard-coloured vinyl seemed to condone repulsiveness in general.

Rashani launched Violet's suitcase into the vehicle's hungry boot. She was about to attempt a burnout in the driveway when Violet cried 'WAIT' and raced back into the red-brick house. 'I forgot my lip liner,' she called over her shoulder. In reality, she'd returned to fill her mother's empty nest-egg vault with a wad of elderly devon. That'd teach the old hag for having varicose veins and outlawing flirting.

'This car smells funny,' she said as Rashani ground the gears. 'Could you two wind down your windows before I become ill?'

Rashani Bail's winding arm was on auto. She couldn't decide if she was jealous of Violet's date with destiny or relieved it wasn't her who had to arrive in a foreign country with nothing but a single portfolio shot taken in the photo booth at the train station and a letter from some photographer in Amsterdam she'd never even met. Not that you could blame Violet for doing a runner. Mrs Opus-Worthington's strictness with her daughter was legendary, even at Wart's. The tyrannical wordsmith was spoken about in the corridors of the school in tones bordering on the reverential.

Did you know Mrs Opus-Worthington would only allow her daughter to leave the house in skirts as wide as they were long?

Did you know Violet was forced to spray air freshener in the toilet for a slow count to five even after *a number one?*

Still. Violet had broken Thou Shalt Not Steal. Rashani didn't want anything monstrous to happen to her best friend but she was curious to see whether God would do any smoting in revenge. He had every right. There was no denying that.

'Mon dieu, it really is getting *disgusting* in here,' said Violet. 'Did someone let off or is Mandy's BO playing up again?'

BO was a convenient short form for the condition known as Body Odour. There'd been a time when Violet thought it meant Badger Operator (that guy with the beard down at the corner store had a lot to answer for). But the days of not knowing what was what were over. The world wasn't going to know what hit it. It was going to kneel to worship at her feet then leap up to buy her one of those drinks with the olives and the party umbrellas. What were they called again? Gin and tonics? In all likelihood Shift Randhorn would make her a household name before the week was out. 'Get here now!' he'd written in response to Violet's photograph. 'You angel! You Madonna! You impossibly heavenly nymph! [Cheques and cards not accepted].'

Violet interrupted these pleasant musings to ahem theatrically.

'Please consider spraying yourself with something, Mandy. You really are starting to smell quite vile.'

Violet's other best friend, Amanda, consulted her armpit. Mrs Opus-Worthington might have been a complete and utter warlock but at least she let Violet wear BO killer. (Mrs Joint thought female deodorants were spiked with pheromones.) Mandy's attempts to decrease the smell by keeping her arms pressed tightly against her side were next to useless. This was because the stench wasn't really emanating from her crevices.

It was coming from a block of butter that had fallen into an inaccessible corner of the car's interior. Blasts from the car's heater were sending it septic and the assault on the girls' nostrils was nothing short of sensational.

'I don't think I can stand much more of this,' Violet said, fanning her nose with a motivational brochure claiming 72 per cent of birds were promiscuous.

'Fine,' said Rashani. 'Try walking the rest of the way to the airport. You'll freeze to death in that microscopic ensemble.'

'It's summer in Europe.'

'And are you sure you're wearing enough make-up?'

Edna's nest egg had covered more than the airfare and suitcase. It had also stretched to three twin sets, eight pairs of shoes and a lipstick in Flaming Rubricate. The rest of the money was put aside to pay for a portfolio by Shift Randhorn. Well. Most of the rest. It was quite possible Violet had also invested in one small bottle of Casino Pink nail polish and one quite large bottle of Violent Ruby Highlitz hair shampoo. Blame Edna Opus-Worthington and her commitment to the colour beige. Thanks to Edna's conviction that drabness was next to Godliness, Violet had pledged to surround herself with only beautiful things. When she grew up she was going to be Amera Suspender. She was going to drink gin and tonics and go to parties and accept cigarettes from positively everyone. Children were out of the question. Who wanted to have to wear an industrial-strength bra day in and day out like her saggy mother?

Mind you, she thought, craning to catch a glimpse of herself in the smudged rear-vision mirror. Maybe it hadn't been such a great idea to use the new lipstick as rouge after all.

'Rashani,' wheedled Violet in a voice as sweet as sweet apple pie.

'Dewey?' Rashani wheedled right back.

'For the millionth zillionth time could you *please* do something about this smell?'

'Well,' said Rashani in her own voice again. 'Apart from sticking a couple of Meds up your nose, I don't think there's a whole lot I can offer you.'

Violet blushed. If she used tampons there was no way she'd tell the world about it. People might think she was loose. Her flat stomach gargled beneath the panels of her new skirt. Was it the cluster of musk air fresheners draped from the rear-vision mirror in a cardboard bouquet or the awful smell they failed to erase? She wondered about the last thing you'd see if you fell from the sky in a burning jumbo. What if you died before you ever got married? That would be worse than dying without being Christened. You'd go to the worst limbo of all.

Her smooth throat pulsed with nausea.

'Pull over,' she screeched. 'I'm going to throw up.'

Plastic perfume from the air fresheners swirled round Violet's nostrils as she gagged delicately in a side-saddle position.

'Bubble gum bubble gum bubble gum,' Amanda sang along to the radio, trying not to inhale the smell of vomit. 'Come on and dance for me my chewy one.'

'I hate this song,' said Rashani, spitting an oyster of chewing gum into a drain. 'It's fucking inane.'

'Stop using that word,' Violet managed between spasms. 'It's grubby.'

'It's not as bad as the c-word.'

This prompted Violet's very first projectile vomit. (Don't worry, there'd be plenty more in future.) Breakfast sprayed all over a bunch of flowers marking a highway grave as she made bitter projections about the future of her expleting friend. Brothels. Female prisons. Probably even motherhood.

'I love being a Catholic,' Rashani mused from behind the steering wheel. 'Everything's such a fucking drama.'

Now Rashani was in Year 12 she thought she could say anything she wanted. Now she'd finally French kissed a boy she thought she knew everything. But Rashani didn't know about Glynn French, Ian Beanland and Davo Kellogg, even if Violet had weakened and told her about Dylan, Alan and Frank. You'd think going all the way would be a tad more memorable but anything was better than being a frigid slut like Sofia Eight or Jennifer Luston. Violet couldn't believe she'd just used an expression like 'frigid slut', even in her brain. Thank God she was leaving high school and running away to Amsterdam to become a model before it was too, too late.

Rashani resumed her odorous streak down the highway and sped straight past another green and white exit sign bearing a picture of an aeroplane.

Violet was beside herself.

'Well that's it, isn't it.'

'That's what?'

'That's it. You've passed another airport exit. That's the *third* one you've missed. Do you realise now I'll miss the plane? Do you realise we might as well turn back now? Do you realise my mother's going to kill me and it's going to be all your fault?'

'Relax,' said Rashani, giving her passenger a medicinal jab in the shoulder. 'The flight's not for another two-and-a-half hours.'

'But the ticket *says* you have to be there at least two hours before the plane leaves. It *says* you have to check in *two hours* in advance or they might allocate your ticket to *someone else*. That's what it *says*.'

'Relax,' said Rashani, removing Violet's plane ticket from her eye before she ploughed into a eucalypt. 'They only say two hours for complete anal retentives. If you've confirmed your ticket they let you on board right up until the last minute.'

'*Confirmed*?' shrieked Violet.

'You did ring to confirm didn't you?'

'*Of course I didn't ring to confirm*. There was nothing *about* confirming on the ticket and I know, because I *read* it right *through*. I read the whole thing and if there'd been a single *thing* about confirming I would have been the first . . .'

Rashani dreamed of a personal volume control that could dim Violet like a chandelier. For the past five years she'd spent every Saturday and every Sunday working in her father's laundry. Her deeply religious mother received personal messages from numberplates and ate her own hair, her deeply religious father beat her sisters with his athletics awards and twice now her deeply religious Uncle Hector had cornered her drunkenly in the bathroom and demanded that she 'suck it'. All this and not once had Rashani ever cried the way Violet Opus-Worthington was crying now. She turned up the radio and twisted her tongue to keep from telling her best friend to find her own fucking way to the airport. The last thing they needed at this stage was another fight.

Amazingly enough, even when Rashani took the wrong turn-off, every second street had a blue sign with a plane.

'All roads lead to the airport,' observed Amanda.

'Don't they think anyone wants to do anything else besides get out of here?' Rashani grouched to no-one in particular.

The pilgrims arrived at the international airport's short-term car park with time to spare and Rashani tugged at the handle of Violet's luggage. The suitcase had wedged itself into the boot of the ugly yellow car like an impacted wisdom tooth.

'You pack the fucking kitchen sink in here?'

Violet told Rashani for the millionth zillionth time it was only a matter of time until her bad language caught up with her. It was a scientific fact that women who swore were five times more likely to become prostitutes, three times more likely to give birth out of wedlock and twice as likely to get cancer of the feminine region. She knew it was true because she'd read it in *Gush*.

'Don't tell me you believe that shit.'

'Don't tell me you don't. I'm only passing this information on for your own good. What sort of friend would I be if I didn't alert you to the dangers of your own behaviour?'

'That's a good one coming from Miss Responsible. You want me to run a criminal check on this Amsterdam photographer before or after you spread your legs on the casting couch?'

'You are revolting, Rashani. You are absolutely revolting. And he's not from Amsterdam. He's Dutch, all right. *Dutch*.'

It might not have been obvious to the outside observer, but Rashani, Violet and Amanda had been best friends for ever. They'd said 'no way do you look fat in that' and argued about who was going to marry Dick Lyndon for

14 years now. Over-the-top castigations had always been part of their arrangement, but lately the friendship had developed the tedium of a chore. It would be many years before Rashani could face up to the fact that the trio's legendary bond had more to do with their mutual internment at the hated ladies' college than any real convergence of interest.

'Location, location, location,' Rashani was to tell her therapist bitterly after she had indeed become a hooker and survivor of cervical cancer (single motherhood was not an option on account of her hostile womb). 'Same place, same time. That's all it's really about. No-one wants to put themselves out for something as irrelevant as a platonic friendship. Mandy and I have been meaning to get together for six years now. We really must catch up, we say. We really must. And then we break out the champagne when no-one calls.'

But there would be plenty of time for unsettling personal growth later. On that icy Thursday in May, Violet Opus-Worthington, Amanda Joint and Rashani Bail were still officially best friends. Rashani might have even had the bloodstained paperwork to prove it (where *had* she put that pact?).

'All right then, Dewey?'

'You got your passport?'

'You got your traveller's cheques?'

'You got your visa?'

'You ready for that anal probe at customs?'

'You can *not* tell it's lipstick. It looks exactly like blush. Honest.'

Violet, Rashani and Amanda chastised each other through the car park, trying to ignore the smell of burning rocket fuel, the wolf-whistlers and the phantom of impending upheaval. Violet pictured in pornographic detail the face of her mother when she got home and discovered her daughter and all her illegal shoes gone. The note on the kitchen table was carefully worded so as to leave the reader in doubt as to whether its author had run away or taken her life. This masterpiece of emotional blackmail was Rashani's work. She'd spent a week getting the tone just so, and charged Violet 12 back copies of *Gush* and an autographed pin-up of Dick Lyndon for the privilege. The look on Edna's face would be priceless, it really would.

'Are you sure you can't hide behind the door then jump out and take a photo so I can see the look on her face when she reads it?'

'Ask your father.'

'Brilliant idea. It'll be a week before he even notices I'm gone.'

And even the usually family-friendly Amanda thought it an optimistic estimate.

Violet checked in her luggage in a perfumed tsunami. She lost her boarding pass, found her boarding pass, then found her boarding pass again. Had anyone seen her boarding pass? The three girls squeezed, shouting, into a brown booth in the bistro in the international lounge. Rashani asked a stranger to take their photo and calculated how much time she'd save if she never brushed her long hair ever again. (Her estimate was two-and-a-half years by the time she was 70.) Amanda considered warning Violet once more about bag snatch, rape and black-market organ trading then wondered whether she should call her first daughter Charlene, Chantelle or Amera. (Why not have triplets and use all three?)

Violet was paralysed with the realisation it was actually about to happen. At no stage during her preparations had she suspected the escape would become a real live event. Now the entire world felt like it was wrapped in Gladwrap.

What if she'd left it too long and Shift Randhorn had found another international catwalk model? What if she got chickenpox like Amanda and was scarred for life? And how about the size of those jumbo jets? Violet counted 17 big planes shaking heavily into the winter sky and imagined how they'd look pelting into the ocean. The night before she'd dreamed a doctor had pushed a light bulb into her privates and it had shattered into a million pieces inside her.

'This potato salad tastes like pus in scab sauce.'

'That's lovely, Rashani. That's just lovely.'

'It's true! If you could bring yourself to eat something once in a while, you might know when something tastes like pus and scabs and when it doesn't.'

Rashani swallowed another load of mayonnaise and scurf and told herself she would *not* get all blubbery just because Violet Opus-Worthington was leaving. She kept busy inventing a new game called Flick Lid.

Step One: Flick Amanda's orange juice bottle lid pinball-style at Violet's boobs.

Step Two: Award points for collisions with said boobs.

Step Three: Deduct points for missing and sending lid flying across the room into weird suit man's eyeball (egads!).

Step Four: Don't get blubbery, *OK? Just don't*.

Violet was struck by the sudden conviction she had accidentally packed her cat.

'But I distinctly remember him going to sleep in my suitcase. What if he didn't get out before I shut it? What if he's in there now? What if he's got no air? What if something happens in the case and I've got no clothes in Amsterdam?'

Amanda and Rashani debated the effect of a low-pressure environment on an animate body, relieved to think about something other than the silent trip home in the symphony of hideousness.

Amanda's position: Blood boiling.

Rashani's position: Blood freezing.

'He'd explode.'

'No he wouldn't.'

'He'd implode, then.'

'Maybe he'll be fine and set some sort of record.'

Violet started to cry. She confessed everything — her fear of the big plane, her fear of the suitcase, her fear of dropping from the sky and leaving no trace whatsoever.

Amanda said flying was the safest mode of travel in the world. She said if you caught one commercial flight every day for the rest of your life you'd have to fly for 28,000 years before you had a stack.

Rashani said 28,000 seemed a little unlikely and Violet cried even more.

'Budweiser,' said Rashani helplessly. 'What kind of name is that for a beer?'

And by the time they embraced at the gateway to customs, they were all in ruins.

Violet queued in the metal funnel injecting passengers into the jet with her heart knocking against her blouse. As she took her last steps on solid ground, the spike from her pinkest, most illegal pair of high-heeled shoes caught on the metal lip of flight RA 865 and she collapsed into the pilot.

'Watch your step,' he said in a heavy accent and adjusted his cap. The falling girl reminded him of a reflection in water. A trick of the light with rippling red hair and blue eyes glittering in and out of focus. The pilot thought of the falling girl and girls in general and felt his orange skin stretch with the reassuring weight of himself. Women were so insubstantial he imagined he could fly a plane straight through them.

'Thank you,' said Violet feeling her face burn and her arms drip. 'I mean, I will. Watch my step, that is.'

The pilot picked up a lipstick in a floral case that had rolled from Violet's handbag as she tumbled. (Thank Dieu it wasn't one of Rashani's tampons.)

'Thank you,' Violet said, and for one unfortunate moment lost complete control of her lips. 'Are we going to be all right?' she cawed. 'I mean. Is it safe? Will I even live?'

'You will be fine,' the pilot said with genuine conviction. If a girl like this ever fell from a plane, she'd float to earth like a leaf. He returned to the cockpit imagining what it would be like to arrive home from a walk in the park and find a woman tangled in his hair.

'There will only be a short period of darkness on this trip,' he announced over the plane's loud speaker system as it shuddered over the city.

But Violet had ears only for the roar.

Things to do, she wrote manically from her seat, trying to ignore the luggage chattering in the ancient cargo nets and the walls fermenting with pink and gold wallpaper.

1. *Stop thinking bad thoughts.*
2. *Be own person.*
3. *Change hair?*
4. *Do something about money.*
5. *Don't ever use lipstick for rouge ever again.*
    (You _can_ tell).

Violet drank white wine out of a bottle from a doll's house. Next to her was an American insurance salesman whose chins fretted during the turbulence and whose pronunciation of the words 'mobile home' caused her actual physical pain. Violet drank red wine. The omelette the air hostess served for dinner had the consistency of a greasy esky. She drank tiny tequilas while the American squelched with laughter at the sit com on the in-flight television receptors. She drank tiny complimentary liqueurs until she barely registered her neighbour's clumsy kneadings at her fluffy jumper.

Violet sped towards her destiny snoring, with a stranger's tongue lapping at the side of her neck like a goat at a salt lick.

6

Up In Smoke!

The rest of that awkward Tuesday morning passed without incident. Jackson Kiss dustbusted the remains of the shattered koala and left for his job at the Local Government Authority. As chief sewerage engineer, he was in the midst of making vital progress on the computerisation of Tantanoula's solid waste disposal services.

Violet retired to the couch to suck dissolvable aspirin and fan herself with the latest edition of *Working Woman*. She had to find Cheryl new friends before Donna Vulpine, the daytime newsreader, discovered her daughter was a loner.

Out in the room off the carport, Cheryl reached Short Digest and Warning Number 512 in the marijuana book. It was titled: *Can Destroy Our Young People In A Couple Of Years*.

'According to Phyllis Schlafly,' cautionary note

number 512 read, 'marijuana can destroy our young people in a couple of years before they ever have the chance to know life and the excitement of confronting its challenges.'

'What a tragedy,' Cheryl thought, tossing away the educational publication in favour of *Pillow Biter*'s Advice For The Terminally Disturbed. She wondered whether she was terminally disturbed and remembered some of the atrocities she had committed upon her pillow. The answer was undoubtedly yes.

Pillow Biter was a magazine which came with 3D glasses for use on its patented Titzapoppin' section. It was a Category 1 Restricted publication. That meant it was not available to persons under 18 years of age and had to be displayed in newsagencies in a plastic sheath. *Pillow Biter* sometimes contained black slashes over certain aspects of its models' anatomy. These aspects had no category because they weren't available to anyone. Not unless they had X-ray vision, anyhow.

'Some parents should have to obtain licences before having children.'

That was what Violet Kiss said when she saw a stack of *Pillow Biter*s in the back corner of Mr and Mrs Spudic's newsagency. In her opinion, the Spudic children automatically qualified as teenage delinquents because their parents had seen fit to include *Pillow Biter* and other equally distasteful publications in the Health and Lifestyle section of their shop.

'Some parents should have to obtain licences before having children,' was also the catchphrase she'd used the time she'd seen Samuel Leadhead and all six or seven of his sisters waiting like cattle dogs outside The Conspiracy Hotel.

'I don't want you going over there,' Violet told Cheryl on more than one occasion. 'The Kisses and the Leadheads might live on each other's doorsteps but that's no reason for us to live in each other's pockets.'

This was a disappointing development. The image of the absolutely ironed Violet Kiss sitting down for a cup of powdered coffee with the grizzled explosion that was Grandma Leadhead was an appealing one. Cheryl was also curious about the family's maze of interconnected caravans, depronged tractors, limping bitzers, unrinsed ice-cream buckets, tool scars and epidemic of rejected rubber boots. She and Zeus often spotted Samuel sprinting between the scrub along the creek behind the hill behind their houses, vanishing in a flash of orange and red school uniform. Once or twice they'd called 'hey', and heard only the farts of beef cattle in reply.

Samuel Leadhead never had much to say to Cheryl Kiss.

Not that that stopped her leaving a love letter on his collapsible wooden desk three years earlier when they'd both been in Year Five at Tantanoula Primary School.

The note was so short it hardly qualified as a letter.

In truth, it was more of a short digest or warning.

Samuel (I love you more

No punctuation as per the infamous Kiss World War II poster technique and the last-minute addition of 'more', which Cheryl hoped would suggest she was responding to some previously aired overture as opposed to making one herself.

Cheryl's decision to opt for a single consonant instead of Samuel's full last name was because she wasn't 100 per cent sure what his real last name was. The boys on the bus called him Leadhead but, as far as she knew, it could have been Leapyear or even Leberwurst (which Nana Jean had said was a kind of sausage). Cheryl hadn't wanted to get their love affair off to a bad start by revealing her ignorance of such a crucial topic.

The newsreader's daughter had no idea why she'd suddenly become interested in Samuel's toothbrush black hair, wide black eyes and mysterious habit of talking only to the gabbling Bradley Spam during lunchbreaks. One day he'd been just another face in the canteen line and the next he'd become impossibly alluring. Maybe it was something to do with the contents of his lunch box. Cheryl battled through brown bread sandwiches the weight of barbells while Samuel dined on chocolate biscuits, packet cake and all-day suckers. Once he even arrived with a tupperware container full of melted ice-cream.

He obviously had the best mother in the world.

As luck would have it, Samuel was never able to take personal receipt of Cheryl's memo because it was intercepted by the lay psycho-sleuth Mrs Stint who was then the commandant of Tantanoula Primary School's trembling Year Five class.

'Watch the reaction of the guilty party,' Marilyn Stint announced to Mr Nuys in a trumpeted stage whisper after finding the note. (Nuys was a visiting school inspector whose deep infatuation with Mrs Stint was matched only by his pathological forgetfulness to fasten his fly.)

'Observe the four stages of guilt. One: Fear of discovery. Two: Fear of retribution. Three: Fear of public exposure. Four: *Whammo!*'

'Holy muddy bucket of pitch,' Cheryl mouthed beneath her breath. 'Holy muddy bucket of pitch.'

The only students spared Stint's patented hand-writing tests and guilt identification procedures that day were Samuel Leadhead and Bradley Spam. Samuel because he obviously hadn't written a love letter to himself. And Bradley because he had been transferred from an institution for children with divergent personalities and was spared everything except sitting up the back of the class producing line drawings of a Murder Child which made repeat appearances in his nightmares. Detective Grippa's stepson seemed to have as much aptitude for drawing as he did for not shouting '*Flaps*' during assembly, but in the interests of his absorption into the wider community, it was school policy to always award him a B+ for his efforts. Stint's attempts to resist these rulings proved useless.

'Your technique is fascinating, Marilyn,' the school inspector chipped in with trademark failure to notice that the top inch of his trousers was gaping the windscreens of speeding orange Ferraris. 'Absolutely fascinating.'

'*Flaps*' shouted Bradley in what may or may not have been heated disagreement.

Then: '*I like liver.*'

On the day Stint identified Cheryl as the authoress of scandal, she dragged the wretched girl elbow-first out to the scalding demountable classroom's storeroom. The teacher's eyes popped like a swollen fish and even Mr Nuys was not permitted entry.

Pyramids of glue pots. Wedges of floor crust. A porcelain sink bubbling oil paint and windows lashed with black steel rims.

'You're a sick and disgusting little pervert,' Mrs Stint spat at Cheryl in that hoarse woop of hers. 'Imagine if your poor sick mother ever discovered her only daughter was regurgitating this type of filth. Love letters! Imagine her poor face. It'd be the death of her this instant.'

At the time, Cheryl only reached the belt of Mrs Stint's solid floral maxiskirt and found herself agreeing most keenly.

'Is that a nod, Cheryl Jane Kiss? Or is your mind off in lavatory land as per usual?'

This exchange took place before Dr Razz Salmon began prescribing Marilyn Stint high doses of emotional anti-inflammatories, back in the bad old days when the ill-favoured old buzzard went off like a Roman Sparkler. Mrs Stint's hunchbacked husband suffered as much as the next man. Deformo (as he was widely known) often lost meal privileges and was reminded on a daily basis that he was not long for this world. Mrs Stint regarded her husband as being no higher up the evolutionary ladder than ewe slag and thought nothing about telling everyone he was likely to be dead before the month was out.

'Then God can deal with the old muddy bucket of pitch,' she'd shout in supermarket aisles, bingo halls and gardening meets. 'See how *He* likes it.'

Interestingly enough Deformo was to exist for another four decades — a development that would have caused tremendous marital stress in the Stint family if anyone had known in advance. In fact, if either party had been privilege to this piece of information back when Cheryl was one-more-than-nine at Tantanoula Primary School, they would have undoubtedly erupted with one or more of a number of common euphemisms for 'fuck'.

Sugar! perhaps.

Or: Far East.

Or: Gosh and golly.

Or: Muddy bucket of pitch.

But back in the demountable classroom on the day of the intercepted love letter, Mrs Stint was in her element and Cheryl's ability to divine the future was severely hampered by the fact that she could see no further than the storage shelf Stint was using to prop up her huge right leg.

The Tantanoula newsreader's fat daughter gazed into thick, white thigh as Mrs Stint whooped on.

'. . . we won't pay a visit to your mother in the hospital this time around, you disgusting little trout, but if I ever find out that you have been responsible for such putrid rubbish *ever* again . . .'

Cheryl wondered how her teacher knew Violet was in the Tantanoula Base Hospital being desexed but assumed, quite rightly, it was safest not to ask.

'Are you listening to me, Cheryl?'

'Yes.'

Cheryl wasn't sure how she felt about her mother's plumbing being cut off at the pass. Nothing was worth the risk of producing another dead sister, but she didn't need reminding that the human body could be taken to pieces as easily as a demountable black classroom. Once, Cheryl had arrived back at school after two days at home with impetigo and 5K's classroom had vanished. All that remained was a slimy piazza of flattened yellow-and-white grass. Five minutes passed before she realised the thing had been relocated via industrial crane to E Block. It was only five minutes, but it didn't do much to suspend a girl's disbelief in the illusion of motherly permanence.

'Yes what?'

'Yes, Mrs Stint.'

'All right now go back inside and help Mr Nuys with the mercury. And next time you think you're interested in a boy remember God is looking over your shoulder. Especially if it's that nasty little Samuel.'

As Cheryl trudged towards the door of the classroom, a muffled cry came from deep within the glassy steel oven.

'*I like liver. My mother likes bacon but I like liver.*'

It was Bradley Spam, baying up at the fluorescent light like an incredulous, landlocked moth.

After that, Cheryl's crush on Samuel Leadhead took a rapid turn for the non-existent.

Back in the present in the room off the carport, Cheryl scribbled violently in her Personal Pocket Journal. 'I hate Mrs Stint,' she wrote. 'I hate Mrs Stint as much as cooked broccoli. I hate Lou as much as vomit. I hate Murray Ramsbottom as much as rotten cow. I hate Tantanoula and I hate Jackson and I hate Violet fucking Kiss.'

Cheryl stopped. She stared at the biro gashes of her mother's name across the page and felt as if she'd been slashed in two with a bread knife.

Violet, meanwhile, was calling excitedly from the lounge room.

'Quick, Cakes. *Look.*'

It was the latest Before and After photographs on her favourite dieting show, *Miss Mass at Midday.*

Cheryl dragged herself inside just in time to see Miss Mass introduce a dieter called Marcia Limp who'd managed to halve her body weight by simply replacing two meals a day with grated celery.

'And how do you feel when you look at those photographs of the fat Marcia, the Marcia who couldn't fit into her clothes, the Marcia whose ugly weight problem stopped her from making friends?'

'*Do I talk now?*' Marcia Limp screeched, fiddling with her collar microphone and looking at someone to the side of the set.

Violet sighed and demanded her iron tablets. She demanded the fan be turned up to four. She demanded Cheryl turn down the television. She demanded more ice in her scotch. She said: 'Be a lifesaver and run up the road for more cigarettes would you? No, I don't have any money you'll just have to use your allowance until I get paid. What? No you may not buy a pocket knife. And don't loiter around that terrible Knockers woman any longer than you have to, either. Apart from the obvious, she's got the private life of a damn bookkeeper.'

The obvious, when it came to the fish and chip shop woman, was her enormous artificial chest.

Cheryl tried not to stare at the vast mounds in Dora Knockers' bunny T-shirt as she paid for her mother's cigarettes and made a point of not stocking up on chocolate for later.

In her race for the exit she snagged herself in the sticky plastic fly strips over the door.

'Shouldn't you be at school, Chezza Jane?'

'Tonsillitis,' Cheryl called over her shoulder as she disentangled herself and began the long hike home.

Cheryl kicked melting wads of bitumen off the side of the road and wiped sweat from her top lip with her forearm. The fish and chip shop woman was a freak. What happened if she wanted to sleep on her stomach? What about metal detectors? And why would anyone want to make their chest *bigger*?

Back at the Kiss residence, Violet took the cigarettes gushing thanks ever so, Cakes, you darling girl, then made the fatal error of reading the side of the packet. The tar content was wrong wrong wrong. Hadn't anyone noticed she was on 25s now, not 30s? Didn't anyone listen to a word she said? It was no wonder Cheryl didn't have any friends it really wasn't.

Violet Kiss shuddered off in an easterly direction, mistook a wall for the toilet door and left a brand-new dint. She left for work without saying goodbye but also without any further mention of the School Slash Friends situation

All in all a good result, thought Cheryl, returning to her room to make her bed.

Under her mattress were the latest copies of *Irregular Intruder*, *Big, Bigger and Bigamy* and *Accent On Anal*.

Five minutes later.

It was all right because it would never happen again.

Tins of baked beans and tins of caved apricots and cartons of cream and packets of biscuits sharp and prick cornered, cracking, scraping, cracking and scraping, and salt and vinegar Crispy Cracks and sickly thick Nutmad and eat through your teeth Chocorocko and neverenough Nicerice and Lutbutter straight from the jar and old Christmas cake pressed into plastic blocks and sweaty meat with green pepper and three plates of ice-cream with strawberry syrup and chocolate milk direct from the carton and more ice-cream and more milk and another plate of whipped Beam Cream and another plate of ice-cream and that fucking silver spoon always tasting of steel and meat.

Cheryl lay spreadeagled on the lounge-room floor. She crouched over the toilet like a spider around an egg sack. She iced her arm and used Jackson's tomato knife to cut railway lines into her flesh. Then she and Zeus made a run for it.

Cheryl would later explain to the police that walking down the hill to Advantage Creek was something she and Zeus did most afternoons.

'And if they're not at the creek, they're playing Cowboys and Indians in that damn stand of bamboo,' Violet was to add, smiling her special half-smile at the fop with the double chin and the uniform.

'Well, the carrot has turned now, Mrs Kiss,' Detective Grippa would reply, adjusting his uniform and fidgeting. 'Oh, and can I just add (between you, me and the black stump) that you're looking more beautiful than ever?'

'I'd always said the city was no place to bring up a child,' Violet sighed, sniffing visibly in a dramatic loss of her journalistic objectivity. 'And then this happens right on our own doorstep.'

'We can organise protection if you want it.'

'That poor, poor darling boy.'

'Someone to watch over the house.'

'You'd think someone in my line of work would be used to this sort of thing.'

'But at this stage we really don't think it's necessary.'

'When I heard what happened I froze right over.'

'Mrs Kiss?'

'You catch that bastard, Detective. You catch that bastard and put him away for good. Now you wouldn't happen to have a scotch on hand for a shocked mother would you, darl?'

Cheryl couldn't count the number of hours she and Zeus spent alone at the creek or encased in the creaking, itching, rat-lined circle of bamboo. Every afternoon after school they walked through the buffalo grass, around the grey stones and down the hill to where the creek skulked through the bouldered cut of the valley and goannas rap-danced through the weeds.

The beef cattle on the land around the water belonged to the Wetherills and were mustered three times a year so the calves could be trucked off to the abattoir and murdered. They had a lot more eyes than the Leadhead's poxy drove but that didn't stop them dying beneath the trees and melting into exhilarating skulls and rib cages. This had as much to do with Zeus as natural selection. One afternoon he latched onto a calf's face and held on until its jaw began to rip right off. Cheryl hit Zeus over the head with a broken fence post to try to make him lose his grip, but the herd charged in waving their antennae and she could only sprint up the hill whimpering for help. Cheryl didn't speak to Zeus for a week. She knew he would have been lynched by farmers if it wasn't for the fact that one of his mistresses was the enigmatic Tantanoula newsreader. A month later, the Wetherills rounded up the mangled calf with all the others and trucked it down to the abattoir to be turned into burger. Nothing stood a chance at the abattoir. It was more relentless even than Zeus. Once, Violet's car had stalled outside the big brick meat factory while she and Cheryl were driving home from river aerobics and their nostrils filled with the hot smell of blood, ground bones and bleating. As mother and daughter arrived home to peel off their leotards and stare from a variety of angles into their separate mirrors, neither could erase the nightmarish vision of what might lie beneath their skin.

That calf's jaw had been no bigger than an egg cup.

A clarification: Cheryl did not travel the brutalised scrub behind the Kiss residence for exercise. It did not get her heart rate into the calorie-burning zone recommended

81

by Violet (she spent more time sitting on rocks than utilising her cardiovascular system). In fact, when it came to the crunch and she was questioned by the local constabulary, she couldn't say what drew her back to the creek afternoon after afternoon.

'But what do you *do* there, Cheryl?' the detective was to ask Cheryl much later that night. 'Not much action down there for a lass your age I wouldn't imagine. Mind you, I know what you young'uns are like. You see the whole of Tantanoula as the dead edge of the wedge.'

Violet gave Cheryl a look that stopped her daughter from sharing, in a quite physical way, her exact feelings about Detective Grippa's line of inquiry.

'I keep an eye out for the goanna,' Cheryl said. 'And I talk to my dog.'

'To your God you say?'

'*Dog*,' said Cheryl, instantly regretting the admission.

'No need to wail down the wrecking wall over that one,' Detective Grippa shouted over his own laugh. 'I talk to myself all the time. It comes out better at the other end if you know what I might be meaning. But aren't you ever afraid, walking down there all by yourself?'

'All the time,' said Cheryl, and once again was at a loss to fully explain.

There was no doubt the halfway land behind the subdivisions on Panorama Way was a terrible place. Cheryl was often overwhelmed by the dark uneasiness of the vines clinging to the creek's three waterholes. Sometimes it was possible to disappear into those murky depths and completely lose sight of the stretching paddock and the trail home. The splash from an aging platypus. The sound of a gunshot. Another downstream stranger in another beaten hat.

Walk half an hour from home and anything could happen.

The other thing Cheryl hated was the goanna. That giddy bastard launched itself from the scrub and swayed over the grass when she was least expecting it. Sometimes she heard it first — an insane thrash through the tangle. But other times the black-and-yellow stripes appeared from nowhere. Nana Jean had told her to drop to the ground or it would mistake her for a tree and start climbing. Cheryl imagined the monster lizard scrabbling her eyes with its puppet teeth and paddling claws and lay awake at night panting.

There was no doubt the halfway land behind the subdivisions on Panorama Way was a terrible place. But it was there, wasn't it? What were you supposed to do? Stay at home?

So.

At 4 p.m. on Tuesday, 13 November, Cheryl Jane Kiss (schoolgirl) and Zeus Thor Idol Kiss (canine) left Lot 28, Panorama Way, to walk to Advantage Creek. It was 32 degrees Celsius and there was a weighty, storminess about the wind. In other parts of town, Mrs Stint enjoyed a spectacular Scrabble-related coup against her partly conscious husband and Dora Knockers slid a pencil behind her synthetic ear and considered abandoning the hospital industry altogether. Once again, the casualty department at Tantanoula Base Hospital overflowed with the sunstruck.

On the way to the creek, Cheryl and Zeus stopped at the bamboo to check on their life raft. It was a little something they had prepared earlier from snapped cylinders and twiggy branches broken in the last big storm. Future role yet to be determined. There was a brief sighting of the rat, an unremarkable pursuit orchestrated by Zeus, three mosquito bites to the knee and one suspected green ant attack. There were brown-and-white calves with eyelashes to their knees and a sudden change of trail to avoid the bull.

Cheryl was palpating her massive belly and formulating hate mail to Lou in her brain when she heard the scream. A spine-chilling sky-splitting TV scream from deep down in the blood and guts of the Advantage Creek waterholes.

How Cheryl could have thought that sound came from a calf was beyond her mother, beyond the detective, beyond the police counsellor with the ASSUMING makes an ASS out of U and ME poster behind her desk and even beyond Cheryl when she thought back on it.

'But there's calves screaming down there all the time,' she'd said, appalled to find herself blubbering in the presence of a gaggle of police flunkeys with belts full of swollen leather pouches. 'There's always calves or their mothers screaming down there even when there isn't a muster.'

But the truth was that after those late-afternoon crammings in the kitchen, Cheryl's mind was like a computer struck by lightning. For all she knew, the shocking sound had come from her own dangling mouth.

'No need for the waterworks, Cheryl,' Detective Grippa had said with a sympathetic offering of scotcheinated coffee to her mother. 'You're as bad as my stepson, Spam. He's been crying over his mother's shoulder ever since he heard the news. It's a heart-rending story, but today is today and tomorrow is tomorrow. You'd have been as much use to that lad as a mad woman's breakfast. In fact, if you'd gone poking your nose where it didn't belong we might have been two kiddies down and not just the one. All we're after is times and observations and such. Anything at all you remember. Anything you saw. A pinch of salt makes a big difference when you're baking a mulberry pie, after all.'

Cheryl's nose dripped and the detective scratched his head.

'Maybe you and I should call it a night,' he said. 'I've been going like a fart in a bottle all day and we've still got the entire family downstairs in Relatives and Grievers. What's the time now without me looking at my watch? I can never find the damn thing because it's always on the other wrist.'

'2.32 a.m.,' yawned Violet.

'Damn and blast. If I had two noses I'd be right. Constable Denning can I have verbal words with you in privacy please? Constable Jergens, you will be required to escort these two young ladies home.'

Cheryl stood to leave but the detective caught her by the shoulder and pushed her firmly into the plastic seat.

'Hold your hearses, young lady,' he said, looking her straight in the eyes. 'It'll take Jergens a few shakes of the lamb to bring the car round. It's raining pepper and salt out there. So before I deliver you into the night, tell me once more what you saw?'

'It was like a shadow,' Cheryl sniffled. 'Like a shadow running along the creek.'

'And what time was that?'

'About 5.30.'

'Thank you.'

'Can I go home now?'

'Just one other thing.'

'What?'

Then Reb's mother showed them both how to apply curlers before making the best chicken soup Cheryl had ever tasted. Back in those days, Reb's dad was still roaming free out of prison. Back in those days, Lou was the shape of a sack of lucerne just like Cheryl.

'It's just puppy fat,' she always told everyone. And guess what? She was right. By the time Louise Frances reached high school she was thinner than Foxy Roxy in all seven of the Kink-A-Ramas.

Life.

Sometimes Cheryl thought it lacked a certain sense of vindictiveness.

The phone rang as she was lying in her usual position beneath the vase of dying flowers.

'How did you get this number?' Cheryl said bitterly into the receiver.

'Is this 831576?'

'I doubt it.'

'Is that you playing silly buggers, Cheryl?'

'Wrong again,' she said, and hung up the phone.

Never in her entire life had she felt so huge, so much of a pea on a mountain. The dread was monstrous.

The phone sounded again and she let it ring for ever before picking up.

'Cheryl?'

'Yes?'

'Was that you on the telling bone a moment ago?'

'No,' she said. 'I only walked in the door this second. Zeus is having problems with his saliva.'

'Well obviously there must be two Cheryl Kisses living in Tantanoula,' quipped Jackson. 'What do you think about that?'

Cheryl said nothing.

Jackson asked Cheryl how school was and the robot said OK. Jackson seemed to have forgotten she was on sick leave.

'OK, what?'

'OK, Jackson.'

'OK *"thanks"*,' said Jackson. 'I'm only asking for some common politeness.'

Jackson said he would be held up in meetings until late and asked if Cheryl thought she could get her own dinner together. Cheryl said she could probably manage.

'Oh, and CJ . . .'

'Yes?'

'Don't tell your mother, will you? You know how she feels about you being home alone at night.'

'OK,' said Cheryl.

'And CJ? In case you haven't noticed, I've left a couple of noteworthy additions to the family library under your mattress.'

Cheryl put down the receiver and ran to the toilet to kneel on the tile floor and scream tinned mango into the stormy blue water.

The phone rang six more times while Cheryl fed three back copies of *Hunch* into the backyard incinerator. She told herself she'd die before she answered it. Then she and Zeus dragged each other into the lounge room to watch *Up In Smoke!*

Up In Smoke! was the television program before the Tantanoula and District Regional news. It was a situation comedy about a debt-stricken middle-aged couple whose efforts to convert their backyard shed into a nuclear fall-out shelter were incessantly (and apparently humorously) thwarted by their neighbours. There was no clear reason for Mr and Mrs Smythe's opposition to Mr and Mrs

Coast's efforts to protect themselves from nuclear annihilation. It was just one of those television things.

Sometimes the Smythes accidentally lunged into the shelter's wet cement during backyard volleyball matches. Sometimes they accidentally backed their car into its fledgling ensuite. And sometimes they quite deliberately threw homemade petrol bombs fashioned from infant formula bottles and methylated spirit-soaked sewing rags into its air recycling unit in revenge for some neighbourly slight or another.

Irony was provided in the form of escalating world tensions in the subplots. These developments suggested imminent nuclear holocaust, which in turn added a wacky urgency to the dispute in microcosm which, in turn, added even further irony as it seemed increasingly likely the neighbours would eliminate themselves without the US or Soviet Union having to lift so much as a trigger finger.

The exclamation mark in *Up In Smoke!*, incidentally, was part of the title. It was to indicate that jokes and other assorted madcappery lay within and was not some witless typo made down at *The Chinese Whisper*'s television guide division. (Producer Beresford Emery Jnr's follow-up series, *Down In Flames,* was nowhere near as popular, perhaps because its title did not contain so much as a full point.)

On Tuesday the 13th of November, *Up In Smoke!* featured a bureaucratic bungle that was *Beyond The Pale!* (This was the exact description of the episode in publicity material sent from the American advertising firm responsible for the program's worldwide media domination.)

That night, the bomb shelter builders discovered — amidst much hilarity — that it was necessary to apply to appropriate local government authorities before taking their shed conversion one reinforced concrete brick further. This meant displaying their plans in a prominent public erection (a sideways jibe at Mr Coast's penchant for naturalism) and seeking approval from the rest of the street, which, you guessed it, included the meddlesome Smythes.

'But when they're sitting in this thing, they'll be able to look straight into our kitchen,' Mr and Mrs Smythe told a law-enforcing adjudicator in prison when their neighbourhood tiff once more deteriorated into an exchange of hurled bean tins and homemade kerosene whammies.

'It's a *bomb* shelter,' Mr and Mrs Coast replied. 'If we ever need to use it, you won't even *have* a kitchen, you'll be *cooking with gas*!'

Much appreciative laughter from the studio audience etc.

Then, with no warning whatsoever, *Up In Smoke!* was interrupted by an urgent newsflash.

It was Violet Kiss, the enigmatic Tantanoula newsreader.

She had infiltrated the American soap opera to announce that 14-year-old Tantanoula High School student Samuel Lightfoot had been found brutally murdered in isolated scrubland behind Panorama Way.

7

No Parental Interview Necessary

TANTANOULA HIGH SCHOOL 'Success through Strivation'				NOTE: The Letter Grade indicates such things as attitude, industry and co-operation in the subject according to the code:
YEAR 9 OR 10 REPORT				A: Excellent — B: Very Good
NAME: Samuel Jonathon Lightfoot				C: Satisfactory — D: Needs Improvement
CLASS: 9–1				E: Poor
ASSESSMENT: Final				The average mark is 65.

SUBJECT	CLASS	MARK	POSITION IN GROUP	LETTER GRADE	
English (Adv)	1	86	11/135	C	Good memory for relevant facts. (Mrs Waist)
Maths	1	67	47/60	D	*Understands most processes and rules.*
Science	1	60	15/30	C	An orderly disposition.
Televisual Studies		75	11/21	B–	Making good process. PRUE BLOCK
Geography		73	16/37	D	Scrupulous when copying from board. CY
Modern History		89	6/65	C+	Despite a somewhat frightening and hallucinogenic approach to essays, Samuel's performance has usually been adequate. M. Stint
Technical Drawing			5/59		Pleasing shapes and formations. Chip Silver

SUBJECT	CLASS	MARK	POSITION IN GROUP	LETTER GRADE	
French		97	1/27	B	A highly aptitudinous student whose ability consistently defies his age. PLEASE contact me re this year's inter school language camp. I can be reached through the school switchboard. Anticipating your call, Rob Bruce
Art		61	31/37	B–	Good but seems to prefer mapping. V
Physical Education			55/56	C	Samuel's approach to physical education is obedient but not particularly enthusiastic. (Pete Scoob.)

No need for parental interview. P. Roper (YEAR ADVISOR)

8

Sex Stars Fav. Positions

The first thing Cheryl did after her mother urgently newsflashed the world about Samuel's death was race through the Kiss residence locking every last door and window. The next thing she did was race through again checking the cupboards. After that it was simply a matter of curling into the foetal position in her mother's wardrobe and sitting pretty.

'Zeus?' she squeaked through the hems.

The dog was reluctant to leave his post by the double glass doors. For all anyone knew, the murderer was still out there, if not a tasty barrow of bone marrow.

'*Zeus*,' she called, louder this time.

Public Enemy Number One pushed his bristling nose between Violet's empty boots. Cheryl grabbed his collar.

What *was* that noise?

Zeus glared into the twilight. Cheryl felt what she thought was a knife in her side and realised she was lying on a copy of Beresford Emery Jnr's video adaptation of *Twelfth Night*!

'In the tradition of *HeShe!*' read the front cover.

'In the tradition of *Switch!*'

'In the tradition of *She Tarzan, Me Jane!*'

Even hyperventilating with terror, Cheryl was outraged.

'Shakespeare wrote *Twelfth Night* before Beresford Emery Jnr was even born,' she hissed into Zeus's tiny triangular ear. 'The odds of it being in the tradition of his string of gender-bending romantic comedies, therefore, is highly unlikely. Where do these copywriters get off?'

Zeus barked so hard Violet's mauve jacket vibrated itself right off the hanger.

'Two men are coming up the driveway,' he howled. 'Don't you realise? What this means?'

'Still,' said Cheryl, weeping with the effort of keeping the pig dog from bolting. 'There's no getting around the fact that *HeShe!*; *Switch!*; *She Tarzan, Me Jane!* and Beresford Emery Jnr's *Twelfth Night!* have a number of features in common.'

'We're dead,' said Zeus, tearing his hair out.

'All starred feted Hollywood actresses of the era performing in masculine roles, all were spectacularly successful at the box office and all contained cameo performances by Lurex Imperial — widely tipped as The Next Big Thing.'

Crunch crunch crunch came the footsteps up the gravel.

'In fact,' Cheryl blubbered. 'Beresford Emery Jnr didn't produce a single dud until his second television series and by then it was widely accepted that the celebrated playboy had well and truly lost his marbles. If

Down In Flames didn't prove it, his attempt to trademark the exclamation mark did.'

Cheryl — who'd recently completed an assignment on Beresford Emery Jnr for Televisual Studies — shrank to flea-size. Her attempts to insinuate herself into the wardrobe's fibro backing were thwarted by a bloated plastic bag. She scrabbled sideways and one of Jackson's secret magazine stashes discharged over the floor.

Dr Pauline Messemer & Dr Johann Hauser's World of Good, Safe and Unusual Sex! read the brochure on Phwoar's $1 Adult Book Sale. *Sexual Positions (Book 1)! Sexual Positions (Book 2)! 40 Plus Pleasure Chests! Intercourse Illustrated! Encyclopedia Sexualis! Sex Stars Fav. Positions! Interracial Sex!*

'Go away,' screamed Cheryl as the knocking on the front door grew louder. 'Leave us alone.'

The footsteps crunched along the front of the house then down one side. There was cigarette smoke and a stifled cough. Cheryl informed Zeus via telepathy that *Interracial Sex!* was a 100-page 8-by-10 inch book explicitly revealing men and women of all races engaged in erotic, passionate sex, with rare and startling photos in vivid colour. She explained that volume two of the *Sexual Positions!* was undoubtedly in the tradition of volume one. Then Zeus finally broke free and hurled himself into space.

'Cheryl Kiss?' came the voice at the window. 'We know you're in there. We can see your ski pants.'

9

The Missing Finger

Police were rocked by the brutality of Samuel Lightfoot's murder.

This was the joyless and not very original particular supplied by Cheryl's mother during the lead item of the 7 p.m. news bulletin.

But the two young constables tapping at the window of the master bedroom at Lot 28, Panorama Way, weren't rocked. They were stunned by the vision of Violet's black bustier skylarking in the half-dark on the clothes line outside the bedroom window.

'Mind if we take a bit of a look around, outside?' one said through the glass.

'A standard reconnaissance of the dwelling home?' added the other.

And 15 minutes later, there they still were, goggling up at the loaded line in awe.

Cheryl extricated herself from a rope of tangled

dressing gown. She stacked Jackson's magazines into a corner of the wardrobe while Zeus skidded up and down the hallway demanding a briefing. It was all she could do to return zombie-like to the television to wait for the police officers to regain their senses. Her relief that the intruders were police and not Samuel's killer was so strong it verged on disappointment.

Petrol, Violet read from the screen with what might very well turn out to be award-winning gravity. An unknown person or persons had doused Samuel Lightfoot with petrol and set him alight down at the creek behind neighbourhood homes on Panorama Way.

Violet Kiss was a dab hand with a media cliché. Slashed in relation to spending, smear in relation to campaign, shock in relation to decision, war in relation to torn and doused in relation to the forced evaporation of Samuel Leadhead down at Advantage Creek.

'The 14-year-old Tantanoula High School student, described by friends as cheerful and outgoing with a big future in football, struggled valiantly for a full kilometre back to his family residence on Panorama Way,' Violet continued from the studio as two officers of the law ogled her undergarments on the other side of town. 'Tragically, however, he died shortly after reaching hospital, leaving behind a town as shocked as it is grieving.'

Photographs of Samuel. A murky family Polaroid beside an out-of-focus Christmas tree. A school portrait of the whole of Year Nine. A wiry, bobby pin of a boy with marbled knees, slicked black hair and enormous black eyes.

'Members of the dead boy's family have made an emotional plea for anyone with any information on Samuel's death to come forward.'

A shot of the Leadhead grandmother snapping her fingers like lobsters in boiling water while Old Man Leadhead held his burning birthmark in both his hands.

Cheryl's mind was full of the high-pitched shriek she'd heard at the creek and the black shadow inching its way beside the water. There was a photograph in the school library of a burning girl running napalmed in Vietnam, her mouth spread into a vicious black wound.

And had there been a smell, a dreadful bouquet inching in and out of the breeze as she'd turned her back on Samuel?

For the fourth time that day, Cheryl Kiss vomited.

'Samuel Leadhead didn't have a big future in football,' she choked from deep within the porcelain well. 'He went to Special Arrangements with me and Bradley Spam on sports day because he had dicky ankles.'

Constables Keaton Jergens and Bang Denning were unaffected by the alleged inaccuracies in the Tantanoula newsreader's reporting. But they livened considerably when Cheryl said she thought she'd seen Samuel at the creek that afternoon.

'We're supposed to interview the entire street but I think it's best we take you down to the station straight off the mark.'

'Of course your mother will have to be alerted.'

'The responsible course of action and all that.'

And between them their smile could have lassooed a reservoir.

'Mind you,' said Bang Denning.

'Mind what?' said Keaton Jergens.

'Someone should really tell Violet Kiss to do something about this dog.'

Cheryl pulled the still humping Zeus off Constable Denning's calf and clipped him to the chain beside the laundry. She was ready to slide across the warm upholstery in the back of the police car but the two officers were feeling chatty. No point rushing back to the station when you were only going to be sent straight out to interview civilians again. The Chungs across the road were pleasant enough but the fillings in those dumplings certainly had been on the pink side.

'You wouldn't happen to be adopted, would you?' asked the one with red hair, ravelling up his sleeves.

'Not unless you know something I don't,' said Cheryl, using the reply suggested by her mother. Impressively enough, Zeus's boyfriend was missing a finger while the red head appeared to have lost an elbow.

'Speedway accident,' said Constable Jergens waving his damaged elbow in Cheryl's face. 'I was led in a Mexican hat dance by a Zip Frisker 900 outside the marinade stand at demolition derby.'

'It was your own fault, Keaton.'

'Can't argue with that, Bang.'

'Never understood why you were loitering outside the Albertini marinade stand in the first instance.'

'The aroma, Bang. Haven't you ever been party to seduction by aroma?'

'Never understood why the Albertinis were allowed to purvey that ethnic carrion at speedway in the first instance. Not that I've got anything against our foreign friends. Mrs Denning having the Maltese terrier and all. But you might as well suck on a garlic crusher for all the subtlety of flavour in a bolognaise.'

'Ever considered it might be just a case of the devil you know, Bang?'

'Not at all. Flavour is flavour after all.'

'Ah but when the first westerners arrived in China the locals thought they smelled of regurgitation.'

'What's that got to do with the price of tea?'

'Everything and nothing. But I'd have to agree with you on the slicing of fruit on onion boards.'

'Completely uncalled for.'

'The mark of a civilisation is the employment of two.'

'One for sweet and one for savoury.'

'Marked with tape if need be.'

This affectionate waltz was interrupted when the two men remembered Cheryl.

'My colleague wasn't meaning to be rude when he asked about the adoption issue,' Constable Denning said with startling lack of reference to food. 'It's just that Violet Kiss looks a little on the young side to have a daughter your age.'

Down in the valley, the Tantanoula sewage works were outdoing themselves.

'Would you look at that,' said Constable Jergens standing on the gravel driveway with his good hand on his hip. 'That sunset is straight out of a landscape. It's a work of art, just the way it is.'

'Bushfires,' answered his partner. 'That's what'll do it.'

'Belongs up on a restaurant wall.'

'You Kisses sure know how to put on a view.'

As usual, Zeus bellowed clarification from the clothes line and as usual, no-one was interested. He was terrified at the pinwheel of colours in the sky, at the fire in the air. He demanded to know what had happened to the meat.

But the only reply came from the gum tree where the brain-dead mate of the koala he'd shredded that morning bawled insults through the crepuscular fog.

Violet was predictably hysterical when she and Cheryl were reunited in Detective Grippa's office. Oh my darling, isn't it terrible, say thank you to the nice policemen, I tried to ring, really I did, Keaton and Bang how very nice to see you again, nudge nudge wink wink, I didn't realise Jackson was working back, couldn't get away from the station, breaking news and all, but don't worry, Cakes, never fear, we're getting protection, imagine that!

Arid smiles all round et cetera.

'What happened to Samuel?' Cheryl asked in a small voice.

'I'm sure there was a packet of cigarettes down here yesterday,' shouted Violet, shadow-boxing her salmon suit jacket. 'Do any of you young men have anything to smoke that isn't an Aquamarina?'

'What happened to Samuel?'

'Who would have imagined,' her mother barked back. 'And right here in Tantanoula? That sick, sick animal.'

The enigmatic Tantanoula newsreader was overexcited. Her eyes were bright and glittery and her voice reflected light like broken glass. Shrill, she was. Shrill like . . . like . . . But Cheryl couldn't think of anything that rhymed with shrill and still made sense. Krill would have been good but the high school drop-out doubted whether planktonic crustaceans wore nail-heeled stilettos and flirted at the armed forces in three strident octaves.

When she'd done work experience down at *The Chinese Whisper*, Genevieve Flash, the editor, had said she used too many animal similes anyway.

'Much as I'd love to stay and chat I'm afraid I'm going to have to love and leave you girls for a moment while I find out whose done what with my batteries,' said Detective Grippa. 'On a night like this we go through the things like dead dogs. The work practices of this station should be put under the microphone, they really should.'

Grippa left with his tape recorder under his arm and words still tangling in his throat. He was trying to summon the courage to break the news to Violet Kiss. The detective was as big a fan of the enigmatic Tantanoula newsreader as anyone was. Always had been. But that newsflash of hers bordered on the irresponsible.

'Did you tell Violet Kiss we were rocked?' he asked Bang Denning outside the nut dispenser.

'I doubt it,' said the constable. 'I'm not even a hundred per cent certain I know what it means. A reference to your music interests perhaps? She really is a heavenly creature, though. World class in fact. Tantanoula is lucky to have her.'

Back in Detective Grippa's office, Violet paced the rubber off her pumps. There was a killer on the loose and she'd broken the story. Before the radio, before the paper, and even before the daytime newsreader Donna Vulpine.

The stimulation was driving her crazy.

What did it all mean? Who'd done it? Did killing a 14-year-old count as infanticide? What *was* infanticide? What was *patricide*? And why did it feel like she'd just sat in a pool of battery acid?

Oh yes. The incident with the scissors.

THERE WAS NO INCIDENT.

THERE WERE NO SCISSORS.

Phew. That was a close one.

Either way, the daytime newsreader had clocked off and the night-time newsreader had clocked on just as the anonymous tip-off from Constables Jergens and Denning came through.

'Cigarettes,' Violet broadcast before twitching her way towards the door. 'Must find cigarettes.'

And her daughter was left alone with her brain.

Cheryl worked the room in her swivel chair. She kicked the walls for momentum and read a note in upside-down handwriting on the police officer's desk.

get dick lyndon sextet cassette back off of
bloody claudette
call head office about Lightfoot request for lie
detector test
milk?

Cheryl thought about the way people in the olden days shook hands to prove they weren't carrying knives. She picked a sliver of paint off an exposed pipe and listened to the noise in her head as loud as a plane crash over the ocean.

Lightfoot was Samuel Leadhead's real last name.

Who wanted the lie detector?

'I see you're admiring my artwork.'

It was Grippa, back with a plastic packet of batteries and a doughnut belching jam. Did he know his prisoner had been snooping through the papers on his desk? Probably not. The detective was pointing a gooey finger at a poster on the wall, a local flora and fauna identification chart in the shape of a bull's-eye. Smack bang in the centre was a stooping ape with long hair and rubies for eyes.

'What's that?' asked Cheryl.

'A reminder not to make the same mistake twice. Trust your institution, young Cheryl. Don't look for external threats when the rot lies within. That way no-one will ever be able to pull your twit.'

'I see.'

'Surely you remember the terrible Tantanoula yowie?'

'I've seen a chimp smoking a pipe on television.'

'Probably before your time. Your mother's colleague, Mrs Vulpine, could tell you one or two things about our infamous abominable snowman. Ask her one time. That'll put the noose up her sleeve, mark my word.'

Cheryl shrugged. Right now, her interest in the Big Foot taped to Detective Grippa's wall was less than zero.

'Detective Grippa?'

'Yes, Cheryl?'

'What happened to Samuel?'

'He passed away this evening, I'm sorry to say. Hung in as far as the hospital then slipped away from us. A heart-rendering affair if ever I heard one.'

'Who did it?'

Grippa rummaged around in his top draw. He pulled out an autographed copy of Shift Deadly's latest album, *Virgin Tractor*, with a sigh of satisfaction.

'Heard the latest single by Babylon Tattoo?' he asked. 'It really hits the Turk on the head.'

Ever since the terrible Tantanoula yowie debacle, Detective Grippa had devoted himself to self-improvement. His latest project was effective communication with juveniles and he'd made it his business to listen to Big Jack Profile's Top 40 program on the local FM station every Saturday morning for the past six months.

'Not bad,' was the detective's verdict on modern music. 'No Amanda Cabaret and The Velvet Staircase but not bad at all.'

Max Grippa was the proud owner of all seven Concrete Cancer albums. He even had a collector's edition copy of *Striptease Policy*, which had been declared illegal on the grounds of extreme nudity.

'Who burned Samuel?' asked Cheryl.

'This rain will be the end of Dirt City's outdoor concert at the football oval. Who would have guessed we'd cop a westerly after such a scorcher? Funny. They usually blow from the other direction.'

Who burned Samuel?

Who burned Samuel?

Was it Mort Ramsbottom he said he would too on the bus . . .

'Now, now, Miss Kiss. Let's not conduct a heresy hunt. The truth is I'm as much in the dark as the next bloke. Unless the next bloke happens to be young Samuel, that is. The truth is we don't know exactly what happened to the boy. That's what we're hoping you can help us work out.'

After that, the detective's questions went on forever. They went on and on until even Cheryl couldn't remember what happened next.

Violet paced in and out of the room chain-smoking. There were plastic cups of grey hot chocolate. Crying from the corridors. Scuffles. Window diamonds of hot summer raindrops hurling themselves against the black glass in endless Kamikaze missions to join the living.

'But what time was that what approximate time was that what time did you do that when that happened the scream how can you be sure did you look at your watch right at that second are you telling me everything but you heard a scream tell me one thing high or low the scream was it high or low could it have been two screams BUT WHAT TIME WHAT APPROXIMATE TIME?'

105

When Grippa decided to give the prisoner a break and ask her opinion on Adulterous God's change in drummers, she burst into tears.

'Don't worry, darling,' Violet said with an ostentatious ruffle of her daughter's hair. 'You just answer the nice detective's questions the best you can and everything will be fine. We'll have protection don't forget, darling. You and me will be like a couple of superstars with all those police watching us round the clock.'

'Actually, Mrs Kiss,' Detective Grippa said, clearing his throat. 'That's something you and I need to have a bit of a chinwag about. It won't take longer than two stabs of a tail I promise. Bang? Could you escort Cheryl to the little ladies' room so she can wash her face and blow her old English rose?'

Constable Denning and Cheryl single-filed through a maze of pale-yellow corridors. They passed battleship filing cabinets and the soup fog of the canteen. They passed a window framing the raging sockets of Grandma Leadhead. The old woman shouted something and threw a coffee cup at the wall. In the room next door to Grandma Leadhead were two other little old ladies, twittering excitedly into tape recorders.

'You're allowed to ask how it happened,' Constable Denning said as they tapped through the poisonous silence that followed. 'Curiosity might of killed the cat but it's not going to relieve me of another finger.'

'How did it happen?' asked Cheryl, certain he meant Samuel.

'I won't bore you with the whole story, but Jergens and I were on the Savvy waterslide,' said Denning with a nostalgic flinch. 'I was wearing my wedding ring and the next thing I know. Flash. It gets caught on the rim at the top of The Juggernaut, doesn't it? Rips right off, don't it? Mrs Denning said "litigate" but she would. "Litigate or die" is her motto. "I wasn't conscious at the time, your Honour, but I *believe* I was sexually assaulted" . . .'

Cheryl nodded thickly. The newsreader's daughter was wondering whether Samuel had been burned after all, whether she had imagined everything.

'I won't bore you with the whole story, but if you ever see a sign that says No Jewellery, make sure you take off your wedding ring,' the policeman called after Cheryl as she pushed the heavy door of the women's toilets. 'Because if something can happen, it probably will. And if it doesn't happen to you, it'll happen to your wife.'

A lady police officer was massaging brown make-up into a mark on her neck in a room full of sanitary disposal units and graffiti. Next to her on the floor was a motorbike helmet and a bunch of roses.

'You OK?' she asked.

'Yeah,' Cheryl said.

What other answer was there?

She and Bang Denning queued beneath the fluorescent glare of the canteen.

'The cook'll be with you in a minute,' said her escort. 'It's the burgers that slow him down. Sometimes I think the local connoisseurs get themselves arrested just to get their hands on a subsidised meat patty. Perhaps you're wondering about the pain . . .?'

Finally, thought Cheryl. Finally someone is finally going to talk about Samuel Leadhead.

'Everyone asks so there's no need to be shy. Without boring you with the whole story, the fact of the matter is I knew I'd been injured, but I thought it was just a nick so I rode the entire slide, even let out a shout round Dead Man's Corner, if I remember correctly.'

The cook handed Cheryl a polystyrene cup smoking with pea and ham soup.

'I shot out the mouth of The Juggernaut like a ping-pong out a drainpipe, and there was my colleague, Keaton, staring at my paw with this priceless expression. And that's when I looked down and realised the finger was gone. Flash! Ripped right off. Strong words, you might think but clichés become clichés because they do the job after all. Even Mrs Denning had to agree with me on that one. "Bang," she said. "What have you done to yourself this time? I haven't seen a joint ripped as severely as that since Motocross."'

The soup was terrible and Cheryl turned back to the canteen for a bag of the doughnuts.

'I don't want to bore you with the whole story, but my belief is Keaton took it worse than I did. Him having just lost the elbow and all. But someone had to climb back up The Juggernaut to retrieve the misplaced digit and damned if I felt that way inclined. "Snap out of it, Jergens," I told him a dozen times all in a row. "Snap out of it and fetch my finger." But I could of been talking to the Maltese terrier for all the intelligence I received in return. Eventually someone had the foresight to give the man a slap on the chops and he was up the slide and back with the missing finger before you could say Dick Lyndon.'

The constable was speeding up, his brain tape chewed by a broken machine.

'Reattachment should of been the first thing on my mind but all I could think of was locating the wedding ring before Mrs Denning noticed it was missing and suspected any sort of funny business. Without boring you with the whole story, stitching was out of the question. "Too difficult, vascularly speaking," the doctor told me. "All well and good, ma'am," I replied. "But why do I feel no pain?" "You will," she said. "You will."

'Reassuring in a way. The human body's protection racket. If you ever get shot through the chest it'll be the same. Won't feel a thing. A knife through the belly, on the other hand . . . now he'll hurt like hell. And not where you expect it either. The pain is referred, you see. The human body sends it all over the shop. Like a passed buck so to speak.'

Cheryl stared at the floor. She wished she'd accepted a plastic bag to hide the doughnuts.

'Feel the stump if you like. Everyone wants to even if they think they don't. You'll discover the scar tissue is surprisingly soft.'

Cheryl said thanks but no thanks. Constable Denning's gnarly trunk looked like the punchline to some repulsive joke.

'The only problem I have now is with change. I'm left-handed as luck would have it. I still extend old lefty for change and flash! the coins fall straight through. Bartenders? They're mute with embarrassment. Me, I just marvel at the strength of human instinct. Or is it habit? I'm just fortunate it wasn't my thumb. Seven more where that finger came from, I say. The thumb is the key to the prehensility caper after all. Mind you, Mrs Denning says if it was my thumb they would of made the effort to sew it back on. But she would say that, wouldn't she. "Litigate," she says every morning when I leave for work and every night when I get home. "Litigate or die." She's a good woman, my wife, but jumpy as a grassfire since she started legal studies.'

'Hey Bang,' called the woman police officer with the roses and the neck marks.

'With you in a minute, Claudette,' said Constable Denning.

They'd reached the door of Detective Grippa's office.

'I guess what I'm trying to tell you, Miss Kiss, albeit in a sideshow sort of way, is that your little friend Samuel wouldn't have suffered as much as you might of thought from looking at him.'

Cheryl was so shocked someone had actually mentioned the murder she dropped her cup of soup and splattered lime chuck all over the linoleum.

'It's the one good thing about this whole sorry business. First degree burns. Second degree burns. Those blokes he would of really known about. Those blokes would of really got him hopping. But third? Your young Samuel wouldn't have felt a thing. No nerves left, you see. All burnt off. Me and Keaton have seen pilots pull themselves out of light plane wreckage black as burned sausages and all they can think of is the passengers. "Anyone injured," they ask. "You find your handbag, madam?" The poor buggers are on the way out. They're dying right before your eyes. But all they can think of is ringing the wife because they feel no pain. It's a slow way to go, I'll grant you that. Not my choice of an exit. But not too bad in the pain department. Your friend Samuel would have walked up that hill in what you literary types might refer to as a dream.'

Cheryl couldn't move.

'You have to look on the bright side.'

'You sure you're all right?'

'Look sharp Cheryl Kiss, if the wind changes your face'll stay like that forever.'

Constable Denning gave Cheryl a friendly pat on the shoulder while she was still trying to imagine what a nerve looked like, a nerve that had been barbecued back to its stump.

'Don't worry about the mess,' he said, pointing to the spilled soup. 'I'll get the lads from the kitchen onto it and no-one will know we were ever here.'

Cheryl shakily opened the door to Detective Grippa's office and the conversation stopped as abruptly as if it had been shot. There was a long pause then the detective said: 'You hear about the boys from Concrete Cancer on that pleasure cruiser, Cheryl? According to *The Chinese Whisper*, they threw three models and a bar fridge into a dolphin pool. It sends me down the wrecking wall, it really does.'

Violet crossed her legs with a scowl.

'We were just talking about Save The Mini,' the detective continued uncomfortably. 'That lead singer was on the radio for ages a minute ago. It was the same thing I told that woman this morning as I said to you a minute ago.'

Cheryl studied the two faces for clues to the secret conversation. Violet was no longer animated. She was pale and tetchy and her cheeks had faded to an opaque puce. Cheryl was an expert on her mother's moods. She registered small changes in the temperament of the Tantanoula newsreader with all the sensitivity of a wall instrument and then failed, absolutely, to act on the information.

'Can we go home now?'

'Just one other thing.'

What could it be? The Eye Doctor's chart topping EP? The scandalous death of Unnatural Carlotta's drug-addicted lead singer? Furio Sullen and the Rampant's ongoing law suit against Beresford Emery Jnr?

'My stepson, Bradley, tells me you're no longer an associate of Louise Frances and Rebecca Michaelson.'

Cheryl mumbled something non-committal while Violet grew darker by the minute.

'I trust this means we're going to see an end to those five-finger bargains of yours?'

'It's five-finger discounts,' said Cheryl, turning as red as a lit candle.

On the way home in the police car she asked Constable Jergens if he was going to be their guard.

'For God's sake don't *yap*, Cheryl,' Violet yapped louder than any of them.

'Well,' demanded Cheryl in an unnecessarily ovoid whisper. '*Are you?*'

'Er . . .' said Constable Jergens, massaging his missing elbow.

'Listen darling,' snapped Violet in the tone she used when she thought she knew a whole lot more than Cheryl did. 'Detective Grippa and I had a little chat and we decided it wasn't necessary after all.'

'What wasn't?'

'Protection.'

'Does that mean they've caught whoever did it?'

'Must you screech so, Cheryl? Must you bleep and yelp and screech so CEASELESSLY?'

'Does that mean they know who it is? Does that mean they had him down at the station? Was he in the next room? Was he right next to us? Was it Mort Ramsbottom and Murray? They said they'd get him on the bus, you know. They always say they'll get him. Are they going to get us, too?'

'All you need to know is everything is under control. The police know exactly what they're doing and for reasons best not known to 14-year-old girls they have decided the Kiss family do not require a guard.'

'Do the Leadheads get a guard?'

'Enough, Cheryl.'

'Is it true his nerves were burnt off?'

'CHERYL!'

'Looks like you've got another investigative reporter in the family,' Constable Jergens said, wrestling with the car. His driving had not been the same since the accident at the speedway. It was six whole months before he could bring himself to get back behind the wheel. Now he was haunted by visions of losing control. Now he lived in fear that one day he would no longer be able to resist the urge to swerve into the backs of pedestrians, pushbike riders or teen gangs loping aimlessly across badly lit zebra crossings.

'Looks like I've got a goddamn 14-year-old,' Violet replied, lighting the wrong end of a White City in her grief.

'We were all 14 once, Mrs Kiss.'

'Not all of us, Constable.'

Outside the car, Tantanoula jolted past in dark, oily flashes. Torrential rain had turned the 3 a.m. world to porridge. Cheryl stared into the immense immobility of the Bi-Mart's cement acres, into the yellow-brick houses serving endless sentences in the suburban prison. Any other life, she thought every time she was conveyed up this long sweep from town. Any other life but this.

'But what if the killer comes to the house?' Cheryl shouted at her mother. 'What if Mort Ramsbottom knows I know it was him and comes to the house and we don't have a guard?'

'Don't be such a goddamn drama queen,' snapped Violet. 'Mort Ramsbottom did not kill Samuel, I'll tell you that for free. Do you honestly think I'd deliberately put you in a danger after spending 14 years and God knows how much in dental bills raising you? Do you know how many children in Tantanoula would kill to live in a house with a VCR? Do you?'

Violet had a sudden memory of white sunbeds on the Beach of the Dead in Cabo Roto. Frank Anderson telling her she was astounding, saccharine cocktails the size of footballs, the third-world sun burning holes in the ocean. Beneath the tight tarpaulin of her belly Cheryl Jane and Sarah Beth had been knitting themselves together out of nothing.

Goddamn you, Cheryl. Goddamn you.

As Constable Jergens deposited mother and daughter at Lot 28, Panorama Way (managing not to skittle a single bystander in the process) he couldn't help noticing the way, up close, the Tantanoula newsreader's skin was finely textured like imported writing paper. Her hair exuded fragrant smoke and her hands fluttered around her face like pigeons startled off a ledge. No, he thought, not like pigeons. Pigeons were flying rats. That was hardly fair. Violet Kiss's hands were more like dragonflies around the thick waters of the Savvy Everglades, like sleek puffins sliding on ranges of ice, like the warbles of magpies with wings elegantly extended, black to the point of impenetrable green.

She was a one in one hundred woman, that one.

Now.

About that drive back to the station.

In the lounge room, Cheryl slouched in agitated freefall as her mother called attention to her endless melodramas, her tiresome exaggerations, her attention-seeking lies, her ascribing of human characteristics where human characteristics were not deserved, her sickening consumption of cheese and dairy products, her disgusting untamed flesh. It was as if there was an excess of Cheryl Jane Kiss, an invasion of daughter and Violet didn't have enough room to breathe. Jackson woke up, said he would have come home earlier if he'd known, then resumed snoring.

'Anthropomorphism,' Cheryl whispered to Zeus out in the room off the carport when it was all over. 'There must be a word for the reverse. For reducing human forms to inanimates. That's what she's doing, you know. She's turning me into something that's not even human.'

Zeus sighed and admitted he may have filed a koala leg behind the compost heap.

10

I Killed The Boy

Down in the industrial quarter, unseen by any of them, the old depot guard slipped into a raincoat and a pair of his late wife's black legwarmers and walked into the night. He'd been dreaming of typhoid shots and had woken aching and fevered, disconcerted by the siren drum of rain on the old depot's tin roof. Now he wandered the abandoned town trailed by a shadow he presumed to be his dog.

What was that?

The streets were unrecognisable beneath the black sheaths of rain.

What was that?

Strange objects, as if a wild party had been abandoned at the exact moment of the downfall.

What was that?

A trail of curly bread rolls, exquisitely sodden. A

discarded piano, shooting water. Dirty arcs from overloaded drainpipes. Flooded bike seats.

A shadow he presumed to be his dog.

The moon drowned and slowly the old man's boots filled with water.

'It was never my intention to reside in a depot,' he said when he found himself outside his own back door with dripping knees and swilling feet. 'What I wanted was to live in a shopfront on the main street. That way whenever my wife drew the curtains she'd have an audience of thousands.

'Digger?' he said, turning at the cry behind him. 'Digger?'

But it wasn't the dog.

It was a man whose face had been dug into a grave.

'I killed him,' he choked. 'I killed the boy.'

Then the ghost with the blazing cheek let out a cry and dissolved into the rain.

At the time, Ernie imagined he had been speaking with the grim reaper himself.

But the next day he stared at his ruined clothing and remembered nothing.

11

Say Goodbye To The Boys, Cheryl

Cheryl had only ever seen one photograph of her father — a single mute image of a blond-haired green-eyed stranger in a bar in the Mexican resort town of Cabo Roto. Next to him was Violet and a fat man with freckles whose arm seemed to be attached to the camera. 'Violet with the famous Anderson brothers,' someone had written on the back. 'Who were those masked men?' For years the photograph lived in the suitcase under the bed. Then Violet came home late one night and caught Cheryl looking at it and that was that.

Incineration.

Cheryl's mother was sensitive about the subject of Cheryl's father. Sensitive and inconsistent. According to Violet, Frank Anderson had been flying at least five different airlines when he'd fallen out of the sky and drowned in the ocean. Usually it was Mexican Connected or US Prime but as the years went by, she'd also mentioned Royal Air, United Oz and even Statewide, which wasn't even an international carrier.

No wonder she didn't remember whether or not she'd been to his funeral.

Cheryl's early memories were like Polaroids trapped beneath the tight plastic of a photo album. Everything appeared in unforgiving stills. Princess the Cocker Spaniel who lived next door to their house in the city: Was she always frozen in a flaming front lawn roll? Grandma Edna: Surely she did something other than arrange pilfered church flowers in that disinfected kitchen. And Violet. Cheryl knew for a fact her mother didn't spend every minute of every day draped glamorously over a statue of a beaming mermaid in Rome.

'Mummy?'

'Yes, Cakes?'

'Can you wipe my bottom, Mummy?'

'No Cakes, you're a big girl now.'

'*You're* a big girl.'

'That's why I don't ask you to wipe my bottom, isn't it?'

Cheryl's early memories were like insects pinned to a board, but her recollections of the day she and Violet left the city to drive to Tantanoula ran as smooth as molasses.

She was seven years old when she and her mother had driven for days through tunnels of silver eucalypt and postcards of farmland and singing bridges and orange streetlights and corkscrew playgrounds and the tail of a fox slipping shark-fin style through the mist. Violet had sat in the front seat tossing cigarette ash into the wind. Sometimes she croaked along to alien radio stations wound from the car radio but mostly she was silent. In the back was Cheryl, balled between a canvas cosmetics bag and a clothes basket full of kitchen utensils. Cheryl not asking How Much Longer? because that was her side of the Keeping Nylon bargain.

Nylon?

The glowing white mouse churned his plastic wheel in the chipboard cage on the car seat beside her. First he lived in a scientific laboratory then he lived in Miss Carlos's classroom in the city school and then he lived with Cheryl and Violet in the car.

Did you know they rubbed lipstick into rabbit's eyes in scientific laboratories? Did you know monkeys were forced to wear underarm perfume? Did you know mice like Nylon were deliberately given brain cancer?

The teacher from Texas was full of useful information. She gave Nylon to Cheryl on her last day at school even though the rest of the class wanted him to stay.

'Sometimes the best gifts are the ones that are hardest to give,' Miss Carlos told 1R, swishing her wild brown hair.

'I *like* Thanksgiving,' shouted Tabitha Bleisch. 'Is it Thanksgiving again *soon*?'

'Last night eight little dogs came out of my big dog, Princess,' said Leeroy Evensly. 'They were asleep in Princess's bottom but three of them didn't open their eyes and now they're dead.'

'My mother said American is bad,' said Sharon Holly. 'She says Thanksgiving is bad and Halloween is bad and Catch and Kiss is bad because they're America and this is *Australian*.'

'Nylon told me he doesn't *want* to go to the country with Cheryl. He said he wants to come *home* with *me*.'

Miss Carlos told everyone to finish cutting faces into their pumpkins and relax. Miss Carlos told everyone to relax, even when people were yelling. She had her own saddle and said y'all whenever she felt like it.

'I'm Mexican,' Cheryl told the teacher on the first day of term.

'How's that, cowgirl?'

'Mum was on holidays. She was expanding her horizons then I got born then she came home and I was Mexican.'

'What a dee-lightful story,' said the teacher. 'And how long had your mother been on vacation?'

'Eight years,' said Cheryl.

Cheryl didn't mention Sarah Beth Anderson while she was telling Miss Carlos the Mexican story. She tried not to talk about her dead sister to anyone because Violet said it was morbid and would bring them all bad luck. Miss Carlos didn't ask what had happened to Cheryl's father, either. That was just as well. Thanks to her mother's sensitivities, Cheryl didn't know the first thing about the man. Not his middle name or what sort of car he drove or even whether or not he had a dog. If it wasn't for the photograph under Violet's bed, Frank Anderson would have appeared in her brain as a big question mark curling out of a shirt collar.

'For Christ's sake, Cheryl, open the window. That damn rat is stinking up the car.'

'Nylon's not a rat, he's a mouse.'

'Of course he's a rat. Look at the size of him.'

'He just eats a lot.'

'Open the window anyway. The smell is making me smoke too much.'

Cheryl wound down the window and Nylon spat a half-digested sunflower seed onto the carpet of wood shavings on his cage floor. He sat back on his dimpled haunches to inspect his work. Outside the car window were ink-spot lakes and green hills the texture of satin. Cheryl thought of Miss Carlos and had a quiet sniff.

Violet had been furious at the teacher's present. She yelled and stamped and then she got sly and told Cheryl it was their moral duty to release Nylon back into the wild, shaking his cage over a city drain to make her point.

Nylon's short life had left him deeply institutionalised. He clung action hero-style to the top rung of his exercise wheel while Cheryl yowled.

Eventually Violet said Nylon could stay on the condition that Cheryl not utter one word, not one single word of complaint during the entire drive to the country.

Cheryl had nodded, pressing Nylon against her face. The moment she felt the warm pill of the rat's body, she wanted another. If not an entire colony.

'What sort of name is Nylon, anyway?'

'It was the name of the horse that won Miss Carlos all her money,' said Cheryl. 'San Antonio is in Texas. It has horseraces and bingo.'

'Do you even know what bingo is?'

'Texas is in America.'

'What is it, then?'

'America is in the U S of A.'

'Australia has horseraces too, you know.'

'In Texas the cars have Texas numberplates.'

'America isn't so special. Believe me, I should know.'

'I'm going to San Antonio as soon as we've finished moving to the country. It will be fine in San Antonio as long as they don't push the button and make the nuclear winter.'

'For God's sake stop *revving* Cheryl. I'm getting a nervous twitch.'

On their last day in the city, words shot back and forth between them fast enough to shout scores.

It was time to start driving and the removalists hadn't arrived to pick up the silver-lined tea chests draughtsboarding their front yard. What if it rained? What if strangers went through their underwear? What if the removalists didn't come at all and they got stuck in Tanta whatever it was with nothing but the clothes on their backs?

'Say goodbye to Cheryl, boys,' said Mrs Evensly, the next-door neighbour.

'Cheryl smells,' said Leon Evensly.

'Cheryl copied the plans to my space sack,' said Leeroy Evensly.

'You should take it as a compliment,' said their mother. 'Imitation is the highest form of flattery.'

Violet stood next to her Apex 60 staring at the shell of their house while Princess and her surviving puppies defecated on the footpath.

'You will be all right, won't you Vi?'

Mrs Evensly was wearing a macrame poncho with beaded waterfalls dripping from each sleeve.

'I'll be fine,'

'You sure?'

'Positive. I need to make a new start. To get my head together for once.'

'Those ungrateful bastards should be shot for giving you the flick. What would they know about sophistication?'

'Not in front of the children, please Deborah.'

'And Winston?'

'Finished.'

'You told him it was over?'

'I told him we were lying low for a few days because Cheryl had the mumps. He'll turn up in a week or so and wonder where he went wrong.'

'Are you kidding?' said Deborah Evensly. 'That arrogant pig would think you'd been abducted by aliens before he'd imagine you'd ever leave him . . . *There must be some sort of misunderstanding* . . .' she said in Winston's voice (the nightclub trombonist had a distinctive nasal whine built for parody).

Mrs Evensly laughed and shuddered macrame rain all over Leeroy's head.

'An aviary is a big house for birds with holes in the roof for air conditioning,' said Cheryl.

But Mrs Evensly and Violet were too busy putting on their sunglasses to reply. They were getting ready to cry. Violet had bought Cheryl sunglasses for covering up crying, but most of the time she forgot to use them — especially in bed at night. She had no need for them now, anyway. Leeroy and Leon stank of cat food and Mrs Evensly drank Scotch straight from the bottle then washed her dishes in the bathtub. The only person Cheryl was really going to miss from the city was Miss Carlos.

Deborah tugged Violet's arm and whispered 'you got anything left for the trip?'

Violet mix-mastered her hair. Back then, it was red not blonde and she and Cheryl were Opus-Worthingtons, not Kisses.

'I don't need anything. I'm giving all that away, remember?'

'I'm not talking about gear,' said Mrs Evensly pushing a wad of rolled money into Violet's conveniently open fist. 'I'm talking about cash.'

'I can't take your money, Deborah,' said Violet.

'Of course you can.'

And guess what?

Mrs Evensly was right.

Both women cried under their sunglasses while Leon and Leeroy performed human somersaults across the lawn.

'Say goodbye to Cheryl, boys.'

'Goodbye, piggy.'

'*Boys.*'

'Goodbye, Cheryl.'

'Say goodbye to the boys, Cheryl.'

But by then it was too late. By then she and her mother were on the road.

Violet, Cheryl and Nylon passed grey oceans and messy webs of prawn trawlers and a giant tourism lobster constructed from crimson fibreglass and perspex. They passed looming semitrailers and devastated picnic spots and rhino four wheel drives and flimsy tin humpy homes and matchstick forests in Nazi lines and kangaroos smeared in question marks across the bitumen and hours upon hours of nothing.

Sometimes they got tired and slept in the back of the car. Other times, they stayed in motels with beds made of aluminium tubes. In all these rooms, Cheryl had to turn the volume of the television all the way to 10 to drown out the roar of the highway.

One night, the woman and the girl came across a forest truck stop beside a freeway roundabout as big as an upended ferris wheel.

Violet installed her seven-year-old daughter in a stiff red booth.

'Wait here,' she said.

'But it's haunted,' whined Cheryl as a tidal wave of semitrailers hissed to a stop outside the dirty windows.

She had just woken up. Her legs had pins and needles and there was a wedge in her waist from the seatbelt. The journey wouldn't end. The night was as thick as gravy. Who wanted to go somewhere it was always summer, anyway?

'Eat your dried fruit,' said Violet. 'I have to go to the bathroom.'

'Can I buy a Super Sucker?'

'Not unless you have a spare $500 to pay the dental bills. Do you want to grow up to be a toothless old crow like Mrs Evensly? Is that what you want? A mouthful of black fillings?'

Wolf-whistles sang into the night as her mother's shoes clipped across the greasy cement to the padlocked toilet. In the red booth next door, a truck driver with black tattoos on his palms read a magazine full of women wearing no shirts. He was picking from a styrofoam cup full of sweets and studying an advertisement for a doll.

'Introducing the next best thing to a woman,' it read. 'Delilah! Absolutely the most humanlike life-like doll ever created. Disregard all the other ads you've ever read about any other doll because Delilah has them all beat by far! Delilah is at least ten years ahead of her time. Besides having an iron-clad money-back guarantee, Delilah comes complete with the following extremely realistic features: Natural beautiful hair implanted on Delilah's beautifully shaped head and body; a very pretty face and head with soft kissable lips that part; and (and!) soft fleshy vinyl skin that warms to the human touch and is more life-like than ever!'

Delilah looked a lot like her mother and Cheryl was disappointed when the man turned the page. She wondered what she'd say if he offered her a lolly.

Everyone said not to take food from strangers but Violet was in another one of her health food frenzies and Cheryl would do anything for sweets. The day before they'd left the city she let Leon Evensly pull down her pants and spread her bottom in exchange for a single brick of bubble gum.

Behind the counter a woman in a grey uniform chewed on her chalk then wrote numbers onto a blackboard dripping with cooking grease. The song on the radio reminded Cheryl of her bedroom and she pressed her face to the glass. Outside, above ghostly rows of petrol pumps and metal-fanged towel dispensers, the night sky reeled with the weight of the galaxy. Never in her life had Cheryl seen so many stars. In the city there was just a smattering in the yellow night, but here something had exploded. Stars were raining onto the truck stop and its huge roundabout in the middle of nowhere and in no time at all they would all be sliced into a trillion quinmillion slivers.

'What the hell are you doing?' Violet croaked when her daughter burst into the baby changing room of the toilet block. Her eyes were red and she was smoking a big cigarette.

'The stars are falling.'

'I told you to stay put,' Violet said, putting out the white bullet on the plastic bench and disappearing beneath her sunglasses even though it was night and she wasn't even crying.

'But they're sharp, they're coming down to peck us with their swords. I want to go home.'

'We can't go home. We've got a new job and a new house waiting in Tantanoula, remember? Christ Cheryl, what happened to your pants?'

'Wee,' said Cheryl, staring up at her mother through a veil of salt. 'I weed myself when I saw the sky.'

Violet's face thawed.

'Oh, Babycakes,' she said, holding her leaky daughter to her chest. 'There's absolutely nothing to worry about, you know. There's more stars in the sky because we're in the country, that's all.'

Cheryl couldn't remember the last time her mother had held her so tight. It was hard to breathe, that close to her mother's body.

'I thought it was the nuclear war,' she sniffled into the hard bones beneath Violet's throat. 'I thought they'd pressed the button and it was the nuclear summer.'

The next morning, the two were woken at dawn by a man in a blue uniform.

'Sorry,' the police officer said when Violet stretched out of the front seat and unfolded herself into an adult. 'We had a report that two children had been abandoned in a car. My mistake, folks. Merry Christmas. And welcome to Savvy.'

Violet had parked beside a long, flat ocean. She had woken in such a good mood, Cheryl was almost certain she would be allowed to eat hamburgers for breakfast.

Here was the rule about junk food: No junk food, not even on birthdays.

Here were the times Violet forgot about the no junk food rule: When she was in a really good mood, when she was in a really bad mood, when she was in that silent, hair-winding mood, when there was something she wanted to watch on television, when she slept through lunch as well as breakfast and when she had a new boyfriend. When Violet had a new boyfriend, Cheryl was allowed to do pretty much whatever she wanted as long as it didn't involve knocking on the door when it was closed, or yelling into the night anything along the lines of: Mummy, are you sure you're all right?

Here was the rule about bubble gum: No bubble gum, not even if you were breaking the junk food rule just this one time. Later, Violet would discover the sugar-free variety and insist Cheryl take a packet after every meal because chewing burned valuable calories. Cheryl didn't mind Anti Dint Stick-O-Mints, but the laxative effect was incredible.

Violet left Cheryl in the car and came back with a silver necklace wrapped in shop paper.

'Merry Christmas,' she said.

'But I don't have anything for you.'

'This weather is enough of a Christmas present for me. Don't you love it, sweetheart?'

'It sure is hot.'

'What about your new necklace. Don't you just *adore* it?'

'It's enchanting,' said Cheryl.

'That's a nice word, sweetheart.'

'It's extra sparkly.'

'That's lovely. Have I wished you a Merry Christmas, darling?'

'I think so. It doesn't really feel like Christmas.'

'But there's reindeer up all over town. And didn't Santa just bring you a necklace?'

'I guess.'

'Believe me, babycakes, you could do a lot worse than this, you really could. On Christmas Day my mother made me sit in church from morning until night. There was no pretty jewellery for me. We didn't have a tree surrounded by presents or a big turkey dinner.'

Cheryl wanted to point out that she and Violet were unlikely to enjoy either of these festive staples but wound her new necklace round her thumb instead.

'Christmas is basically just a day like any other,' said Violet. 'It starts and then it ends. So what? New Year's Day, though. New Year's Day is special. That's the day you should make your biggest plans of all.'

'New Year's revolutions.'

'Especially this year, Cheryl. Because this is the year everything's going to change. This is the year I'm going to get my big head together and you're going to get your little head together and we're both going to land on our feet. You better get ready, sweetheart. This is really going to be our year.'

Cheryl wondered what made a year more yours than anyone else's. And was it stealing? Miss Carlos would have known but Miss Carlos was five days' drive in the other direction and there was no way Cheryl wanted to pass by that truck stop again ever.

'Was your mummy Grandma Edna?'

'Yes she was, Cheryl.'

'Why doesn't she come over any more?'

'Because she's dead, Cheryl.'

'Is that why she lives under the ground?'

'It's a lovely day, babycakes. Do we really have to discuss dead people right this very instant?'

A car with a surfboard on the roof pulled up and two boys and two girls got out and ran down to the sand. They raced to the edge of the water and jumped about splashing each other squealing. After a while they got up onto each others' shoulders so they could push each other into the big salty mirror. The boys wore brightly coloured shorts and the girls had tiny triangles tied to their chest with pieces of string. They were the happiest people in the world.

'Mummy?'

'Why don't you try calling me Violet, sometimes? Most people think we're sisters when they first meet us, you know.'

Violet's mood was disintegrating.

'Can we still get hamburgers for breakfast?'

'If you keep eating hamburgers you'll never be able to go to the beach in a bikini. You'll have to hide under a big T-shirt like Mrs Evensly, even when you're swimming in the water. And when you come out it'll stick to your body so everyone will see all your rolls of fat anyway. Is that what you want?'

'No.'

'Good. Because I certainly don't want to go to the beach with a daughter who gets mistaken for a whale and refloated every time she tries to get a suntan.'

The two boys and two girls who'd been swimming walked back up to their car. They had no towels and shook off the water by dancing.

'Merry Christmas,' they shouted out the window before they drove off.

'Merry Christmas,' muttered Violet behind dark glasses and a cigarette.

Without the swimmers, the ocean was as flat as a line.

'Why is the sea here so sick?'

'That's a stupid thing to ask.'

'But it has no waves.'

'It's probably having a rest.'

'Why is the sea so tired?'

'Maybe it's like mummy and has to work day and night looking after its ungrateful daughter.'

'Will it die if it doesn't open its eyes?'

'That's right, Cheryl, it'll die. It'll cough up blood for a couple of hours and then it'll keel right over and die.'

Cheryl left her mother in the car and ran to the edge of the wide flat sea to shout.

'Hey, Princess,' she yelled at the sleeping ocean. She wished the Evenslys had given names to the puppies that hadn't woken up.

'Wake up, Princess.'

But the sea stayed flat.

'I don't like it here,' said Cheryl. 'Can we not get hamburgers for breakfast somewhere else?'

Incredibly enough, Cheryl got junk food after all. That was Violet for you. One minute you weren't allowed to eat anything but dried fruit and the next minute she was pulling up outside a milk bar and handing you $5 saying 'get whatever you want' and staring out the window like she was 1000 miles away. How about that?

It was good ordering things for yourself in milk bars. The owners always threw in stuff for free because you couldn't see over the top of the counter.

'Two hamburgers with cheese, bacon and extra sauce and a takeaway black coffee, please.'

Violet didn't have to know about the extra burger. And it *was* nearly New Year's Eve. After New Year's Eve, Violet got impossible about food for ages. One New Year's Day, she'd put them on a cleansing diet of soup made out of nothing but vegetable peelings. It looked like something you might see in the toilet.

Violet and Cheryl drove through the town until they found a park beside a river. They unfolded one of their blankets next to an oyster-encrusted bridge pylon and

Cheryl made sure she leant over the grass so meat juice wouldn't wreck their bed.

After one-and-a-half secret burgers, she threw the leftovers into the air and a flock of seagulls fought for the meat in a screaming white fire.

'Look Mummy,' Cheryl said, 'They're having a public meeting in the sky.'

But Violet was too busy smoking and wearing her sunglasses to answer.

Cheryl played in the grass and on the swings. The skin on her hands had been X-rayed with beetroot so she played operations with sticks underneath the slippery dip. On one side of the park, away from the equipment, was a small pond surrounded by stones. It was covered with waterlilies and right on the edge was a green tree frog with bulging eyes and creases beneath its armpits. The frog had a pale stomach and cling-on sucknaps instead of toes. It was easy to catch, but wet itself on Cheryl's arm.

'Bad frog,' said Cheryl, stopping short of a smack because that would be cruel. Also because the frog might burst.

Leon and Leeroy Evensly had run down a frog to make it explode. It was only plastic but they'd filled it up with green jelly and detonated it all over the footpath. Leon and Leeroy didn't live here by the river but there were at least three other boys with scooters — Cheryl had spotted them out the car window while she and Violet were driving to the park.

Cheryl took the frog down to the edge of the water and threw it out as far as she could without squeezing too hard. Leon said frogs had four interconnected hearts, each more full of pus than the next. But it was cruel for a frog to have to live in such a small pond so close to so many boys with scooters. It should swim to the other side of the river where the bush began. That's where it could make a new start and get its head together for once in its life.

The frog rose to the surface blinking frantically. Its legs flapped exactly the way frogs' legs did on TV. It was very exciting.

'Swim the other way,' Cheryl shouted as the yellow eyes motored towards her.

But the frog was stupid. It kept paddling back towards the picnic and Cheryl kept hurling it back into the river.

'There's plenty of food on the other side,' she said and threw it out again, partly annoyed and partly pleased at the extra opportunity to watch it swim.

Cheryl had just thrown the frog into the water for the umpteenth time when someone wrenched her shoulder backwards.

'What are you doing?' said the stranger. He had matted hair and smelled funny.

Cheryl glanced up at her mother who gave them an uncertain wave and slipped her sunglasses up her nose so she didn't have to peer over the top.

'I don't know,' said Cheryl.

'That's a freshwater frog,' the man said.

'I was returning it to the wild.'

'This is a saltwater river.'

'I didn't want it to explode.'

'To that frog this water would feel like an acid bath.'

A wind came up and peaked the water into depraved meringues. The frog, still metres from the shore, now kicked so irregularly it was blown back further that it was able to propel itself.

'Even if it makes it back to shore it won't live more than an hour or so,' said the stranger.

Cheryl scratched a scab on her leg.

'Happy?' he said, releasing Cheryl's arm and walking off in disgust. 'Fucking tourists.'

Cheryl was devastated.

An hour later, she and her mother drove into Tantanoula. Well, they would have driven into Tantanoula if the highway hadn't been blocked by police cars.

'Brush your hair, Cheryl,' said Violet, craning to apply lipstick in the rear-vision mirror. 'And for God's sake do something about that bottom lip. It was only a stupid toad.'

Next to the car was another stretch of the same river Cheryl had murdered the frog beside that morning. It was dirty and brown and seemed to shrink from its own banks. Next to it was a gang of people with rolled up shirts who were pulling a giant package from the murk. Everything was in slow motion. The buffalo grass slouched with ticks and the faded Welcome to Tantanoula sign said: The Land That Winter Forgot.

'Hot enough for you, ladies?' asked one of the policemen. Across the road from the river was a boarded-up wooden depot reading Tantanoula Medals and Militaria. 'This heat's enough to drive you up the cart, I reckon. Why do people keep ringing me up after 5 p.m. all day, anyway?'

'What seems the problem, officer?' asked Violet with a toss of her head and a European accent.

'Floater,' said the policeman. 'Got snagged on some kid's new boogie board and there goes Christmas Day. You'd think he could have waited until the 27th. Had a little consideration for those of us on a rostered day off. But they're self-centred, these sewer-ciders. My advice is to stand well back from them.'

'Tragic,' sighed Violet.

'It's a long street, but it still goes from one end to the other. You ladies are not from round here are you?'

'That's right.'

'Visiting this fine country of ours for long?'

'Oh no,' laughed Violet, speaking with more of an accent than ever. 'I'm not a foreigner. I've just spent many years abroad.'

'Good for you, young lady. I'd be OS quick as asking if it wasn't for the job. In the meantime I have my phrase books. Thanks to our new tourist centre, I know how to ask for a Devonshire tea in seven different mother tongues.'

If Violet hadn't been quite so devoid of martinis, she might have made a remark about mother's tongues that would have left Senior Constable Max Grippa the colour of meatloaf. As it was, everything remained remarkably civil.

'You don't happen to have a cigarette do you?'

'For you, young lady, anything. Give me two minutes to disorganise myself and I'll be right with you.'

'What's a floater, Mum?'

'Mind your own business, Cheryl Jane. It's very rude to listen in on other people's conversations. And it's Violet, all right? Not Mum. Violet. We're making a fresh start, remember?'

Cheryl watched through the car window as the police gang covered the package from the river with an orange plastic sheet and laid it out on the grass next to the wooden leg of a picnic table. The orange plastic sheet slipped sideways and Cheryl caught a glimpse of curly black hair and a single bloated eye swarming with blue flies. A police officer drinking chocolate milk from a cardboard carton opened on both sides pulled the orange plastic sheet back over the face.

'Digger,' came a yell from across the street. It was an old man leading a big black dog with a plastic bag of groceries tied across its back. 'Digger — get in behind boy.'

Someone said something about the funny farm and there was a high laugh from Violet. She'd never heard Digger sing along to the old depot guard's harmonica.

'The new newsreader?' the policeman said, pumping her mother's hand. 'I should get your autograph before you get too famous. We don't get many celebrities in this neck of the woods. What's the latest? Or isn't it out yet?'

Up in the sky, a plane sketched out the words Buy Bi-Mart. The sky was blue and the sun was relentless. Cheryl stared at the huge hand laid palm-up beneath the orange plastic and wished someone would try to wake the floater up. Maybe he was a freshwater man and had fallen into the salt by accident. Or maybe he was just tired. Violet said Christmas could be just as tiring as a divorce. And she should know. She'd had plenty of both of them.

'I want to go back to the city,' Cheryl said. 'The country looked a lot better while we were still driving.'

That night, Cheryl sat with Donna Vulpine backstage at the television station while her mother read her first ever Tantanoula news bulletin. Donna wouldn't let Cheryl bring Nylon inside the green room and made her wash her hands twice before she was allowed to eat her crackers and French onion dip. Donna had no adequate explanation for the plain brown room being called green and didn't even know the location of the nearest zoo. Telling Cheryl she had a daughter her age at Tantanoula Infants School was hardly adequate compensation.

'Why wasn't the floater on the news?' Cheryl asked her mother in their new house later that night. 'He was dead, wasn't he?'

'It was because he put himself in the water,' said Violet. She still had her television make-up on and was slurring slightly. 'No-one laid a finger on him, Cakes, he did it all by himself.'

'Isn't it on the news when someone puts themself in the water?'

'No. Now go to sleep.'

'I don't like the floor.'

'Bad luck. The beds won't be here till the day after tomorrow so you'll just have to put up with it.'

'Mum?'

'WHAT?'

'There sure are a lot of trucks for the country.'

Cheryl and Violet stayed in the red-brick house on Tantanoula Highway for the rest of the Christmas holidays. The highway had four lanes and split the town from north to south. Refrigerated trucks used it. Petrol tankers plastered with danger signs used it. White caravans lurching their way to the beaches used it. Tantanoula was the biggest town for miles but no-one stopped unless they lived there or couldn't hold their bladder for another hour until they reached the coast.

Next to the red-brick house on Tantanoula Highway lived a woman with long grey hair called Jean who looked after Cheryl while her mother was having her hair dyed blonde or braying *where is our goddamn furniture* down the telephone line.

Jean had three ducks flying up the wall of her lounge room and a dog with hairy legs called Barky.

'Parsley seeds have to go to the dead and back seven times before germinating,' Jean told Cheryl as they shelled oysters beneath the fragrant shade of a frangipani. 'And they must be planted on Good Friday by a pregnant woman or else.'

'Or else what?' asked Cheryl, slipping another handful of oysters to Barky. She'd rather be at the epicentre of a nuclear blast than eat anything so slimy.

'Or else your good fortune will disappear up the chimney.'

Cheryl helped herself to shortbread from a masking-taped bottle marked Raisins. Jean was the gravesmith's daughter. It was hard to imagine anyone so old being someone's daughter but there was no arguing with the awesome black-and-white portrait hanging over Jean's automatic piano. The gravesmith's big stick was called a rifle.

The other case against oysters, of course, was that they came out of the middle of rocks.

'Is there anything else?'

'My word there is. Once planted, parsley plants must not be moved or you won't see the year out. And don't ever move into a house without parsley plants growing or your beasts will be struck down by the pox.'

Violet laughed.

'Jean is from the country,' she told Cheryl. 'She's just superstitious. Nylon isn't going to die because we don't grow parsley.'

In Jean's backyard were strawberry plants, manacled flowers and a tree with round silver leaves.

'But where is the parsley?' asked Cheryl.

'Wash your mouth out,' the grey woman replied. 'It takes an honest woman to grow parsley but if she succeeds she will have no daughters and only barren sons.'

Jean said it was fine for Cheryl to stay with her during the afternoons and evenings for the rest of the school holidays while Violet worked. They shelled oysters and baked shortbread and stole industrial debris from building sites. One afternoon they constructed a spy satellite from electric cable spools, polystyrene and blue ice-cream containers in the backyard. Jean named the satellite 'Cheryl' and launched it by crashing open a bottle of Cold Duck. Cheryl laughed so wildly at the splinters of glass and sparkling wine that she weed herself and automatically began to cry. Jean said don't worry. She said the bladder was nature's pharmacy and urine was a better cure for blue-bottle stings than anything you could buy in a tube.

Cheryl said yuck but Jean only cackled.

To touch her long white hair you had to wait until she'd fallen asleep in front of the wireless and started to snore. To see a photograph of the first woman in New Zealand to ride a bicycle you only had to ask. But to watch her hurl the largest of the three wall ducks at her adult son required an invitation to lunch on Sunday.

'The boy's infuriating,' she told Cheryl one Sunday evening as they re-glued the duck's webbed foot for the second week running. 'I've tried to take an interest in the wretched creature, I really have, but he bores me witless. It's no wonder his wife left him for another man. I'd leave him for another son if I could.'

Sometimes Cheryl thought Jean was a witch. She'd never heard anyone say such horrible things about their own flesh and blood before. But she didn't like Jean's son either. He had no hair and a big fat face like a baby. He came home on the weekends and lounged around the house reading magazines with rude pictures in the over-elasticised white underwear his last wife had sewn for him on her faulty Singer sewing machine. Three times he had been struck by lightning without noticing.

There was no doubt about it. Jean Kiss's son, Jackson, was like the hot air of a Tantanoula summer — there was a nasty nothingness about the man.

The removalists didn't ever arrive with the furniture. They gave Violet some money instead and Cheryl never saw her posters of the seasons or Miss Carlos's beginner bingo set ever again. What she did see plenty of was Jackson Kiss.

Personally, Cheryl had her money on the policeman they met at the river on the first day and said as much to Jean Kiss at the wedding.

'She did see him first,' she explained over the icing of her third slice of wedding cake. 'And he did give her a police escort up to the television station.'

'Ah well,' Jackson's mother said gruffly. 'There's no accounting for tastelessness.'

Jean Kiss found the wedding inconceivably depressing. She drove her moped down to the river to drink Cold Duck, load her pipe and watch the river inch past like a brown snake trying and failing to shed its skin. She thought back to her own wedding and the 30 years of marriage that followed. Every day Jean Kiss worked at the Liquor and Associated Beverages Union and every night she rode home on her motorbike to bring in the clothes, clean the house and prepare dinner. Her late husband had never done anything more productive after work than whisk the jazz drum kit in the romper room.

Jean got married thinking boredom was not knowing what to do with the hours between lunch and dinner on a Sunday.

'I didn't have a goddamn clue,' she crowed at the dirty river. 'I didn't have a goddamn clue.'

Two week's later, the old woman died in her sleep. Cheryl cried but Violet said it was for the best. 'Jean wasn't a very happy person, darling. She didn't even buy us a wedding present.'

During the wake, Violet toasted Cheryl with a bottle of scotch and reminded her not to mention her previous marriages in public. She wasn't ashamed of having A Past, as it were. But four husbands sounded so terribly ancient.

The funeral lasted until two in the morning.

'Stop trying to hug me,' Cheryl whined as the red-brick houses of Panorama Way flashed past the Kiss car window on the way home from the crematorium function room.

'I'm only trying to be nice,' Jackson replied from behind the steering wheel.

'Rashani Bail's a slut,' slurred the figure on the back seat.

Once again, Violet Kiss hadn't landed on her feet so much as her face.

12

The Man From The School

Sun. Brazenly enough, the 14th of November dawned as clear as an eye. So much for the deluge the night before.

'So much for the macadamia crops,' said Jackson.

'What the hell would you know about macadamia crops?' snapped his wife.

Violet Kiss was in one of her states. After arriving home from the police station and fighting with Cheryl, she'd spent the rest of the night writhing in furious nostalgia, sweat dripping from her forehead and sheets wringing her lovely neck.

'Where's my suitcase,' she'd demanded at 4.30 a.m.

'BTC–269,' Jackson replied sleepily. 'BTC–269?'

But Violet would not take her numberplate for an answer.

She'd leapt from the ruins of the mattress, turned on the light and began digging beneath the bed. Discoveries included a cardboard box of scarves marked scarves, three fancy-dress masks made of inner tube and a saucy novel called *Jasmin's Secret* she'd purchased while expanding her horizons in Amsterdam. It was a goddamn anthropological site down there.

Violet reeled from a sudden burst of perfume and mothballs. She dragged the old suitcase beneath a cone of light in Jackson's study and shook a battered postcard of the Chicas Chicas Chicas bar in Cabo Roto from the pages of Cheryl's passport.

Violet's second born was so small she'd been photographed in a doctor's palm.

'Get out of here,' the Mexican nurse had told Violet in the hospital. 'Just get your things and go.'

When Violet left Cabo Roto, she cried so much the nurses said she was at risk of pneumonia.

Not that you could believe everything the nurses said.

After all, their last words to Violet were: It's better this way.

Cheryl walked in and slouched over the breakfast table in pyjamas. Her mother had stopped dwelling on the past and started with the eye thing.

'Is so,' said Violet.

'Is not,' said Jackson.

'Is too.'

'Is not.'

'CHERYL?'

Cheryl went through the motions of examining her mother's face.

'I don't know,' she said finally. 'The left one is looking a bit creepy.'

'See,' said Violet.

'This is ridiculous,' said Jackson.

'One of my eyes is definitely turning green.'

'You'd look like a rock star if you had different coloured eyes, Mum. Lance Seldom has one blue eye and one green one. His changed after he got herpes.'

'Please don't say that word at the breakfast table, Cheryl.'

'Why not? Mr Scoob says it during PE all the time. You'll get herpes if you do this, you'll get herpes if you do that.'

'Cheryl.'

'You don't just get herpes down in your darkroom, either.'

'I'm warning you, Cheryl . . .'

'You can get it in your eyes and your ears and even up your bum . . .'

'That's it, young lady. Go to your room at once.'

'Herpes,' Cheryl shouted as she left the table. 'Herpes, herpes, herpes, herpes, herpes, herpes, herpes, herpes, herpes.'

'What have I done to deserve this?'

Jackson flapped *Keeping The Romance Alive* open at the cooking pages. 'You think *you're* in trouble,' he said. 'I hate to argue with the experts, but serving eggs without tomato sauce is just a waste of time. It'd be like trying to eat lettuce without sugar.'

Out in the carport, Cheryl retrieved her Personal Pocket Journal from the slit in her mattress.

Cheryl Kiss — Girl Detective, she wrote at the top of a new page.

Case One: Who Killed Samuel Leadhead?

Samuel's Enemies: Mort Ramsbottom, Murray Ramsbottom, Mrs Kiss and most probably Lou.

Unanswered questions: What happened when Leadhead took the lie detector test? Which Leadhead was it anyway? Did Bradley Spam have an alibi? Why didn't Detective Grippa give anyone a guard and how can you tell if someone is watching your every move with binoculars from up at the fig tree?

'I don't want to stay here by myself today,' Cheryl said, as her mother ironed herself into a yellow work envelope. Violet's television clothes were so stiff it was a wonder they needed coat hangers at all. She was leaving for work early because of Samuel's murder.

'Go to school then.'

'I don't want to go to school either.'

'Well, stop complaining.'

'I'm not complaining. I keep hearing noises, that's all.'

Sometimes Cheryl wished Violet's eye did change colour, that it turned as bright green as the tassels on her new suede boots. Then she could tell everyone that, like the rest of the fine Kiss views, Violet's beautiful new green peeper was the product of disease, the product of the herpes virus eating away her corneas.

'Nothing can touch us,' Cheryl said as her mother drove away and Zeus bolted the last of the windows. 'With the girl detective in charge, we're completely safe.'

A line of black ants streamed beneath a crack in the door.

Was nothing impenetrable?

Outside, beyond the curve of her vision, a dry branch snapped underfoot.

Zeus sprang to all fours.

'See!' he honked. 'Ballistics! Invaders! The end of the world!'

A human shadow crept along the coiled hose dribbling over Jackson's banksias.

'Shit,' said Cheryl. 'Not again.'

She grabbed a bread knife and peered through the flyscreen.

Christy Leadhead had never looked worse.

Samuel's older sister stood squinting in the Kiss driveway with fried streams springing from her knees and rheumy red eyes. Her crowbar was so enormous it was hard to tell which was wielding the other.

'What do you want?' Cheryl yelled.

'I'm looking for the man from the school,' said Christy, jabbing the crowbar into Violet's umbrella stand. 'He's the man who killed Sammy. Have you seen him?'

Christy sat at the kitchen table smelling of oily hair and soap. Her face was olive like Samuel's and the rest of the Leadhead sisters. It was dark and thin and supported the mandatory mushroom cloud of wiry black hair. Her eyebrows were plucked to scratches and there was a tan line across her jaw line.

Foundation.

Maybe even rouge.

Christy Leadhead probably wasn't even a virgin.

'You don't look so fat close up,' she said to Cheryl.

'I'm not,' said Cheryl. 'It's only puppy fat, anyway.'

'Why don't you go on a diet?'

'I've got big bones.'

'Your face is all right. You could be a model if you went on a diet. Look at this . . .'

She kicked off a rubber boot to reveal a set of erratically painted toenails.

'I'm going to be a foot model. Gran wants me to learn shorthand, but my sister Alice reckons you can earn $200 an hour just by taking off your shoes. Imagine that.'

'Models are shallow,' said Cheryl, wondering how Christy Leadhead got her eyeliner looking so much like Lurex Imperial's. 'It's superficial to judge people for how they look on the outside. The important thing is what's on the inside.'

'You're sick,' said Christy. 'You're going to marry a doctor so he can cut you open to see how nice you look under your skin.'

There was a deafening shriek from the wall of cicadas in the garden.

'Gran calls me a tapeworm 'cos I eat and eat and only get thinner. She says no-one's going to marry a parasite but I'd rather be too thin than too fat any day. What are you looking like that for? This dog ever shut up? You got any grog?'

Cheryl pulled a bottle of her mother's Scotch from behind the jug of bleeding purple flowers.

'This?'

'What else you got?'

From behind the fridge.

'This?'

'What else you got?'

From the back of the saucepan cupboard.

'This?'

'That'll do.'

Christy poured a slurp from each bottle into a glass and swallowed.

'Firewater,' she said, wiping her mouth. 'Have some.'

Christy's lips were crusted and broken. What if she had herpes? Cheryl brought the glass to her face and gulped. Samuel's sister was right. The grog was liquid fire sloshing around her stomach. It was like being burned alive.

Was it?

'You want a cigarette?'

'Got my own,' said Cheryl lighting one of her mother's White Cities from a crushed packet on the fridge. Gas sank from her mouth in a limp puff.

'You got to force yourself to inhale,' Christy said. 'If you want to learn to drawback, it's the only way. Look. Like this.'

Christy Leadhead didn't go to Tantanoula High School any more. She'd left to go to work at the Bi-Mart. Before that she was in class 10–5 which was how you knew straight off she was dumb. The highest class in grade ten was 10–1. That was for brainiacs. The lowest was 10–5. That was for retards. Once there'd been a 10–6 but then Bi-Mart opened and advertised for night fillers and the class disbanded. Christy and her sister Stacie were the last to go. They got moved up to 10–5 when 10–6 died, but parents wrote in to complain. They said the infiltrators were low achievers who would destroy 10–5's averages. 9–1 thought this was hilarious. 9–1 was Cheryl's class. It was also Samuel's. When Samuel first started at Tantanoula High School, he'd landed in 7–7 like the rest of the Leadheads. Then Mr Nuys the school inspector made everyone sit IQ tests and Samuel shot up to 7–1 like an express elevator.

What was the result of Cheryl's IQ test?

Violet wouldn't say.

She'd obtained her daughter's results after sharing an entire bottle of white rum with Mr Nuys during a parent liaison evening.

But she wouldn't tell Cheryl because she said it might give her a swollen head.

According to Violet, getting a swollen head was one of the worst things that could happen to a person.

'Stop looking at me like that.'

'Like what?'

'Like that. You can't smoke but you think you're so good.'

The latter half of this remark was so far from the truth Cheryl spluttered grog all over her lap.

'Anyway,' said Christy. 'I know you saw Sammy. I know you saw him and didn't do nothing. But I don't care. You didn't want to get burned by the man from the school. I can understand that. There's a crowbar outside. There's a rifle at the house. I'm gonna find the man from the school and make him pay for what he did. Don't look at me that way. It has to be your own brother. To really understand it has to be your own flesh and blood.'

Cheryl thought about telling Christy about her dead twin. Sarah Beth wasn't identical so maybe she wouldn't have even grown up fat. Was there an afterlife? Could you learn how to smoke there? Twin sisters were supposed to be connected. But Cheryl didn't feel like she was only half a person. She felt like she was three or four of them. Especially on vinyl bus seats when she took up half, more than *half* the damn seat.

'You're not even listening.'

'I am too.'

'When I saw Gran carrying Sammy down the hill I didn't even know who he was. She was up the fig tree collecting cow pats for the garden and I thought she had a bag of shit. Gran walked right up to me with the shit over her shoulder and said where's your father and I said out in the ute somewhere and she said call a fucking ambulance and that's when I realised the sack was my brother.

'Gran lay Sammy down in the shade and turned on the hose. Stay awake, she kept saying, you got to stay awake. Then Sammy opened his eyes and told us it was the man from the school. He said it was the man from the school what came to the house and made him go down the creek and burned him.'

'What man?'

'Dunno what man, do we? The man from the school. That's all he said. Then he started breathing real funny and Gran made me go get peas from the freezer and when there was no peas left we covered him up with packets of corn.

'Gran wouldn't let me go down the hospital in the ambulance. She told me to wait there for dad. Then the doctor rang and said he's real sorry but Sammy he died on the way.'

Christy started crying. It was as if someone had pulled a switch. It only lasted a minute and then it stopped. She gave Cheryl a funny look.

'How come you're not at school, Kiss?'

'I'm sick,' said Cheryl.

'Bulldust,' said Christy. 'You're wagging.'

Then: 'You ever sat The Frigid Test?'

'I don't know. Is it like Spin The Bottle?'

Christy fell around the floor holding her stomach and laughing.

'God, Kiss. You *are* frigid. You are *so* frigid.'

'All right,' said Cheryl. 'What do I have to do?'

'Take off your clothes.'

'Get out of town.'

'Freaking hell, Kiss. I haven't even started the test yet and you've already failed.'

'I thought it was only boys who could give The Frigid Test.'

'That's total bulldust. Anyone can do it. Now get 'em off.'

Cheryl didn't want to make Christy mad. Not while the crowbar was right there in the hatstand. So she put Zeus outside and drew the curtain. Her clothes made a huge pile. There was a parka and a singlet and two long-sleeved shirts and a pair of figure-shaping tights (purchased by her mother) and dark grey trousers and finally her shoes and socks. In the gloom her skin looked very white. Cheryl wondered about the strange feeling on her back and realised it was her hair.

'You sure got big tits for Year Nine.'

'Shut up.'

'It's true. You shouldn't cover them up so much. You could pull as much dick as you wanted if people knew you had tits like that. Dick Puller. That's what they'd call you. Ha! Now keep still. I'm gonna start.'

Christy put a finger on the top of Cheryl's head.

'Aren't you supposed to take your clothes off too?'

'Christ, Kiss. What are ya? A freaking lezzo?'

Cheryl squeezed shut her eyes as Christy ran her finger in a straight line down her forehead, down her nose, down her lips, down her chin, down her neck, down the little bones in the centre of her chest, down her stomach and *gross out* right down the middle of her privates.

Christy's finger went all the way down the inside of Cheryl's legs until it reached the floor.

Cheryl breathed out.

'You passed,' Christy said matter of factly. She washed her hands with soap while Cheryl dressed. 'Now let's go look for the man from the school. If we find him we'll kill him. Come on. I'll show you where the man from the school laid out Sammy's watch and his ring and his clothes and everything.'

'Down at the creek?' mumbled Cheryl. (She was still in shock.)

'All in a line. Before he burned him. When we find that cunt we can shoot him right through the face.'

Cheryl's mouth opened and closed all on its own.

'You coming or not? You owe it to Sammy. You got a dog. I got a stick. No-one will dare come anywhere near us.'

'You going to carry that crowbar all the way to the creek?'

'Why not.'

'It's a long way down.'

'Bring a knife as well, then. Just in case.'

It was strange walking to the creek with someone else. Time passed differently and Cheryl hardly noticed a thing. Zeus felt it too. It drove him crazy. 'Together,' he yapped. 'Stay close. Round up. *Quick*. Keep tight.'

'You want to look in here?' Cheryl asked as they passed the bamboo.

'No way,' said Christy. 'It's full of yowies.'

Cheryl peered through the towering bamboo trunks. They creaked and groaned even without a wind.

'Here. Give me the crowbar.'

Cheryl used the weighty black pole to golf a cow pat into the air then plunged through the shiny yellow curtain.

Fuck Reb and Lou. She'd just passed The Frigid Test. Fuck the man from the school. He probably didn't even know what a frigid test was.

As usual, the centre of the bamboo stand was the eye of a cyclone. An empty cell surrounded by noise and chaos.

There was no killer on the run.

There wasn't even a rat.

'I've got four boyfriends,' Christy said as they continued walking down the hill towards the creek. 'Nicandro, Phillip, Donkey and Filthy Drew Skritch. Where's that pig dog of yours? He chicken out? Gran says one day that pig dog of yours will end up with a bullet through his skull.'

'If anyone touches Zeus I'll kill them.'

'You still got a pet rat?'

'He died of old age and science.'

'Gran says you gotta be mad to keep a rodent in the house.'

'Nylon wasn't a rodent. He was domesticated. Once a rat gets domesticated it isn't a rodent any more.'

'Bulldust.'

Christy Leadhead wouldn't know. What would Christy Leadhead know? Christy Leadhead wore a rippy blue dress with football socks and rubber boots. She had black bracelets, ratty hair and biro love hearts scrawled tattoo-style over each thigh.

'You'll go to jail if you shoot the man from the school.'

'No I won't. It'll be self-defence. Self-defence of my brother.'

They passed a reading group of cattle beneath the shade of a camphor laurel.

'It's a long way down,' said Christy.

'Haven't you even been to the creek before?'

'Only on Dad's trail bike.'

They passed the rotting corpse of a calf. Fortunately Zeus was distracted by crows and didn't eat it in front of them.

'Sammy went down the creek all the time. Mostly at night. Gran was always at him for pissing off, but Dad said let him go. He said Sammy would learn soon enough that pissing off don't get you nowhere. Me and Stacie always thought the Tantanoula yowie was gonna get him. Gran said if we didn't stay in our room at night the Tantanoula yowie would come and get us while we were asleep.'

What a ridiculous warning, thought Cheryl. If something was going to come and get you while you slept it made sense to be as far away from your bedroom as possible. It was an incentive to escape if ever she heard one.

There was a long silence as they reached the creek and trudged through the jungle by the waterholes. The rain from the night before made the water roar. Or was it just the rusty spaghetti tin rattling along the rapids? Then they rounded a corner and saw them, two women and a man in uniform crouched over a black splash in the grass, a huge black scar as if someone had ground out the biggest White City in the world. There were three police motorbikes, a ribbon of yellow police tape and a huge pile of metallic instruments.

Christy froze.

'Come on,' said Cheryl.

'No,' said Christy.

'Don't you even want to have a look?'

'No,' said Christy.

'Hey,' called the man, straightening up over the scorched grass. 'Is that you Cheryl Kiss?'

'Shit,' said Cheryl. 'It's the policeman with the missing finger.'

'Christy Lightfoot?'

'Run for it!' said Christy, suddenly coming to life. 'He was down the station last night. Wouldn't shut up about his freaking finger.'

'Flash!' said Cheryl.

'Flash!' said Christy. 'Rips right off, don't it?'

And they galloped through the buffalo grass laughing hysterically.

'Girls?' Constable Denning called after them.

It was a spectacular about-turn. The two cacklers sprinted back up the ridge, back past the dead calf, back past the cows and back past the bamboo until they collapsed under the fig tree on the hill overlooking both their homes.

'Freaking hell, I think I just had a heart attack.'

'I think I just had two heart attacks.'

Christy lay back on the fallen fig leaves.

'Did you know your house used to be up on this hill? Those posts over there were for the gate and that cement block was the front door.'

'Bulldust.'

'It's true. See the stumps? Your house used to be right there. They pulled it down the mountain on rollers when I was little. Mum brought us up to watch. Sammy came in the rucksack and everything. It was freaky. The whole house slid down the hill. Sonya reckoned she rode it but she was lying. She didn't even have a helmet.'

'Where's your mum, now?'

156

'Dunno. She got sick after Shona was born and after that she went. Gran said she died so I carved her name in a stone out the back of the vans and put on flowers. Gran says we can't say her name but the only grave is the one I made for her.'

'Maybe she went on holiday and lost her memory.'

'Maybe.'

'Maybe she got kidnapped and brainwashed.'

'Maybe.'

'My real dad's dead.'

'I know.'

'He died in a plane crash.'

'I know.'

'How do you know?'

'Everyone knows. Everyone knows about Violet Kiss the big celebrity. When I'm a foot model I'm going to live in a big mansion with 100 slaves and no-one's gonna know a thing.'

'Mum used to be on television in the city. Once she got a backstage ticket to a Lance Seldom concert.'

'Did she get his autograph?'

'He got held up at the airport and couldn't make it.'

'*He got held up at the airport and couldn't make it,*' she mimicked. 'You Kisses think you're so good.'

'Stop calling me Kiss.'

'All right, Kiss.'

'Kiss isn't even my real last name. Jackson Kiss is only my stepfather.'

'I know. Gran says Jackson Kiss is a cuckoo. She says he sits on everyone else's eggs. He did it before, you know. He married Mrs Shorter from Savvy with three boys and then Mrs Shorter went and left him, anyhow.'

Cheryl wanted to say something nasty about Christy's mother but decided against it. She didn't want Christy telling everyone she couldn't smoke.

'Shit,' Christy said, leaping up. 'Holy freaking shit.'

'What?' said Cheryl, jumping too, in case they'd been lying in a green ant nest.

'The bloody crowbar,' Christy said. 'I left the crowbar down at the bloody creek. Dad'll kill me.'

Cheryl watched Samuel's sister sprint back towards the creek, knees flying behind like hair bobbles. She looked down the hill at the mess of the Leadheads' caravans and then at the stretched elastic of her own white home.

Zeus.

Cheryl had been so absorbed with Christy during the expedition she'd forgotten Zeus completely. Couldn't even remember the last time she'd seen him. She turned from the fig tree house and began to trot down the hill. Maybe Christy had tricked her. Maybe Grandma Leadhead was busy doing something terrible to Zeus down at the caravans. Maybe someone had put a bullet in his skull in revenge for all that shredding.

Far off in sewerage valley, tornados of bushfire smoke spiralled toilet rolls against the sunset. It reminded Cheryl of the smell she'd glimpsed the afternoon before. The smell of Samuel's death.

Cheryl reeled in disgust. She was less than human, she really was.

She found Zeus rolling in the shrinking hide of the dead calf but was in no mood to celebrate his salvation. It had become terribly important to return home before the three officers climbed the hill on their police issue motorbikes. Terribly important to vanish before Christy returned with her metal pole. Critical to escape the smell of burning.

13

The Terrible Tantanoula Yowie

'Stay in your bed at night or the terrible Tantanoula yowie will come and get you while you sleep,' was Florence Lightfoot's standard goodnight to all eight of her son's abandoned children.

'Will the yowie come and get Alice if she doesn't stay in her room?'

'Shut it, Sonya.'

'Is the yowie that dead cow underneath the fig tree?'

'Shut it, Stacie.'

'Will the yowie come if I'm in bed but not asleep? Was the yowie the one that came and got Mummy? Is the yowie God?'

'Stop being daft and go to bed.'

Samuel Lightfoot shivered. For a minute he thought the yowie had laser-iced his feet. Then he realised it was only Shona hogging the blankets.

Florence left the last batch of her petrified grandchildren and seized the crowbar in preparation for the dark walk between the second children's caravan and her own. Only that morning, the old depot guard had seen the terrible Tantanoula yowie tear a pensioner limb from limb up on Mount Slight. Thank God for the old depot guard. If it wasn't for him, Florence wouldn't have the foggiest idea about the dangers in the outside world. And who else was supposed to escort her to the Bi-Mart when she went to town to stock up on tins and shit paper? Her good-for-nothing son? Ha. That'd be the day.

The old depot guard hadn't really seen the Tantanoula yowie. None of them had. But thanks to Senior Constables Grippa and Spam, the mythical beast had taken the blame for an entire half-decade.

Here's how it happened:

It was nineteen hundred and something or other. It was stinking hot (just for a change) and a notorious macadamia nut grower by the name of Oxford Christian had just swan-dived into the flesh-braiding blades of her plantation's sorting unit in the badlands between Tantanoula and the beachside town of Savvy.

What prompted the eccentric heiress, convicted transvestite and grandfather of five to voluntarily shred her own evidence?

She'd just become the first person to be tackled by the terrible Tantanoula yowie, that's why.

That was Senior Constable Grippa's theory, anyway.

'Well, bang me backwards with a Wellington,' the youthful officer was heard to remark after arriving at the crime scene with his brooding partner, Spam. 'This one's as dead as a mad woman's breakfast.'

And at that very moment he spotted, or could have sworn he spotted, a massive he-ape run drooling into the brushed maze of Ms Christian's sprawling plantation.

'Bridges alive!' he shouted as *The Chinese Whisper's* two new cadet reporters arrived at the door taking notes. 'Ask me what we're supposed to do with that manifestation of mutancy and I'll give you a nun on a bicycle. Did you see it Spam? Tell me you saw it before I die of bewonderment.'

But Grippa's laconic sidekick offered nothing more than a putrid whinny.

By the next morning, the word on the street was that Oxford Christian had been mustered into her high-speed mechanised bundler by a half-man half-ape the height of a traffic light. These words had been put on the street by *The Chinese Whisper's* two new girl reporters, Genevieve and Donna.

Untimely Demise Of His/Her Nutter Linked To Predatory Primate

(read the headline).

Police Predict Prehuman Plague

Genevieve was beyond disgust.

'When exactly would Ms Christian's demise have been timely?' she asked her fellow cadet. 'Next week? Next year? How about Tuesday? And I love the prehuman plague. You ask the policeman whether the ape has a mate, he says he doesn't know and you predict a pandemic.'

'He didn't rule it out did he?' said Donna. 'Everyone knows yowies breed like rabbits. If there's two of them out there, it's quite possible there could be a plague. I'm sorry, Genevieve, but that's science.'

'I'm sorry, Donna, but that headline was still complete crap.'

Genevieve Flash and Donna Vulpine went back to inserting the dollar signs into the *Whisper*'s market report. They had another hour-and-a-half of fruit and vegetables to do before moving on to the greyhound results. Then there was all that seething to get out of the way.

Of course, Donna Vulpine wasn't Donna Vulpine then. She was Donna Meetlove and she gave as much thought to marrying Kevin Vulpine and changing her name as she did to *The Chinese Whisper*'s battered old copy of *Grammar Fundaments*. After only two weeks on the job, the 17-year-old rhythmic gymnast was hard-pressed to tell the difference between alliteration and electrocution. But she had just read a book about dressing for success and knew for a fact that the average career was made up of 90 per cent twin set.

Genevieve disagreed.

She said if the average career was made up of 90 per cent of anything it was likely to be cock.

Donna was beyond disgust.

Where did that foul-mouthed lemon get off? And what was the story with the button-up skirt? If Donna had one dollar for every time Genevieve's tacky buttons popped open to reveal an equally tacky undergarment, she'd own a floor-length leather coat. Or at least a half-decent briefcase.

There was only room in that newsroom for one new cadet and it wasn't going to be button girl. Employing two cadet journalists in that era of shrinking circulations and atrophying advertising bases was irresponsible, anyway. Donna was working on a proposal in which the company could save $5000 a year by eliminating her colleague's salary (and hopefully, therefore, her colleague).

'That other new cadet thinks she's pretty smart,' the future daytime newsreader told the chief subeditor after masticating his privates in *The Whisper*'s staff bathroom. 'But if Genevieve Flash is so smart, why does she think your headlines are, and I quote "complete and utter crap"? I've always thought your headlines were giants of the genre.'

'Who?' said the chief subeditor.

He was feeling a little faint.

Donna wasn't. Last time she'd retired to the men's toilets with the chief subeditor she'd tried masturbating standing up and passed out. This evening she'd kept her hands to herself and emerged feeling like a million dollars. Like the speedway racer whose head had caught fire beneath his helmet, the young woman had learned a valuable lesson.

'Genevieve Flash is her name,' said Donna as she removed a hair snarl from between her front teeth. 'I'm not surprised you can't place her. She's hardly memorable.'

'Yes,' said the chief subeditor. He pulled his pants up and attempted to use his wallet as a comb. 'Right you are, then.'

Donna could tell he'd appreciated her use of the phrase 'giants of the genre'. It had appeared several times in the office copy of *The New York Hurrah* so she knew it was a winner.

Untimely Demise Of His/Her Nutter was Donna and Genevieve's first front-page story. It carried both their names in full. Donna's series of investigative follow-ups also carried her photograph and led to her first taste of fan mail.

'*In one of your endlessly crapulous stories on the discovery of yowies in Tantanoula you wrote "poke that pussy",*' read the typed note. '*I would like to poke your pussy with my big dick and bounce off your big tits at the same time. Perhaps we can get together, literally speaking? I imagine you look something like these photographs.*'

Donna was scandalised. The pornographic snapshots accompanying the letter were all snipped from *Hunch For Men*'s inaugural Fataholics edition. And to think she hadn't eaten dessert for six whole months.

'"Poke that pussy",' mused Senior Constable Grippa after the astonishingly lipsticked cadet presented the letter for inspection down at the station. 'Can't say I remember reading that particular line in the papyrus. But what I never knew never hurt me, I'm afraid.'

'Of course you can't remember that particular line,' Donna erupted. 'Do you really think someone like me would write something like that in a serious newspaper report? Do you really think the editor would allow it to be printed even if I did?'

But Senior Constable Grippa was absorbed in a photograph of an absolutely enormous young Hunchette standing in a shower cubicle. Her flesh was pressed against all four glass walls and had been transformed into a sort of cube.

'I can't believe you actually thought I came up with a phrase like "poke that pussy". I should report you for sexual harassment.'

'Mmm?'

And Senior Constable Grippa was as surprised as anyone when he discovered young Donna's tongue down his throat.

Act Two of the terrible Tantanoula yowie show commenced a week after Donna received the Poke That Pussy letter.

Here's how it happened:

Once again, Senior Constables Grippa and Spam were called to a mysterious death in the new and as yet to be improved beachside town of Savvy. And once again, Grippa caught a glimpse of the beast's bristling thighs and draping earlobes as it sauntered behind the late Max Laundry's fibreglass carport.

'The first time I could hardly believe my eyes,' he announced via megaphone to the small crowd gathered on Mr Laundry's manicured front lawn. 'Now I can hardly believe my nose.'

It was a fair call. Even Senior Constable Spam was retching at the smell.

'The carrot has turned like two phrases passing in the night,' said Senior Constable Grippa, aware that the last of the listeners had left some hours ago and he was now just enjoying the sound of his own voice. 'Helloooo? Echo Alpha Bravo. Hey, Spam. Can you hear me? Have a go at this.'

The Coroner had two things to say on the subject of the deaths of Max Laundry and Oxford Christian: Heart attack and industrial accident. No suspicious circumstances whatsoever.

Or was that three things?

Either way, Donna Meetlove would not be stopped.

A cover up! was her verdict.

By whom or for what reason was irrelevant.

The point was, she'd worked around the clock to produce an exposé on the terrible Tantanoula Yowie in *The Chinese Whisper*'s coveted Saturday feature section and now the editor had the nerve to ask whether the story had legs.

'Ha ha,' tittered Donna. 'Does *my* story have legs? *Legs*? That's really very amusing, Mr Stint.'

But the hunchbacked editor of *The Chinese Whisper* wasn't as easily pacified as certain chief subeditors. Partly because blondes gave him hives and partly because he was a card-carrying celibate. Mr Nicholas Bartholemew Stint hadn't had a sexual urge for seven years, four months, one week and three days, now. Not that his schoolteacher wife had noticed.

'Legs,' Nicholas Bartholemew Stint read from the *New Shorter Oxford English Dictionary* (which ran for two hard cover volumes and 3801 pages). 'Each of the limbs of support and locomotion in an animal body. "Shake a leg" — make a start or hurry up. "Get one's leg over" — engage in sexual intercourse. "Have no legs" — have insufficient momentum to reach a desired point.'

Donna wanted to tell the crippled old retard her investigative feature story had pins going all the way up to its arse. The words that actually emerged from her mouth were: 'Why of course the story has legs, Mr Stint. Are you sure I can't get you a tea or a coffee or a nice little bun?' Then she dropped her notebook and flashed her bottom while picking it up for good measure.

Donna's exposé on the terrible Tantanoula yowie didn't really have legs — or even supportive wooden crutches. The 'expert sources' she'd quoted in paragraphs three, four and seven were none other than the old depot guard who'd also sworn blind that quiche was genetically engineered by the United Nation's Supra Government as a part of an undercover campaign to disarm the masses (Donna had decided to edit out that part of the quote). The woman on the switchboard at the local Federation of Reserves and Wildlife didn't exactly agree that the Terrible Tantanoula Yowie was a communist conspiracy, but she didn't exactly disagree either. And Razz Salmon would do anything to get his face in the paper. Even if it meant calling for exhumations and re-autopsies.

Genetic Travesty Terrorises Tantanoula

(read the headline).

Who the hell will be next?

The satiated chief subeditor had never used the word 'hell' in a headline before. It was a calculated risk that paid off. Sales went through the roof, Donna got promoted, Genevieve Flash decided natural justice was a vicious rumour and from that moment on, the evil yowie's reign of terror knew no bounds. Lost children. Floods. Tapeworm infestations. Militant weed stock. Road kill. Pensioner passings. The yowie took the blame for it all.

Yowie Plague Linked To Bushfire Carnage

Possible Yowie Town Hall Sighting

Yowie Claims Three Lives In Shock Pedestrian Crossing Slam: Housewife

It didn't matter that no-one except Max Grippa had ever seen anything even remotely resembling the notorious feral ape. For four glorious years, there was an explanation for everything.

Then Senior Constable Peter Spam made a shocking deathbed admission.

It was in the Lung Ward of the Tantanoula Base Hospital. Spam had been bagged and tubed as a direct result of his addiction to unfiltered tobacco cigarettes. As his time drew near, he instructed his wife to make the necessary calls. One was to his partner, Max.

'Spam,' said Grippa when he entered the room.

'Grippa,' said Spam.

And as the two men shook hands, the dying man used the last of his strength to haul the stocky sergeant down to his concertinaed lips.

'Revenge may not be a dish best served half-dead but it's better than not serving it at all,' he said.

'I'm sorry?'

'I believe you're acquainted with my wife.'

And out of the hospital ward's tin wardrobe stepped the terrible Tantanoula yowie.

'Well I'll be thorped,' said Grippa.

'Fuck me dead,' said Donna Meetlove, who'd received a tip-off from a woman identifying herself only as Mrs Y.

'And so we meet again,' snarled the yowie.

And pulled off its own head.

No-one said anything for a full minute — an eternity if you're standing beside a hospital oxygen tent staring at Mrs Yvonne Spam in a Big Foot costume.

'Oooh,' sniggered Spam. 'Oooh save me, I'm so frightened of the terrible Tantanoula yowie.'

Max Grippa and Donna Meetlove could only gape.

Apparently, *The Chinese Whisper*'s cadet pool was not the only pit of seething internecine rivalry. Apparently, Pete Spam had been in the force a full 18 months longer than Max Grippa and had suffered terribly when the talented youngster was promoted to the status of equal. Did no-one else hear the verbal diarrhoea splattering from his mouth day in and day out?

When Grippa had two things, he said: 'I'll give you both except one.'

When Grippa came to the Spam's Christmas barbecue, he said: 'That's funny, all my trees grow up from the bottom.'

When Grippa was busy he said: 'If only the one half would let the other half know what the other half was doing, the other half would know what's going on.'

After a few drinks one Friday night after work, Pete Spam told his partner the things he did to the English language were cruel and unusual.

'I should have been born twins with two noses,' Max replied jovially. 'Then you'd have a lot to put up with.'

Pete Spam wanted the man slit. Or at the very least taped shut.

But what of his good wife, Yvonne? What of her role in the deception? Could anyone confirm rumours that Grippa had once rebuffed her infatuated request for a jig at the Tantanoula High School reunion barn dance?

Pete Spam never stopped to wonder why Mrs Spam had agreed to dress-up in an ape costume and loiter round so many crime scenes. He had absolutely no idea that within a year, his wife and archenemy would marry and bring up his gabbling son, Bradley Spam, as their own.

'It's a short world,' his partner could have told him.

Or: 'It's a short world like a mad woman's breakfast.'

Or: 'It's a short world but it's usually quicker that way.'

Yvonne held the yowie's huge hessian skull beneath her armpit as if she was about to use it to score a goal.

Spam couldn't stop giggling. Even the fact that he would be a worm factory within the hour was extremely amusing.

'Detective skills deschmective skills,' he chortled as his blood pressure soared and his vital signs flattened. 'Oh. And you there in the corner with the notebook. Does the phrase "poke that pussy" bring back any memories?'

Donna did not need to be a mental giant to realise she was in deep shite. As news spread that the yowie was a hoax, the ambitious cub reporter did her damnedest to discredit the dead Spam's dying words.

'Attention-seeking fabrications are completely consistent with his condition,' said a psychiatrist who often prescribed the consumption of the dried leaves and blossoms of the Indian hemp, *Cannabis sativa*, for stress. 'Therefore it is highly likely that this police officer's confession has no basis in reality.'

'Then again,' continued the mental specialist, whose advice to local schizophrenics was to stop wearing shorts that exposed so much backdoor cleavage, 'the acting out of such attention-seeking fabrications are also completely consistent with his condition. Therefore it is highly likely that his wife was indeed getting about town dressed as an ape. When she wasn't working here answering my telephone, that is.'

Down at *The Chinese Whisper*, the brand-new editoress was about to let her feelings about the 'let the cleavage do the talking' techniques of young Donna be known to the world. Nicholas Bartholemew Stint had retired at the height of the yowie scandal in order to aggravate his wife by becoming as ill as possible. Stunningly enough, his replacement was none other than Genevieve Flash. Like so many others before her, the frustrated young lady had decided if she couldn't beat them, she might as well join in. Unlike Donna, however, she'd set her sights further afield than the subediting circle and had popped the buttons of her skirt all over the board of directors. Well. Not over the entire board. Most of them ricocheted off the heaving bosom of managing directoress Ms Beverley Fringe if you must know. Was it any wonder the usually hard-nosed Fringe had decided to stick her neck right out and appoint the youngest editor in local newspaper history?

Genevieve's first decision in her new role was to publish a large clarification stating that any and all suggestions that the Tantanoula yowie actually existed were regretted. Her second was to celebrate briefly with Beverley in the car park stairwell. Her third was to tell Donna Meetlove to pack up her journalistic integrity and go.

'Shouldn't take more than a couple of minutes,' she said to her former tormentor. And then she got down to making her benefactress impossibly large sums of money.

Donna sniffed as loudly as was possible under the circumstances and took the first cab to the downtown address of Television Station 10–11. She was about to learn the ins and outs of office coffee-making.

All this left Florence Lightfoot well and truly up shit creek in the bedtime threat department.

'Stay in your bed at night or the terrible Tantanoula yowie will come and get you while you sleep,' she shouted somewhat tentatively after the Spams' scandalous practical joke had been exposed on every media outlet in the Upper North.

In the first caravan Alice, Sonya, Stacie and Christy gazed back at their grandmother with matching black eyes and flowing noses. They'd spent another evening in The Conspiracy Hotel watching television through the window of the beer garden and had seen the pretty woman with the blonde hair pulling the yowie head on and off for the cameras.

Whatever it meant was bound to be bad.

'Maybe it ate her and died while she was still alive,' Christy whispered through the dark.

'Fucked her more like,' said her 12-year-old sister, Alice. 'More likely it was fucking her then died while it was fucking her.'

'Fucking,' chorused Sonya and Stacie. 'Fucking fucking fucking.'

Florence Lightfoot thrashed her way through the dark towards the second metal carton of grandchildren.

'Stay in your bed at night or the terrible Tantanoula yowie will come and get you while you sleep.'

There was no answer.

Florence gripped the caravan's metal doorway for balance and strained to see through the vinegar slosh. Her daughter-in-law had vanished on a night like this. Dissolved into the world like dirt in bathwater.

'STAY IN YOUR BEDS AT NIGHT OR THE TERRIBLE TANTANOULA YOWIE WILL COME AND GET YOU WHILE YOU SLEEP.'

Deathly silence.

Florence let out a lopsided roar that kick-started the babies like old motorbikes. Over the orchestra Shona cried for her mother.

First baby.

Second baby.

Shona.

THE BOY, THE BOY, BUT WHERE WAS THE GODDAM BOY?

'I'm right here, Gran,' came the thin voice through the dark. 'I'm right here in my tent sleeping.'

Florence thumped through the van's narrow aisle crushing shoes and showering firewater. There was only one way to beat sense into a wife and her useless son should have done it years ago.

'WALK OUT ON YOUR GODDAM KIDS? I'LL TEACH YOU LIBERATED YOU GODDAMN WOG BITCH.'

Yewwarrgh!

Later, when his face had stopped burning and his grandmother had passed out on a splash of nappies between the bunk beds, Samuel crept out of bed.

The pretty lady inside the monster looked a lot like his mother, he thought, packing toys into boxes and folding his clothes into a skyscraper in the corner. Except that his mother's hair was black as well as yellow.

Samuel stacked and folded and sorted by the light of the moon until the caravan was full of straight lines and angles. He touched his broken cheek and tucked in his sisters' sheets until the only mess left was his grandmother and her floor raft of chaos.

Samuel Lightfoot was only four years old the day the pretty woman burst out of the monster on television, but the image remained with him. Later, when he started school, Bradley Spam took him home to meet her.

'You can't judge a book by its cover,' the former Mrs Spam told the two boys as she used a stick with a hook to yank the yowie head out of its hole in the roof. 'Deep down even the ugliest person can be beautiful inside — even if they've got scars or no hair or rolls of fat around their wrists.'

Yvonne was a different person since she'd hooked up with Senior Constable Grippa. She'd stopped perming her hair and believed that if you looked hard enough you could find the good in everyone.

But Samuel returned home from his visit to the Grippa's feeling deeply disturbed.

If beautiful women could live beneath the skins of monsters, any hideous thing on the street could be his mother. And what of the reverse? What if someone pulled off *his* head and discovered the terrible creature lying beneath?

Samuel washed his mouth out with his grandmother's Blisterine and swallowed to make sure even his insides were clean.

He tidied his room, he tidied his room and he tidied his room again.

For a while, the monster inside of him slept.

14

It's Up To Us

Tampons were things girls put inside themselves when they got their periods. Cheryl knew this to be a fact. So why wasn't she able to do it? She tried sitting in different positions, she tried using butter and she even tried ringing the advice line on the outside of the packet.

'Have you ever had intercourse, dear?'

'*Have* you *ever had fucking intercourse?*'

Christ.

It wasn't fair. Christy had been right about Cheryl's boobs. They had a life of their own. But no matter how big she got up top, nothing seemed to happen down below. She had hardly any hair, she couldn't use a tampon and she didn't even have her periods.

'Are you sure you wouldn't like me to make an appointment with Dr Salmon, Cakes? It can't be normal given the state of the rest of your, ahem, *developments.*

[A knowing snort.] Oh. Any luck in the boyfriend department, yet?'

In books when girls first got their periods, they thought they were dying. It wouldn't be like that for Cheryl. It would be a relief. Then she could stop pretending and get on with using tampons like everyone else. It was hard lying about something you'd only ever seen in a blue line drawing on an instruction sheet.

Cheryl had heard a lot about periods from Mr Scoob. He was the PE teacher who believed in providing students with a total education. He was wider than he was tall and had big potato knees and rolled hams for thighs.

'All right then, class,' Mr Scoob said one afternoon when it was too hot for the medicine ball. 'Who here masturbates?'

No-one moved.

'All right then, class,' he'd said. 'Who at least knows how to masturbate?'

There was a guffaw from down the back and someone called Murray Ramsbottom a wanker.

'All right then, class. Let's start with the girls.'

Cheryl and Reb cringed as Mr Scoob jacked up the pant of his ironed shorts and planted a sweaty leg on their desk.

'Now pay attention,' he said with one hand over his fly. 'Your parents never had the benefit of the information I'm about to share with you, so listen up. Basically what you have to do is jiggle the first chickpea you come to. Like this.'

Cheryl could hardly move with embarrassment.

Worst of all, he hadn't said a thing about pillows.

Lou was away with a broken arm so they filled her in the next day after signing her cast.

'Girls masturbating?' she'd said. 'That's ridiculous. What are we supposed to do, *finger ourselves*?'

Cheryl lay on the couch in the Kiss family lounge room gasping. It had been a long day. First she'd passed The Frigid Test, then she and Christy had hunted the man from the school, then she'd seen where Samuel had died, then she'd got home and eaten her body weight in cheese and canned fruit. The nutritional panel on the side of the family-sized tins warned that lychees in heavy syrup might contain traces of peanuts. It was a complete and utter disaster.

Cheryl's stepfather stormed out of the kitchen and stood between Cheryl and *Up In Smoke!* with his frilly apron tucked into the top of his trousers. He said just because Cheryl was upset about Samuel and her friends didn't mean she could snub his eggs poached in moselle and bacon straws.

'We've all got to keep the romance alive remember, CJ. For the sake of your mother, you should make more of an effort.'

'Could you keep it down please?' said Cheryl in a sweet voice. 'I'm trying to watch the news.'

The chief sponsor of Station 10–11's nightly bulletins was the Tantanoula and District Tourism Advancement Commission. Thanks to its generous sponsorship arrangement, TADTAC received a mention in practically every item. Spokeswoman Barbie Sling even had the last word during a report on the most recent Cold War missile crisis. 'Why not forget the troubles of the world by checking in for an extended stay at the Tantanoula Motor Inn?' she'd beamed after a shot of US marines on full alert. 'The sausage casserole at Russell and Judy's new bistro simply must be tasted to be believed.'

When Cheryl did work experience at *The Chinese Whisper*, she'd written a scoop identifying the exact percentage of TADTAC-related items on Station 10–11's news and condemning the priority given to feel-good local coverage in lieu of stories of national importance. She'd blasted its shallow cult of personality and even lampooned the newsreader's beloved headatorialising.

Right eyebrow: human interest.

Left eyebrow: political intrigue.

Forehead tilt: breaking news.

Vodka screeching: any encounter with that goddamn lino.

Genevieve Flash — whose independence was also severely compromised by TADTAC advertising dollars — was impressed by Cheryl's ability to maintain a metaphor of news organisations as all-knowing, all-powerful, beyond criticism, I-know-best parentalists. She said she was sorry she couldn't publish the scoop ('a union thing, I'm afraid') but said Cheryl was welcome to come by and learn how to write 23-word first paragraphs any school holiday.

'You remind me of me at your age,' the editor said sadly. 'If you were a couple of years older and cut down on the animal similes I could give you a job.'

'Eat Up Your Dinner', read the headline on Cheryl's scoop.

'That's a pretty good headline,' the sports cadet had remarked. 'How'd you come up with that?'

The sports cadet was new in town.

TADTAC's long-standing sponsorship arrangements with Tantanoula's evening news bulletin and daily newspaper had also drawn stinging criticism in *The Chinese Whisper*'s weekly satirical column, 'My Word', penned by retired former business editor Woodward Face Jnr.

Face didn't only have it in for TADTAC and the Tantanoula news bulletin. He had it in for everything. Modern music. Local government. Women's undergarments. Decaffeinated coffee. Communism. New settlers. Old settlers. The infamous Tantanoula yowie. Sex education. Tourists. Locals. The Conspiracy Hotel. Facial hair. Imported succulents. Big Jack Profile. Dr Razz Salmon. Even the populist Television 10–11 newsreaders found themselves crucified on the point of his poison pen.

'Fluttering eyelashes belong in harems not serious news bulletins,' he wrote on one occasion. 'Chattering prattlers like Violet Kiss and Donna Vulpine should save their endless odes to their sex lives for weekend Tupperware parties.'

Violet and Donna had never once mentioned their sex lives during their respective broadcasts, despite making regular appearances on the morning show's 'Meet Your Media' segment. But Woodward Face Jnr was a celebrated misogynist who once said, off the record, that women were just another example of feminism gone too far.

Genevieve Flash had little choice but to let Woodward Face Jnr keep his column. He was the husband of the managing director — her close companion, Beverley Fringe.

On 14 November, there was a 23-and-a-half minute wait for news of Samuel Leadhead.

Intervening Item A: The revelation that it had been another uncharacteristically scorching day, even for Tantanoula.

'Amid fears of devastating grassfires and failing crops,' the newsreader read with impeccable palette work, 'the Tantanoula and District Tourism Advancement Commission reminds locals that every cloudless sky has a silver lining and that the continuation of such superb beach weather could very well result in a bumper Christmas for tourism.' A round of applause for the station's wacky fishing-hat-wearing weatherman et cetera et cetera.

Intervening Item B: The latest update on Dora Knockers' attempt to bring the notorious Feels on Wheels Revue on tour to Tantanoula as a novelty drought relief fundraiser.

'We appreciate this colourful local identity's interest in the district's cash crops,' chinked TADTAC spokeswoman Miss Barbie Sling. 'However we fail to see the connection between Californian strip rollerskating squads and relieving the Tantanoula water shortage issue. Sadly, we believe Miss Knockers' plan has more to do with fulfilling the unwholesome desires of perverts and deviants than filling the water troughs of our dear, suffering farmers.' Meaningful looks down a nose that should have carried Slippery When Wet signage et cetera et cetera.

Intervening Item C: The obligatory national news story with regional slant, to wit, a declaration by the national tourism minister that his department's series of one-off regional grants for the purpose of erecting giant fibreglass monuments at themed rural service stations would continue for another year.

'Contrary to the views of our critics, this is not a macabre monument to the slow death of ruralism,' said the minister. 'These two-tonne sheep, eight-foot crustaceans and larger-than-life corn cobs fill visitors with the glory of the great outdoors and the hard-won glamour of the man on the land. Only last week, I spoke to a critically ill youngster whose dying wish was to be photographed alongside The Big Lobster. If his request had been made in more solvent times, we might even have been able to oblige.' One last shot of the minister shifting unhappily in his eight-piece suit and on-loan Akubra hat et cetera et cetera.

Intervening Item D: The obligatory international news story with national slant, to wit, further, terrifying rumblings from one superpower about rumours of the other's development of a nuclear stockpile so incomprehensibly large it could wipe out the world four times over.

'If those commies think we're going to sit around on our behinds while they spit on freedom then they've got another thing coming,' said an average American soldier with admirable ability to read his autocue. 'Did you know they barbecue their own children?' Off-the-cuff quotes from Barbie Sling saying these latest developments should not affect the national forecast for overseas visitors providing, of course, that there still was an overseas ha ha ha et cetera et cetera.

Intervening Item E: A human interest story on a proposed outdoor rock concert by sleepy Swedish death metal band Misspelt Yoof.

'The local law enforcers have nothing against rock and its compatriot roll,' Detective Grippa told the camera. 'On the contrary, I have always found Misspelt Yoof's early work to be very enjoyable. Perhaps local ensembles such as The Dying Butchers and Mexican Breakfast could take a leaf from their book and lay off the wacky backy for a night or two. Just joking, people. The last time I caught The Innocent Handgrenades down at The Conspiracy they were cooking with jelly.' TADTAC spokeswoman Barbie Sling reminding concerned locals that despite the noise pollution, an outdoor rock concert would attract an estimated 10,000 burger buyers et cetera et cetera.

Cheryl knew her mother was about to begin reading the Samuel story because she stopped doing the infamous half-smile and assumed her Serious Expression.

'In other news,' Violet read, 'police are continuing their inquiries into the tragic death of Tantanoula schoolboy Samuel Lightfoot and have urged residents to remain calm.'

'On a brighter note,' she continued, 'the Tantanoula and District Tourism Advancement Commission's annual Sponsor A Pansy day will see local gardens erupt in a riot of colour as TADTAC pushes to have Tantanoula declared the Florid Capital of the Upper North.'

And that was it.

That was the height of Tantanoula's interest in the death of Samuel Leadhead.

Cheryl couldn't believe it.

It was scandalous even for Station 10–11. Samuel might have been a Leadhead, but murders were practically unheard of in Tantanoula. The town didn't even have a drive-in, for God's sake.

Cheryl ignored Jackson's repeated requests about how school had been and wracked her brain for answers.

Was Violet protecting the killer? Did that mean Detective Grippa was in on it too? Who in Tantanoula was so important they'd be allowed to get away with murder? Not the Ramsbottom brothers. Was the man from the school the principal? Mrs Stint in a moustache? Lou's father? Detective Grippa himself?

If Cheryl was in a Becky Swift mystery she'd be able to solve the crime all by herself. Becky wouldn't lie around trying to use tampons and worrying whether Samuel Leadhead's killer was hiding under her bed. She'd put on her red-and-white chequered shirt and catch Samuel's murderer all by herself. It might get hairy when her evil uncle and aunty tried to send her away to English boarding school and sell her horse for dog meat, but in the end Becky would always triumph.

'It's up to us,' Cheryl whispered to Zeus through the security door on her room.

She opened her Personal Pocket Journal to the Cheryl Kiss — Girl Reporter page she'd started that morning.

Evidence: she wrote in big letters.

Then she underlined for a while trying to think of something to write other than Cheryl 'Fuckface' Kiss. Then she thought about Lance Seldom and rode her pillow for a while. Then she fell asleep and dreamed her mother sliced so much of herself off with sewing scissors, there was nothing left of her but rissole.

15

God, Marilyn Stint Had Realised, Was As Incompetent As The Next Man

On Cheryl's first day at Tantanoula Primary School, the principal led her across a fiery cement playground to a squat city of steel and glass.

'It's so shiny,' she said.

'It's all new,' said the principal. 'All brand new demountables.'

'It hurts my eyes.'

'Look away. That way you won't be dazzled. We're here now, anyway. Cheryl, this is your new classroom. And this is your new teacher.'

The fury in the long, grey dress was dangling two children by their collars. 'Show the new girl the toilets, girls,' she bawled. 'And make sure she washes her hands.'

'Yes, Mrs Stint.'

'How many times must we wash our hands, 2K?'

'THREE TIMES,' exclaimed the class.

'And what must we use?'

'ANTIBACTERIAL SOAP.'

'Antibacterial soap what?'

'ANTIBACTERIAL SOAP, MRS STINT.'

'Otherwise the exercise is as good as what?'

'MAGIC, MRS STINT.'

'Exactly, 2K. If you do not wash and rinse your hands three times with antibacterial soap, you might as well be a nigger casting a spell for all the good it's doing your germs. This is a scientific fact, 2K. Washing once with regular soap has no scientifically proven effect whatsoever. You might as well be a tribe of leprosy-ridden savages who believe in magic. Do you want to be a tribe of leprosy-ridden savages, 2K?'

'NO, MRS STINT.'

'Do you want to have to wear your mother's thigh bone through your nose?'

'NO WE DON'T.'

'No we don't what?'

'NO WE DON'T, MRS STINT.'

'Flaps,' yelled a boy up the back behind an art pad. 'HOW ABOUT SOME FLAPS?'

Cheryl could still hear the teacher shouting at the Flaps boy by the time she and the two girls reached yet another black metallic building with yellow metallic trim and blazing windows. The toilet block looked exactly the same as everything else in the new school. What if she couldn't find it and weed herself in front of the giant teacher?

Once they were away from Mrs Stint, the tour guides talked in silly voices and looked at each other giggling.

'This is where you go to the toilet,' said the girl with the black hair.

'This is where you wash your hands,' said the one with the brown.

'And this is where you look underneath to see the whizzers,' they shouted, poking their heads beneath a door that was closed.

The girl in the toilet shouted while the other two jumped about the tiled floor laughing and singing.

'Rebecca's in the biscuit tin. Looking for her safety pin. She can lose but she can't win. 'Cos she's got maggots up her thing.'

Louise Frances and Rachel Roulette raced into the glare leaving Cheryl kneeling on the floor looking up at a face covered in freckles.

'What's a *thing*?' asked Cheryl.

'It's that scab between your legs,' said the girl, pulling up her pants. 'What's your name?'

'Cheryl. What's yours?'

'Rebecca, but you can call me Reb. I've got a skipping rope with sparkles and magic handles.'

'I've got a pet mouse called Nylon.'

'I love Murray Ramsbottom,' the girl replied, flushing the toilet. 'Who do you love?'

'Miss Carlos,' said Cheryl. 'Once when she was camping in Africa she went on a lion safari. Then she went to the toilet in a bush and a hyena licked her bum.'

'You can't love a girl you have to love a boy. Don't you have a boyfriend?'

Cheryl thought about it.

'Leeroy Evensly,' she said eventually.

'What's so good about Leeroy Evensly?'

'He has a real bike not just a scooter.'

Reb washed her hands three times with pink fluid from a pump-action wall pack.

'Everyone has a real bike,' she said in a businesslike fashion. 'Murray Ramsbottom has two and a minibike. He's in third class, anyway.'

And that, for the time being, settled it.

The lesson that morning was sodomy and what God did to anyone caught sodomising anyone else. By lunchtime, Cheryl still had no idea what Mrs Stint was going on about, but she felt awestruck at the news that God's son, The Baby Cheeses, had the power to send grown men to hell to be burned alive.

The bell sounded for big lunch and 2K liquefied into the playground like a fizzy vitamin tablet in a glass of water. Everyone knew who to sit with except Cheryl and the red-headed girl from the toilet.

'Are you new, too?'

'Nah,' said Reb. 'I came one week before the school holidays started.'

'Did you drive up from the city?'

'Nah. We moved up from Savvy when Dad got transferred.'

'Do you ride a horse to school?'

'Nah. Horses are illegal. The police said they all have to go to heaven. But if you give me 50 cents, I'll let you play with me for the rest of the week.'

Rebecca Michaelson had been sent to the storeroom twice that morning for telling lies, but Cheryl didn't care. She knew all about the cost of living from her mother and thought 50 cents was a bargain.

During the rest of big lunch, Cheryl and Rebecca ate salad sandwiches with beetroot and cheese extra and told each other some of the biggest lies of their careers. Reb said her dad was Lance Seldom and owned four speedboats. Cheryl said Violet was Lurex Imperial and owned a herd of Angora goats.

By the time the bell signalled the resumption of lessons, they were exhausted.

Mrs Stint, on the other hand, was ready to kill.

The notorious educator hated young children with a vengeance. But for 15 years now she had been unable to progress beyond teaching second class. Tantanoula was a region with high unemployment. As with most local workplaces, the primary method of advancement was to wait for someone higher up the food chain to die. This allowed everyone to climb one rung while a newcomer slipped in at the bottom.

Good news for Mrs Stint: By the time Cheryl joined 2K, she would only have to wait two more years before being transferred to Fifth Class (courtesy of Miss Essex's habit of riding car bonnets along the beach during full moons). Then it would only be 18 more months before she was able to relocate two kilometres up the road to Tantanoula High School as a history teacher. (Three cheers for Mr Davy and that bucket of infected oysters.)

Bad news for Cheryl: At the time she joined 2K, Mrs Stint was livid. In fact, Tantanoula's sole competitive cactus grower was so overwhelmingly spleeny that at night the grinding of her enormous teeth could be heard metres from her house. Could you blame her? All 37 full-time staff ahead of her at Tantanoula's primary or high schools were in rude good health and she had just been struck down by The Change of Life.

'Don't try to wriggle out of it,' Marilyn Stint shouted at the Lord during private prayer sessions. 'I can't so much as close my eyes without suffering another power surge or formication fit and you know it.'

God rarely got a word in edgewise during such counsel. This was probably just as well. Interjection rivalled hygiene lapses when it came to inciting the good Mrs Stint.

'Get that look off your face . . .' she'd bellow towards the ceiling. 'There's only one person to blame for this state of affairs. And who might that person be, I wonder? That's right, my so-called Saviour. It's You. And what might You be intending to do about this sorry state of affairs? What might You be planning in the way of restitution . . .?'

(Here she'd pause for dramatic effect.)

'Nothing. That's right. In all your infinite wisdom you won't do a damn thing.'

God, Marilyn Stint had realised, was as incompetent as the next man.

Mrs Stint sublimated these disturbing cognitions by directing an even more athletic attention towards her sluggish career. It was a curly one. What with the invention of fluoride and the discovery of cholesterol, the good citizens of Tantanoula were living longer than ever before. The teachers at Tantanoula Primary School, in particular, had never looked livelier.

'But accidents will happen,' Mrs Stint assured her hunchbacked husband with stinging enthusiasm. 'Biscuit Essex told me last week she didn't feel the best and Donald Fish only has to be in the same room as kiwifruit to suffer a life-threatening allergic reaction.'

The former editor of *The Chinese Whisper* convulsed politely. For all his love of the physical world there were times (chiefly every minute his wife occupied their residence) when his prayers included a most heartfelt plea to the Lord to permit him a speedy curtain call.

But the Lord had been sent to His room and was not to be let out until He'd thought about what He had done.

Cheryl, meanwhile, was adapting to life as a Lugworm. 2K was divided into six groups, each named after an important-to-learn animal. This was not Mrs Stint's idea. It was in a thing called a District Educational Syllabus, which happened to be a legally binding document and therefore one that was not supposed to be torn up and ignited in the school quadrangle. ('*MRS STINT. RESTRAIN YOURSELF. PLEASE.*')

Mrs Stint had no say in the matter of whether or not to divide 2K into animal groups, but she possessed all the executive choice in the world over which particular species they drew for their names. That was how Cheryl Kiss and Rebecca Michaelson became Lugworms, Louise Frances became a Cockchafer, Rachel Roulette and Samuel Leadhead became Weevils, and the remaining students became either Hornets, Mites or Aphids.

'Do you have some sort of a problem with insects . . .?' Mrs Stint bellowed at the school principal after he discovered her class did not include a single wombat or wallaby. 'Do you think they are somehow inferior to marine life, amphibians or mammals? Do you think when God created insects he intended for them to be scorned by Tantanoula . . .?'

The principal said 'no' and then, after being corrected, 'no, Mrs Stint'. Marilyn often accused the poor fellow of stifling her career on account of her gender. But this could not have been further from the truth. Had the principal been in charge of such matters he would have expedited Mrs Stint's departure from Tantanoula Primary School for good. She was not the only one to hope someone higher ranked would suffer a fate if not worse than death then at least equal to it. Once, in his darker moments, the principal had even considered sending the allergy-ridden Donald Fish a gift-wrapped box of kiwifruit brownies. This evil thought left him so disorientated with guilt he forgot his own name while introducing the School Talent Fest.

As a Lugworm, Cheryl's responsibilities were a) washing paint off the classroom sink after Artistic Expression, b) distributing bibles during Morning Prayer and c) reporting back to Mrs Stint with any and all breaches of Handwashing Duty. Handwashing Duty involved queuing before the mighty white of the 2K sink and completing three consecutive soaps with Bacto-Hinder, a hospital grade disinfectant manufactured in three shades of thunderous pink. Mrs Stint was a firm advocate of the advantages of Intra Peer Espionage. This, along with Handwriting Tests and Lie Detection, were Stint originals. But they never made an appearance in the District Educational Syllabus, despite numerous agitations by their inventor.

2K filed into the classroom in neat lines and washed their hands three times before sitting down. They began and ended each day with a prayer to the Lord to salvage their unsavoury souls (and our unsavoury sausage rolls, Louise and Rachel would chant when Stint was out of earshot). At the end of the week, all 32 of the tiny wooden chairs were inverted on the tiny wooden desks and 2K stood at attention waiting to hear which animal grouping had performed most adequately during the previous five days. The District Educational Syllabus recommended awarding a packet of dried fruit, pencil set or perhaps even an early mark. Mrs Stint, however, had opted for a points system aimed at scoring 2K's inclusion on Noah's ark.

'100 points are required for a ticket to ride,' said Mrs Stint. 'Otherwise it's into the flood waters with the rest of the sinners.'

Those of 2K who had lived in Tantanoula for any length of time knew all about floods. The last was six months earlier when the foamy brown waters of the river ate the traffic lights and teen gangs conducted air-mattress races through the CBD. Those houses fortunate enough to remain above ground were invaded by brown snakes. Under any other circumstances, floods would have been a bad choice for inspiring fear in 2K. Those who remembered the rising waters the year before recalled not only thrilling spectator sport, but the closure of all schools for a full week. But Mrs Stint was so terrifying, 2K would have trembled if she'd threatened a day at the beach.

Once Mrs Stint started up with the flood and the leprosy business, Cheryl suffered a radical religious rapid conversion. She'd heard of God before, of course she had. But no-one had warned her that at any time He could swoop down and send you to a colony where your fingers rotted off.

To make matters worse, there was the scripture problem.

On the first Thursday of Cheryl's first week of school, a bell sounded and the entire school fractured into strange new formations. Baptist. Presbyterian. Roman Catholic. Church of England. The names came from a foreign language. In the city, Cheryl had attended Non-denominational when the bell rang for scripture. These sessions were supervised by Miss Carlos and included a great deal of bingo. But on the first Thursday of the first week of term at Tantanoula Primary School, Reb said she'd never heard of Non-denominational and dashed off to Roman Catholic to crayon a picture of God's son, weeping, onto a paper hat.

Cheryl didn't know what Noah or The Baby Cheeses thought of girls who went to Non-denominational but had no intention of finding out from Mrs Stint. She hid in the toilets checking between her fingers and toes for signs of leprosy. Leprosy started as a rash, then spread all over your body until your arms and legs fell off as easily as a plastic Brenda doll's. You couldn't argue with leprosy.

One of the cisterns sneezed blue water and Cheryl thought dejectedly of Miss Carlos's long hair.

'Bingo,' she called aloud. Then she opened the door and walked straight into the blazing undergarments of Marilyn Stint.

That Friday afternoon, all the animal groups were allowed to leave except for the Lugworms.

'So,' said Mrs Stint. 'Who'd like to tell me why you're all here?'

'Because Monica Slather got her ears pierced?'

'Because Colleen McTabloid ate dirt?'

'Because Guy Silverside threw his mother's shoe?'

'DO NOT MAKE ME SICK, LUGWORMS. I DID NOT HOLD YOU BACK AFTER SCHOOL BECAUSE I WANTED A LITANY OF YOUR DISGUSTING EXTRA CURRICULAR ACTIVITIES. I HELD YOU BACK BECAUSE ONE OF YOU HAS BEEN CAUGHT WAGGING. *WAGGING.*'

The Lugworms flinched en masse.

'I could report this to the principal but I believe it's you, her wormy companions, who must accept ultimate responsibility so I'm subtracting 10 points from all your Ark Passes.'

An audible tremor.

'Remember, worms. Next time you see Cheryl Kiss misbehaving, I want you to think about what it feels like when you're swimming and you swallow a mouthful of water. Because when the flood comes, it won't be a mouthful, it will be an entire ocean.'

On one hand, Cheryl was sure if the world really was about to flood, her mother would have said something about it on the news. On the other hand, she couldn't remember ever feeling quite so alarmed.

Late the following Wednesday night, she wandered into the main house from her bedroom to converse with her mother.

'Mum,' she said. 'This year I want to go to scripture.'

Violet didn't answer. Her face was parked in the hairless chest of her new husband — its permanent garage since the three of them had moved to Panorama Way four weeks earlier. Whenever Violet and Jackson were in the house at the same time they had to be in constant physical contact to avoid losing their superhuman powers. That was Cheryl's theory, anyway.

'Are you listening Mum?'

All that emerged from the human tangle on the lounge was a choked slurp.

'Mum?'

The only thing worse than watching Violet and Jackson maintain their superhuman powers was reading the letters they left each other on the coffee table or jabbed romantically between the toilet paper rolls in the lavatory. Violet got wet just thinking about Jackson Kiss. Cheryl knew this for a fact, although she didn't know what rain had to do with anything. For love letters, they certainly contained a lot of swearing.

The newlyweds extricated themselves from each other and commenced watching a video recording of that night's edition of *Up In Smoke!* followed by the 7 p.m. news. The Kisses were one of the first families in Tantanoula to own a video cassette recorder or Vee See Ah as they were known in the shops. Cheryl had been informed of this fascinating piece of news at least once a day for the past two weeks.

'Mum,' she yelled into her mother's small but perfectly formed right ear. 'If I don't go to scripture I'm going to end up at the bottom of the ocean.'

'Keep the volume down, darling. I can hear everything you say perfectly well without you shouting.'

'I know you see me as a threat, Cheryl,' Jackson murmured without looking up from the television. 'But I want you to know that I know I will never take the place of your father.'

Violet scrabbled onto one elbow with all the grace of a pelican snapping for bait. She squinted dashingly at the flickering light of the television, then finally looked up and caught her daughter's eye.

'For God's sake, Cheryl. Your face is as long as a donkey's. What on earth is the problem?'

'What religion are we, Mum.'

'Didn't we go through all this when you started kindy?'

'But Rebecca said Non-denominational isn't a religion.'

'That's because Non-denominational is for atheists and agnostics.'

'What's an agnostic?

Jackson snickered. 'According to my late mother, the height of cowardice.'

195

The next day Cheryl studied the chart of available scripture classes in desperation. Sometimes she thought her mother was two separate people. One during the morning and one during the night.

'Non-denominational definitely isn't on the scripture list, mum,' she said the following evening.

'Incredible. Alert the armed forces.'

'Where am I supposed to go? Today I went with Rebecca to Roman Catholic but everyone looked at me funny.'

'Listen, Cheryl, I didn't raise you alone for seven years to watch you get brainwashed by the first bunch of rednecks you came across. Religion was what drove me and your grandmother apart. We don't want it coming between us now do we, darling?'

'But Mrs Stint said . . .'

'Tell her she's required by law to provide an alternative.'

Cheryl squatted against the wall watching her mother's face on the videotape of the news.

'My God,' gasped Violet.

'What,' asked her new husband.

'My God,' gasped Violet at the screen.

'*What?*'

'I look *ancient* in yellow, that's what.'

'You look very glamorous if you ask me.'

'Don't be ridiculous I look hideous.'

'Hey Mum, did Noah let two atheists go on the ark along with two of everything else?'

'No, he didn't Cheryl. Atheists don't get to go on the ark and we don't get to go to heaven either. Do you know why? Because when we die that's that. We turn into worm food like Grandma Edna and Grandma Jean.'

'Take it easy, darling,' said Jackson. 'You're spilling your drink.'

Later, Jackson paid a visit to Cheryl's bedroom in the carport. He appeared at the doorway shortly after Violet began yodelling the theme song to the news at top volume on the verandah.

'What on earth are you doing, CJ?'

'Nothing,' she said, leaping back into bed. 'No-one even calls me that, anyway.'

'You were praying, weren't you.'

'No.'

'That's certainly what it looked like to me.'

'I was picking something up from the floor.'

'Your mother'll have your guts for garters.'

'I *wasn't.*'

'Whatever you say, CJ, whatever you say.'

Jackson scratched his pants for a while.

'I tell you what, Cheryl,' he said eventually. 'If the scripture thing is that much of a big deal, tell them Church of England. That was Jean's religion. I'm sure she'd be relieved to know someone was carrying on the family tradition.'

Cheryl lay in bed imagining that the house caught fire and she was able to move every piece of furniture alone before rescuing her mother. It was incredible. She was able to move every last piece of furniture onto the lawn before her mother even woke up. In the dream, Violet's gratitude was the size of the sky and Cheryl imagined the fire over and over until she could smell the flames.

Being Church of England turned out to have fringe benefits. For example, did you know you could also be called Anglican? Cheryl found this most interesting. Also of note was Captain Kevin, the Church of England scripture teacher. Captain Kevin had bright blue eyes and a light aeroplane called Lurex Imperial. He never talked about floods or leprosy but did have a lot of exciting stories about ultralight crashes and windsurfing with sharks down at the surf beach at Savvy. Once, he was spotted wheeling Miss Biscuit Essex, the librarian, at high speeds through the Bi-Mart in a shopping trolley, but that was neither here nor there.

'Maybe you kids think God's not on your wavelength,' Captain Kevin said on Thursday mornings. 'Maybe you think he's old hat, yesterday's news. Well take *Up In Smoke!* Please, take *Up In Smoke!*'

Cheryl clicked her thighs with amusement. The rest of the class seemed unsure whether to laugh or flick another rubber band at their instructor's wiry goatee. The big joke was to call him Captain Kangaroo.

'Every week each family attempts to deal with the spiritual wasteland of the nuclear age in their own way,' he continued. 'The Coasts are fatalists, yes? They believe an earthly response is the only protection whereas the Smythes are spiritualists. Their interference in the bomb business is their way of saying "hey you guys, the Lord is our umbrella, even under the mushroom cloud".'

'What's a spiritual wasteland, Captain Kevin?' asked Louise Frances in her 'this is where you wash your hands' voice.

'Will Mr and Mrs Smythe's skin peel off after the A-Bomb?' asked Rachel Roulette.

'Can mice get leprosy?' asked Cheryl.

'FLAPS,' yelped Bradley Spam.

'Can I please be excused?' said Samuel Leadhead.

Cheryl Kiss wouldn't even have noticed Samuel Leadhead in second class if he hadn't been such a

Problem Child. Everyone in 2K knew Samuel was a Problem Child because Mrs Stint said so all the time. Also because it was April and the Weevils were sitting on minus 12 points in the ark race.

'The Weevils are in the red,' Louise told Murray Ramsbottom in the playground one lunchtime. 'Do you know what that means? It means they're in the negatives. Do you know what that means? It means they have even less points than *zero*.'

Murray Ramsbottom ate a meat pie without removing his chewing gum. It reminded him of the noise his minibike made when it first started. You can't ride it, you're not licensed, he said whenever anyone came over. Louise was like one of those coloured birds that flew into aircraft engines and crashed planes.

'An Indian Myna,' he said. 'Or maybe just a butcher bird.'

The sauce on the pie reminded Louise of the dusty pink of Mort's cheeks. She smiled for all she was worth.

'When you Weevils meet your maker, you'll know who to blame,' Mrs Stint announced on Friday afternoon when the group inched another step backwards towards the flood waters. 'You can blame The Problem Child's rudeness.'

Personally, Cheryl thought Louise Frances and Rachel Roulette were much ruder than Samuel Leadhead. But Mrs Stint never seemed to notice the silly voices they used to ask unanswerable questions. She was more concerned with the fact that Samuel Leadhead said nothing. A sullen child was the work of Satan. It said so in one of the Testaments. (Testaments sounds like TESTICLES, giggled Louise and Rachel.)

'Look at me when I'm talking to you, 2K. Rebecca Michaelson get that finger out of your ear. If God wanted your finger to burrow into your head he would have given it front teeth. Aphids, whatever you're doing, stop it. If Bradley Spam was supposed to have his face taped you can be certain I would have taken care of it before now. Cockchafers about-turn. Lugworms straighten those chairs. And anyone thinking of skipping weekend prayers remember winter is leprosy season. Class dismissed. Samuel Leadhead stay back and see me in the storeroom.'

Samuel's silent rudeness wasn't the only thing making Mrs Stint roar. Three times now he'd left the school grounds without permission and been caught wandering through a boutique clothing shop in his grandmother's lipstick.

'What's your name, girlie?' asked the policewoman when Samuel turned up in the main change room of Hollywood Wives.

'Blackshot,' said Samuel. 'Blackshot the bushranger.'

'Bushranger, eh? You best be chopping down a few trees to stop the coach.'

'I must have been careless about my tracks,' answered Samuel. 'I was in my hide-out when I heard horses' hooves. Expecting it to be friends I went outside. Policemen grabbed me and took me to prison. I will be hanged today.'

Constable Claudette told Samuel to return the red shoes and python skin handbag to the Hollywood Wives shopgirl and took him straight back to Mrs Stint.

'What's your name, son?' asked the old depot guard when Samuel turned up beneath the dismembered ute in B section. Samuel wasn't wearing lipstick that time, but his satchel was overflowing with supplies of stale bread.

'My name's Lightsabre,' said Samuel. 'Lightsabre the space boy. I dropped out of the space machine when the gravity plus ran out of orbit, but the road and the streetlights broke my fall. What I use is a helmet made of glass and a jet-powered knee board.'

The old depot guard made Samuel drink a cup of tea and listen to the race results on a portable wireless. He insisted the boy admire his old dog, Digger, and explained in exhaustive detail their attempts to patent a side-saddle scooter for ladies. 'Listen to this,' he said and started up on the harmonica. For 10 minutes, Digger sang his heart out, then the old depot guard delivered Samuel back to the bosom of Mrs Stint.

'Sorry, Lightsabre,' were his final words. 'I'd keep you on board but I'm under surveillance. The Reds and the coffee shops are springing up everywhere. Watch your back, space boy. Thanks for straightening out the linen cupboard. And drop by any time you're in need of a singalong.'

Mrs Stint threatened to bring in the Regional Administrators. She threatened to tie Samuel to his chair with elastic ockie straps. But even her stories about men with guns who put runaway schoolchildren in their cars didn't stop Samuel Leadhead from wandering.

'Samuel is going to be a floater,' Cheryl said from the back of Donna Vulpine's eight-seater Nymphovertible the morning she and Violet shared a lift to river aerobics.

The daytime newsreader and her husband lived on a farm that used to belong to Kenneth's father. They had an in-ground swimming pool, plastic outdoor furniture and lots of children.

'You'll have to excuse my lack of vibrance this morning,' Donna said to Violet in the front seat. 'I was up the entire night, literally, the *entire* night.'

'The children?'

'No — "American Hits and Misses". I started watching when the baby went down and the next thing I knew it was 4.30 in the a.m.'

'Addictive, isn't it.'

'Just one more song, you tell yourself. And the next thing you know Mrs Gosling's at the front door ready to start on the cleaning and there you are, crouched over a jigsaw in your jim jams like you were 14 all over again. The home shopping network, on the other hand, is absolutely dreadful.'

'Absolutely,' said Violet, who'd found herself watching the late-night advertorials at strange angles from the floor more times than she cared to mention. 'Those programs should be banned.'

'What about the infinite dress,' Cheryl chipped in from the back seat. 'You bought the infinite dress from the home shopping network.'

'Don't miss a thing do you,' Violet said under her breath.

'An infinite dress,' tittered Donna. 'How very amusing.'

'It's one dress but you can wear it 100 different ways.'

'Thanks for your contribution, Cheryl, I think Donna gets the point.'

'And to think I've never seen you wear it, Vi. You really must bring it into work one day for a fashion parade.'

In the back seat, the Vulpine baby fixated on Cheryl from its space capsule. Cheryl pinched the back of the baby's fat leg and made it cry. When the baby stopped crying, she pinched it again. Hurting the Vulpine baby made her feel ugly and excited both at once. She didn't know how she first got the idea to pinch it on the leg but once she started she couldn't stop.

'Did you hear about Genevieve Flash and her new lady friend down at The Conspiracy Hotel last night?'

'Now that you mention it, I did hear something,' said Violet. 'Apparently Beverley Fringe is officially yesterday's news.'

The two women raised their eyebrows at each other across the front seat. With her blonde hair standing to attention up in the wind, Violet looked like a startled rooster.

'What's wrong with Mrs Flash,' asked Cheryl.

'I think you'll find it's *Ms* Flash, Cheryl.

'Ha ha.'

'HA HA.'

And the four little piggies went wee wee wee wee all the way home. Well. All the way to river aerobics anyway.

Despite the constant threat of the storeroom, Cheryl and Reb were telling more fibs than ever before. During Weekend Report one Monday morning, Cheryl told 2K she and her mother had gone fishing on an aluminium boat and caught an electric ray with three eyes on stalks. Fibbing was great. The moment the words came out of your mouth you could actually believe they were true.

Mrs Stint was about to tell Cheryl to meet her in the storeroom when she narrowed her gaze and sniffed the wind. The silence was astronomical.

'2K,' she said with deadly elocution. 'Where is Samuel Leadhead?'

But once again, no-one knew.

Mr Wiblen from Clerical and Ancillary searched for the missing Weevil all day. The old depot guard dropped by and offered to set Digger dog on the trail, but after a whole day passed with nothing there seemed little choice but to alert the police.

'It's S-A-M with a U-E-L, is that right?' asked the burly policeman.

'Mind your mouth,' said Mrs Stint.

'Ah, well,' continued Senior Constable Grippa. 'They usually are, but kids are kids. Now let me get this all down in a nutshell in a couple of goes. Do you happen to have any batteries? It's not for me to rhyme, reason or wonder, but sometimes I think I could see better through these glasses if I took them off.'

Cheryl found it difficult to sleep the night Samuel disappeared. She hoped Satan hadn't come to get him early. That would be very unfair considering the Weevils hadn't had a full year to get their ark points up. Cheryl pulled the sheets up to her chin and mentally ran through the house fire plan. Would she be able to push the fridge out of the burning house or would it be necessary to use a wheelbarrow? It had taken three removalists and much squealing from Violet to manoeuvre that fridge through the poky kitchen door. Maybe she'd have to leave it behind. Cheryl listened to the creaks and cries of the night. Those koalas sure made a racket. She wondered if The Baby Cheeses would have silver hair and a briefcase like her father in the photograph.

'Cheryl,' Jesus said. 'Do you think I meant to fall out of the sky and die? Do you think I wanted to leave you and your dead sister all alone?'

'I don't know,' Cheryl cried. 'I really don't know, Dad.'

Samuel stayed missing all the next day and some of the next evening. At 8 p.m., a cleaner found him beneath Mrs Stint's demountable classroom, wedged right up the back beside a wet wall of brick and dirt.

'Don't hit me anymore,' Samuel said when he first spotted the cleaner's feet.

No-one saw Samuel at school the next day. In his place was a nervous woman from the Department of Youth and Community Affairs who told 2K it was time for a little heart to heart. 'If you ever have any problems at home,' she said, 'I want you to know there are always people you can talk to.' The woman wore a coloured cheesecloth scarf and sounded distracted, as if all she could think about was where she might have left her teeth.

'2K know exactly who to turn to if they have any problems,' Mrs Stint raged. 'God. And if God happens to be away on business, they turn to me.'

'Excellent,' the counsellor said vaguely. 'That's all settled then. And now if you will excuse me, I have a dental appointment.'

When Samuel returned from his adventures, he had red stripes across one of his arms and a bleeding fig for a nose. He didn't talk to anyone about what had happened. He just sat next to Bradley Spam at recess and lunchtime and ate quietly as his retard friend yelped obscenities at a game of handball.

16

Grade 10 School Social With V And A — Gross!

The first two suspects in the investigation into Samuel Leadhead's murder were the old depot guard from the Medals and Militaria Warehouse in town and Dora Knockers from the fish and chip shop at the top of Panorama Way. The Kiss girl had no concrete leads as such. She just happened to run into them while wandering the road in search of supplies. Dora Knockers couldn't really be classed as 'the man from the school' unless she wore some sort of coat and beard but Cheryl had seen the old depot guard hanging round the bus stop plenty.

It was the hamburger hour.

The old man arrived at the fish and chip shop calling for his dog then sat wheezing in the thin breeze swishing the plastic fly veil over the door. He ordered a pineapple melt with the crusts cut off and a dollar's worth of chips. Dora Knockers' neon sign squinted Free Sauce into the sunlight. The fly veil flapped synthetic rainbows and the new blackboard menu leered over the trench of boiling oil.

'What's that when it's at home?'

'Camembert.'

'What's that when it's at home?'

'Brie.'

'What's the difference?'

'Camembert is from the region of Camembert and brie is any sparkling cheese. You got any more questions Erns or are you going to let me finish draining the beetroot?'

'But what's with the deep-frying?'

'That's how camembert and brie are served, Ern. Crumbed, deep-fried and served with a side of cranberry sauce.'

The radio announced a maximum of 35 degrees in Tantanoula as the shop thermometer hit 40. Dora sponged her forehead with a singlet draped over a nail below the cash register. The old man was a worry. He was withered enough as it was. Any further evaporation was bound to kill him.

'Drink this.'

'I don't touch Coke.'

'It's not Coke, it's iced tea.'

'You're an angel, Doors. Iced what?'

'*Drink it.*'

The old man sniffed the rim of the glass and put it down on the table.

'I once ran a lawnmower on Coke.'

The plastic ribbons across the front door slithered, but for the life of him Ernie Estrich couldn't feel the breeze.

It was as depressing as anything else that had happened that week.

'Used to be a milk bar town, Tantanoula. Used to be a time you could get an eye in the sky with sauce and a chockie milk shake at a family-run milk bar. Now though. Now the place has gone to the dish lickers. Now it's all coffee shops this and coffee shops that. All cafe oh lays and sandwiches with the crusts still on. Flour outside the cakes instead of inside of 'em where it belongs. Get that hair out of your eyes, I tell the hooligan with the pigtail. And see someone about those nails. You collect things as a child, Doors? There's archetypes, you know. Those that did and those that didn't. Collect, isn't it? Used to be a time you could find a family-run milk bar on the nearest corner. Now you can't walk out the front door without falling over a bottle of fizz water or a sandwich with the crust left on. A dollar twenty is what they charge for a mug of Nescafé down at Antonio's nowsadays. God only knows what they want for a dollar's worth of chips.'

'A dollar twenty for a coffee you say, Erns?' Dora thought maybe it was worth forking out for one of those cappuccino machines after all.

'This is the only true blue milk bar left in town. What are you mucking about with those foreign cheeses for, Doors? What's cheddar ever done to you?'

'I'm moving with the times, old man. The diners of today aren't interested in Vegemite sandwiches and lamingtons. They want fried camembert with a side of cranberry. It's a health thing.'

'Lamingtons. Now they're something you'd keep for a Sunday. Lamingtons. Used to be a time you couldn't set foot outside your depot without stumbling over a tray of the bloody buggers. But when was the last time you saw a lammo in Tantanoula? So? Stale sponge cake is how it's done. Stale sponge dipped in chocolate and coconut. That's how my late wife did it, any road. What do you ladies do with your stale sponges nowsadays? Straight down the bra, I suppose. I've always suspected as much. "Are they real or are they cyber?" I ask the girlies out the front of the coffee shops. But they're too busy with their grass clippings. "No wonder you're all so bloomin' thin," I say. "All you eat is fizz water and grass clippings." "What's the point of grass clippings on your steak sandwich", I reiterate to the hooligan, "what's the point when you can't even get a decent chockie milk shake to wash it all down?" Alfalfa, God help me. Which cap-wearing chrome-polisher came up with that miserable excuse for tucker I wonder?'

One dollar's worth of chips made its way through the wilting loop of Ernie's stomach as his suit pants crimped dejectedly beneath his belt. It was official. The world had officially become a mystery. Sometimes he and Digger walked out the front door of Medals and Militaria and didn't recognise a thing.

Where were all the supplies? The war? His wife's brown stockings with pink lace beneath the meat safe?

'Digger?' he called suddenly. 'Digger? Get in behind.'

'I don't want to name names but personally I blame the fountain,' he continued emotionally. 'Before they put in that fountain everything was the way it'd always been. Hot, you realise? Everyone back and forth to the war, the girls stopping off for a bit of a fish of a Saturday. Perch, isn't it? A system to the thing. Tantanoula. Then the fighting's over and sooner or later some communist in pleated pants whacks a cement angel piddling bloody goldfish in the middle of the road and all of a sudden no-one's interested in the milk bars or the soldiers any more. All of a sudden every dog and his missus wants to take his fried cheese and his eggs with orange peel in a coffee shop at a table stuck right out in the middle of the road. You're lucky to be able to park a ute in the CBD these days the road's that full of chairs and tables. And who in their right mind would put orange peel on an egg and bacon? Yesterday in the Bi-Mart I tripped over a meatless sausage. That's what the world's come to, Dora. Vego Tarian sausage. Boys didn't burn alive in the backyard before the Vego Tarians and fountains.'

Dora frowned. It was a peculiar look. Parts of her face were mobile but other sections had permanently stalled. Her big stiff lips were especially creepy. They quivered above her chin in a solid unit.

'What are you talking about old man?'

'The boy what got burned. Young Samuel. The Lightsabre isn't it? We were acquainted quite by accident. Years back he dropped in on me. Out of nowhere it could have been. He turned up in the depot and I gave him an art lesson. If you can draw a piece of fruit, I told him, you can paint anything. Then I took him backwards. Back to that big lady teacher with the curly hair and the mouth like the business end of a rooster, God save us all. Terrible business that burning, Doors. If the night ghost with the birthing mark hadn't confessed I would have thought it was the big lady teacher what was the guilty part. "I killed the boy," the birthing mark said to me in the rain on the night of the day. "I did it with my own two hands." That big lady teacher, though, Doors. That leapy old bitch had a murderous walk.'

'Watch your language, Erns. There's schoolgirls present.'

'Sorry, Doors.'

'And leave Samuel Lightfoot to the police. They got a hell of a lot more neurones synapsing than you do.'

'The police don't care about no boy, Doors. He wasn't a governmentician. He didn't sit in the coffee shops eating fried camemberry with Mediterranean sauce. I went in and told the boys in blue I knew who killed young Lightsabre and they didn't give me so much as a cup of soup.'

Years since the old depot guard had seen a boy burned alive. A kraut. Dancing in the top floor of a building alive with fire.

'You were wasting your time down at the police station, Ernie Estrich. If it was soup you wanted you should have come to me.'

The bandy legs of the old man's white plastic seat splayed lower towards the big black-and-white squares on the shop floor. Black-and-white squares covered everything these days. Anyone would think the world had gone off, the way the governmenticians kept wrapping it up in plastic. Anyone would think it was rotten to the core.

'What're you pulling faces for girlie? You want for the wind to change direction and the rest of us to be stuck with that look for the rest of eternity?'

Cheryl hadn't been pulling faces. She'd been cringing from the dripping spatula the fish and chip shop woman was waving for emphasis.

'If I hear one more person come in here saying they know who killed Samuel Lightfoot I'll commit an act of violence,' Dora said, swinging her oily baton like a

211

reckless conductor. 'Tina Krueger comes in yesterday saying it was the father. Beryl Ramsbottom comes in here saying it was the long lost mother. Razz Salmon doesn't care as long as someone fries. "It's just a signature," he says to me over this very counter. "What's all the fuss about one little signature?" I told the good doctor to stick his petition where the sun didn't shine.'

'What petition?' asked Cheryl.

'Bring back the death knock, isn't it?' said the old depot guard. 'Bring back the penalty so whoever did Lightsabre fries like one of your chips and your fishes. An eye for an eye, what? I signed the partition, Doors. I told Dr Salmon I should have electrified that night ghost with the birthing mark myself while I had the chance. I should have rung in once I saw him on the telly. No-one deserves a flaming like that. Not at such a tenderised age, before the chance to experience life and all her many and various marvellous. I told Razz Salmon what do you mean there's nothing can be done about this gout? I said, you ever seen the way they kill cockies nowsadays? It's the miniature coffee shops that do it. The cockies pop in for an Anzac biscuit in the poison dream home and the next day their intestines are out under their wings.'

Dora tch tch-ed and flipped open a copy of *Working Woman*. The headline on page seven read:

They Said My Husband Was A Killer
And I Called Them Liars.
Then Even I Began To Doubt.

'Mark me, Dora Knockers. Someone'll fry over this Lightsabre business just you wait and see if they don't.

What I'm trying to say is you know where you stand with lamingtons. Digger? Where are you Digger dog?'

Cheryl watched the s-bend of the old man stagger up the flat road as if it was as steep as Everest. Violet was always going on about the benefits of raising children away from the lunatics in the city. But she obviously hadn't queued for a sugar-free beverage in Dora Knockers' shop any time recently.

'It's a dirty shame,' sighed Dora, looking up from her magazine. 'That dog of his was run down two years back now and no-one has the heart to remind him. And the shrinkage. Each time he comes in he's lost another inch. What am I going to do with him, Miss Kiss?'

The colourful Upper North identity was bursting out of ankle-tight denim jeans and a naval-length strip of bubble wrap housing the biggest set of bosoms Cheryl had ever seen. Her eyelashes were as stiff as iron filings and her eyeshadow slashes the blue of hospital blankets.

'I think whoever killed Samuel was someone he knew,' said Cheryl, trying and failing to avert her eyes. 'Otherwise he would have made a run for it. It had to be someone he trusted.'

'For God's sake don't you start. It'd kill me to sit through another conspiracy theory in this heat. Doesn't anyone in this town have anything better to do than pretend they're Becky Swift? What'll it be then, Chezza? Cancer sticks for that celebrity mother of yours or the usual bag of potato scallops?'

'I'm on a diet,' said Cheryl. 'I only want a diet lemonade.'

'Diets are the opium of the masses,' said Dora. 'They kill off your brain cells and make you go out with weirdos. There's a lot to be said for being on the fuller figured side. At least you'll always have a decent bust. You ever seen a thin woman with a decent bust, Chezza?'

'You,' Cheryl blurted.

'Yeah right,' scoffed the fish and chip shop woman. 'These are the work of mother nature and my name's Lurex Imperial.'

Cheryl already knew Dora Knockers' chest was made of plastic. She'd seen X-ray photographs of her operations in one of Jackson's magazines. There was a picture of Dora Knockers swinging off a pole with seven other freaks, each with a set of bowling balls bigger than the next. Cheryl had brought the photographs along the day they'd played Spin The Bottle in Lou's mother's carport.

'That one's the lezzo,' said Cheryl. 'That one's the swinger. And that's the one who likes to take it up the backdoor.'

'You're disgusting,' Lou had said. 'How'd you get so incredibly disgusting?'

Thanks to *X Spot* magazine's Fuct Files, everyone in Lou's mother's carport knew Dora Knockers had joined the Bazookas or Bust dance troupe as an Indian Girl when she was 21 years old. They knew her favourite colour was pussy pink and her favourite pastime was pow-wowing with cowboys with great big guns 'just like you'.

'When girls ask what my number is,' Mort Ramsbottom announced after inspecting the photographs. 'I say sex, sex, sex and sex.'

Behind the counter, Dora Knockers was giving Cheryl a funny look. Come to think of it, Dora Knockers was always giving Cheryl a funny look.

Slut, thought Cheryl. Stupid slut. The word had power, even when you only said it in your head. It was deadly. Like calling someone a dick wipe. Or a fuck face. Cheryl crossed her arms over her chest, making sure she didn't squeeze anything over the top of her T-shirt. According to Lou, sluts had sex with old men and even with retards.

When Dora first came to Tantanoula, she got a job at the only pub in town allowed to stay open after midnight. It was the Party Hard Capital of the Galaxy and it was on the main street right next to the council chambers where Jackson worked. Jackson said Dora Knockers didn't take all her clothes off at the Party Hard Capital of the Galaxy. He said she just did topless Go Go in a cage next to the band. Then Violet had walked in and said what are you two talking about and Jackson had said we haven't been talking about anything, have we Cheryl.

Cheryl had overheard both her mother and stepfather whispering on the phone to Dora Knockers when the other one was out of the house. Then Dora came to Violet's New Year's Eve barbecue and she and Violet fought and after that the whispering stopped. There'd been a hundred members of the local community at that barbecue. Cheryl had spent most of the night in her room but she'd heard the crash of breaking bottles and she'd smelled the burning hair.

Dora leaned forward rocking her manufactured womanhood ominously across the front counter.

'Hey Chezza.'

'Yeah?'

'Come out the back for a sec.'

'Why?'

'There's something I want to show you.'

The little flat behind the fish and chip shop stank of stale oil and was covered with grimy photographs of seascapes. Even the fruit in the bowl wore a film of grease and dust. Dora rifled through a pile of papers on her kitchen bench.

'And to think Razz Salmon had the hide to call *me* superficial,' she grumbled. 'That man would draw up a petition banning himself if he thought it would win him a vote. Everyone's Samuel Lightfoot's best friend now, of course. But the truth is that boy had an attitude. Ask how he was and he'd ignore you completely. How much does it cost to say "hello"?'

Hundreds of dollars, thought Cheryl. On some days, thousands.

'Here it is.' Dora dangled a stapled collection of foolscap pages in Cheryl's face. 'Have a look at this for me would you, Chezza? It's uni through the mail. Two months in and I'm already going mental. Serves me right for fucking about on campus when I had the chance.'

Dora's essay drooled with loopy blue writing. Big circles perched heavily over the i's and there were a great many exclamation marks. She obviously carried an aerosol can of the things.

'What's it about?'

'*Twelfth Night*. The role of the comic butler in Shakespeare's romantic comedies. Women's lib. The usual suspects.'

'I don't know anything about Shakespeare.'

'My dad once told me Shakespeare was a boong who waved his spear above his head before fights,' Dora mused. 'I spent half my life thinking the Bard was a darkie.'

'We don't do Shakespeare till Year 10.'

The fish and chip shop woman reversed out of memory lane with a screech.

'Fuck me dead, Cheryl. I'm not asking you to subvert the goddamn dominant paradigm or anything. Just run an eye over the essay and tell me whether it scans. There's a bag of potato scallops and crab sticks in it if you do.'

They both turned as a yowie head tangled in the sticky rainbow over the doorway.

Cheryl waited for Bradley Spam to yell 'flaps' or perhaps even 'bacon liver' but Samuel's best friend just pulled off his mother's disguise and stared into the empty shop with pussy red eyes.

'Shouldn't you be at school?' Dora called through the fug.

Bradley let out a garrotted peep and fled.

'Maybe he's got the same bug you have, eh Chezza?' Dora said as the half-yowie made an agitated retreat down Panorama Way. 'Now get to work.'

Cheryl was temporarily spellbound by the sight of Dora Knockers wrestling a sack of frozen chips, her big pink lips contracting like salted slugs. Then she commenced a grim wade through the inky tropics of the essay. Terrifyingly enough, it contained a large number of words she had to look up in the dictionary on the fridge. Admittedly, one of them was 'dramastic' but there were quite a few others that actually existed and even appeared to have been used in context.

'A little overdone with the exclamation marks though, don't you think, Dora Knockers?' Cheryl eventually wrote in the margin.

She didn't want her protégée to get a swollen head.

Outside the shop, a canine and car horn squealed a duet. Cheryl wondered if it was the old depot guard's ectoplasmic dog. She put the essay to one side and opened her Personal Pocket Journal to the Evidence section.

'Whoever killed Samuel was someone he knew,' she wrote. 'He would have made a run for it, otherwise. It had to be someone he trusted.'

That rules out Mrs Stint with a fake moustache, she thought. Samuel hated the Year Nine history teacher almost as much as Cheryl did. The heavily sedated old tyrant probably didn't have the strength to lift a can of petrol, anyway. Unless she'd made Samuel carry it down to the river Baby Cheeses style, that is.

The Old Depot Guard, Cheryl wrote across the top of a new page.

EVIDENCE: Says he knows killer. Is clearly insane. Fiddles with fly. Doesn't wear underwear. Smells bad. Shouts in street. Thinks dog is alive. Gave away $1 notes in Bi-Mart.

MITIGATING CIRCUMSTANCES: Can barely walk.

Cheryl re-examined her notes. As the assistant solicitor in Mrs Stint's Mock Trial team (school uniform breaches and fringe length excluding her from a coveted barrister position) she knew the case against the old depot guard was breathtakingly weak.

Nothing for it but to commence investigations against Dora Knockers.

Cheryl shuffled through the papers on the kitchen bench. There were three earlier versions of the *Twelfth Night* essay, a brochure about the importance of attaching cats' phone numbers to their collars and a recipe for garlic bread. She had better luck with the cardboard box beneath Dora's bed.

Six years old! read the scribble on the back of the first of the loose photographs. *Lion Pants! Me and V! Me, V and A putting Choo Choo in sack!*

Strangely enough, the portrait on the front of *Grade 10 School Social with V and A — Gross!* contained nothing more animate than a still life of a bunch of flowers.

Cheryl put the photos on the bed and peered out into the front of the shop where Dora was cleavering lettuces at a rate of knots. There was only one lettuce and a bag of tomatoes to go. Cheryl had to move fast.

Beneath a stapled collection of parking tickets was a ripped, hand-written reference from the Central City Freshwater Sharkarium. It described a cheerful and willing worker whose care with the sharklings was a thing to write home about.

'Of course under the current circumstances we have regretfully decided to let this young lady go,' the reference continued. 'As you will no doubt appreciate, this step must be taken to avoid adverse publicity at a time when large marine life aquariums throughout the world are really "doing it tough". Nevertheless we trust you will take note of her scrupulous at-work conduct during sentencing. In conclusion, the entire Johnson family and board of trustees wish this bright young woman all the very best with her rehabilitation and recommend her without hesitation to any and all future employers.'

The reference was addressed to: The Police Prosecutor, Central City Local Court.

The rest of the box was like a cross section of the continental crust.

Layer one: A manilla folder marked R for receipts.

Layer two: A photograph of Genevieve Flash, the editor of *The Chinese Whisper*, in a bikini.

Layer three: An Apply To Small Test Patch hair bleach instruction sheet.

Layer four: Three battered editions from the *Becky Swift* mystery series.

Layer five: An unopened packet containing a perished version of Delilah, The Most Life-like Female Doll Ever Created.

Layer six: A letter addressed to Mr Robert Bail of Bail's Laundromat marked Return to Sender.

Then, BINGO: a battered diary strapped with dozens of old rubber bands and leaking letters.

Cheryl slipped the diary into her bag and returned the rest of Dora's bits and pieces to the cardboard box. She reached the loose photographs and stared again at *Grade 10 School Social with V and A — Gross!* The picture of the bunch of flowers was thicker than the others. Quite possibly it was two photographs stuck together. Cheryl picked at a corner and began to peel.

On the back of the newly freed flower photo was the smudged scribble *From Mum's funeral.*

On the front of the newly exposed *Grade 10 School Social with V and A — Gross!* were three girls wearing old-fashioned dresses down to their calves. The one with the headband on the far left was Dora Knockers before her operations. Cheryl had seen a cut-out version of the exact same image in *X-Spot*. The one in the middle had small, smiley eyes and could have been anyone. And the one on the far right was Violet.

Cheryl felt a choking claustrophobia. She made a dash for the door, but there, leaning against the counter in exaggerated poses of relaxation, were Lou and Reb and the rest of them.

'Give us 5 cents worth of rats,' said Lou.

'Rats *are* 5 cents,' said Dora.

'Well. Give. Me. One. Then.'

Lou rolled her eyes at the others while Dora used a pair of plastic tongs to detach a single specimen from the tangle. After she'd put the gangly sweet in a white paper bag, Lou spoke again.

'I don't want a blue one I want a red one.'

Dora adjusted the plastic apron she'd put on to tackle the lettuce. It had fake hair printed on the chest and a slogan reading: Tough Guy and Ladies' Man.

'Tough titties,' Dora said. 'Why aren't you kids at school anyway?'

'Closed,' said Reb. 'The police are interviewing the teachers over Samuel Leadhead.'

'I reckon it was Mr Scoob.'

'I reckon it was Christy Leadhead.'

'I reckon it was Cheryl Kiss.'

'I've got a joke for you,' said Lou, eyeing off the fish and chip shop woman's yellow waves. 'What do blondes call brown hair dye?'

'What?' asked Dora.

'Artificial intelligence,' said Lou, lowering the rat into her mouth by its tail.

'Ha ha,' said Reb.

'Ha ha,' said the rest of them.

'I've got a joke for you, too,' said Dora.

'What,' said Lou, teeth covered in blue rat slag.

'What smells worse than an anchovy?'

'What?'

'An anchovy's cunt.'

Lou and Reb and the others backed slowly out of the shop shaking their heads in disbelief. Cheryl waited until Reb's plaits were a good 50 metres up the road, then made a run for it.

'But what about your scallops and crab sticks,' Dora called after her.

Cheryl sprinted into the midday sun without looking back.

17

Special Arrangements

The reason Cheryl went to Special Arrangements instead of sport wasn't because she made Carmine Steinem swallow her tongue during surf lifesaving practice. It was because of the change rooms. Or the lack of them, to be precise.

When Cheryl first started at Tantanoula High School she thought the open plan dressing sheds next to the school auditorium were *hilarious*: a) anyone could flick rubber bands at Pat Elevator's fat backdoor while she was changing into her school-issue school bloomers; b) someone always had an open tube of fake leg tan ready to rub into someone else's face, and; c) who needed a c? That fake leg tan was *incredible*. Half the time Lou played netball looking like she stood too close to *detonating nuclear bombs*.

The dressing shed stopped being quite so amusing in

Year Nine when Lou noticed something funny about the top of Cheryl's legs when she was changing for netball.

'What's that?'

'Nothing.'

'It looks like cheese.'

'Does not.'

'Does poo.'

Cheryl tried to stretch the uniform another inch lower. Thanks to her planet-sized girth, the pleats on the skirt gaped like unstitched wounds.

'Hey Reb! Check this out. Cheryl's got stalagmite!'

'It's cellulite, stupid,' Reb said, coming over for a look. 'Stalagmites are cold sores. Ha! It looks like cheese.'

'Does not.'

'Does poo.'

'Alien cheese!'

'Mince in glad bags!'

'Whale spit with spoof!'

Reb and Cheryl were supposed to be officially in hate with Louise Frances on account of the fact that her mother wore sundresses without shaving under her armpits, but lately Reb seemed to be finding Lou funnier and funnier. Cheryl consoled herself with the knowledge that she hadn't eaten so much as a jar of Lutbutter since the afternoon before and would soon be as skinny as one of Rachel Roulette's skinny legs.

In the dressing shed the following Sports Day, Lou noticed something amusing about the rolls around Cheryl's belly. The week after that she noticed something burlesque about the skin cuts caused by Cheryl's huge new bra. The week after that she surprised everyone by observing that Cheryl was developing a farcical triple chin. Cheryl Kiss came second in the 50-metre sprint at the Sports Carnival to the sound of Lou singing fatty boomsticks.

'That's nice,' Violet said late that night when her daughter presented the sliver of blue ribbon on the tiny gold safety pin. 'But carrying all that extra weight is like running with a sack of potatoes strapped round your waist. It's amazing you even finished your little race, darling. Did anyone try to refloat you at the finish line? Ha!'

Cheryl ignored Mr Scoob's suggestion that she commence after-school track and field training and concentrated on entertaining Reb.

First she ploughed a medicine ball into the abdomen of the unpopular Diana Crypt. Then she used a hockey stick as an electric guitar and 'accidentally' blasted the cauliflower earhole of the enormous Anzac Trent. Then, during a particularly insipid soccer game, she yanked Pat Elevator's bloomers so that half the team got a flash of her blubbery backdoor.

Reb howled with laughter. She'd never seen anything quite so funny in her entire life. Except maybe Lou's impersonation of Cheryl bouncing off walls like a pin ball.

'Restrain yourselves, girls,' Mr Scoob said from the sidelines. The forward-thinking PE teacher was wondering whether Year Nine needed more information about their hormones. He was willing to bet his entire knee-high sock collection that if adolescents spent more time engaging in guilt-free self-gratification, they'd throw less newspaper-wrapped bricks through car windows.

The last time Cheryl participated in a high school sporting event was the second Tuesday in March: the afternoon 9–1 was scheduled to brush-up on its surf lifesaving skills in the chlorinated waters of the Tantanoula Memorial Baths. Even Mr Scoob could see the advantages of actual surf when instructing in ocean rescue, but the region was in the grip of a bluebottle epidemic and he'd already received an official caution about advising students to urinate on their stings. (God only knows what the district inspectors would say if they discovered he'd golden-showered half the allergenic Under-13s open sea polo team. What was he supposed to do? Leave them writhing? Even delaying to squirt his First Aid supplies into an Orchy bottle behind Tom Valve's towel had caused his inflamed young charges additional distress.)

Cheryl loved surf lifesaving no matter where it was held. This was because surf lifesaving required swimming fully clothed. Regularly sized students protested bitterly but the Kiss girl had been bathing in smart casual to cover her bulges all her life and thought nothing of the suffocating drag of denim and wet synthetics.

Cheryl's unfair advantage in the surf lifesaving pool reminded her of *Blind Rage* — the movie where Lurex Imperial played a glamorous blind codebreaker on the run from the KGB and assorted infiltrated American agents. Who would have thought a blind woman stood a chance against a crack squad of assassins armed with heavy artillery? Not cornered in a Transylvanian mansion with the phone lines severed, the security dogs silenced and the maid strangled by a rope of her own intestines. Then Kate Wonder cut the electricity so everyone was in the dark.

Even blind codebreakers and fat girls come out on top when the swimming pool is a level one.

In surf lifesaving, Cheryl ploughed through the water in a parka and thermals while everyone else flailed. Only other fat students like huge Pat Elevator in her hand-me-down polo necks got anywhere near her. In surf lifesaving, Cheryl was the champ. Cheryl was the man. Best of all, the reward money for bringing the traitors to justice was enough for Kate Wonder to pay for the operation to restore her sight and allow her to live happily ever after with her true love, millionaire adventure balloonist He Newman (played, spectacularly enough, by cinematic newcomer Lance Seldom).

It was the second Tuesday in March and Mr Scoob was pairing 9–1 up for mouth-to-mouth resuscitation down at the pool. When he called Cheryl and Carmine Steinem's names together, Cheryl turned to Reb and put her fingers down her throat, pretending to gag. Carmine was more unpopular than Diana Crypt, Pat Elevator and Anzac Trent put together. She had the shoulders of a bulldozer. She had Vesuvius pimples, pig eyes and sideburns. Mort and Murray Ramsbottom called her Bucket because they said that's what she must have escaped from at the abortion clinic.

But being teamed with Bucket for mouth-to-mouth was nothing compared to the sick feeling in Cheryl's stomach when Reb and Lou were also required to join forces. Mr Scoob called their names and Cheryl turned to Reb to perform the pretend gag. 'Sucked in,' she hissed. 'Look out for nits and herpes. And ask how her mother's ape legs are going.'

'Louise Frances is all right,' Reb whispered back.

And within minutes Cheryl's best friend and worst enemy were down the deep end giggling at each other's see-through blouses.

Bucket was waiting for Cheryl beneath the No Running No Dive Bombing sign.

'We're supposed to start practising,' she said.

'Yeah yeah,' said Cheryl. 'But don't breathe on me. And stop leaning so freaking close. It's not LEZZO practice.'

After a few half-hearted mouth-to-mouth movements to the sides of each other's faces, Mr Scoob told the resuscitation group to swap with the water-treaders.

Reb was so busy giggling at something Lou was saying she didn't even see Cheryl walk past.

'Fuck face,' Cheryl said under her breath.

'What?' honked Bucket.

'Sit on this,' said Cheryl, sticking her middle finger up at Lou's back.

Cheryl and Carmine stood at the deep end staring into the fuming blue reservoir. Cheryl suddenly had a great idea. She told Carmine to stop taking her shoes off. She said the laces had to be tied together into feet handcuffs.

'It's new for Year Nine.'

'Are you sure?' (Carmine Steinem almost had a facial expression.)

'Of course, I'm sure. Look, I'm doing it. Foot cuffs. IN A DOUBLE KNOT, CHICKEN.'

Cheryl made clucking noises as Carmine toyed with the laces on her big black boots. Lying always made her heart beat gratifyingly faster.

'Buck buck buck.'

'I'm doing it.'

'BUCK BUCK BUCK.'

'Look. It's done, all right?'

And before Carmine had time to ask why everyone always called her Bucket, Cheryl pushed her into the water.

Carmine was a big girl. Like Cheryl, she was used to swimming with her clothes on. But Bucket was no mermaid and could do little more than flail her bound feet recklessly as she plunged to the bottom of the pool.

Cheryl jumped into the water herself so as not to attract attention. She'd tied her laces with a slip knot and separated her legs with a single kick.

Carmine surfaced with a gargle.

'You all right?' said Cheryl.

Carmine thrashed her way to the side of the pool, still spluttering.

'Hello?'

Bucket's eyes bulged, her body convulsed and her mouth stretched into a useless yawn. Cheryl screamed for Mr Scoob and the foreshortened teacher moved faster than anyone thought possible. He yanked Bucket out of the pool, pulled back her head and jabbed two hairy digits down her gullet.

His patient's breath returned with the force of a jet plane's engine.

'You swallowed your tongue,' Mr Scoob panted when she had finished savaging the atmosphere. 'You should get an award for that one. In all my 72 years in show business I've never seen a tongue jammed so far down a human throat.'

And then he caught sight of Carmine's shoelaces.

The spray of saliva went for metres.

'Are you insane? Are you a complete bloody fruitcake? Did I say the lesson today was to drown yourselves? DID I?'

Carmine tried to speak but couldn't. Her throat had been scoured by the steel wool on Mr Scoob's fingers.

'No, Mr Scoob,' she mouthed.

'JEEEESUS.'

The PE teacher had just noticed Cheryl was wearing dripping footwear as well.

'Did anyone else here decide to take their lives into their own hands by tying their shoelaces together in the swimming pool? Wipe that smirk off your face, Louise Frances. Regardless of what you and Rebecca Michaelson might think, water safety, is NOT a joke. Am I making myself perfectly clear?'

'Yes, Mr Scoob,' Lou said in her perfect girl voice.

'Rebecca?'

'Yes, sir.'

'Good.'

Pete Scoob dropped into a meaty squat.

'You feeling OK?' he said as he wrestled with the knot in Carmine's laces.

Bucket nodded.

'Is there anything else you want to tell me about how this happened?'

Carmine shook her head. She heaved up from the damp cement and walked to the phone to ring her mother, convinced that yet again she'd failed one of life's vital tasks.

Lou, meanwhile, was busy pointing out to anyone who'd listen that Cheryl Kiss even had fat on her *ankles*.

Cheryl didn't think about the fact that Bucket had nearly died. She thought of another four years of open plan dressing sheds and Lou's endless jibes and the stand-up comedy routine of her figure and decided the time had come to make a dignified retreat.

'Say no more,' Mr Scoob said after reading the forged note Cheryl brought in the following week. 'I thought something might have been brewing — what with that unfortunate business down at the pool and all. They've probably been brought on by post-traumatic shock. Nothing else you need to ask while you've got me here? Nothing you're wondering about the facts of life? No concerns about any of the changes happening to your body? No boy problems?'

Cheryl wondered whether the fact that Mort Ramsbottom had started calling her Hunch ranked as a boy problem and thanked Mr Scoob for his concern.

She was to bring in a forged note saying she had her periods every sports afternoon for the rest of the year. Mr Scoob seemed to think this was perfectly normal. He was deeply distracted by his new sexual transmitted disease education kit, which included actual slides of actual herpes ulcers.

'Not that I'm trying to put you off expressing your feelings for each other in a physical way, Year Nine. Take reasonable precautions and the sky's the limit. After all, just because your parents were taught to feel guilty about perfectly natural physical urges doesn't mean you have to make the same mistake. Now what we have in this illustration is a typical outbreak of genital herpes affecting the penis . . .'

Students who went to Special Arrangements instead of sport spent Tuesday afternoons in the big glass classroom usually reserved for drama.

The supervising teacher was Mrs Stint whose ability to wrangle sporting events had been severely compromised by Dr Salmon's calming medications. During her last call of duty she'd fallen asleep during an amateur martial arts afternoon and woken with barely enough time to prevent Murray Ramsbottom from kung-fu chopping Anzac Trent's testicular sack.

My word, that was a close one. SNHGRRGGGGH . . .

Mrs Stint's role as Special Arrangements supervisor also ensured that Tantanoula High School's Sports Afternoons were the most highly attended in the region. Once, Miss Strip the arts teacher had assumed the position and the exodus from the rugby team was a thing to behold.

Cheryl reported for duty at the big glass classroom with her school bag slung over her shoulder and the hem of her school uniform safety-pinned to within an inch of its life (*Working Woman* had just published an exposé on the slimming powers of the micro skirt).

The only other students in the classroom were Samuel Leadhead and Bradley Spam.

Neither looked particularly happy to see her.

The two boys watched Cheryl walk into the room and give her Non Sports pass to Mrs Stint with grim expressions. They listened to Mrs Stint extol the virtues of the Tantanoula newsreader without a word. Finally, after Cheryl had slung her yellow school bag over a seat up the back of the room and struggled in vain to sit without showing any underpant, Bradley let out a subdued 'FLAPS'. The detective's stepson didn't shout as much as he had done at primary school but still spent most of his time drawing increasingly elaborate fantasyscapes in his large yellow art books. Cheryl had a vague recollection of Miss Strip organising an exhibition of his work at the Tantanoula Town Hall but couldn't remember whether she'd gone to see them or not. She and Reb were probably disco dancing or looking for UFOs or hating Lou or something.

Bloody Lou.

As soon as Mrs Stint's enormous head hit the desk, Samuel and Bradley glanced at each other, swept their books into their bags and began playing cards.

The game was elaborate. There were Jokers and Wild Twos and Bonus Red Threes and secret families snaking in every direction.

For someone who'd yelled FUCKING LIVER through the minute's silence at his father's funeral, Bradley sure was quiet when he played cards with Samuel Leadhead.

He wasn't that bad looking up close, either.

Spam's bony face jutted between his yellow bangs like a rock in a rapid. But there was something exciting about his wide mouth and green eyes, about the trail of bones up the back of his neck and the fluorescent surprise of his teeth.

Cheryl hoped she wouldn't develop a crush on the school retard and become the laughing-stock of Year Nine. The mileage Louise Frances would get out of that one didn't bear thinking about.

Sitting next to Bradley, Samuel looked very small and dark, with a face a bit like Zeus's. Even when he was playing cards he spent most of his time staring out the window, so Cheryl had plenty of time to examine his profile.

Get this: Samuel Leadhead shaved. She could tell by the prickles. They weren't just in dribs and drabs like Murray Ramsbottom's, either. They were all over his cheeks. Samuel's chin certainly was square all of a sudden. And his skin was terrible. Probably from shaving the tops off all those pimples. Cheryl could sympathise. Once she'd shaved over a stretchmark inside her thigh and haemorrhaged all over her mother's Queen Sheba bath mat.

Samuel looked up and caught Cheryl staring.

'What,' he said in a loud voice. 'What are you looking at?'

'Nothing,' said Cheryl.

'CUNT HAS A C NOT A K,' Bradley erupted in a panic.

And all three Special Arrangers looked up at the heaving figure of Mrs Stint in unison.

Snhgrrggggh.

Snhgrrggggh.

SNHGRRGGGGH.

Mrs Stint was dreaming she was waxing God's back.

Samuel gave Cheryl a suspicious look and returned to the card game. Cheryl doodled on a Geography assignment about international agriculture and wished she'd brought something to read. Her mother's copy of *Working Woman*, perhaps. There was a whole section on vertical stripes she hadn't even got to yet. Cheryl wondered whether Mrs Stint's anti-depressant medication would turn out to be carcinogenic so the history teacher would develop an ox-heart tomato tumour right in the middle of her forehead. Jackson's mother, Jean, used to grow ox-heart tomatoes. They were the most disgusting things Cheryl had seen except for oysters. Both looked like something you might find down someone's disgusting pants.

Cheryl giggled.

Samuel looked up.

'Don't worry,' she said. 'I wasn't laughing at you. I was thinking of something else. It sure is boring in here. Does anyone else ever come? Is it true about Miss Strip? What's the card game.'

'Canasta,' said Samuel.

'CANASTA,' yelped Bradley.

'Can I play?' said Cheryl.

Samuel shook his head.

'Why not?'

'It's too hard.'

'TOO HARD,' came the echo.

'It can't be too hard if he can do it.'

'A C NOT A K,' Bradley shouted, looking genuinely offended.

That afternoon Cheryl and Reb waited for their buses on the hill next to the bus shelter the way they always did.

'How was it?'

'How was what?'

'You know. Special Arrangements.'

'It was OK. What about sport?'

'It was OK. It was rollerskating. Murray Ramsbottom tipped a bottle of Coke down Pat Elevator's dress. That was about it. Diana Crypt tripped during speed skate and everyone saw her arse. I dunno. Mr Scoob kept going on about pheromones. Whatever. Murray Ramsbottom pashed Rachel Roulette up the back of the bus. Nothing happened. You coming down the Bi-Mart tomorrow? Lou reckons there's new Lance Seldom earrings. With guitars.'

Cheryl looked down the hill and caught a glimpse of Bradley's praying-mantis amble and hose-length fingers. She realised with a whoosh of relief she was safe.

'Bradley Spam's skeleton is too big for his body,' she said to Reb. 'It's going to burst through his skin and then there'll be pus and flesh all over the bus stop.'

'OUCH,' Reb hissed. 'That freaking HURTS.'

She was getting her ears pierced by Lou so she had somewhere to put the Lance Seldom earrings she and Cheryl were going to steal from Bi-Mart.

'Fucking Mr Scoob,' Lou said when she was finished. 'Fucking rollerskating. Fucking Rachel Roulette. She's such a fucking slut. Murray Ramsbottom pashes SLUTS. Where were you anyway, Cheryl Jane Kiss?'

'Special arrangements.'

'Didn't miss much. Wish I was too fat for sport.'

'You coming down the Bi-Mart next Tuesday?' asked Reb. 'Me and Cheryl are gonna nick a pair of those new Lance Seldom earrings.'

'They've got guitars,' said Cheryl.

'DUH,' said Lou. 'I only nicked seven ENTIRE pairs last weekend.'

'Well, me and Cheryl are going down after sport next Tuesday. If you wanna come, come.'

'I'll think about it,' said Lou. 'Mort Ramsbottom asked me to come round to see his trail bike so I'll have to think about it.'

'Whatever,' said Reb. 'We can go another afternoon.'

Cheryl fumed. Lou seemed to think she could hang round them any time she felt like it. The whole point of a best friend was that you only had one of them.

That night, Cheryl held an ice cube on each side of her earlobe and attacked it with a sewing needle. She worked slowly. When Lou pierced ears, it was over faster than you could say MRS STINT'S COMING. But Cheryl was a slow mover. Very slow. In fact, by 2 a.m. she'd only done one-and-a-half ears. Cheryl left her room and walked into the house to look in the bathroom mirror. Her ears were traffic lights and her collar was soaked.

'Cakes? Cakeybum, is that you?'

Cheryl could smell her mother through the chipboard wall.

'Yes mother.'

She slid the door. Violet was half-in and half-out of her work clothes, holding a champagne glass and a bottle of vodka. She kept trying to knock even though the door was wide open.

'Oh hello,' Violet shrieked, when she finally realised she was drumming on thin air. 'Can I borrow a cup of sugar? HA HA!'

Cheryl turned her face at an angle, but Violet was too busy cackling to notice the needle sticking out of her daughter's bleeding right ear.

Also, she seemed to be trying to perform a handstand.

Two days later, long red fingers clawed their way down Cheryl's throat and Violet had to cart her off to Razz Salmon for antibiotics.

The piercings had gone septic.

'Where do you get off, Cheryl?' said Violet. 'Where do you get off?'

But Cheryl had no idea.

On her second week of Special Arrangements, Cheryl came prepared. She'd harvested a plastic bagful of change from the floor of her mother's car during the trip to Dr Salmon's and had purchased a brand new, gold-embossed Personal Pocket Journal.

'I'm writing my memoirs,' she told Samuel and Bradley once Mrs Stint had gone to sleep. 'One day I'm going to be a world famous novelist. Or Lurex Imperial's ghostwriter. Or one of those people who writes the stuff on Lance Seldom's yoyos.'

'What happened to the side of your neck?'

'Nothing.'

'I thought you'd tried to hang yourself,' said Samuel and returned to the card game. He had another purple moon beneath his eye and what looked like two missing fingernails. Cheryl lost a fingernail once. Violet accidentally slammed it in the car door and it grew back black and eventually fell off. Cheryl was so used to seeing Samuel Leadhead come to school with broken arms and pulled hair she hardly noticed any more.

'I, Cheryl Kiss,' she wrote on the first page of the Personal Pocket Journal. 'I, Cheryl Kiss was born in Mexico. I had a twin sister called Sarah Beth. I had a father called Frank Anderson. Now I live on Sunset Stripe with my mother and my dog. I used to have a stepfather but someone poisoned his peas and he died coughing up organs.'

Cheryl examined the paragraph then coloured in all the e's, o's and a's.

She stared aggressively at the card players, hoping Samuel would look up and yell at her again.

But he was too busy claiming victory.

'I'm out,' he said, arranging the last of his cards on the table.

'ROTUNDA,' Bradley bawled affectionately before commencing a reshuffle.

That afternoon after school, Cheryl and Reb caught the bus down to the Bi-Mart. Lou had arranged to meet them at the Super Cream afterwards, but the shop detective got them before they reached her.

'It was Reb's idea,' Cheryl cried in the windowless room out the back of the store. 'It was always Reb's idea.'

How was she to know her best friend was in the next room listening in?

'But it *was* your idea,' she'd said to Reb on the phone after their parents had picked them up from the police station and paid for the jangle of earrings secreted down their bras.

'Mum said I'm not allowed to talk to you for a while.'

'I'll give you my Lance Seldom poster.'

'I've already got one.'

'I'll give you my pogo stick.'

'You'll get in trouble.'

'I already am in trouble.'

'All right,' said Reb after a while. 'But only if you bring your passport to school so we can show Lou. She'll *spew*.'

After that Lou and the rest of them started hanging round Cheryl and Reb pretty much full time.

Months passed.

Cheryl's pierced ears healed into grisly scabs. Mrs Stint grew another mole. Carmine Steinem changed schools. And then it was summer again. Another endless Tantanoula summer when the newsreader's temper blazed, Mrs Stint's armpits chafed themselves into mine shafts and stained babies rolled in the rocky orange sand along the beaches until they were mistaken for the deep-fried camembert wedges Dora Knockers served with a sprig of parsley and a generous side of Long Life cranberry sauce at lunchtimes and up until 8.45 p.m. on Thursday nights.

Cheryl had stopped taking much notice of Samuel and Bradley on Tuesday afternoons thanks to the magazines that had begun materialising beneath her mattress.

Pillow Biter. Irregular Intruder. Big, Bigger and Bigamy. Busted. Accent On Anal. Hunch For Men. X Spot. Splat.

Cheryl didn't want to read them but she couldn't help it — crouched up the back of Special Arrangements with *Readers' Wives* half-in and half-out of her school bag in case Mrs Stint conducted a surprise raid.

Hear 2 Housewives Fuck My Shaven Cunt

Dirt Cheap Anal Sex

30 Second Jerk Off Line

**(Wank Your Cock To Hardcore, Dirty Kinky Phone Filth
With Girls Who Like It Deep In Their Holes)**

Cheryl wondered why anyone would want to spend $5 a minute ringing a telephone service where all anyone ever did was swear. It'd be OK if you got to chat with Lance Seldom or something, but the girls in the pictures weren't even celebrities. Plus they were ugly. They didn't smile at the camera and half of them looked like they had rashes.

Still, there was something irresistible about their primary coloured promises.

SPUNK OVER MY HUGE TITS
(0099 235 876)

YOU'RE SO BIG IT HURTS
(0099 120 935)

Double Dildo Lesbian Fucking
(0099 765 298)

Cheryl wrote down 'jerk', 'spunk' and 'dildo' to look up in the dictionary later, then cast a guilty glance upwards, in case someone was watching. That was when she realised she and Mrs Stint were the only ones left in the classroom. Samuel and Bradley's bags were still at their desk, their cards still on the table. But the players had vanished.

Over the course of the following weeks, Cheryl identified a pattern. At 2.30 p.m. the mid-afternoon siren sounded and Mrs Stint woke with a roar. 'Carry on,' she'd shout, staring wildly into the middle distance with her grey hair on end. Then her big head would fall back onto the desk with a thud and Bradley and Samuel would look at each other, lower their cards and slip out the door.

Cheryl assumed it was cigarettes. That's what people usually did in the gloomy toilet block next to Special Arrangements. Cigarettes or maybe texta sniffing. (Lou said it got you high AS, but Cheryl only ever got stained nostrils.)

'Got a spare durry?' Cheryl asked them one afternoon when he and Bradley returned from the toilet block manically chewing spearmint gum.

Samuel looked confused. He looked like he was about to shout then retreated into an urgent huddle with Bradley.

It's only a lousy cigarette, Cheryl thought. What's the big deal about a lousy cigarette?

She shoved *XXX Jailbirds* back into her school bag and flipped open the Thesaurus.

> fleshy beefy hefty paunchy bloated puffy blowzy overfleshed distended swollen abdominous gorbellied pussle-gutted fubsy rotund pudgy podgy portly elephantine hippopotamic colossalas fat as a quail as fat as a pig as fat as a pork hog

How many synonyms for 'Cheryl Jane Kiss' did the English language bloody well need?

Cheryl drew a picture of Mrs Stint with no clothes on, then a picture of Bradley Spam with no clothes on, then a picture of Samuel Leadhead with whale spray coming out his donger. She used a black texta to colour in his eyes and fingernails and tried to remember the last time she'd felt happy.

What she didn't understand was why some girls had to be thin and other girls had to be fat. What she didn't understand was what Reb saw in Lou. What Violet saw in Jackson. Why Sarah Beth had to die and how come Violet didn't even know whether the fucking airline had even found her father's body.

'Don't interrogate me, Cheryl. You know I can't stand it when you interrogate me.'

'But can't we ring them up, Mum? Can't we ring them up to see if they made a grave?'

'I'm warning you, Cheryl.'

'He was on his way to live with you and me, though. Right Mum?'

'SEE, CHERYL? SEE WHAT YOU'VE MADE ME DO? VODKA ALL OVER MUMMY'S NEW SUNGLASSES. ARE YOU HAPPY NOW?'

The next Tuesday, Cheryl wandered out of Special Arrangements in pursuit of Bradley and Samuel.

The boys' toilets looked pretty much like the girls' except for the white pissing wall. No wonder it smelled so bad. Half that piss probably evaporated and hung round the roof in a big yellow cloud. Imagine piss rain. That'd be way worse than acid rain. It'd stink even worse than the dead koalas Zeus hid in his well up near the old chicken shed.

Would it have killed Violet to keep just one photo? Just one lousy photo of Cheryl and Sarah Beth's father?

Bradley and Samuel were behind a cubicle door advertising Rachel Roulette's home number for 'a slut what goes all night'.

They weren't making any noise and there wasn't any cigarette smoke, but Cheryl knew it had to be them because it was the only locked door in the building.

She slunk into the cubicle next door and tiptoed onto the toilet seat, trying not to choke on the stress of spying.

'BUSTED,' she was going to scream.

Then 'GIVE US A DURRY, SCABS.'

That's what Lou said to Mort Ramsbottom's gang when she bludged cigarettes off them behind the ag shed at lunch. By rights she was the scab, asking for cigarettes for free, but Mort Ramsbottom's gang didn't seem to mind and always gave her as many as she wanted.

'Have mine,' they'd say, jostling to offer their pack first. 'Don't touch his. They've got the pox.'

But Samuel Leadhead and Bradley Spam didn't offer Cheryl cigarettes or beverages when she poked her head over the cubicle wall.

In fact, they were so busy they didn't even see her.

Bradley Spam was sitting on the toilet with the seat down and Samuel Leadhead was sitting on his lap with one leg round each side of his waist. And they were kissing. French-style with their mouths pressed together and their eyes closed and their tongues out and EVERYTHING.

18

Unbridled Licentiousness

During the long sprint home from the fish and chip shop, Cheryl thought she caught a glimpse of the yowie head lurking behind the Kruegers' hydrangeas. She thought she saw it darting behind the Hatts' people mover and the Ketteringhams' water tank and the Surfs' histrionic washing line and finally behind the bamboo stand up on the hill behind the Kiss residence.

'Hey Bradley,' Cheryl shouted from the Kiss family fence.

But the sound withered in the heat and the bamboo poles were still.

Cheryl collapsed on her bed and pinged the rubber bands off Dora Knockers' stolen diary. Inside were four photocopied letters, all dating back to the New Year's Eve when Violet and Dora had the fight.

Violet Kiss
Lot 28 Panorama Way
Tantanoula
January 3

Dear Violet

Please accept my apologies for my actions on
New Year's Eve. I truly believe what happened
was nothing more than a series of
misunderstandings which, under ordinary
circumstances, would have amounted to nothing
other than a friendly disagreement. However,
being the festive season, people tend to become
full of beer and bad manners and things get
taken out of context.

I certainly did not mean for you to take
badly my feminist views and obviously I
underestimated your sensitivities about your
age. I was genuinely surprised when you said I
was 'attacking' you as a mother. Just because
I think it's wrong to lie to your daughter
doesn't mean I regard you as 'an evil witch'!
However, after thinking things over, I agree it
was probably the wrong time, place and company
for such a discussion.

Also I would like to apologise for writing my
opinion of you numerous times in your new
Visitor's Book. As you know, I am not in the
habit of reneging on my views. Nevertheless,
repeatedly writing that you were a 'fucked up
alcho' on a number of pages was wrong.

I am prepared to offer you restitution for
any other damage to your property and hope my

behaviour does not reflect badly on Genevieve Flash who is a relatively new acquaintance of mine and hasn't spoken to me since experiencing the full force of my, ahem, more excitable side.

When I first came to Tantanoula, I sincerely hoped we could pick up where we left off. Now I realise that's impossible. Too much has changed. Not even Cheryl recognises me any more. Whatever we had between us is obviously over.

Once again, I am sorry if you confused my open and forthright attempts to have creative discussions with 'attacks'.

They were not and never have been.

Yours sincerely
Dora Knockers

PS. Don't worry. I'm not going to tell anyone anything. Blackmail isn't my style. Give me a minor drug infringement any day! Just joking! You won't hear from me again.

PRIVATE AND CONFIDENTIAL

Jackson Kiss
c/o Tantanoula Shire Council
16 Short Street
Tantanoula
January 3

Dear Jackson

Obviously you'd rather I didn't write to you at work but I've got a few things I need to get off my chest (please refrain from guffawing if you possibly can). I'm sorry you feel badly towards me. I honestly did not mean to harass your family at the party. Perhaps the inimitable Violet is right — if women aren't spoken for by the time they are 30 they will be left on the shelf. Then again, I'm quite a few years past my use-by date and I still get my fair share of offers as you of all people should know!

I guess your wife's barbecue was the wrong New Year's Eve party to gatecrash in my advanced state of chemical affliction. But I'm willing to make amends. I've already written to Violet apologising and I'm prepared to replace your entire sprinkler system even though parts of the hosing were obviously damaged beforehand.

Anyway, while I'm sorry for causing such a stink, I honestly don't believe my behaviour on New Year's Eve amounted to a 'jealous and twisted persecution' of your wife. And I still think I have a point about the bullshit she feeds everyone about what really happened in Mexico. Or does she feed you the same crap?

Oh well. This is the point where I say goodbye and good luck. It was fun while it lasted but I've met someone else and the therapist keeps lecturing me about the dangers of triangles. Don't worry about returning the Atlas and the jumper leads. Consider them parting gifts.

Once again, I hope you accept my apology and manage to restrain your life partner from vilifying me in the seven o'clock news.

In a long line of Knocker-isms, New Year's
Eve definitely takes the cake!

Yours sincerely
Dora

PRIVATE AND CONFIDENTIAL

Genevieve Flash
c/o The Chinese Whisper
15 Hoick Street
Tantanoula

Dear Gen

Aaaaahhhhhhhh . . .

I'm sorry, OK? I'm sorry I'm sorry I'm sorry
I'm sorry I'm sorry I'm sorry I'm sorry I'm
sorry I'm sorry I'm sorry I'm sorry I'm sorry
I'M SORRY . . .

How many times do I have to say it before
you'll end this wall of silence thing and
answer the phone?

Just so you know, I have written to the
middle-class Kiss family with an apology and an
offer of restitution for making the middle-
class mistake of telling the truth.

But it's you who deserves the biggest
apology, Gen. You're the only person in this
fucked-up little town who hasn't treated me
like a complete and utter freak. Then I had to
go and screw everything up by embarrassing you
in public. So much for my win-over-the-local-
community campaign.

I told you I'd make a lousy date!

Still. With friends like me who needs enemies, huh? And you have to admit there is a humorous side. God, the look on Violet's face when that precious collar of hers went up was priceless (she looked like a frill-necked lizard caught in a bushfire!). How was I to know Kenneth Vulpine would believe me when I said flaming Sambucas were supposed to be drunk while they were still alight? At one stage I looked around and everyone was either burnt or burning!

Anyway, you'll be pleased to know I am finally re-evaluating my use of recreational drugs. Clearly cocaine, marijuana and champagne reveal the darker side of my otherwise sane personality!

It's all over with J now, by the way. I didn't get a chance to tell you this at New Year's, but we had a shocking row on Christmas Day. He came round to the shop after doing the family lunch thing and I started accusing him of being with you-know-who and he said of course he'd been with her, she was his effing wife and if I wanted her to know he was effing her best friend then I should go right ahead and tell her!

I guess I was still jumpy after that licensing court business. (Though as you pointed out in your editorial, if crab sticks were required by law to contain actual crab they wouldn't cost 30 cents a piece!)

I haven't told you this before, but me and Violet go back a real long way. Maybe you think

that makes the J thing worse but me and Violet
have so much history, I don't know what's right
any more. I'm not at liberty to go into details
but that woman's got so many goddamn skeletons
in her closet, it's amazing she can still shut
the door! You can't blame the daughter for
being so screwed up. On Saturday night I
overheard Violet telling Razz Salmon and his
squeeze that motherhood was worse than jail.
'You get less for murder,' were her exact
words. And the daughter's standing right behind
her! Obviously I'm in no danger of qualifying
for mother of the year but the look on that
kid's face drove me fucking nuts.

I'm writing this from the caravan park at
Savvy. I drove down on New Year's Day to lie in
the sun and detox. I thought I'd be able to
straighten up just by moving out of the city,
but country living isn't quite as cleansing as
I'd anticipated.

Take two, eh?

Savvy was where we used to come for holidays
before mum got too out of hand. After that, we
went to a motor inn in the city. It was only 10
minutes from home but she got so stressed about
forgetting something, she'd swallow half a
bottle of Valium before we even pulled out of
the drive! One time we had to go back to check
the oven twelve times before we reached the end
of the street! My sisters haven't spoken to me
since we buried her. I could kill my uncle for
sending them those fucking videos, I really
could.

I miss you, Gen. I miss your sanity. I miss your stupid smile. I miss the way you yell at the telly during the adverts. You ever going to speak to me ever again?

Hopefully by the time you get this letter you will have rung and said everything's cool between us and I can go back to ogling you over port and brandies at The Conspiracy after work like I used to!

Infatuated?

Me?

Never.

Yours as ever

Dora

xxx

Big Waters Typing and Secretarial Agency

Main Street

Savvy 3097

Dear Miss Knockers

Enclosed please find the three letters you requested typing and our invoice which must be paid by the close of business on the 8th. A small surcharge has been added to cover the correction of spelling and grammatical errors — which you requested. We did our best to maintain the sense and integrity of your correspondence. Mrs Bystein's decision to change 'resuscitation' to 'restitution' was made only after a consultation with me.

We hope you are happy with the professionality of our work and will consider using the Big Waters Typing and Secretarial Agency again in future.

Please take note, however, that it is not our agency's policy to handle material which contains obscenity or any references which may indicate a breach of the law. The ladies in our typing pool pride themselves on their open-minded nature but wish you to know that the unbridled licentiousness to which you may be accustomed in the city is not welcome here in Savvy.

We can only wonder what your poor dead mother would say if she knew the depths to which you have sunk. I personally enjoyed a game of 500 with your father on three separate occasions and remember him as a fine and upstanding man who would find your behaviour abhorrent to say the least.

Yours sincerely
Edith Pratt
Manageress, Big Waters Typing and Secretarial Agency

19

Give It To Her

Cheryl's mouth had been hanging open so long it crackled. She returned Dora's letters to the diary as Jackson's car tortured the gravel in the drive. Another car followed. Did there have to be visitors? *Now?*

Cheryl pulled off the stretching sundress she'd stolen from her mother's room and dragged on a pair of wide elastic trousers, a man's long-sleeved white shirt and the least woollen of her cardigans. She knew it was too hot for so many layers. But the alternative was to expose the guests to the acres of flesh and the pussy white lumps covering the backs of both her shoulders. The arm lumps had been there for a year now. Violet said it was from eating too much meat and dairy.

'One day a boy's going to want to rub his hand on that part of your arm and all he's going to feel are those pimples,' she said.

'I doubt it,' said Cheryl.

But she remembered Christy running her fingers down her stomach in the Kiss family lounge room and wondered whether Samuel's sister had noticed the lumps. Bloody frigid test. It seemed like a good idea at the time, but now she couldn't get the stupid Leadhead girl out of her head. The night before when she'd been riding her pillow she'd even had a vision of Christy's spotty face.

Ugh.

Cheryl hauled on the last of her disguise and stepped outside.

'Hello, Cheryl,' said Kenneth Vulpine, levering himself out of his rusting utility.

'Hello, Mr Vulpine,' said Cheryl, slipping her hand up her sleeves and scratching the tops off her white arm lumps like it was going out of fashion. She glared at her stepfather.

'Cuppa?' said Jackson.

'You read my mind,' said Kenneth.

Kenneth Vulpine had married Donna Meetlove shortly after she'd been sacked from *The Chinese Whisper*. The disgraced cadet had embarked on a series of late-night rendezvous with the salami-coloured pig-hunter in the interests of cultivating crucial new farming contacts for the television station. As luck would have it, all she was really cultivating was the first of Kenneth's burly offspring. Before the year was out she found herself at the wrong end of a shotgun wedding in a dress with elastic stomach panels. Had the shock of it ever left her face? Cheryl couldn't have cared less.

Grain Fed Beef was what the good citizens of Tantanoula called Kenneth Vulpine behind his back. He hunted pigs with three dogs who lived in upended water tanks. He made his money buying and selling weed kill.

He charged $20 to shoot any animal of any size through the brain. He owned a single tuxedo custom-made to accommodate his monstrous neck. He was here now in the Kiss family kitchen.

'Ken's brought Tiddles over to see Zeus,' said Jackson when the two men emerged with steaming mugs of beige.

'Why?' said Cheryl.

'Because she's on heat, stupid.'

Kevin lifted a small red tube out of the back of the ute. The tube wriggled, then collapsed panting onto the ground. Falling over was fine when you were a dachshund. There was only an inch between you and the gravel.

'Don't tell my wife I made precious ride in the back. She'll want to send her off to therapy again. Women, eh?'

'Women,' agreed Jackson.

'You can't live with 'em and you can't shoot 'em.'

'You can say that again.'

'You can't live with 'em and you can't shoot 'em.'

'Ha ha.'

'Ha ha.'

'Zeus,' called Jackson. 'Zeus? Get over here, boy.'

Zeus snarled at his own anus while the daytime newsreader's dachshund hauled itself to its stumps and waddled in circles round the carport. The sausage dog had a needle nose that could stitch buttons and legs no larger than scones. It was the most ridiculous thing Zeus had ever seen.

'Can't wait to see the look on my wife's face when Tiddles drops her bundle all over the shag pile. She'll think it's the goddamn virgin birth.'

'You'll have to call them all Jesus.'

'Ha ha,' said Kenneth.

Jackson called Zeus one more time, then hauled him, backpeddling, towards Tiddles.

Cheryl couldn't watch but she couldn't walk away either.

'Get into her, Zeus,' said Kenneth

'Yeah Zeus,' said Jackson.

'Sink the sausage.'

'Bury the bishop.'

'Pound the mound.'

'Spear the bearded clam.'

'Poke that pussy.'

'Give it to her.'

Zeus, jumped at Tiddles's head. He jumped at her ribs. He jumped at her ridiculous right ear. He jumped absolutely everywhere except the portal Jackson directed him towards.

Tiddles just stood there. Her stomach had gravel rash. In general, she'd realised it was better not to move.

After a while, Zeus licked Tiddles's eyes and lay down in the shade.

Kenneth poked Zeus with his foot.

He and Jackson looked at each other.

'Sorry, Ken.'

'Don't apologise.'

'This is really embarrassing.'

'It's all right. Tiddles seems to have been taking sex appeal lessons off my wife.'

'Ha ha,' said Jackson, weakly.

'Has Casanova here ever got it up before?'

'Of course he has. Once he even had to be hospitalised.'

'Get out of town.'

'I kid you not. The lunatic got it up but couldn't get it down.'

'NO!'

'YES!'

'NO!'

'Mind you, that day seems to be well behind him now.'

Cheryl disagreed. She would never forget the swollen persimmon between Zeus's legs and the howling from beneath the door of the vet's surgery. If that was what sex was about she didn't want a bar of it. Mind you, it hadn't stopped her from swallowing Murray Ramsbottom's tongue a week later during Spin The Bottle.

'His old fella got stuck outside the sheath,' said Jackson.

'That'd bring a tear to a man's eyes,' said Kenneth.

'Tell me about it.'

'Sheath!'

'Christ!'

'Now that's something you wouldn't read in the papers.'

'Not in *The Chinese Whisper* any road. A pack of lemons the lot of 'em.'

'It cost $400 in vet bills,' said Cheryl. 'And Zeus couldn't walk properly for a week.'

But the two men had forgotten she existed.

'That emu of mine is a funny bugger,' said Kenneth. 'I told Donna I said Donna that emu of ours is a real funny bugger. I said he could make us some money if we put him in that news bulletin of yours. Not often you see an emu romantically inclined towards a goat after all. Once I saw a duck giving it to a one-legged rooster. But an emu and a goat. Now that's really something.'

'You said it,' said Jackson.

'An emu and a goat!'

'Ha ha.'

'Ha ha.'

'You're killing me Ken, you really are.'

'Obviously Zeus's plumbing is in working order,' mused Kenneth Vulpine. 'Maybe all he needs is a bit of privacy.'

'Or a bit of a helping hand.'

'I hope you're not suggesting what I think you're suggesting.'

'Why not? It's worth a shot. It never fails with yours truly, after all.'

And Jackson dragged Zeus up behind the shed and got to work between his hind legs.

Cheryl slammed her door and buried her head beneath her pillow. There was a yelp from the backyard. She loathed her stepfather so much she was gagging on it.

'Terrible business about the young Lightfoot lad,' said Kenneth Vulpine when it was all over.

'Shocking,' said Jackson.

'All that was left of his face were his teeth.'

'Tell me about it.'

'That's what that wog mother gets for running off with her own kind. The police know who did it, you know.'

'Mrs Vulpine your source on this one, is she?'

'The little lady paid a visit to the cop shop yesterday afternoon and said the investigation unit's dead minimal. No more door-knocking or nothing.'

Jackson couldn't restrain himself.

'I'll tell you a thing or two about the death of Samuel Lightfoot,' he finally erupted. 'If you really want to know what happened I could tell you a thing or two that'd make your skin crawl.'

Kenneth and Jackson leaned into each other whispering until Kenneth emerged shaking his head.

'Bullshit,' he said.

'I kid you not.'

'That's fucking unbelievable.'

'It's all true,' Jackson said smugly. 'Violet got it off Grippa himself.'

The two men walked side by side to Kenneth's ute, one bristling and red, the other spongy and white. Jackson might have been almost bald but Kenneth Vulpine had enough hair for both of them. It was snow white and shot out in every direction like an unsecured garden hose.

'Kids today, eh?' said Kenneth. 'A bunch of fucking delinquents.'

'Too true,' said Jackson looking back at Cheryl's room. 'Oh. And I'm sorry about Zeus this afternoon, Ken. I don't know what got into him.'

'Well I certainly know what didn't get into Tiddles.'

'Ha ha.'

'Have a word with that dog of yours would you, darling,' Kenneth called over his shoulder at Cheryl as he backed the utility down the driveway. 'After this afternoon's performance, I'm starting to think he's a goddamn queer, as well.'

20

What Exactly *Is* Bum Jacking?

Cheryl had been crying beneath the fig tree hating Jackson Kiss for a good 10 minutes before she realised Christy Leadhead was standing beside the trunk watching her.

Christy didn't say anything about Cheryl's whimpers and sniffles. She smashed a few fallen figs into the ground and split a root in half with a stick. She said: I'm closing in on the man from the school. She said: I've got four real cigars in a plastic bag. She said: The old depot guard's the only one in this town with a fallout shelter. She said: Come down the hill and maybe I'll show you Sammy's room.

Cheryl wiped a trail of snot onto her cardigan sleeve.

'Why are you wearing an ice-cream container on your head?'

'It's a magpie helmet. I've got a spare if you like.'

'I don't want one.'

'Those bastards can split your head open if they swoop hard enough.'

'I've never got swooped by magpies.'

'Shona did. They pecked her so hard she nearly lost half her brain.'

Cheryl glanced warily up to the sky and strapped the Neapolitan ice-cream container to her skull. If Christy Leadhead thought birds could drop from the sky and crack open their heads she was probably right. In this fucked-up place, anything could happen.

There were seven old caravans parked around the Leadhead's dark dam. Some sprouted brick and canvas, others had complex root systems of pipes and electrical leads. The Leadhead's caravans were forgotten plants that had grown through their pots. They were overflowing and barely portable. There'd be blood if the old death boxes were ever moved along. Blood and sap and broken veins.

'Do you have a van each?'

'Very funny, Kiss. Very, very amusing.'

Cheryl trailed Samuel's sister between the rectangular shadows, still wearing her plastic helmet. The bare dirt was awash with an ocean of empty bottles, it was an ocean of headless dolls, plastic pegs, leather straps and chained yellow dogs chewing unripe avocados that had fallen from the tree beside the dam. Cheryl reached out a hand to the closest canine and Christy slapped it back.

'You crazy?'

'What's her name?'

'I dunno,' she said. 'Dog I suppose.'

The animal drooled green flecks. Cheryl didn't like to think of Zeus having a girlfriend, but this Leadhead dog was definitely more his type than Tiddles. They could go all the way then shred each other's ears off. It would be a beautiful thing except Cheryl didn't like to think about Zeus having a girlfriend.

Jackson contaminated everything.

The first Leadhead caravan had fingerprinted windscreens strangled by anaemic floral curtains. It had a flaking sign that said 'Mum's Taxi' and a walking-stick made of black pipe leaning up against the door.

'Nan's,' said Christy.

Christy's father's van next door was in even worse shape. Newspaper was gaffer-taped across the single window and the towbar had disintegrated into a vile orange stump.

'Dad's working on the rust,' said Christy. 'Once he's done the rust we're gonna sell it and buy a new one.'

Of course you are, thought Cheryl.

'And this here is the kitchen.'

Christy yanked the screen door on the third van and slipped into the dirty shade.

'Coming?'

Cheryl paused. Rocking on the front steps of the third van was a fractured motorbike helmet. Next to that was a black bin overflowing with grey chicken bones. For the first time in her life, she experienced a true and genuine appreciation of the plastic bin liner.

'Do you want some Tang or what?' came Christy's call.

'*KISS?*'

Cheryl slid along a vinyl bench circling a long red table freckled with white and gold. Every crack was a dirty fingernail, every corner a refuge for crusts and cores and peanut-buttered knives.

'One night we had to camp under the fig tree because

Nan lost the keys. It was unreal. I ate marshmallows on a stick and threw up bark.'

Christy opened the chipboard cupboard and produced a congealed bottle of Tang. She ate a couple of spoonfuls then used a fork to dig crescents into a husky Tupperware bowl.

'We're gonna share a plate, OK? I can't be bothered washing anything up.'

Sometimes, when Christy turned her head at certain angles, she looked like the girl from the King of Clubs in the playing cards Jackson kept in his filing cabinet.

'I'm gonna serve it with ice-cream, OK?'

The King of Clubs girl wore a pair of denim jeans and a stripy woollen snake round her neck. Her boobs were like fried eggs superglued to her chest.

'Nan used to buy us chocolate topping for the ice-cream but then Sapphire got allergic and her throat blew up and Nan had to drive her down the hospital. The old depot guard was in the bed next door with ice on his throat too and he pulled back the curtain and he looked at Sapphire and he said "did you get strangled, as well?" and we laughed and laughed and laughed.'

Christy also looked a bit like the Eight of Diamonds. The Eight of Diamonds girl wore a celluloid sun visor and had a target painted on her chest. In the foreground was a hand holding on to a dart.

'I love ice-cream,' said Christy. 'Sometimes I even eat ice-cream with Vegemite.'

'I'm not allowed to eat sweets because I'm on a diet,' said Cheryl. 'All I eat is fruit and health food.'

'Nan won't buy us fruit. She says it bungs you up.'

The Leadhead's fridge was huge. It was yellow with rounded corners and a long silver handle that had probably once been part of a shark. Christy opened the door to an ice shard and frozen pea shower. She shook the snow from her hair and put an entire bucket of ice-cream in front of Cheryl on the table. Cheryl felt her heart beat faster. It was stupid to start your diet when you were there at the Leadhead's surrounded by ice-cream and whole walls of mobile kitchen cupboards full of who knew what.

One more time that afternoon and then tomorrow never again.

How bad could it be?

'Maybe I'll just have one plate of ice-cream.'

Christy groped round the back of the fridge and pulled out a milk bottle filled with brown fluid.

'You ever tried magic mushroom coffee?'

'I don't know,' said Cheryl. 'Once my stepfather made spaghetti carbonara with mushrooms from out the back and we all got cramps.'

'Carbon what? Gold tops don't give you cramps. They make you feel unreal. Once I had gold tops and rooted Nicandro and he grew a whole other head out his other shoulder. It was unreal.'

Cheryl gulped. Nicandro Ridley was ugly enough at the best of times. Two of him at once would be totally gross. Before he'd left Tantanoula High School, Nicandro squirted a zit into Lou's eyes down at the bus shelter and Lou swore she went blind for five whole minutes.

Had Christy Leadhead just said root?

'So?'

'So, what?'

'Do you want some gold tops or what?'

'I don't know if I should,' said Cheryl. 'I've only ever taken cigarettes and alcohol.'

'You are such a dag, Kiss. You don't take cigarettes and alcohol. You take trips or speed. You *drink* grog and you *smoke* fags. Got it? Didn't Louise Frances teach you anything?'

'Lou's only taken cigarettes and alcohol, too. Once she had a bite of a hash cookie from Mort Ramsbottom but she threw up straight afterwards so she couldn't tell if it worked.'

'Louise Frances told Shona on the bus she'd taken two whole tabs of acid.'

'Lou wouldn't know what a tab even was.'

(In truth it was Cheryl who was unsure what a tab might be, but that fact was available on a need-to-know basis.)

Talking about Lou made Cheryl's ears sweat. She changed the subject so Christy would stop giving her such a weird grin.

'Is that a photograph of your mother?'

'Fuck off!'

'Well how should I know what she looks like?'

'Use your brain. She'd look like Alice, wouldn't she? She'd look like Sonya or Stacie or Shona or Sapphire or Minnie or me or even Sammy. That's a picture of Gran. She doesn't even look like Dad.'

'What about the rest of the photos?'

'All Gran.'

'Even the ones from the magazines?'

'That was when she was Miss Dairy Queen.'

'She looks young.'

'She looks stupid. Anyone who wore dresses like that must have been fucking mental.'

Christy kicked her foot against the steel leg of the kitchen table and lit a cigarette. She smoked in between mouthfuls of Tang and ice-cream, curling her top lip when the ice particles froze her teeth. Cheryl tried not to stare at the magic mushroom water in the milk bottle as she swallowed orange ice-cream. It had an inch-thick film of scum across the top and the same again in sediment resting on the bottom.

'How old were you when your mum went away?'

'Four. Sammy was three. He remembers her better than me 'cos after she left she used to drop through the ceiling and speak to him while he was sleeping. Once I thought she came to me too, but it was only Shona stealing ciggies from under the pillow.'

'Don't take this the wrong way,' said Cheryl, 'but this ice-cream tastes like rubber. I'm actually having to *chew*. Is it past its use by?'

'Alice bought it on Tuesday when Sammy died,' Christy said matter of factly. 'She and the rest of my sisters got home from Bi-Mart in the ute and then I told 'em what happened to Sammy and then they forgot about the groceries till the next day. When I put the ice-cream back in the freezer it was fully melted.'

Cheryl felt like she had just eaten human flesh.

'I don't want any more.'

'Suit yourself. You comin' to look at my brother's room or not?'

Samuel Leadhead's bed was in the last caravan in the row and jutted from the wall with three others. His sisters' beds were detonations of tangled sheets and grey blankets, but Samuel's had been made with geometric precision. The stiff sheets were bound so tightly round the thin little bunk they looked like they needed a can opener.

'This is where Minnie, Sapphire, Shona and Sammy

sleep. Me and Alice and Sonya and Stacie got the one next door.'

'Who did that to his bed?'

'Sammy. That's how he always does it. He washes his own sheets whenever he wants. He says when he shut his eyes, all he can see are machines.'

'What's that got to do with his bed?' Cheryl was trying to ignore the present tense.

'I don't know. Sammy's weird. He likes everything back in the same place. Nan says you're an idiot to do anything you got to do again in a week's time. She says clean the floor today, it's only going be messed up again tomorrow. But Sammy is always real neat.'

Cheryl wondered how best to bring up the topic of the unopened packet of Chocolate Phantoms on top of the Leadhead family fridge. She looked around, fidgeting. The walls beside the girls' beds were covered in collages of cut-out pictures of Lance Seldom and Lurex Imperial, just like hers. Samuel's was empty except for a single poster of a motorbike flying through the air over a dirt mountain.

'I didn't know Samuel was into Motocross.'

'He wasn't,' said Christy. 'Dad put up that poster. He got it from one of his bike magazines and put it up before the police came.'

'How come?'

'I dunno.'

'Who cares if Samuel likes bikes or not?'

'I dunno. The police took everything. They went off with his school bag and his books and his clothes and his packs of cards and all the boxes under the bed. They even took stuff out of the bathroom he used. Soap and shaving gear and stuff. Nan said they probably would of cut down and taken his flowers if they'd known.'

'What flowers?'

'I'm not s'posed to tell.'

'Go on. Maybe we'll find a clue.'

Christy thought about it. Or was she only scratching?

'All right,' she said. 'But if you tell my Dad I'll freaking kill you.'

Christy led Cheryl through the swamp of discarded clothing on the floor. She zigzagged through beer cans and burst balloons and discarded spray jet nozzles and rusting tins of half-eaten dog food. She pulled up abruptly at the last caravan and covered Cheryl's face with her hands.

'Close your eyes and don't look until I tell you.'

When Cheryl regained her vision she'd been led into the scrub behind the Leadhead caravans and was dizzy from the curry of Christy's palms. There, in the afternoon heat and the red dirt, was an explosion of colour. Sunflowers usually fell over each other like drunks round a pool table. But Samuel Leadhead's stood at attention like lead soldiers.

Cheryl didn't know what to say. She removed a thorn from her nose under the pretence of rubbing while Christy levered her underpants from her bottom with two painted fingernails.

'Sammy had a chicken once,' Christy said eventually. 'It was the most perfect chicken you've ever seen. Most chickens have warts on their legs or bald necks or something sticking out of their feathers, but this one was perfect. It followed Sammy everywhere.'

Cheryl dreamed of a pet that loyal. Zeus always seemed like he had something better to do, even if it was only eating cow pats. Nylon was even worse. The one time Cheryl had forgotten to bolt his cage door he'd vanished. If Violet hadn't decided to wear her knee-high boots to the Vulpine baby shower, they might never have found him again.

Cheryl banged her head on top of her magpie helmet to see if it still hurt. It did.

'Do sunflowers really turn their heads to look at the sun?'

'Nan says it's like they're watching you. She says their eyes follow you up and down the hill. She said Sammy was only allowed to water them when Dad was out.'

Samuel's flowers gave Cheryl the creeps. Their hairy stalks were strapped at every inch to steel poles and the black pies of their heads looked too big for their bodies. They looked like starving children in Kampuchea. That's what Lou used to call Samuel on account of him being so thin.

Kampo.

'Hey, Kampo,' she'd yell across the library. 'Where's your wacko boyfriend?'

Samuel never answered but sometimes Bradley Spam would leap beaming from behind an atlas and gabble at the top of his lungs until Mrs Heche said this was a library not a disco and moved everyone along. Or had Samuel and Bradley been allowed to stay? Terrible. Only two days since he'd died and Cheryl was already forgetting what he looked like.

'How come your brother had to water the sunflowers when your dad was out?'

'Because we told him they were Alice and Stacie's.'

Christy's dress had become hooked up at the back. Each time she moved, Cheryl caught a glimpse of the horseshoe between her thighs and a pair of off-white underpants flopping against a lurid streak of white skin.

'Why did you tell your dad that?'

'Why do you think?' Christy said and spun one final time on her heel. 'I don't like it up here. I'm going back down to the kitchen to make chips. We got the ones with the vinegar flavour already cooked in. Come back down to the kitchen when you're finished looking for clues.'

Christy jiggled back through the scrub towards the caravans. Who would have thought a thin girl would jiggle so much when she moved? Violet's legs were the same. They were nothing but skin and bone but they still had stretchmarks at the top and they still cheesed up when she sat down. Cheryl had spotted a new blue lizard vein on her mother's thigh the previous summer and sprayed it with mosquito repellent for a joke. That was the last time she'd seen Violet wear anything shorter than long pants in public.

Cheryl picked a handful of seeds from one of the sunflower heads and smoothed a finger along the white stripe running from end to end. She and Reb once grew a marijuana seed in a pink cotton ball in one of Violet's shot glasses. Then they got caught shoplifting at the Bi-Mart and Cheryl flushed it down the toilet in case her bedroom got raided by some sort of squad. Then Reb had demanded Cheryl bring her passport to school to show Lou and the others.

'Freaky,' Lou said, studying the baby in the palm. 'You look like a witchetty grub. Mort said you had an identical twin but you absorbed it into your body before you were born. Is that true?'

'We weren't identical. We were premature,' said Cheryl. 'We came early and then my sister got a virus.'

'Virus schmirus,' said Lou. 'You ate your twin sister.'

'Give that back.'

'I want to show Mort.'

'GIVE IT BACK.'

After school that day, Cheryl had returned home and eaten two frozen banana cakes without even waiting for them to thaw. She'd grown so enormous she had to use Jackson's skinning knife to release the pressure. Cheryl was such a coward she used ice to numb her skin before cutting herself. But there was something immensely satisfying about the red scores down her inner arms and legs, something that almost made up for the gorging that came before.

Cheryl found Christy in the kitchen cooking chips on the Leadhead's grisly gas stove. She served them in newspaper just like Dora Knockers.

'Did you know chips are actually vegetables?'

'Bullcrap.'

'That means you could eat nothing but chips and still be on a diet.'

'That's absolute bullcrap, Kiss.'

Christy finished eating and threw her plate frisbee-style towards the sink. It clattered satisfactorily amongst the cutlery and tin openers.

'Now for the Christy Leadhead speciality,' she announced. 'Mushroom coffee with rum, cream and hundreds and thousands.'

The brown sludge in the tin mug tasted exactly how it looked. Cheryl hoped she'd throw up before she ingested any arsenic. Or was it strychnine? Violet explained it all on the news once but Cheryl had forgotten.

'Either way, that's what you're getting,' she shouted. 'A non-lethal dose of poison.'

'What?' Christy shouted back. She'd put The Lady Doctors on the ghetto blaster and was dancing on the dirt outside the kitchen door like a nut in a blender. 'DID? YOU? SAY? SOMETHING?'

Halfway through the song, Christy collapsed on the caravan steps, huffing. She took a deep swig from her tin mug and lit a cigarette.

'Every time I stop smoking I get as sick as a dog. Nan smokes two packets a day and hasn't ever been down the hospital. I give up all the time and go in more than anyone. Last time it was mushie burns. Me and Shona were making mushie coffee to watch the floods and she put it in the blender while it was still boiling and I turned it on and it sprayed all over my face. I got second-degree burns here, here and here. But I didn't cry or nothing. Down the Bi-Mart, the day after Sammy died, they said: "What are you doing in? Don't you even care?" And I said: "Who moved my cash box?" And I didn't cry or nothing. But inside I felt like someone had ripped out my lungs.'

Cheryl and Christy stared down the hill into the sewage plant's single flaming eye. There was a strangled crow from the rooster dump. After a while, Cheryl realised she'd been drawing back on her cigarette without even noticing. After a while, the sun disappeared and the Leadhead dam switched off with a sizzle. After a while, Cheryl realised the decapitated pink ballet slipper beside the kitchen caravan stairs was the funniest thing she'd seen in years.

'What's so hilarious, Kiss?'

For someone who didn't cry her eyes sure were puffy.

'Nothing,' snorted Cheryl.

'You're out of it.'

'Am not.'

'Are so.'

'Am not.'

'Walk in a straight line, then.'

Cheryl wasn't really feeling giddy enough to fall over but suspected Christy would appreciate the gesture.

'You're fucked, Kiss,' Christy screeched as Cheryl pedalled invisible bicycles upside down on the ground. 'You're fucked out of your tiny brain.'

'Am not,' said Cheryl pedalling again for good measure. 'I'm 100 perschent straight.'

Cheryl Jane Kiss wasn't the fat girl from school with no friends any more. She was fucked out of her tiny brain. Best of all, she'd tipped most of her coffee out when Christy was busy using a toilet roll as a microphone. Cheryl had been drunk before and knew for a fact that pretending to be drunk was a far superior experience. That way you could act like a complete idiot and still enjoy it. That way you could impress Samuel Leadhead's sister and still be alert enough to think of the best way to get hold of the unopened packet of Mint Slaps in the Leadhead cupboard.

Cheryl Kiss the arch imposter.

'You want some more coffee, Christy?'

Cheryl returned to the Leadhead kitchen under the pretence of hostessing. She managed to inhale the entire packet of Mint Slaps and eat another two scoops of refrozen ice-cream before Christy even started asking whether she was all right in there.

Was it Cheryl's imagination or were the gaps between the fridge and the van walls awash with dolls' heads? Had she drunk more of that coffee than she thought she had?

'Coming.'

Christy launched into a new dance move which involved tapping the ground on each side of her feet with a stick. She lasted only a few minutes before wheezing up a whopping green slug.

'I didn't smoke all day yesterday in honour of Sammy,' she gagged. 'See where it got me?'

'You've learned a valuable lesson,' said Cheryl, thinking Christy would like the *Whoops!* videotape in which Richard Variety-Slim's head caught fire beneath his helmet. Then remembering Christy's brother had just been burned alive and thinking 'how could you, Cheryl, how could you be such a disgusting pervert'.

'A valuable lesson,' mused Christy. 'Now that's a good one. If I wasn't so out of it I might even write it down.'

The Lady Doctors ended and Christy put on another tape. It was Furio Sullen and The Rampants. Cheryl was scandalised. She and Lou and Reb and the rest of them had pulled Furio stickers off their pencil cases as early as March. Sure 'Mr Machine' and 'Let Them Be Sexual' were OK songs, but Cheryl had stopped thinking about Furio's long blond hair during pillow-riding expeditions the moment she saw the paparazzi shot in *Working Woman*. There, in devastating full colour, was Furio staggering out of a nightclub wearing lipstick with a man dressed up as a woman climbing each arm.

'Spew,' said Cheryl. 'I can't believe you still own this tape.'

'"Mr Machine" and "Let Them Be Sexual" are OK songs,' said Christy, resuming her stick dance. 'Anyway, it's not my tape. It's Sammy's.'

When Lou and Reb and Cheryl and the rest of them had seen the *Working Woman* photo of Furio Sullen they'd scribbled over his face with a black biro until the page broke.

'What a waste,' Reb had said.

'What a faggot,' Lou had replied. 'I bet his little friends don't think it's a waste while he's bum jacking them.

'What exactly *is* bum jacking?' Cheryl asked Christy. She'd seen at least 15 possibilities in her stepfather's copy of *Accent On Anal* but still wasn't 100 per cent certain. It sounded as if tyre-changing equipment could be involved.

'It's when two men put things up each other's a-holes,' Christy said, dancing on. 'It could be a stick or a beet or anything. Once I saw an X-ray of a man's a-hole with a broken beer bottle inside it.'

Cheryl could believe it. After seeing *Accent on Anal*'s Double Dating section, she could believe anything.

'Dad and Nan and my sisters will be back soon,' Christy said with only a hint of a slur. 'You wanna have a bath or what?'

21

If You Don't Want To Party Don't Come To Fucking Mexico

Violet had been travelling the world for six years by the time Frank Anderson found her washed up in the Chicas Chicas Chicas bar on the Beach of the Dead. She wore a crimson sarong and a lurching cocktail umbrella. He had a pressed-linen shirt and a jaw you could set your watch by. When the fateful couple glanced at each other down the bar, a dozen trumpets sounded in unison.

'Goddamn mariachis,' Frank said by way of introduction. 'They're the natural enemy of the hangover. May I offer you a drink on the house?'

The Beach of the Dead was the main sand strip in the jet-setting sun trap of Cabo Roto at the feet of the jungled Sierra Enemigo. Once, the beach had been the site of a bloody battle between pirates and Indians. But by the time Violet arrived there hadn't been a severed hand washed up in the surf for years.

What she did discover was the highest concentration of post-operative Americans this side of the Amera Suspender Memorial Hospital.

Violet tottered off the overnight bus and was muscled aside by a gigantress with surgical scars on her torso as red and lively as hot plate rings. Contrary to the brochure Violet had rifled through in the LA bus terminal, the beach population of Cabo Roto did not consist exclusively of musclebound youngsters volleying inflatable beach balls to impossible princesses in hipster string bikinis. It was, instead, a race of aging obesities who had been taken apart and reassembled with scant attention to detail. Swimmers tent-pegged the sand with bright steel crutches and elaborate metallic girdlings. Sand castlers wore eye patches, sample bags and vast tracts of missing abdomen. Unmade human beds and scrambled flesh stretched all the way from the sweaty little park at Museo de las Calaveras to the beaming chicken above the hole-in-the-wall of El Camaron Feliz.

It was the eye of a flesh apocalypse.

The first thing Violet did after arriving at Cabo Roto was return to the bus depot and buy a ticket somewhere else. This was nothing new. In six years of travelling, she had remained stationary for no longer than seven months despite true love, burst appendix, true love, diplomatic immunity, true love, live speedway action, true love, that unforgettable quartet of trombonists, true love, musical dedications, true love, several marriages, true love, a Portuguese bullfighter who requested she remove her clothing via electronic interpreter, true love, nude waltzes on the ramparts of the Alhambra Palace and did anyone happen to mention true love?

In her six years on the road, Violet Martinelli née Variety-Slim nee Opus-Worthington had endured more true love than most people managed in a lifetime. But nothing had cured her international fidgeting.

What on earth was she looking for?

According to a computer dating form she'd tipsily completed in Los Angeles a day or two earlier, it was a successful man aged between 18 and 50 who enjoyed looking after himself and earning money. Mr Right would be honest, responsible, spontaneous, open-minded, athletic, *BUILT!!*, tertiary educated, classy, uninhibited, sincere, *involved in the film industry (?)* and have a wonderful sense of humour, *natural* blond highlights, a great personality and a huge ... BANK BALANCE! (ha! ha!) (just joking). No scars, goatees or cheating lying bastard stockbrokers with drug problems. African Americans and smokers OK.

OK?

But what of the international modelling career? What in the name of Amera Suspender had happened to that?

No-one was more surprised than Violet when her chosen profession collapsed in a heap only weeks after her arrival in Amsterdam. Especially since *the* English ex-pat photographer in the Netherlands had signed her up only hours after she hobbled into The Jiggle Bar. Shift Randhorn had taken one look at the crumpled Goddess with the suitcase and the red splattered clothing and demanded to see her sans swimsuit. Violet, of course, had taken one look at Randhorn's inflated waist, grizzled lips and infected neck folds and decided to cut her losses.

'How high?' she asked in a jet-lagged little voice, still mortified by what she was convinced she'd done to her cat.

How was she to know Shift's idea of 'a nice little head shot' varied wildly from the industry standard? How was she to know she would be replaced by an ice hockey cheerleader within a month? How was she to know Shift Randhorn would prove to be just as duplicitous as Richard Variety-Slim, Flavio Martinelli and 170 others?

She wasn't a goddamn clairvoyant.

In other news, Violet's plan never to speak to her mother again lasted exactly one month and two days after her arrival in Europe and exactly one hour and five minutes after her split with Shift. She rang home on a public telephone just down the road from The Torture Museum, as contrite as all hell.

Just one little return airfare, Mother?

Edna said her daughter was dead to her. Also that if Violet dared show her face at the family home again, she'd kill her. Also that if her father died of a heart attack any time soon it would be all her fault. And she'd kill her. Again, if necessary.

Was there something about the baby Jesus crying tears of actual wolf cub blood for Violet's sins?

Probably. Edna's rantings about burning salt, exploding whores and undergarments of actual thorns had been going in one of Violet's ears and out the other for 18 years now.

'Father?' said Violet, ringing back when she was sure her mother was at work.

But Mr Opus-Worthington could barely mumble the words 'test match' before hanging up. To be completely frank, the absentminded cricket fanatic wasn't 100 per cent who he'd just been talking to. He had a vague recollection of a young woman who'd once thrown an egg at the woman he'd married, but that was about it. Now where was that new teapot with the geese? Even the chipped one with the pansies would do.

Violet took the only civilised course of action and learned how to pull a beer. She learned how to froth a coffee and balance a bar tray and record a phone number up her left thigh while carrying five whole dessert plates up her right. She learned that no matter how widely you smiled at female customers, they'd never leave a tip.

Violet saved up enough money to fly home then forgot to buy a ticket. Free from the constraints of her mother she became distracted by a man who engraved her name on a grain of rice, by a man with eyelashes as long as hers were, by a man who rode a monocycle and spat fire, by a man who had written a novel in verse, by a man who did nothing but sit in his squat and read gossip magazines, by the head of the Happy Hotel and Home Supplies chain.

Who?

'Oh *him*,' Violet chastised Rashani long distance over the phone. 'I ditched him *eons* ago. Gotta run, I've got a big audition in less than an hour. Ciao ciao!'

Violet didn't really have a big audition. She hadn't been the one to ditch Norman Cunthrope from Happy Hotel and Home Supplies, either. He'd upped and slammed the door to their Barcelona B&B with no explanation whatsoever. It wasn't as if she'd intended to keep the money. It was Norman's fault for spying instead of going out for fatty octopus like he'd said. What was wrong with men paying women for sex, anyway? Not in a grubby, prostitution way. In an 'I know this won't make up for what you have just endured but please accept it as a humble and completely inadequate gesture of my gratitude and remorse' sort of way. Men were impossible. They were the most selfish, disgusting, odorous, beastly creations on the planet.

Of course that was no reason to refrain from marrying great swathes of the species.

Violet met Richard Variety-Slim at a nightclub in Monaco. The Formula One test driver proposed to her from deep within the panther skin waterbed flooding his trackside motor home. Violet was barely conscious when she answered in the affirmative and completely catatonic by the time he consummated their union.

'Sugar!' she cried late the next morning when she finally woke. 'That was the worst night's sleep I've had in years.'

Then: 'Who the hell are you?'

Richard thought she was being amusing and introduced himself as her fiancé. Violet double-taked at the ginormous rock on her finger and decided to keep her mouth shut. The happy couple were married and divorced within six months. Violet commemorated the death of their love by taking up with Variety-Slim's chief engineer, but her ex-husband did not deal with the separation so productively. His driving became nothing short of maniacal and he was dropped from the team after mowing down a clutch of autograph-seekers at a racetrack in Japan. Happily, he discovered stunt driving and — thanks to the *Whoops!* video series — achieved a level of fame and fortune that put his former Formula One peers to shame. The footage of Richard Variety-Slim learning a valuable lesson with his head on fire beneath his helmet became the most watched episode in *Whoops!* history.

'She'll be sorry,' he thought as the surgeons removed the bandages from the last of his skin grafts and he signed up to become the face of Hollywood Fire Extinguishers. 'She'll come crawling back.'

But by then Violet was teetering on the brink of her second marriage.

This time, of course, it was true love. The fact that she'd just used up the last of the money she'd got hawking her engagement ring had nothing to do with it. Flavio Martinelli might not have spoken much English but he was by far the most charming man Violet had ever met. Apart from holding down a respectable job as a taxation accountant, he performed stunts in the boudoir Violet had always assumed were urban myths.

'Was good?' he'd ask after emerging slavering from between Violet's depilated thighs.

Signora Martinelli was never able to bring herself to answer. But in her conversations with Rashani, she couldn't help but drop the odd hint.

'He's very *effective,*' she said long distance from Milan.

'Great,' said Rashani, who'd just hung a tampon from her rear-vision mirror because her father had said they were disgusting (she told him it was going to stay right where it was until he got used to it). 'You don't know how unbelievably thrilled I am for you.'

'You should hear him try to say my name. He can't do it. He sounds *so* cute.'

'Great,' said Rashani, who'd also just dropped out of uni and turned her first trick in order to help support her decaying mother.

'He calls me "America" because he thinks that's where people speak English. He's *so* cute.'

'Great,' said Rashani whose next client was standing outside her front door in flared jeans and an I Heart Spam T-shirt. (At least Mistress Vanda only sent customers from the university campus.)

'When he's away on business he always rings when he gets back to his hotel even if it's 3.30 in the morning and he's a little bit drunk.'

'I hope you don't think that's cute,' said Rashani.

'But I can't sleep until I know he's home.'

Violet divorced Flavio after discovering his frequent business trips were actually a transsexual prostitution addiction. She declined to provide her friend with these details, even though Rashani would have sympathised completely. The fledgling sex worker had decided there was no accounting for men and their sexual proclivities. Winston Birch, Duke Blazer and Mike Le Cornu now had permanent weekly bookings, even though all three had girlfriends who routinely put out and — she knew this to be a fact — sometimes even swallowed.

The night the divorce came through, Violet drank a gallon of strawberry liquor in a Milanese bar with a waiter who introduced her to the rest of the staff as 'name name-name' because he couldn't pronounce Violet Opus-Worthington.

'You want to get on this?' she'd shrieked, shoving her knee into a stranger's face while dancing. 'You want to get on this?'

For the life of her, she could not recall his reply.

The marriages slowed after The Italian Incident, but Violet continued processing gentlemen at a rate of knots. The messiness of these liaisons necessitated constant relocations and Violet saw the world without realising it. She caught buses and trains and planes and taxi cabs in emotional El Niños. Her only connections to the outside world were occasional calls to Rashani and Amanda and the headlines on other traveller's newspapers:

Probe Lifts Lid On Mystery Death

There Are Two Dogs In Amera Suspender's Life

PUSSYCAT AFGHAN LOUNGER!

'What's that when it's at home?' Violet asked the man reading the newspaper attached to this extraordinary announcement.

'What do you want it to be?' replied Percy Slang — soon to be the inventor of The Most Life-like Female Doll Ever Created.

And off she went again.

The years went by. In Thailand she was arrested by the police for walking drunk on a freeway. In Poland, a tourism official said 'why did you come here if you didn't bother learning the language?'. In Kingston she got food poisoning after snapper stew and cigars. A Jamaican doctor in surf gear pulled her eyelids over the back of her head and compressed her stomach. He asked 'what happened to you, man?' while she vomited and laughed while the one living fish in the hospital tank picked the ribs of the two dead ones.

Fellow travellers asked where she was from. They asked what accent was that, was her hair a wig and could their little girl have one of her rice cakes. (Inevitably it shattered and the child would howl like a hyena). Violet travelled alongside a woman with eyeshadow as thick as paste, alongside a Russian poodle called Bella, alongside a Gypsy cardplayer whose backside was as wide as his banjo, alongside wrestlers with flashing lights in their shoes, alongside a Ukrainian juggler with a Canadian accent, alongside a black man with a cigarette who danced by putting on his coat and letting it slip off his shoulders.

Reeking of duty-free perfumes, Violet flew behind a child with a huge hairstyle to cover the fact that she was missing an ear. Mid-flight the child turned to speak to her through the gap in the seats.

'What do you do all day?' she said as the air hostesses performed a fashion parade down the aisle. 'How come I've never seen you around?'

Violet told the child she'd been travelling so long she'd realised the world was nothing but soup.

People she didn't know began to tell her she looked tired.

On the main street of the Mexican resort town of Cabo Roto, Violet shoved a bus ticket to New York into the compost of her handbag and turned a full 360 degrees on the spot. There were seven-and-a-half hours before the bus was due to leave. Her high-heeled sandals drilled holes in the dirt. Her head swam. Eventually her eyes thickened against the glare and she was able to see past the sea of scrabbled shoulders down the road to the fringed awning of the bar. Violet saluted and disappeared in a puff of dust. Behind her, the madman from the bus terminal bellowed as he squatted to examine the two bite marks her shoes had left in the road.

Once again the earth had been savaged by giant snakes.

The first thing newcomers noticed about Cabo Roto's infamous Chicas Chicas Chicas bar was that it had seen what was known architecturally as 'better days'. The new management team was attempting to transform the former strip joint into a family-friendly eatery, but even without the nipple-tassled dancers and their trained chihuahuas, there were still plenty of reminders that the monthly promotion at Chicas Chicas Chicas had not always been Third Child Eats Free. Its phones were tapped and its foundations bubbled. A flaking mirror ball shed dandruff diamonds over what had once been Pussy Podium. The lighting box was filled with medical-strength pornography. Weathered leather g-strings had fallen (or been hurled) behind the soft drink dispenser and were slowly insinuating themselves into the machine's arthritic innards.

'If I'd wanted a can of lukewarm soda I would have asked for one,' clacked a hugely wounded American as the temperamental dispenser choked on another pair of elderly undergarments. 'Now apologise to my wife. After everything she's been through, the last thing she deserves is to be insulted with a room-temperature beverage.'

To date, no customers had complained about the taps in the shape of women's bosoms or the beer levers in the shape of erect male organs. This was not because they were open-minded or the least bit 'swingy'. It was because the vast bulk of Chicas Chicas Chicas customers were half-blind with sunscreen or disease or from living far longer than they really and truly deserved.

Violet knew none of these things as she walked into the bar, kicked her suitcase into the booth furthest from daylight and ordered a breakfast tequila.

Actually, make that three breakfast tequilas.

Seven-and-a-half hours in crapulous, third world freaksville. How would she cope? The bar was filled with raw chickens in Hawaiian shirts. Did none of these surgical exhibitionists have any shame in their appearance at all? Once, in Turkey, Violet had overscratched a mosquito bite and hadn't left her room for a week in case strangers thought she had the pox.

She stared deeply into her glass to avoid making eye contact. The last thing she wanted was to get caught up in a conversation with a patchworked retiree or some plate-faced Mexican who only came up to her cleavage.

Then she took a second glance at the stranger in the immaculate shirt beside the We Use Boiled Water In Our Ice sign and realised there wasn't a hint of a sweat moon beneath his armpits.

'Where am I?' she thought in a sudden rush of bus-lag. And for a full five seconds, her brain offered nothing but blur. Then the mariachis sounded and Frank Anderson introduced himself and before anyone knew any better, Violet was taking her fourth tequila in the hotel suite Frank shared with his younger brother, Ben, 30 minutes south of the city.

Destiny is always easy to identify with hindsight.

Violet, for instance, was to write in a postcard to Rashani that she knew from the outset Frank Anderson was The One.

'The moment I laid eyes on him,' were her exact words. 'Oh. And don't forget you promised to let me know if Dad dies.'

Violet had just told a whopping great lie. She hadn't thought Frank was The One any more than she thought she'd be screaming for her mother in the emergency ward of a Cabo Roto hospital a mere 10 months down the track. The woman lurched into men's lives like an L-plated rollerskater.

But fatal errors in judgment are always easy to identify with hindsight.

At 4.30 p.m. on her first afternoon in Mexico, Violet untangled herself from Frank's tan and rifled through the bathroom cupboard. She wasn't entirely sure what she was looking for, but knew for a fact that if she found syringes she was walking out immediately.

'Violet Opus-Worthington is not,' she announced to her reflection, 'I repeat, *is not*, getting mixed up with another merchant junkie.'

Not after Buzz Instrument and that interminable queuing out the back of The Barbados Bar.

Buzz was the reason Violet had left LA as well as the reason she had placed her personal advertisement for Mr Right right in the middle of *The Financial Champion* where he'd be sure to notice it. Sure, Buzz knew exactly which cocktail lounges would ring up cocaine on his company credit cards. And sure, his company had paid through the nose for Violet's sudden taste in 'assorted refreshments'. But nothing made up for the humiliation of discovering Buzz and a cocaine waitress in flagrante delicto in The Barbados Bar's unisex bathroom. Buzz insisted the moaning redhead had simply been investigating a malignant mole, but, by that stage in her career, Violet knew a blow job when she saw it. She had nothing but contempt for women who faked orgasm during fellatio. Men were stupid but they weren't that stupid. Except, perhaps, for Buzz Instrument.

The cupboard in the Anderson brothers' bathroom contained hair dye, aftershave and eyebrow wax. Every towel was geometrically arranged over the rails and the end of the toilet paper was folded into an arrow. There was a sign on the bathroom tap which said Do Not Drink and a perfect pyramid of mineral water bottles beneath the sink.

'Well,' Violet concluded while soaping her nethers in the shower. 'If Frank Anderson has any skeletons in his closet, they're certainly going to be very tidy ones.'

Despite what she would later tell Rashani, Violet didn't think her liaison with the Chicas Chicas Chicas barman would continue longer than a night or three at the most. Cabo Roto was a dump and Frank Anderson was only a barman. Even if he did drive a convertible car, live in an expensive hotel and look disconcertingly like a young Dick Lyndon. ('Onion Tears' was Violet's absolute favourite song in the whole world. It was so KICKY.)

Violet studied herself in the bathroom's vast range of reflective surfaces and tilted the door until she'd multiplied herself to the power of infinity. She struck a photogenic pose and reminded herself to keep her lips apart when she smiled. The worst thing about shacking up with a new man was trying to hold onto your Number Twos until they'd left the house. You needed an interval of at least an hour to be on the safe side. Frankly, she was amazed she'd never blown a bowel.

Violet returned to the bedroom to scrutinise the sleeper. The resemblance with Dick Lyndon was truly uncanny. He had big hands and a chest like an anatomical model's. Taller than she was by maybe a head and a half. When he'd whispered to her in Spanish, she'd swooned right on cue, even though he admitted he'd only recited the Chicas Chicas Chicas lunch menu.

Frank opened his eyes to find Violet's tequila breath hovering all over his face.

'Wow,' he mumbled. 'You're so intense.'

'I was just looking for my hair clip,' said Violet.

'Don't worry. I like intense.'

'But I really was looking for my hair clip.'

'Oh. Right. Is it long and thin with a spike on one end?'

'That's the one.'

'I think it may have set up permanent residence in the back of my neck.'

Violet averted her gaze as he rolled over and performed a citizen's extraction.

'Why don't you go down and take a look at the beach?' he said, closing his eyes. 'I've got a couple of phone calls to make up here, then I'll be right down.'

He was snoring again in seconds.

Violet swung away, then returned to pull a stiff hotel sheet over Frank's exposed bits. Men's private parts were disgusting. They were the missing link between water and land life. Give them four scrawny legs and they'd be right at home in a fish tank eating raw meat off the end of a skewer. Shift Randhorn had owned an axolotl. Apart from looking repulsive, it had all the personality of a rubber sandal.

Out in the lounge room, Violet dug a bikini out of her suitcase and commenced one last search for Frank's wallet. She clearly remembered seeing it at the bar. It was new, black, and raining credit card receipts. Surely he hadn't hidden it during their brief dodgem from bar to bedroom? It was hardly worth sticking around if he was the suspicious type. Violet valued trust in a man above all else except maybe the ability to tango. And answer the phone pleasantly even if he'd just woken up. And not open taxi doors and expect a woman to scramble over to the far side of the back seat. And of course to provide adequate financial compensation for sexual favours.

Lovely Drake Barb had once given Violet $1000 to buy herself something nice after she'd provided nothing more strenuous than a little light hand relief. Drake Barb was one of Buzz Instrument's colleagues down at Sunset Boulevard Securities and Investments. She'd felt terribly guilty about the hand job in question but it wasn't as if either he or Buzz were The One or anything. Then she'd caught Buzz with The Barbados Bar waitress, and realised it had all been fate. That's why it was important to follow your instincts. That's why it was important to do the very first thing that came into your mind without ever worrying about the consequences.

'Live first and worry later,' she thought as the lift descended through the spinal column of the white hotel.

'Actually,' she thought, emerging in a lobby studded with immaculate guests in pastel-coloured linen. 'Live first, then live *more* later.'

See? Who said you needed to go to university to know what was what? Who cared that the freshly snubbed Ian Beanland had called her a bimbo in front of the entire inter-school social? Who cared about Rashani always getting higher marks in English even though all she did all day was talk about FUCKING? (It's not as if she could do anything BUT talk.) Edna told the neighbours her daughter was too stupid to do anything but end up barefoot and pregnant in a home for delinquent girls and Violet couldn't have cared less. She barely remembered the time her mother had forced her to use a potty as a grown up so she could see the filth her body produced. She thought nothing of her mother's flaking hair line and her obsession with girls who smelled between their legs and the way she insisted on taking showers in your underwear and bra even though the wet elastic rubbed welts into your flesh and and and . . .

The private sand strip out the front of the Hotel Josefina was nothing like the human stew at The Beach of The Dead. There were chlorinated pools in flowing ink spots and four neat rows of plastic beds beneath twig and bark umbrellas. There were uniformed attendants offering beach towels, cocktails in half-coconut shells and, in Violet's case, incredulous wolf-whistles.

Violet arranged herself on the sunbed nearest the attendants and ordered an afternoon tequila. The white beach stretchers weren't nearly as comfortable as they appeared from a distance. Their cross strappings were made out of plastic rope and dug into her flesh. But at least it was hot. Four-thirty in the afternoon and the sun was still blistering. Violet hated the cold. What was the point of having a body like hers if you had to hide it beneath layer upon layer of clothing? That was the problem with Europe. In winter you ended up looking like a zeppelin. Thermal underwear wasn't an option. Violet had tried it one year in Warsaw and nearly given a Fiat salesman a heart attack from the static electricity. Also it pilled. If a man ran his hand up a woman's thigh he didn't expect an obstacle course. And what if he thought those hard fabric pimples belonged to *her*? Christ, what a nightmare.

Violet adjusted her sunglasses and gazed down the runway of her stomach. The Hotel Josefina's private beach strip was a reserve for men who looked just like Frank. They rolled up from the sea still smelling of aftershave, their silver hair shining and the skin around their eyes creased like a bull elephants. Violet watched them stamp their feet in the sand and shake the gravel from their investment magazines, wrapping their wide hands around invisible steering wheels. The women hadn't deteriorated as badly as the ones on the public beach in town, but Violet was still shocked at the dimples and stains. These were the sort of women who gave wives a bad name. Did they not own mirrors? Full body sarongs? An overprescription of sleeping tablets to put themselves out of their misery?

Ha!

If Violet ever reached an age when she let herself go and no longer cared she'd do herself in for sure.

A wobbling snake in a jewelled one-piece narrowed her eyes on her way from the beach to the pool.

Bitch, Violet muttered under her breath. Fat bitch.

She ordered another tequila, then fell asleep with a lit cigarette still burning between her painted fingernails. In her dream the snake woman with the jewels emerged shining from the pool and lay beside her on the plastic beach bed. They kissed on the lips and it was like an electrocution.

Violet woke with a shudder. The only thing worse than going to seed and no longer caring was waking up one day and discovering you'd turned lesbo. Women who turned lesbo could kiss male attention goodbye for good. No-one was going to look twice at a crew cut and boilersuit. Except maybe another homo.

'I just rang Amanda and she says you're living in a share house and playing the acoustic guitar,' Violet said into the phone in the hotel lobby. 'You haven't turned lesbo have you?'

'Do you know what time it is here?' Rashani croaked after the delay. She could hear the crash of the surf in the background and the electronic drone of foreign nature between the words.

'Well are you?'

'Actually for the last week or so I've been an official radical celibate. Where are you, you bloody pisspot?'

'Mexico.'

'Good for you. Are you ever going to wire me back that cash I lent you last year?'

Violet slammed the receiver down in disgust. Here she was, travelling the world on a shoestring and Rashani was asking *her* for money. She wasn't fooling anyone with that radical celibate crap, either. Everyone had always suspected Rashani was a closet lemon. She was always pulling up her dress and streaking through the half-built housing block out the back of the school. Once, during a game of Truth or Dare, she'd said that if the only other person left in the world was another woman she'd probably let her eat her out.

'Don't have a spaz attack, Dewey,' Rashani had said, trying to open a second bottle of beer with her eye socket. 'I'm sure it'd feel roughly the same if you kept your eyes closed.'

Violet had been sickened beyond belief.

High up in the hotel, Frank Anderson watched the vision in the tiny black bikini stroll from the phone booth through a pair of duty-free binoculars. He balanced on the white plastic table on the verandah to get a better view and tried to remember where he'd left his wallet.

In his slapstick way, his brother phoned from the cafe wanting to know whether Violet had a pouch.

'She's Australian, isn't she?'

'She's better looking than you are.'

'Find out whether she's part marsupial and report back to me at once.'

'Can't. She's gone back to sleep on the beach. I think she's jet-lagged.'

'What about tonight?'

'What about tonight?'

'Am I right in presuming you will be standing me up for dinner?'

'Are you kidding?' Frank said without a pause. 'Eight-thirty. Muchos Tacos. You've *got* to meet her.'

Frank used the Trojan-Enz brand of condoms.

Ben alerted Violet to this fact during dinner when he produced one over the chilies en nogada (he'd discovered Frank's wallet making a pass at the underwear beneath the Chicas Chicas Chicas drink dispenser).

'Surely you think the brand name a stroke of genius?'

Frank and Violet blushed.

'I mean, who, apart from me, would voluntarily go into a chemist and ask for a packet of Micro-Tips?'

Violet would have liked to answer, but was still speechless at the discovery that Frank and his weird brother weren't bartenders at all. They were aspiring property developers who owned two bars on the west coast of the U S of A. Chicas Chicas Chicas was their first venture into foreign territory and they planned to stay in Cabo Roto until its transformation was complete. In all likelihood, they were loaded.

Violet hoped the sea breeze wasn't blowing her hair into too hideous an arrangement. The tables at Muchos Tacos were outdoors on the beach, right down near the water. She would have preferred air conditioning but Frank obviously got off on the nature thing. Violet could live with that. At that precise moment she thought she could live with just about anything. Except for the goddamn sea breeze. And maybe Frank's weird brother, Ben.

'There's no sour cream,' she said, pushing an immense green chilli round her plate with a fork.

'That's why we come here,' said Ben. 'This place is authentic. No Tex Mex dairy extras here. Not at Muchos Tacos.'

Strings of cheese dangled from each side of his mouth like tentacles.

'I think you have some food on your face,' Violet said quietly.

'WHAT?' bellowed Ben.

'Some food. On your face.'

'WHY THAT'S A BALD-FACED LIE.'

'Oh, leave her alone,' said Frank. He was laughing so hard his eyes had disappeared. (You'd think by now the novelty of his little brother would have worn off.) 'If our guest wants sour cream I'm sure we can find her some.'

'I'm all right,' Violet smiled bravely.

'She's all right,' Ben repeated in exactly the same voice. 'Isn't that the meat on a stick man?'

The old Mexican had a wide chest and hairless armpits. He wore a sliver of meat sticks over a singlet with an iguana singlet. He said something in Spanish and waved an arrow over the loaded plates on the table.

'Trojan-Enz are yesterday's condom,' Ben said. 'Micro-Tips, on the other hand, are a man's passport to integrity. Do you happen to stock any Micro-Tips, my good fellow?'

'Ben,' said Frank. Laughing.

'No? Well how about Fumbly Guys or Stay Downs? Could you sell me a packet of Living In Eternal Hopes or

Quite Honestly This Packet Hasn't Been In My Wallet For More Than Five Years?'

The meat-seller gave Ben a quizzical look then reached into his bag and produced a beef-sized slab of chicken.

'At last!' said Ben. 'I'll take half a dozen.'

He did too. What's more he ate every last mouthful even though he'd ordered more food than Violet and Frank put together.

'What do you think?' he said, popping his shirt and extroverting his white belly into a full moon.

'Very nice,' said Violet wishing she had someone to roll her eyes at.

'It's my nest egg,' said Ben. 'It'll be worth a fortune one day. Please don't touch the exhibit, madam. All breakages must be paid for.'

That night, Violet and Frank had sex three times in rapid succession. Afterwards, Violet asked whether Ben had any, you know, problems.

Frank laughed.

'Only other people,' he said. 'They just don't get him.'

As the couple embarked on their fourth mission for the evening, Violet promised herself she'd start getting Ben immediately. Frank would appreciate her efforts and realise that if they got married it would be fine for his little brother to drop by whenever he wanted — provided he gave them enough notice, of course. Imagine Ben at the wedding, Violet thought, slurping drunkenly at Frank's . . . *God what was that?* . . . Oh well. Anderson Junior might have to be restrained during the speeches but at least a tux and cummerbund would cover the nest egg.

The next morning, a maid knocked on the hotel door while Violet and Frank were still at it. 'Ahorita no, por favor,' Frank shouted.

Ben had already left for the bar. Violet had heard the clanging.

She spent the day on the beach, making a special effort not to fall asleep in the sun in case she dreamed of the snake woman again. In the afternoon she climbed into her best yellow dress and caught a cab to Chicas Chicas Chicas.

'I looked up the CIA file on Australia,' Ben whispered while Frank was smoothing down his hair in the office.

'How did you do that?'

'I can't say for security reasons. All I am at liberty to reveal is that I know who you are and I know what you've done.'

Violet panicked. There were so many things Frank didn't know. Her marriages. Those photographs. Delilah, The Most Life-like Female Doll Ever Created. Percy Slang really had turned out to be a piece of work. When the alleged artist had asked Violet to model nude for a new range of inflatable women, he'd said it was only for biological reference points. Then she'd passed a sex shop six months later and come face to face with her identical twin in full polyvinyl.

Shocking was hardly the word.

Violet desperately wanted to be one of the people who *got* Frank's younger brother but clearly Ben was insane and jealous and downright spiteful enough to expose her before she even got a foot in the door.

'Hello, beautiful,' said Frank.

'Hello, darling,' said Violet.

'Has Ben been making you feel at home?'

'Of course, darling.'

'I told her your nickname is Stinky Linty,' said Ben. 'Also that you fart in spas.'

'He's the original cupid isn't he, babycakes,' said Frank, putting an arm round his date's shoulder.

'I need a drink,' said Violet.

Frank asked the waitress to fix everyone cocktails then showed Violet his collection of photographs of him and his brother with famous people. Somehow Ben had managed to take the pictures as well as appearing in them. You could see his arm arcing into infinity at the side of the frames. Frank said their father had offered to invent some sort of arm-extender so both his boys could stand at ease in their celebrity photos, but so far the old man's efforts had all been too bulky to incorporate in after-five outfits.

Did the Anderson brothers really know so many film stars, singers and lycra-clad dancers?

'Not really,' said Frank. Sometimes we get invited to things because of the bars. That's all. Really we're just a couple of glorified autograph-seekers.'

'But it certainly makes us look like we're in the loop, doesn't it? Isn't that Him? Her? Those Guys from That Thing? MY GOD THERE'S FRANK AND BEN ANDERSON!'

Violet was impressed. Amera Suspender appeared not once but three times in Ben and Frank's collection. *Violet Opus-Worthington was drinking cocktails with people who got invited to the same parties as Amera Suspender.*

'Here,' Ben said, putting his arm round Violet and extending his camera arm in front of them like a boom. 'No-one back home will believe we met the charmingly beautiful Violet Opus-Worthington unless we have documentary evidence.'

Maybe he wasn't so bad after all.

'What till I fix my hair,' Violet said, fiddling urgently while looking into the bar chrome.

'Say queso!'

And simultaneously their pupils cringed at the flash.

Later, Cheryl would steal the photograph from beneath her mother's bed and study the tall man in the suit and the short man with the belly looking for clues. Later, Violet would look at the strange shape the word made her mouth and berate herself for not sticking to the new smile she'd developed in the gymnasium in West Hollywood. 'Queso' reduced what she liked to call her Visible IQ by at least 20 or 30 points.

Frank and Ben moved as a unit. They ate in at The Fajita Republic (Our Motto Is Great Everything) and took out from The Happy Shrimp and Mr Fish. They carried their bottles of tequila down to Playa de los Muertos to watch the wounded Americans rotate their plastic sunbeds to reduce the shade on their overflowing bodies and to cheer on the short men selling Coco Bananas or carrying dogs beneath their arms like briefcases.

Ben said The Beach of the Dead was better than colour television.

But what about the gasoline, the sewage and the urine? What about the lost children trapped in pink inflatable rings and the endless parade of butchered flesh?

'Yesterday I saw a woman on the beach with one of those *bags* hanging out of her body,' said Violet. 'What about her?'

'It's all good,' said Ben.

He turned to stare as a girl in white shorts crossed the road.

'Tell your brother he's a perve,' Violet said to Frank.

'But I'm just watching shapes against light,' Ben said, genuinely taken aback.

Frank bought Violet a silver hipflask with green jewels. He didn't buy it from one of the thong-wearers by the market road. He bought it from an air-conditioned shop and made sure she saw the certificate of authentication.

Ben said 'anything you can do' and bought Violet a string of plastic Christmas lights in the shape of boots. As he handed them over wrapped in newspaper, his pointy side teeth shone like a rat's.

'Just One Mexican Minute,' he said.

'Notice my hands never leave my wrists.'

'You call this a Sunday?'

Ben never made any sense at all. Probably he'd been adopted. Frank was tall and clean whereas Ben was short and scratchy. Frank asked Violet was she sure the sun wasn't too hot whereas Ben said 'so what if I like fish?'

'Hey Violet.'

'Yes, Benjamin?'

'Which do you prefer, flour or corn tortillas?'

Then, before she could answer, he'd yell 'SAY FLOUR' and roll round the floor like it was the funniest thing he'd heard all week.

'Well, it was,' he'd say when he finally composed himself. 'How do y'all like those Christmas lights in the shape of boots? From now on they'll always remind me of what's her name.'

Ben spotted Wing Boy while they were eating Super Chicken at The Beach of the Dead. He was a goblin child with curling black hairs over his hunched back and huge plastic floaties tied to his scrawny upper arms. Wing Boy, Ben called him. It's a bird! It's a plane! No, it's Wing Boy! (For all natural emergencies requiring flotation.)

Ben swung Wing Boy in circles while his parents laughed and jabbered in tongues. Violet sighed tragically. A child like that should have been drowned at birth like a puppy. It would have been kinder than forcing it to live in this cruel, cruel world. She hoped whatever Wing Boy had wasn't contagious and tried to ignore Ben as he bowled up from the surf bearing the limp corpse of yet another bikini top shedding supportive cups.

'Yuck,' she screeched as he flicked seaweed strands over her suntan. 'People are looking, Frank. Say something to your brother. He's a grown man, for God's sake.'

But Frank just laughed as Ben paraded past wearing the abandoned bikini as a wig.

Frank's bathers were almost as small as Violet's, but fat Ben always swam in long shorts and a T-shirt. As he pranced about in the bikini cap, Violet wondered what lay beneath the saturated wahooti shirts and dripping yibbida yabbidas. Not stretchmarks, please God. She'd seen a man with stretchmarks once and had to run for a toilet.

The man with the meat on a stick walked up and gave Frank a dinner voucher for two at a new hotel in the resort wasteland in the north.

Ben said: Don't mind me. I'll leave you two lovebirds in peace for the night.

Frank said: You sure, Ben?

Violet said: It's all right, Frankie. We don't want to leave your brother home all on his lonesome now, do we? We can all go together.

And even she was surprised at the high serrations in her voice.

As it turned out, the restaurant on the dinner voucher did not exist. Frank drove round and round the pre-fabricated ghost town on the hem of the town and found only the dark cement shells of unfinished hotels.

'See?' said Ben accusingly.

'See what?' said Violet, depressed by the towering husks and unfinished streetlights.

'Just *SEE.*'

Frank laughed and said if you kids can't keep quiet in the back you can walk. He pulled the rented car up outside a restaurant called Mariachi Loco on the highway.

'Can't we find somewhere quieter?' said Violet.

Ben tilted his head questioningly.

'I SAID "CAN'T WE FIND SOMEWHERE QUIETER?"'

'SOMEWHERE QUIETER YOU SAY?' Ben bawled back.

'YES. SOMEWHERE QUIETER.'

'WHY?' he screamed over a convoy of passing semitrailers.

At Mariachi Loco, Violet and Ben and Frank ordered tres mexicanos platos and tres margaritas sin hielo and then tres mas margaritas sin hielo and then just a few more margaritas without ice to wash the other half-dozen down.

'What's the worst thing that could happen if you actually drank the water?' Violet asked recklessly. 'How bad could a little bit of ice, be?'

'Not bad at all if you enjoy faecal matter with your meal,' said Ben. 'Not to mention the contraction of various exotic gastric disorders that require the digital examination that dare not speak its name.'

Violet squealed and sent her knife and fork flying. She had no idea what Ben was talking about but felt certain it was devastatingly amusing.

'Ben,' said Frank wiping tears from his eyes. 'You really are too much.'

Violet's bladder ached from all the squealing. It was fantastic. She was finally getting Ben Anderson. Not just going through the motions, REALLY GETTING HIM. Was Frank watching? Did he realise what was going down right in front of his own eyes? Violet looked across the table at the tall brown man in the creaseless white linen and the round speckled one swimming in hibiscus. The world was so perfect she could have wept. She could have sung. She could have leaned forward and kissed both brothers right on the mouth.

But at the last minute she thought better of it and danced topless on the table instead.

The mariachi musicians whooped and crowed. The entire restaurant roared. Violet felt two sets of Anderson eyes romping over her body as she twisted and shimmied.

'Never had a lesson!' she pealed over the music and the stream of trucks shaking Mariachi Loco's enormous glass windows. 'I never had a fucking lesson!'

If the Anderson brothers were shocked, they showed no sign of it. The bristling barman had blindfolded them with yellow and lime green ponchos. He'd wrenched back their heads and was pouring tequila straight down the backs of their throats.

The brothers emerged spluttering.

'Guess what number I'm thinking of,' Ben coughed.

'Fifty-seven,' Frank coughed back.

'Close,' said Ben. 'It was 13.'

And then he and Frank were up on the table dancing too, and then a barmaid with a cigar brought a whole tray of shot glasses, and then a wounded tourist led Violet in an unwieldy Lindy hop, and then someone fell into someone else's lap, and then another poncho barman was pouring more tequila and then everything became too fused with everything else to have any sort of shape of its own.

By the time Ben and Frank walked out past the 12-piece band, the whites of their eyes were stitched with blood. Ben said the best thing about Mexico was the way the food tasted just like the music and fell asleep standing up against the car door. Frank said he was just fine to drive then drove slowly and deliberately into a telegraph pole.

Violet thought it was the funniest thing that had ever happened in her entire life.

After that, the days went on and on. Frank and Ben stopped checking in on the Chicas Chicas Chicas bar and Violet accidentally put her postponed bus ticket to New York through the wash. It was as if they were under a spell. Sometimes they started drinking at breakfast and didn't stop until they fell into bed or ran into another telegraph pole. The hire car looked as if it had been beaten up. Frank grew huge black eye circles and Ben wore the same shirt for ten days straight. Were there even days of the week?

There was a night when Violet used Frank's high-powered hair drier and it exploded into a Roman candle of sparks and melted plastic. She'd watched it in slow motion, not letting go for seconds and seconds.

There was an afternoon when a birthday card arrived at the hotel from Amanda.

Happy birthday to you
Happy birthday to you
Happy birthday dear Violet
Happy birthday to you

The card arrived with love from three people Violet had never met. Amanda's husband and two children. Was it possible for Amanda to have given birth? Wasn't she only 17? Had Violet really been in Mexico long enough for mail to arrive?

The glands around her neck swelled up like puffer fish.

There was a night when Ben wouldn't stop staring. Violet lit a cigarette and Ben stared. Violet sipped through a curly straw and Ben stared. Violet went to the toilets to see if she had a disfiguring chunk of livestock wedged between her front teeth and Ben stared.

'Do I look stupid or something?' she cried when Frank went to the bar to buy more drinks. Then, quickly recovering: 'Why don't you take a photograph, darling. They last so much longer.'

Ben drew a squashed circle onto the back of his serviette.

'Does this shape have a name?'

'I have no idea.'

'Me neither,' said Ben. 'But it's an exact replica of the piece of skin showing on your back.'

Then he leaned forward and kissed her.

Violet barely had time to grab the incriminating sketch and shred it beneath the table before Frank arrived back with the drinks.

The next morning, Violet rang Rashani on the public telephone outside The Happy Shrimp. The beaming prawns on the restaurant's sign were euphoric about the prospect of being fried and eaten. They gave the thumbs up as they dived into a cauldron of boiling fat. The glands around Violet's face were as tight as a string of pearls.

'What's up,' yawned Rashani.

'I think I'm sick,' said Violet.

'What are your symptoms?'

'Everything aches and it hurts to open my eyes.'

'Sounds like a hangover,' said Rashani. 'Take another bottle of that Mexican tequila and don't call me in the morning.'

'It's not funny,' said Violet. 'My skin's weird. My lungs feel strange. Maybe I've got cancer.'

Violet was worried about typhoons. She was agitated beyond belief about car crashes, old age and religious vengeance. She knew it was just a matter of time before everyone ran out of money and ended up in Mexican jails full of American retirees with organs on the outside of their body and no boiled water or coloured soap.

The glands around her neck squeezed at her throat in an invisible choker

'Did you know there are rock slides here?' she babbled. 'Did you know there are bandits? Did you know you can actually contract malaria and dengue fever just from being bitten by a mosquito? RASHANI? God. And to think how much he trusts me. What if we go out in the car and the ground opens up and we get sucked into an underground volcano?'

Rashani changed the subject and asked about the food and the beaches and whether Violet had bought any daring new frocks lately. She wondered how long it would take Violet to accuse her of turning lesbo and asked about the Andersons.

'Maybe you can introduce me to the little brother and we can double date.'

Violet's wail was shattering.

'For fuck's sake, do you think you could refrain from doing that quite so close to the phone? What's the problem now?'

'Last night,' moaned Violet.

'What about last night?'

'I think I may have cleaned my teeth with tap water.'

'So?'

'So? *So*? It's the third world, Rashani. The third world. You might be sitting at home where everything's safe but I'm here in the third world. The water's poisonous. It's full of sewage and God knows what else. I'm going to get sick and I'm going to die and get cancer. I just know it.'

Rashani sighed and listened to the snap of coins as Violet fumbled to fund her hysteria. She didn't bother telling her best friend she only had a day to find somewhere to live.

'It's not that we have anything against bisexuals,' Sharon, the Bazookas or Bust Schoolgirl, had said during the critical house meeting. 'But there's no way you fuck as many women as you do men.'

'You're a dilettante,' said Charlotte the Cheerleader.

'A weekender,' added Helen the Horny Housewife.

Rashani had been up in her room packing her trail blazer when Violet had called. She could have told her best friend about the fight with her Bazookas or Bust colleagues or the latest fuck-up with the surgery or the results of her pap smear but in the end it seemed easier to wait until Violet's money ran out and the line went dead.

Violet and the Anderson brothers went back to Mariachi Loco for old times' sake but left before the drinking games. Frank's headaches were now a fact of life. He went to bed early and ate a dozen times a day so he didn't have to take his painkillers on an empty stomach. Violet hoped he wouldn't put on weight. She couldn't remember the last time it wasn't Ben who'd driven them home. In the mornings, she woke terrified she had contracted neck cancer but by the afternoon she didn't have a care in the world.

'Forgive me, babycakes,' Frank said, drilling a finger into his temple. 'But I'm afraid I'm going to have to retire.'

And again he went to bed early leaving Ben and Violet sitting on the hotel verandah drinking warm tequila straight from the bottle. Well, Violet was sitting. Ben squatted and stood and squatted and stood and even tried balancing against the wall on an elbow. If he could remember three good reasons for legs, he was doing a good job of hiding it.

'It's an exquisite evening, isn't it?' Violet said with a clumsy hair swish. Thanks to the Mexican beer and the margaritas and the champagne at the restaurant, the stars swayed overhead like a mobile.

Ben got up and sat down. He muttered into his armpit.

'Speak up, sweetie?'

'Something terrible,' said Ben.

Violet couldn't help but notice the way some of the stars had joined up to form the word 'STAR'. Or was it 'STARE'?

'Something terrible is happening,' said Ben. 'I said something terrible is happening.'

'Now that's a very melodramatic thing for you to say, darling,' she replied vaguely. (START! Or even STAPLE!) 'Wouldn't you say your little brother's being a teensy weensy bit melodramatic, Frankie?'

'Frank's gone to bed.'

'Bed?'

'He's sick again.'

'Poor Frankie.'

'What's happening is wrong.'

'Did we really use the last of the ice?'

'Everything is unravelling.'

Violet scratched absentmindedly at a bite on her leg. Her fingernails filled with blood but she felt no pain. How much of the roar came from the sea and how much of it had always been in her head? Did Rashani ever return those blue shoes with the buckles? Imagine a fish in a hat — or a seahorse with an implant! The thing about Amera Suspender is that her brassieres probably never broke in the washing machine and shot underwire into her chest. Violet felt no pain but could see a long steel claw jutting out the top of her cleavage.

'Isn't it an absolutely beautiful evening, Frankie?' she said, pushing the escaped underwire until it burst through the thin fabric tunnel at the other end of her bra and jutted out her sleeve. 'Isn't it an absolute stunner?'

Ben leapt, muttering, to his useless legs.

'What?' honked Violet.

'I said "not as beautiful as you".'

'Why, that's very sweet of yðu, Frankie.'

'Not sweet. Just a fact.'

Violet picked at the exposed bra wire that had slid back to resurface beneath her chin. Before she knew it, the annoying thing popped into her hand and her right breast dropped a full inch.

'Well, I'm going to take it as a compliment,' she said, wondering whether to even things up by removing the left wire or trying to re-insert the right, 'And let me say you're looking very handsome under the moonlight tonight, too.'

Violet didn't have a clue how her drinking companion looked under the moonlight. Thanks to the Mexican beer and the margaritas and the champagne at the restaurant, all she could see of his face was a clothes-drier blur. Was there even a moon? Ben was going to make her throw up if he kept dancing like that. God, and that nervous, reptilian snicker. Violet couldn't tell whether he had just said 'I love you' or whether she was extracting words from the roar like shapes from clouds. She leant forward to listen and their foreheads clattered over a spilled drink.

'Ow,' said Violet.

Ben repeated his miserable confession, and once again Violet misheard.

'It's all right,' she said. 'There's plenty more in the bottle.'

Then, before she knew it, he was sucking her palm like a dehydrated horse at a puddle.

The next day, Ben drove Violet and Frank to a river high on the side of the mountain. Violet was pale and Ben was bright red. Frank smiled tiredly and said why aren't we dangling our feet. He'd just opened another bottle of champagne when the trees rattled and the ground shook and Violet turned to see an army of huge, dark pigs marching straight towards them. She fainted dead to the ground.

When Violet woke up, Frank was patting someone's head and telling it everything was going to be AOK. Ben, meanwhile, was flicking his teeth and saying 'pling'. Ben flicked his teeth and said 'pling' to represent people who had a star sparkling off their front teeth in cartoons. Normally he did it behind the backs of muscle men without their shirts at the beach. But when Violet woke up on the ground beside the river, he was doing it at the big black pigs.

'You fucking idiot,' she said. 'You complete and utter goddamn fucking freak.'

Ben reeled.

'But I thought you'd like it,' he stammered. 'The pigs aren't dangerous. They follow a path through the jungle. They never reach the river. That's why I brought you here. They walk straight past. I thought you'd like it. *Violet.*'

'It's all right, Benjamin,' said Frank, putting his arm round his brother's shoulder. 'Everything is AOK. Right, babycakes? Tell Ben everything is AOK.'

Violet gasped in disbelief. She pulled herself to her feet and ran back through the vines to the car, right past the line of pigs still carving their way through the jungle in the other direction.

By the time they got back to the hotel, her knees were locked with mud.

'You've got to cut him some slack, babycakes,' Frank said when they were alone. His eye circles were darker than ever and he had a constellation of sores on his forehead. 'The only thing our mother taught us was how to take a joke. "Stay home from school," she'd say. "Don't go. Look, we're all staying home."'

'I don't know who we are any more.'

'All you need to know is that I love you, babycakes.'

'We can't keep living with your brother. I don't get him. I'm just like everyone else. I tried but I really don't get him at all.'

'Sure you do, babycakes,' said Frank.

But he was snoring before his eyes had closed and once again Violet found herself wandering despicably through the hotel dark towards Ben's door.

The morning Frank and Violet tied the knot was hot and cloudy. Ben didn't wear a tuxedo or a cummerbund. He wore his usual uniform of huge coloured shirt and shorts — and still he snorted for air. There were sunglasses marks burned into his face from the hours he'd spent walking up the beach after his brother had told him the happy news.

Frank, Ben and Violet Anderson left the registry office and limped along The Beach of The Dead. A singing woman dug a sand coffin for her blistered husband, Wing Boy danced on an inflated tyre inner tube and the lifeguards put up a sign by the sea warning of dangerous fluents and yelifish.

Rosa's Beach Cantina was hot and deserted.

Frank and Ben ordered huevos rancheros and Bloody Marys. It was only 11 in the morning, after all. Violet drank straight scotch and smoked a dry cigarette. She stared into the globe of green-skinned grapefruit on the plate in front of her and stabbed its dried carrot rounds and glacé cherries with a fork. She couldn't stop kneading the toxic moons beneath her neck.

'To the parents-to-be,' Frank said, raising his glass with a desiccated beam. In lieu of knowing why his wedding day felt so poisonous, he had resolved to leave Mexico as soon as humanly possible. 'To us.'

'To the happy couple,' said Ben.

Violet put on her sunglasses with the intention of bursting into tears but vomited into the cafe's potted plant instead.

The Anderson family didn't return to Texas. Violet got fat and refused to leave the hotel room and then the babies came early, tiny blue sacks smelling of blood, shit and death. It took an eternity. Violet couldn't believe how long it took to expel the silent creatures from her body, couldn't believe she'd actually cried for her mother, couldn't believe the pain and the revelations that emerged when the Anderson brothers dared appear at the hospital door after it was all over.

Frank left first. Furious with grief and disbelief. Slamming the door behind him so the nurses raised their eyebrows. Ben was red-eyed and broken.

'Did you have to tell him?'

'Go fuck yourself.'

'I want to be the one who buries them.'

'Fuck off.'

'They're as much mine as they are his.'

Ben begged and cried and pleaded. He said please let me stay, please let me stay, please let me stay until the nurses called the hospital security.

'The senorita needs her rest,' said the short man with the gun and Ben looked back once and closed the door. It was so quiet in the shadow of the screaming, Mrs Anderson could hear the scrape of Ben's suitcase disappearing all the way down the hallway.

Violet cried for days. She cried until she had no human fluid left inside her at all. She cried until her organs were nothing but currants. And then she did what the nurses told her to do and packed her bags and caught a cab to the airport.

In the airport, Violet wandered among the living with zombie eyes. A flight had been cancelled and two loads of passengers were crammed into a single plane. Dying humans and diseased fabrics pressed in at her from every angle. 'If You Don't Want To Party Don't Come To Fucking Mexico' read the T-shirt sitting next to her.

'You all right, little lady?'

Far down on earth, the grotesque expanse of LA glowed in an enormous switchboard. The pilot switched off the cabin lights and reflections from the city filled the plane with luminous pus. Violet flinched at the yellow shadows and the streams of car lights moving slowly like liquid through UV lines.

'Now that's something you don't see every day,' said the man in the T-shirt, nostrils dried solid from the blasts of the air conditioning.

'I can't see anything,' said Violet as the plane dropped from the sky into LAX in a chunk of infected industrial debris.

Violet queued at the international transfer desk, boarded flight TF–987 for Australia and waited until the new jet had bottomed out above the clouds before swallowing a full bottle of Frank's sleeping pills. It wasn't because she couldn't stand the loss of her twin daughters. It was because even she couldn't live with the fact that beneath the gaping ache in her chest was a thin vein of relief.

22

You Killed Him

By the time Samuel's father walked into the Leadhead family bathroom, Cheryl and Christy had attached empty shampoo bottles to the flaps between their legs and begun a sort of underwater hula. It was a strange thing to do (even Cheryl could have told you that). But after Christy had offered to transfer her chewing gum to Cheryl's mouth without using her hands and Cheryl had said 'try blowing a bubble into my mouth' and Christy had said 'watch this' and Cheryl had lost her balance and both of them had slipped against each other in the soup, nothing seemed strange.

'It's only lezzo if you keep your eyes open.'

Christy's face was soft compared to Murray Ramsbottom's. She could feel every last hair on Christy's face and each one was softer than the next. Even her pimples felt soft.

'No biting!'

Christy's tongue was small compared to Murray Ramsbottom's. It didn't taste like glue. More like cigarettes and coffee and maybe French fries and tomato sauce. Cheryl kept her eyes squeezed so tightly she saw stars.

'I'll show you a trick,' Christy had said, jumping from the bath and pulling out a plastic bag full of empty shampoo containers from behind a cupboard. Cheryl opened one eye and caught a glimpse of skittling thighs and broken ribs laid cockeyed beneath polished wooden skin.

'The more you squeeze them underwater first, the better they work . . .'

Christy forced the air out of the largest of the bottles and latched it suction-style between her legs.

'Have a bash, Kiss.'

It was remarkable. The empty shampoo bottle felt better than thinking about holding hands with Lance Seldom, better than playing Spin The Bottle with Murray Ramsbottom, better than riding a pillow, better than just about anything. Especially if you squeezed it again once it was attached.

'I'm the dancing queen,' sang Christy, wiggling her hips so the bottle waved around on its own between her thighs. 'On my tambourine.'

Christy's eyes were glazed and she waved her hands above her stringy hair. The label on the bottle said: Secret Botanical Shine Complex.

'Look Mum. No hands!'

And that was about the time Old Man Leadhead walked in.

In her hula daze, Cheryl half-expected him to stay. That's what Jackson did when he walked in on her in the

317

bath. He went on cleaning his teeth or shaving or pulling the hair out of his nostrils with Violet's tweezers or asking whether or not Cheryl had been washing herself properly.

'It should tickle,' he said. 'If you've been washing yourself properly. Does it tickle, Cheryl?'

Whenever possible, Cheryl stuck to the shower.

But Old Man Leadhead didn't hang around to chat. The Kiss girl barely caught a glance of the blazing birthmark over his eye before he gave a grim stare and turned on his heel.

'Fuck me dead,' said Christy, flying out of the bath like a fish. 'FUCK ME DEAD.'

'What am I supposed to do?' said Cheryl.

'I'm dead,' she said, throwing on her dress and bolting out the door. 'I'm freakin' dead.'

Cheryl groped desperately through the white murk for the plug. Once there had been bubbles. Now there was only grease and plastic bottles. She looked around for a towel and found a white rag draped over the bathroom sink. She caught a glimpse of herself in the mirror and realised she was still wearing the magpie helmet. She scrabbled into her clothes, dirty underwear and all. Her heart beat so fast she thought she was going to pass out.

Samuel's minced face after he'd run away from 2K and been Lightsabre beneath the school demountable.

The ghost with the birthmark who'd come to the old depot guard in the rain.

The terrible sound of Christy's screech outside.

It all made perfect sense.

The man from the school was Samuel's last lie.

Cheryl inched her way through the dark behind the Leadhead circus, biting chunks off the inside of her mouth and tripping over bones and cans. Christy was sprawled in the dirt next to the kitchen steps. She'd stopped screeching but there was a bright stream coming from her nose and one of her eyes looked funny, as though it had been left out like the ice-cream and had melted. Standing over her was Grandma Leadhead with a belt in one hand and a brown bottle-shaped paper bag in the other. There was a line of olive faces at the rear window of the Leadhead station wagon.

A stick snapped beneath Cheryl's feet and the witch's eyes bucked round in her sockets. There was spit on her chin and a hole under her armpit. Through the torn flowers Cheryl could see all the way through to the dirty rolls of fat over her bra.

'Get off our fucking land.'

Everything moved in slow motion.

'You hear me, girl?'

The old woman grabbed Cheryl by the back of her neck and Cheryl fell to her knees. The earth smelled of dog piss and Tang. The hole in the side of the sweaty tent dress tore even further. Grandma Leadhead marched Cheryl along on her hands and knees and hauled her up between two vans where the light was thin and grey.

'Here. You so interested in the Lightfoots now my boy was burned? You want to see where he lay and died for your sins? Well, God help you. God save your wretched soul.'

Cheryl felt the claw withdraw from her neck. The ground where Samuel had lain wasn't scorched earth, it was a spray of vegetables. A nest of crushed peas and split plastic bags. Everything fell away as Old Man Leadhead's disembodied face materialised through the dark. The back of Cheryl's throat produced an animal gobble.

'You did it,' she squeaked.

'What?' said Old Man Leadhead.

'You killed him.'

And then she was back on the ground swallowing dirt.

Samuel's father hit her twice more across the face before she thrashed out of his grip and ran. Stitches sent lightning bolts through both sides of her chest. The rattle of her breath and the soprano cicadas were deafening. She had intended to take Christy with her but now she'd left another Leadhead to burn alone on the side of the mountain. She was no better than Old Man Leadhead, no better than her mother. There was no man from any school. It had been Cheryl all along.

The Kiss of death.

Violet was in the shower, propped against the wall with water streaming down her face.

'Babycakes,' she slurred when she saw her daughter. She tried to stand but fell against the tiles with a damp slap. 'What's up, Babycakes? I mean, where have you been? I mean, Jackson's out looking. I mean, help mummy up, babycakes. She's been worried sick about her little girl.'

Cheryl avoided the naked body of her mother as she picked up the vodka bottle and turned off the shower. She passed Violet a towel and caught a glimpse of her reflection in the taps. She couldn't tell if her face was swelling or not.

'Old Man Leadhead is the one who killed Samuel,' she said as her mother held the towel in a cha cha, the bandage between her legs, sodden and dripping.

'Old man what, Cakeybabes?' Mrs Kiss had a vague realisation of what she'd just said and cackled hysterically. 'Funny mummy!'

Cheryl couldn't bear it.

'Don't you care? Don't you even care that Old Man Leadhead killed Samuel and now he knows I know he'll come down here and kill me too? Don't you care about anything at all?'

'You're a funny old thing, Cakes.'

Violet retrieved the vodka bottle and suckled, letting the towel slip off her waist.

'Mr Leadlight didn't kill Sam Uel,' she said, exaggerating the syllables.

'What are you talking about?'

'Didn't mummy tell you? Sam Uel burned his own self, Cakey Cakes. Sam Uel did it all himself.'

'You're lying,' Cheryl screamed. She put her fingers in her ears and closed her eyes and screamed and screamed and screamed. Then she realised it wasn't just her screaming. It was Violet as well.

'I haven't got any female friends,' Violet howled into the tiles. 'Why haven't I got any female friends?'

Cheryl turned her back and left her mother twisted in towel on the cold wet floor.

Behind the closed door of her bedroom, she sat beneath her desk with her knees pulled to her chest. Scratched on the underside of the splintered wood was a stick figure of a woman with no clothes and a big chest. The desk used to belong to Jackson. Outside, Zeus barked rock songs and Violet's screams turned into a song.

'I, Cheryl Kiss,' Cheryl wrote in her Personal Pocket Journal in the dark.

The knocking on her bedroom door sounded far away. It was at the small end of a paper trumpet, no louder than the mucoid grunts of the surviving koala raping his new mate in the eucalypt outside.

'I, Cheryl Kiss,' Cheryl wrote again.

She paused, staring at the shapes of the letters until they no longer had any meaning. Typical, really. Minutes, maybe only seconds left to live, and she couldn't think of a single thing to write. No last words of wisdom, no pithy observations, nothing. The pressure was worse than an English exam.

No wonder Samuel hadn't left a suicide note.

Cheryl corrected herself. Samuel hadn't committed suicide. His father had burned him to death because he made his bed instead of riding trail bikes and because he must have found out what happened with Bradley Spam in the toilets even though Cheryl hadn't breathed a word, and because there was no end to the things families could do to themselves.

Cheryl destroyed the I, Cheryl Kiss journal page with the end of her pen as the yelling outside her bedroom door rose in volume.

'For fuck's sake,' she yelled at the door. 'There's no need to have a coronary, I'm coming out, all right?'

Cheryl stared down at the page.

It wasn't right.

She had to leave some final words of wisdom for whoever found her body.

Christy Leadhead's a lemon

she scribbled in a strange burst of rage.

And unlocked her bedroom door.

23

The Silver Lighter

Old Man Leadhead was leaning against the splintered doorway panting, an ingrown singlet flapping over his dirty blue chest.

'Christy said I'd find you here,' he gasped. 'I ran all the way.'

Cheryl handed him a box of matches.

'You might as well burn me,' she said dully. 'I don't care any more. Whatever happens now, I don't care.'

Samuel's father stared down at the murder weapon in his hand. Repulsively enough, a wiry grey forest sprouted from the centre of his birthmark. Zeus whimpered from the clothes hoist.

'Do your worst,' Cheryl said. 'Quite honestly, you'd be doing me a favour.'

'What are you talking about, girl? I came down here to apologise.'

'Excuse me a minute,' Cheryl said, feeling sick. She walked round the side of the house to unclip Zeus. The dog bounded out with an anguished cheer. He was so drunk on freedom he forgot to tear out the interloper's throat and danced instead. Cheryl could have cried at the sight of the deep familiar brindle and the killer, golf-ball cheeks.

Old Man Leadhead pulled a beaten packet of cigarettes out of his top pocket and offered one to Cheryl.

'No thanks, I don't smoke,' she said, putting it in her mouth. She opened the box of matches but they were damp and snapped at the stumps.

'Try this,' said Old Man Leadhead, passing her a silver lighter.

'The wife gave it to me,' he continued, turning it round in his palm. 'Before any of the kiddies came along. That's how long I've had it, you realise.'

'I don't believe it,' Cheryl blurted.

'It's true,' he said, put out. 'Ask Christy. Ask any of them. I've had it forever. Keep it with me night and day. Lost it once for an afternoon and I felt like I'd lost my pants.'

'Not the lighter,' said Cheryl. 'Samuel. My mother said he committed suicide. It isn't true.' Then: 'Is it?'

Old Man Leadhead stared.

'You knew my boy,' he said. 'I seen you on the bus with him. I seen you walking down the creek where he walked. You been in the school with him all these years. You tell me whether he could have done such a thing to himself.'

Cheryl tried to imagine Samuel setting the silver lighter to his trouser cuffs while sitting on the toilet with Bradley Spam and drew a blank.

'They say they got evidence,' Old Man Leadhead went on. 'The police say they got evidence my boy went and burned himself up but for the life of me I can't see it.

'Then they tell me they got witnesses. Bo Deal down the servo what saw him buy the petrol all on his own. Two old birds what saw him taking off his clothes and lining them out down by the river. What were they thinking? I said to the coppers. What were those two old birds thinking to see a boy do such a thing and not stop and go check? They were taking their morning constitutionals, the coppers said. They were taking their morning constitutionals and thought he was a pervert. He was only 14, I told them. How could he be a pervert? And the coppers said I'd be surprised how young they started, I really would.'

Cheryl was deaf and dumb. She couldn't care less any more. Not about Samuel or his dad or what had happened in the toilets with Bradley Spam or anything. She was sitting there on the step in the dark smoking better than Christy Leadhead and she couldn't have cared less. Zeus licked her arm with his foul tongue. All right. Maybe she cared about Zeus.

'You hit him after he ran away from school.'

'I never touched the boy.'

'Whenever Mr Scoob asked, Samuel said he fell down the staircase. You don't even have a staircase.'

'I'd never touch none of my kids.'

'What about me?'

'You weren't one of my kids. And what you said was way out of line. But like I said before, the reason I'm here is to pass on my apologise. Christy sent me. She said it weren't sociable of me to be whacking visitors and I reckon she was probably right.'

Old Man Leadhead stared into the night.

'Funny that. Mum's usually the one what suffers from the short fuse. Deep down she's got a good heart. But after she's been on the turps, she don't know herself. And Sammy was always rubbing her up the wrong way, what with all his troubles and him being the splitting image of his mother and all.

'Not that I blame Antonella for leaving,' he went on. 'She stayed and she stayed and then she just upped and left. I was the one what should of done more to keep it together and God should of struck me down for not doing something to keep the old woman off the kids. Spare the rod and spoil the child, she always said. But some nights I'd get home and those kids of mine looked like they belonged in a bottle.'

Samuel's father dragged hard on his cigarette. The eye above the birthmark twitched. In the background they could hear Violet wailing 'Onion Tears' — the original version recorded by Jose Septiembre before the Dick Lyndon Sextet immortalised it as an instrumental.

> *You say you've never been so low*
> *You say you're sad to let me go*
> *But I break like a chandelier*
> *When I see you crying onion tears*

The tick tick from the water meter next to the carport meant the shower was back on — pelting by the sound of it.

'The old depot guard said a man with a birthmark told him he'd killed Samuel.'

'On the night he went it was all I could think of. It was just going round and round in me head. I didn't save me boy, I didn't protect little Sammy, I might as well of lit that match myself for all I did to keep him from harm. "It was me," I told the police. "It was me what let it happen. Give me the lie detection and you'll know I'm speaking from the heart."'

An oily tear rolled down the obstacle course of Old Man Leadhead's cheeks.

'They didn't give me the lie detection, but. They sent me to the police head doctor. The police head doctor said I could blame meself till the cows came home and it wouldn't bring the boy back. She said I had to hold it together for the sake of the girls. But it makes no sense, I told her. If Sammy had got himself into some sort of trouble he could have come to me or come to his sisters. Why would he hurt himself so bad? Sammy was what you might call a crybaby. He wouldn't of burnt himself if he could of helped it.

'Purification, said the head doctor. The ones what do it with fire do it for purification. A cleaning thing, like in the Bible. Did anything happen? she asked me. Did anything happen to make him feel dirty? That's about the time I walked out. You don't know a thing, I told her. Fire didn't clean my boy. I saw his body after they brought him in and it was as messed up as you could get.'

'But the picture,' Cheryl said lamely. 'Why'd you put up the picture of the bike in his bedroom if you weren't trying to cover something up?'

'Dunno what came over, me,' Old Man Leadhead said. 'I know my boy never had no time for no trail bikes. He would rather have stayed home in his sisters' shoes. But I never cared about none of that. I just didn't want no-one saying nothin' bad about my boy after he was gone.'

By that stage, Old Man Leadhead was bawling like a baby. His nostrils flared and streams of snot drooled out each one. In the movies people would have started putting their arms round each other, but Cheryl didn't want to get any closer than she absolutely had to. It was like a dream. Cheryl there on the step with her mother singing from the bathroom on one side and Old Man Leadhead crying and apologising and crying and wiping the snot away with his deep olive skin on the other. Cheryl didn't put her arm round him but she did touch his back with her hand — just for a second.

'Go home,' she said. 'It's getting late and I've got things I have to do.'

'So you accept me apologise then? I won't hear the end of it if I go home and tell Christy you didn't accept me apologise.'

'Don't worry about it,' said Cheryl. 'It really doesn't matter.'

'Christy said you were all right. It's good she's found herself a little mate. She don't got that many friends since she started down the Bi-Mart.'

Cheryl nodded as Old Man Leadhead pulled himself up and tucked his wayward singlet into his wrinkled pants. He turned to go then turned back.

'I'm not sure we ever were properly introduced as such,' he said, jabbing his hand into Cheryl's face. 'Samuel Lightfoot. Used to have to say Senior but now I don't s'pose there'll be any confusion.'

'Cheryl Kiss,' said Cheryl, shaking his hand. 'I'm sorry I didn't do anything when I heard him screaming.'

'Nothing you could of done.'

'I wasn't sure what it meant and then I didn't do anything at all.'

328

'Story of my life, Cheryl Kiss,' was the last thing she heard as Samuel Lightfoot Senior vanished into the gloom.

Cheryl opened the door to the carport room and changed out of her clothes. They were still damp from the bath with Christy. She strapped Dora Knockers' diary back up with rubber bands and put Zeus on his leash. Violet must have managed to get herself out of the shower because there was a domino of kitchen crashes before Dick Lyndon began blasting out of the stereo. The last thing Cheryl did was pull the 'Christy Leadhead is a lemon' page out of her Personal Pocket Journal and set fire to it with the silver lighter Samuel's father had left on her doorstep. It burned into a velvety crisp.

Cheryl and Zeus listened to Dick Lyndon fade into nothing as they walked up Panorama Way, past the Chungs and the Wetherills and the Towers and the Scrimshaws and the Proudfoots and the Nids and the McMaxwells and the Goslings and the Lavertys and the Knotts and the Domotors and the Surfs and the Ketteringhams and the Okes and the Hatts and the Kruegers and the Ramsbottoms and the Spudics and the Weleslys and the Keefs and the Zaxmaxes and the Spadgeways and the Balstrups and a pair of psychedelic sewing scissors with yoyo DNA beneath its nails and rust already cramping the blades. The thrillseekers reached the shopping centre where a single neon light burned Free Sauce above the front door of Dora Knockers' fish and chip shop.

Dora unbolted the front door in a T-shirt that said Suck My Penis Envy. Her blonde hair had frothed into a helmet and her eyes looked tiny.

'What's wrong with your face?' asked Cheryl.

'No make-up,' said Dora. 'What's wrong with your face?'

'Fell down the stairs,' said Cheryl.

'Very original,' said Dora. 'Are you planning to stand out here all night or are you going to come inside?'

The diary sat between them on the coffee table. Dora drank herbal tea and Cheryl drank hot chocolate. Zeus smelled everyone's legs, then de-fleaed thatches of hair out of his rectum. It was the best idea he'd had in years. Seriously, it was a total revelation.

Dora examined *Grade 10 School Social with V and A — Gross!*

'Me and your mother and our friend, Amanda, in high school,' she said. 'Can you believe those heels? Can you believe we were the coolest girls in school in those ridiculous heels? If your mother knew one day they'd look so lame she would have died.'

Cheryl stared at the ghosts teetering on inches of coloured plastic.

'What really happened in Mexico?' she said.

24

Sarah Beth

A revisionist historian. That's what I used to call your mother. The rest of the time I called her Dewey. In primary school she started a list of how many boys looked at her in the street. Then Edna dragged her off to the country to visit an aunt and she came back with an entire logbook. Dates and times and hair colours for pages on end. You'd think the male population didn't have anything better to do than look at Violet Opus-Worthington when she walked into the newsagent to buy a botany book.

'When did they find time to eat?' I asked.

But your mother was too busy filing to answer.

The truth is I don't really know where to start, Chezza Jane. Everything's so connected to everything else.

You remember your grandmother?

You got photos?

You recall that trouble with the Whang Co. suit?

She was a real shithead, your Nan. Scuse my French, but she was as strong as an ox. The day after your mother ran away to Amsterdam she waited for me and Mandy at the bus stop and boxed our ears till Sister Meredith threatened to call the authorities. We heard sirens for a week. One time I walked in on the old witch in the bathroom and the biceps were hanging off her arms like a sack of tennis balls. I don't know what was worse — the Iron Man physique under those disastrous dresses or the fact she was taking a hot shower in her bra and panties. Can you imagine that? Wet elastic on skin gives me the creeps. In this day and age it isn't civilised. Christ, I can still picture it now.

You were only two when Edna passed away. Terrible expression, that: Passed away. Mind you, the alternative is When Your Nan's Head Got Ripped Off By That Street Sign so it's probably best to stick with the euphemisms. The crash was real nasty. The car your Nan was driving was split straight down the middle. But we still crowded round waiting for her to walk out of the wreck intact. We thought the old bugger was invincible. It didn't sit right — a lousy old chunk of metal getting the better of her.

When the jaws of life arrived, it took an hour to cut her free. She'd been wearing three bras all at once and the wiring was tangled up in the steering column. Sorry, Chezza. Way too much information. But I can't help but see the funny side. It's like that fella who injected cocaine into his python to get a three-day stiffy, then died of gangrene. In one way it's tragic. But in lots of other ways it's totally fucking hilarious. When I first read that story in *The Chinese Whisper* I laughed for an hour straight up. And how about that suicide attempt in Canada? The one where the bullet lodged in the back of the dude's skull and he lived? Three years later, he's got his shit together with the family and the house and the barbecue setting and everything, and the bullet finally explodes and there's brain all over the breakfast table.

You got to laugh.

Not if you happened to be sitting there trying to eat your cereal, of course.

But with a bit of distance there's definitely a punchline.

Did I get round to telling you about your grandmother?

She hadn't exactly mellowed by the time you came along. When your grandfather died she whistled all the way through the funeral then went home and made liverwurst from scratch. But for some reason you ended up in her good books. My theory is that it was because you didn't end up in Violet's. Good books, that is. Someone once told me mothers and babies are filled with chemicals to make 'em latch on to each other, but you two never hit it off. Chalk and cheese, I think is the expression. Pretty stupid expression. If you wanted something real different to chalk you'd go for something wet. Or maybe a duster.

Don't you agree?

You weren't worse than any other poo machine. You were pretty cute for a sprog, actually. But Violet took the whole thing personally. Every little spew was a personal attack. Every poo in a pair of plastic pants a massive 'fuck you'. On the night of your first birthday, you ate a gold button off that zillion dollar Whang Co. suit she was always wearing to interviews and Violet accused you of deliberately trying to sabotage her career. She rubbed your face in the rest of the suit to teach you a lesson (Edna's idea.) Then she spent the next two days scavenging through your dirty nappies. You'll be happy to know you had guts even back then, Chezza Jane. By the time that button resurfaced, it was stripped right back to knuckle.

Is it too stuffy in here? Do you want some fried cheese? Does that dog of yours always do that to table legs? I've got a shocking habit of going off on a tangent. The world according to Dora Knockers. That's what you're enduring, Miss Kiss. Rule one: Never trust anyone who refers to themselves in the third person. Rule two: Are you listening to Dora Knockers?

All right I'll shut up.

Without getting into the whole nature nurture fiasco, the reason I got to tell you about Edna is because Edna is the reason Violet ran away to Amsterdam and what happened in Amsterdam is the reason Violet eventually ended up in Mexico and Mexico was where she met Frank Anderson and his little brother, Ben, and that's how you and your little sister came to be born.

So where were we? High school. The plane to Europe. That bloody photographer with the flatlining signature. (I kid you not — it travelled for miles without a single sign of life.) *What was Violet thinking? I mean what WAS she thinking?* Back in those days, me and Violet and Mandy were real close. We did everything together. Everything we could, anyway. Edna didn't let Violet socialise after school in case Satan tempted her to the drive-in and put a claw down her draws or something, so most of the time we had to bullshit. Trombone. That was Violet's usual excuse. 'Trombone practice, mother. Sorry, gotta run.' You never saw a girl leave for orchestra with so much lipstick. Served Edna right. She made Violet play trombone because it was about the only thing in the world apart from singing that made her look freakish. 'Squid,' we called her in primary school. Me and Mandy reckoned Squid was allergic, her lips swelled that much after she played.

Lucky for us, we only got triangle and maracas.

Like I said, the other thing we used to call Violet at school was Dewey. Edna was the strictest mother at Wart's, she was legendary, but Violet had more boyfriends than all of us put together and added to the number you first started with.

'At least you got a good personality, Rashani.'

That's what she had to say about my luck in the gene pool. To this day I hear those words and want to kill someone. Violet, probably. Pretty girls have no idea how easy they got it. They got no idea what sort of advantage they got over everyone else. After I had my surgery, I could walk into a bar and pick up a fella just by spewing into his drink and kneeing him in the Niagara Falls. But I never forgot it was an unfair advantage and I never used it to the detriment of another girl.

Well. Maybe I used it against your mother. Once. When I first came to Tantanoula. But that was different. That was war. At least I thought it was. To tell you the truth I was re-evaluating my use of recreational drugs at the time so who knows what it was.

Your mum was 18 when she went to Amsterdam. She was older than the rest of us 'cos she got held back a year in primary school. We only had a few months left at high school but Violet saw this ad for models in a magazine and bit the bullet. She said the situation with her wisdom teeth was a sign she needed more room to move. She said Edna had stopped wearing undergarments in the shower and started wearing entire outfits.

I don't know whether this last part was true. It sounded pretty far-fetched even for old Opus-Worthington. But I know for a fact Violet was expected to wear at least a singlet and panties when she showered because your grandmother conducted a spot check the night I stayed over after Glynn French's pool party (sorry, orchestra practice). Mrs Opus-Worthington walked in, discovered Violet nude and chucked one of her black prescription shoes right at her head. Of course these days it would be child abuse. But back then, no-one looked twice at a girl who turned up for netball with heel dints. The good sisters at Wart's said spare the rod and spoil the girl. Thankfully most of 'em had osteoporosis and couldn't flick a cane to save their lives.

When Violet told me she'd stolen her mother's money and bought a one-way plane ticket to Europe I told her she was a fucking idiot. I told her she should finish school so she had something to fall back on. I said if I had as many boyfriends as she did I wouldn't want for anything else as long as I lived. We had a fight. It wasn't as bad as the one we'd had over Frank Stomp the year before but it was still pretty serious.

Violet said I didn't want her to go because she was going to be a hot-shot international catwalk model while I was just a nobody with no boys looking at me back home in the laundrette.

I said it was only a matter of time until Violet was old and ugly like Edna and then where would her fancy modelling career be.

After that I think we pulled each other's hair for a while and after that we made up and after that me and Mandy drove her to the airport.

Violet rang lots the first week she was gone. Turning up in Amsterdam without a cent to her name was a guts call, but all she talked about to me was her mother. She wanted to know what sort of state she was in, whether she was finally sorry for all the horrible things she'd done et cetera et cetera. There was also the situation with her cat, Moses. Just before me and Mandy put her on the plane, she got convinced she'd accidentally packed him into her suitcase. Me and Mandy told her over and over not to worry, that Moses was probably lying on her bed eating pigeons as per usual. But when she arrived in Amsterdam she locked herself in the airport toilet to scrub up for her meeting with the photographic contact and discovered her suitcase was full of slime. I told her it must have been her new red hair shampoo. I told her it couldn't have been the cat. Not without bone fragments or ears or fur or toenails or anything. But Violet was really fucked up over it. She was so fucked up she didn't even bother cleaning the exploded whatever it was off her dress before the big rendezvous.

Don't ever tell your mother this, but the freaky thing is Moses vanished the exact same day she did. When Edna bailed me and Mandy up at the Wart's bus stop she was more cheesed off about the disappearance of that damn cat than she was about the disappearance of the money. Or her daughter, for that matter.

After that first week, I didn't hear from Violet for months. I figured things didn't work out with the Dutch photographer because the next time she rang she was in Spain dating some guy who dabbled in stocks and bonds. I asked if she was a big-shot international catwalk model yet and she said 'virtually'. That was her answer for the next seven years. Once I thought I saw her on telly, drinking champagne at a car race, but apart from that I didn't have a clue what she was up to. She never sent photos from her weddings or nothing.

Back then, I thought there was a limited pool of luck. I thought if other people got too much there'd be less for yours truly. But Violet not making it in the modelling world sure didn't help me any. After she went away, me and Mandy sat round after school and couldn't think of a single thing to say.

We got through our exams all right. Neither of us were what you'd call intellectual heavyweights but we did OK. Then Mandy went off to tech to do child care and I scraped into uni and set about changing the world — with a fucking arts degree, no less. Violet's got this thing about getting old, but me, I look at kiddies today and thank Christ it's all over. No offence, Cheryl, but I wouldn't be your age again if you paid me.

Anyway, I always had this idea that once I got away from my family and the laundromat and had a place of my own, I'd be fine. But uni turned out to be seriously deleterious for my health.

You don't want to know everything that happened. Well. Maybe you do, but I'm not going to tell you. Once I tried to tell your mother, but she was having some trouble with some guy who raced animals and didn't bother listening. She was good at that, your mother. She didn't want to know, she tuned out.

'What guy?'

'Who raced animals?'

'I'm sorry?'

Anyway, so this happened and that happened and after a few unfortunate years hawking my bony arse I left university and got a job in a dance troupe and the guy who ran it took a liking to me and said had I heard about this surgery business because if I hadn't heard about it and I'd like to hear about it he'd be more than happy to fill me in because maybe I could get into a position to earn the both of us a hell of a lot more cashola.

That's how it started. He lent me the money and I went under once and I went under twice and I went under three times and after that I lost count.

Back in those days, the surgeons didn't know nearly as much about plastics as they do now. I was what you might call a guinea pig. One night I was bending over shaving my legs in the bath, and I burst. All this crap spurted out like glue from a tube. By the time I got to hospital, my hand was glued solid to my chest.

Funny, right?

If I hadn't been there I would have laughed myself witless.

So there's Violet, travelling round the world marrying up a storm and there's me, changing my name and pumping myself up and doing interviews with magazines and feeling like the world was finally starting to take notice. It wasn't the whole world, of course — just a dark, shitty corner with not enough bar stools. But I couldn't get enough — even if I did have to put up with the occasional flat tyre. The old airbags earned me a fortune and I had a trail of men after me as long as a highway. If I'd tried to keep a list of everyone who looked at me in the street I would have had to hire a fucking bookkeeper.

Violet didn't know about any of this. She still thought I was at uni and I stopped trying to tell her otherwise. It's no wonder she never tried her hand at tertiary education herself. As far as she knew, a lousy arts degree took seven whole years.

The therapist had plenty to say about me and Violet. But therapists don't know everything. After all, it was the therapist who recommended I ignite the healing fire within. Hello? I said. Have you not noticed that I am highly flammable? If I start striking internal matches, this whole damn couch is likely to go up.

When Violet got to Mexico, she rang me from a phone on the beach to say she'd just met someone. As usual he was this, he was that, he was so good at absolutely everything and me, being kind of antsy because she'd rung in the middle of the night and woken me up, asked exactly what made Frank Anderson so special. What Violet said was that she'd gone through his bathroom and was fairly sure he wasn't an intravenous drug user.

She had standards, you had to give her that.

The next time your mother rang was months later and she was in one of her states. It wasn't because she and the Frank guy had busted up. It was because they were still together and the younger brother was turning out to be some sort of fruitcake. She had one of her panic attacks about the end of the world and I told her everything would be OK, really it would, blah blah blah, then waited till she ran out of money and went back to sleep.

Maybe you think I was a bad friend not to take her seriously but even if I'd known what was about to happen I couldn't have stopped it. I couldn't get on a plane and fly to Mexico. Not with my airbags the way they were. Sheila from the dance troupe tried to fly to Bali for her honeymoon and they blew all over her chicken cutlets. She only got work in the community sector after that.

I don't know how long Violet had been back in Australia before she rang me. I couldn't get a whole lot of sense out of her. I'd always had this fantasy about the look on her face when she came home and saw The New

Me. But when I turned up at that shiny hotel on the freeway near the airport, she barely recognised me at all. She was a real mess. I doubt she'd even dragged herself out of bed to use the little girls' room.

Somehow I got her into a bath. And the fucked-up thing is she still looked as goddamn gorgeous as she always had. Even with her hair standing up by itself and her dress crusty enough to have corners, she still looked goddamn incredible.

And this crap little part of me thought: How could you? How could you look like that and still end up like this?

I left Violet yakking away to herself in the bath and unpacked her suitcase looking for fresh clothes. It was full of sand and dried flowers and lizards without their tails. The flora was dead but two of the reptiles were still crawling. If there hadn't been so much shit going down, I would have rung a zoo or something, but as it was I flushed them down the toilet. The little one went without a fight but the big one got away. Maybe it escaped into the wild and started a colony. Or maybe it just ended up pulverised in the hotel washing machine.

I'd just found a dress with less stainage than the others when the phone rang. That sent Violet completely apeshit. She jumped out of the bath and tried to crawl under the bed after the runaway reptile. She didn't get real far. There was only a two-inch clearance. She butted her head against that mattress until she'd practically knocked herself out.

So I pick up the phone and it's this guy from airport security saying this is the last time he's calling before he alerts the relevant authorities 'cos those nurses who brought the baby over, they got to fly back to Mexico and the plane they wanna catch is leaving in less than two hours and they got families too and how many times does he have to ring before he gets a little co-operation and it sure would make it easier on everyone if you could come by and pick up your baby . . . and are you sure everything's all right there, Mrs Anderson?

How I got Violet off the floor, into a dress and out the door is beyond me.

In the cab she straightened up and started telling me the story. We were only a couple of kilometres from the international terminal, so all I got were bits and pieces. It happened in Mexico, she said. She'd gone to the doctor about some problem she was having with her glands and on the way out he'd said, by the way, congratulations on the happy news.

'Happy news?'

'*Como? You mean you didn't know? Pero senora, you're four months gone . . .*'

Frank did what he considered the decent thing and married her on the spot. Apparently he was over the moon but Violet had a total meltdown. Kiddies had never really been part of her plan, you understand. And as it turned out there was a situation with the fruitcake brother.

'Am I correct in assuming that what you're talking about here is some sort of weirdo love triangle scenario?'

'You do the math,' was all she'd say at the time. 'You do the goddamn math.'

The name of the brother was Ben. Maybe he was as nutty as Violet said he was, maybe he wasn't. Bear in mind she once threatened to have me committed for using aluminium-free deodorant so I took everything she said about Benjamin Anderson's insanity with a bucket of salt.

There was a Polaroid of the three of them in her suitcase. The older one, Frank, was a total movie star. Ben was no oil painting but he looked like he had a sense of humour. He looked like the sort of person who wouldn't mind if you left the toilet door open, if you know what I mean. Mind you, I never go for the square-jawed types. They always want you to cover up your tattoos in shopping centres.

The question on everyone's lips, of course, was why your mother was back in Australia while you were still over in Mexico.

Violet clammed up once we reached the metal detectors at Customer Service. Especially when they brought you out in a box. The blood drained from her gob and she wouldn't say a word. But at least she didn't headbutt anything.

'All by herself she is breathing and drinking now.'

That's what the Mexican nurses said when they handed you over. They were real old, they were dressed like a couple of nuns, but they were nice enough. They certainly didn't seem surprised about having to fly a baby halfway round the world in search of its mother. I kept expecting Violet to be arrested but the security staff just pumped her hand and took photographs.

'I guess you didn't leave her in a garbage bin or anything,' I joked, but Violet wasn't really in the mood.

Everyone always says babies are beautiful but most of the time they're lying. Most of the time babies are red and lumpy with crooked eyes and not enough hair. But you looked pretty good, Chezza. You squawked and shat too much for my liking, but you looked pretty good. God you were tiny. They'd taken your passport photo while you were lying in some doctor's palm. Next to you, he was a fucking orang-outang.

The airport security people made Violet sign a couple of forms (or rather I held her elbow while she shook) and the next thing I knew, me and her were standing in the airport cab rank with a baby, a blanket, a birth certificate and absolutely no idea what to do next.

I still couldn't understand why she'd got off so easy. Couldn't understand how someone could leave their baby in Mexico and not get an infringement notice or something. But Violet had devoted herself to impersonating the living dead. She didn't liven up till later.

Everything got real busy. You and Violet moved onto the sofa bed in my flat above the club and I got real good at mixing powdered milk in the middle of the night without waking up. We took you to a doctor to have you checked out and he said for a premmie you looked fine. I think he thought Violet and I were a couple because he gave us a lecture about the damage deviant relationships could have on good old-fashioned family values. That shocked Violet out of her stupor. It was bad enough being a single mother with no job. Now complete strangers were mistaking her for a faggot.

'Were you giving out some sort of signals or was it just because we went in together?' she demanded when we got back from the surgery.

That's when I realised she was going to be just fine.

I hooked Violet up with one of the regulars at the club and he gave her a part-time job as a receptionist at his television station. You'd think something like Mexico would change a person for life, but when Violet bounced back she was as exactly the same as ever — maybe even more so. By the time you were six months old, she'd changed her hair and was reading public service announcements on weekends.

It was wrong of her to have a go at you over that Whang suit button. If it wasn't for you, she would have only experienced career as a verb. Single motherhood didn't have quite as much currency in the romantic money market, you see. For a long time, her idea of sweet nothings were zeros in salaries. She started work 'cos she knew she wouldn't be able to pull a joint signature on a bank account the way she used too.

That said, Violet moved in with my friend the TV station guy before you could say 'second wind'. You were probably too little to remember Duke Blazer, but he was a decent enough chap. Not too keen on dirty nappies but decent enough. Violet even kissed and made up with your grandmother. Took her a few months before she made the call but the moment your Nana laid eyes on you and Violet clawing each other's eyes out she was a lost cause. Which was just as well really, because Violet was a firm believer in babysitting.

Your mother didn't tell me the rest of the Mexico story until the night of her 26th birthday. Duke was away so we went out for cocktails. I made the mistake of ordering margaritas while Violet was in the little girls' room. When she came back she knocked them all over the floor.

'That's what we used to drink in Cabo Roto,' she shouted. 'How could you be so insensitive?'

Violet said when she went into labour early, she thought she was dying. There'd been a big religious festival and the maternity ward was full of skeletons.

She said: 'Can you believe those foreigners?'

She said: 'It's no wonder Sarah Beth stopped breathing.'

She said: 'Anyone who woke up surrounded by that sort of interior decorating would have realised it wasn't worth the trouble.'

You and your twin sister were premature. By how many weeks I don't know. But Sarah Beth was so frail she only lived a few minutes, and the doctors didn't even hold you up to Violet's face before racing you off to intensive care. Later, they came back and said sorry to be the bearers of bad news but it was only a matter of time before you joined Sarah Beth and God in heaven. They told your mother to be thankful at least one of her daughters would be christened before she made her way to the other side.

Violet had a terrible blue with Ben and Frank, after that. I gather she told them about the meat in the sandwich scenario and they stormed off or she kicked them out or the hospital got rid of them — who knows? It's hard to tell with Violet. She said they pissed off and abandoned her, but it's hard to tell. For all I know the Anderson brothers were sitting in their hotel waiting for her to come to her senses.

Things got real grim in the mental health department. The doctors said 'you should really be with your family at a time like this' and Violet hurled another plate of custard. The doctors said 'excuse me senora, we don't think you fully understand' and Violet shattered another vase. The doctors strapped her to the bed and said 'one more outburst like that and it's off to the hospital for mujeres locas up on the hill'.

'Don't worry, I didn't really go crazy,' Violet told me that night in the bar. 'I just broke the wrong nose on the wrong nurse one day. That's all.'

She checked herself out of hospital and caught a cab to the airport. She told me she honestly thought you were dead.

I don't know if you know about the sleeping tablets.

If you got all the way through my diary you'd know and if you didn't, it's too late now. Did you get all the way through my diary, you little shit? Stealing a diary is a serious invasion of privacy. It's on par with going through someone's garbage. I'll forgive you this once but if it happens again you'll be sorry. Ask your mother. I can be a right cow when I turn my mind to it.

Violet must have been real unimpressed with the inflight menu because an hour or so out of LA she downed a bottle of sleeping tablets. When she told me about it I knew straight off it wasn't what you might call a cry for help. Nothing anyone could have done for her that far from a stomach pump, it was a serious attempt. But your mother's constitution was always on the delicate side. She spent the rest of the flight spewing up then actually managed to walk off the plane on her own two legs. She fell over as soon as she reached the terminal, but at least she'd managed a couple of metres.

Spookily enough, the pilot was the same dude who'd flown her to Amsterdam all those years earlier. She must have made quite an impression because he recognised her straight away. He picked her up and dusted her off and offered to take her to hospital himself. Violet said no hospital so he took her down the road to the airport hotel instead.

I don't know how long Violet lay in that room before she finally rang me. My guess is she would have stayed till she rotted if that hospital security guard hadn't kept calling.

Urgent message from La Santa Maria hospital in Mexico. Incredible news. The doctor says there's been a miracle. Your little girl lived. MRS ANDERSON?

Part of me wishes I'd been round more while you were growing up but most of me knows it would have been a waste of time.

I've always been hopeless with kids. Can't do any of that goo goo gaa gaa shit or tell lies about Father Christmas or the tooth whatsit. Duke Blazer used to say I just didn't have a 'G' rating.

Me and your mother were growing apart again, anyhow. Even when everything was going smoothly there was always this drama or that drama and if I didn't put my clothes back on to make myself available at the exact moment she needed assistance then I was a selfish cow who didn't appreciate how hard things were for her when everything was going so well for me. By well, she meant financially. I earned a shitload of money back when I was dancing but most of it went as fast as it came in. I was a surgery junkie.

The other thing we fell out over was the Anderson issue. I thought those two boys had a right to know they had a living daughter — regardless of which one was actually the father. But Violet said she never wanted to see either of them again. She wanted to forget that Mexico and Sarah Beth and the sleeping tablets had ever happened. Especially with her new TV career. Not a real good look for a newsreader, marinating in your own waste in an airport hotel.

By the time Edna died, we'd stopped talking like we used to (or she'd stopped talking at me like she used to) and your mother had hooked up with the woman next door. That was fine by me. Deborah Evensly was welcome to her. Bazookas or Bust had been offered a season in a club in Japan and I decided it was my turn to see the world. We all had to have reductions to cope with the plane trip but it was worth every last antibiotic. After Japan we thought we might as well do one more tour while we were plane-worthy and after Canada we thought, why not Chile?

And that's what happened to the next ten years.

When I looked up your mother in Tantanoula, I'd just got back from Berlin and was at the proverbial crossroads. Most of the original chicks had left the group and I was having to do schoolteacher and librarian acts — all that elderly shit. You ever heard of a 36-year-old Indian Girl? Deborah Evensly gave me your mother's number. She wasn't too keen but gave in so I'd remove my stilettos from her manicured front lawn. How you managed to live next door to that many garden gnomes, I'll never know. And those appalling sons of hers. Christ.

It was stupid of me to expect Violet would suddenly bend over backwards to help out an old friend at a loose end but time does weird things. It makes you forget the negatives and only remember the positives. Or maybe it makes you invent the positives. Either way, when I turned up in Tantanoula with a bold plan to turn over a new leaf and start seriously re-evaluating my use of recreational drugs, your mother was less than pleased to see me. If you got through the entire diary, you probably know the rest. Violet asked if I'd mind pretending we didn't know each other, I did the most evil thing I've ever done in my life with your stepfather and everything went horribly pear-shaped at that bloody New Year's Eve party.

It was very antisocial of me to set fire to her guests like that, but I think we were both looking for an excuse never to speak to each other again.

You know, after she got back from overseas, and I'd stopped being Rashani Bail and become Dora Knockers, she never said a thing about the bold new me.

Actually, that's not strictly true.

Once I was whingeing about some yodeller in a panel van and she said 'if you don't want men looking at you like that you shouldn't wear such tight breasts'. So maybe she did notice I'd changed, after all.

25

Like The End Of A Bad Airport Novel

It took ages for Cheryl's blood to resume circulating at the correct speed.

'Can I still call you Dora?' she said after a while.

'Call me whatever you want,' said the fish and chip shop woman. 'Everyone else does. But Dora is the name on my driver's licence. It's who my clothes fit.'

Cheryl picked a cuticle until it dripped.

'I'll change and give you a lift home,' Dora said. 'All this confessionalism has worn me out. It's like the end of a bad airport novel where you have to put up with an entire chapter full of plot just so the author can tie up the loose ends. Thrillers are always so predictable. I should know. I've read enough of them. You a Becky Swift fan? I prefer *Barb Piercing — Girl Detective* myself, but I've still got a soft spot for a Becky Swift mystery.'

'I thought my father died in a plane crash.'

'Ah well. No-one's perfect.'

'Can I have their address?'

'Whose?'

'Frank and Ben Anderson's.'

'Can't help you there, Chezza. There's no guarantee they'd want to hear from you, anyway. They don't even know you exist. Let me rephrase that. That you still exist. For all I know there's no such thing as the Anderson brothers. For all I know Violet was bullshitting about the whole thing. Once she lied about having a sixth toe just to get out of netball. Once she rang in sick with a fake abortion. The woman has no shame.'

'I'd rather know than not know.'

'Famous last words.'

'Why did you tell me, then? If you thought it was better not to know why did you go and tell me everything?'

Dora groped for a cigarette and remembered she'd given up two years back. Kids were even harder work than she'd imagined. If they weren't soiling their nappies or swallowing buttons, they were setting fire to themselves or picking you up on inconsistencies. Was it ignorance that was bliss or something else?

'About that lift home.'

'I don't want to go home.'

'Sure you do.'

'I'm running away.'

'Well, you're in the right demographic to be a teenage runway. But I can't help noticing you've packed rather lightly. Where's your army knife and aluminium plate? Where's your cutlery set on a hinge? You want me to strap up your dog in a tablecloth so you can carry him on a stick over your shoulder?'

'Very funny,' said Cheryl.

'Sorry,' said Dora. 'Like I said, I'm hopeless with the tooth fairy stuff. You're — what — all of sixteen years old?'

'Fourteen.'

'Fuck me dead. Even worse than I thought. You can't even walk into a bar and order a port and brandy. How do you expect to be able to earn a living? To pay taxes and life insurance and all that crap?'

'I hate my mother.'

'Everyone hates their mother.'

'I hate my stepfather.'

'That, I can also understand.'

'Jackson makes me sick. He soaks Zeus in vinegar because he thinks it's good for fleas and he keeps giving me pictures of people with no clothes on and asking stupid questions.'

Dora's head exploded with visions of uncles and laundrette drying rooms and a tube of lubricant the size of a rolling pin.

'Hold it right there.'

'There is absolutely NO scientific evidence vinegar works on fleas. It doesn't even work on bluebottles any more. Also it makes Zeus completely BILIOUS. What's bilious?'

'Cheryl.'

'Yes?'

'Can we backtrack a moment please?'

'What.'

'Are you telling me Jackson touches you?'

'Don't be gross. Are you even listening? Jackson gives me books and magazines and posters and stuff and then wants to talk about them. It's stupid because there's hardly any writing, anyway. *Hunch* sometimes has

'Readers Write In' but *Pillow Biter* doesn't even have a horoscope.'

'Is that all he does?'

'Mostly.'

'What do you mean, mostly?'

'I don't know. Sometimes he walks in while I'm on the toilet and sometimes he asks whether he can check my backside for worms. Also he's got a book on how to grow marijuana in his study but he says if he catches me smoking cigarettes one more time, he'll tell Mum. It's not as bad as what happened with Reb — her dad played Spin The Bottle — but I'm sick of the magazines and all the stupid questions.'

'I'll be fucked,' said Dora Knockers, shaking her head. 'Well, I'll be fucked.'

She poured herself a glass of something from a yellow bottle.

'Who's Reb, anyway?' she asked in a monotone.

'Reb and Lou were my best friends at school but on Monday they sent Murray Ramsbottom round to tell me they didn't want me hanging round with them any more.'

'Who's Murray Ramsbottom?'

'This guy I kissed in Spin The Bottle.'

'Little shits,' said Dora, collecting herself. 'Sending the boyfriend's a real low act. Even I've never sent the boyfriend.'

'Murray isn't my boyfriend. He's Rachel Roulette's boyfriend. But that's the reason I'm not going back to school.'

Dora finished her drink then poured two more.

'Here,' she said. 'If you're going to be a high school drop-out you might as well develop a substance problem. Mind you, it's insane to turn your back on education at your age. In fact I think it's illegal. Why don't you enrol in one of the other schools?'

'Because it would be exactly the same.'

'You're probably right. Adolescents are repellent creatures. I certainly was. Make a point of skipping straight to middle age, Chezza. It won't be any easier but it'll make a great party trick.'

'If you're going to let me sleep here, can Zeus stay as well?'

'That depends on whether he stops assaulting my coffee table. I'm not sure I've ever seen a dog do that in its sleep. Mind you, nothing compares with Genevieve's fox terrier. Last week we caught him having it off with the chickens and had to throw out a whole omelette. Great out here in the country, isn't it? Mother nature is so fresh and wholesome. And now I'm going to ring your mother. Call me old-fashioned but I'd rather Detective Grippa didn't arrive at my front door at the crack of dawn with an arrest warrant for teen-snatching if it's all the same to you.'

'She won't answer. She's been taking a shower all night.'

'Fine. I'll keep ringing until she gets out.'

Cheryl went to the bathroom while Dora made the call. She sat on the loopy bathroom rug pulling hairs out of the tomato-knife scars on her leg. Then she took out Samuel's father's lighter and ran it round and round her palm the way he had done. Tomorrow she'd drop it off at the Leadhead's caravans. Maybe Christy would be there.

After the yelling in the lounge room stopped, she came out. Dora was transforming her couch into a bed.

'Did you speak to Mum?'

'I spoke to Jackson. I decided to have a quiet word with him about the magazine business.'

'THANKS A LOT.'

'I'd like to say he won't be bothering you again but knowing Violet she'll be pounding on the door by dawn.'

'I was being sarcastic.'

'Well. Maybe not dawn. If she's been showering as long as you say she has, maybe we should expect her round midday.'

'Mum goes to work at midday.'

'Perhaps tomorrow evening, then. Unless she's still under the weather of course, in which case it could very well be the day after.'

'The day after is Saturday. Mum goes to aqua aerobics with Mrs Vulpine on Saturday.'

'Sunday, perhaps?'

Cheryl shrugged.

'We'll just have to sit tight and see, then. Don't expect me to be a responsible adult in the meantime. Genevieve sleeps over at least four nights a week and I've been known to inhale nitrous oxide through the cream gun after work despite the fact that I've been re-evaluating my use of recreational drugs for some years now. In other news, I'm not going to come over all Barb Piercing girl detective and help you locate your father and I have no intention of giving you a job in the shop to make you appreciate the value of schooling. I've seen your work with potato scallops and I'm not impressed. That said, you and Testosterone here are welcome to stay as long as you want.'

'Thanks,' said Cheryl, climbing into the lounge bed and wondering how old you had to be before you could buy an overseas plane ticket without a mother. Was it possible to get high from inhaling stale fat? Dora's house sure did stink. It was high time someone invented the nose equivalent of earplugs.

'Zeus usually sleeps outside so there might be an accident during the night,' she called to Dora in the other room.

'I can hardly wait,' Dora called back. Then: 'Hey Cheryl.'

'Yeah?'

'What's your opinion of these new cappuccino machines?'

'They're OK. They make good milk for hot chocolate, I suppose.'

Then: 'Hey Dora.'

Yeah?'

'Did you know Samuel committed suicide?'

'Yeah.'

'How do you know?'

'How do you think I know? The police told Genevieve and Genevieve told me.'

'Do you think it would hurt to burn yourself alive?'

'Are you kidding? Of course it would fucking hurt. I got a sunburned neck last time me and Gen went bushwalking and I couldn't move for a week'

'I want to know why he did it.'

'You and everyone else in this town.'

'I think of him all the time.'

'Don't,' said Dora, and turned out the light.

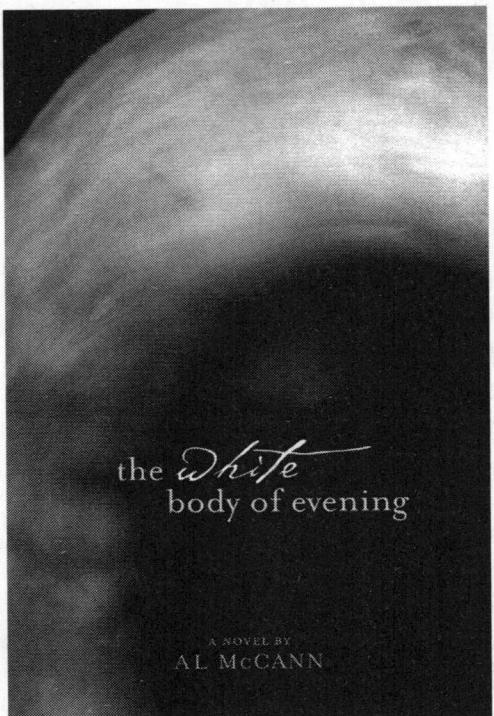

the *white*
body of evening

A NOVEL BY
AL McCANN

The White Body of Evening

A L McCANN

Behind the respectable façade of turn-of-the-century Melbourne lies another, darker city — one of obsession, derangement, dissipation and crime. This is the world that has driven Albert Walters to the brink of madness, that haunts his abused wife Anna and infects the lives of their children, Paul and Ondine.

Led astray by a mysterious charlatan, Paul's artistic ambition conflicts not only with society but with a sister who finds her reflection distorted in the decadence that surrounds her. Spurred on by a shocking murder and fuelled by the absurdities of war and nationhood, Paul is drawn into the darkness that inspires him, while Ondine takes dubious refuge in the light.

Written with an historian's eye for detail and a painter's love of beauty, *The White Body of Evening* is a breathtaking debut.

ISBN 0 7322 7467 2